PREMONITION

AGNES JAYNE

Premonition
Agnes Jayne

www.ellysianpress.com

Premonition
© Copyright Agnes Jayne 2015. All rights reserved.

Print ISBN: 978-1-941637-21-0
Second Edition

Editor: Jen Ryan, Imagine That Editing
Cover Art: M Joseph Murphy

DEDICATION

To Carl:
My husband, my hero, my love

CHAPTER 1

Emily watched from the kitchen window as a light from the far shore played along the waves of the river. As the wind plundered the trees along the bank, the light bobbed, flickered, and was gone. She heard the ghost of a voice whisper in her mind, but she ignored it. The voice would wait until morning. Maybe the sunlight would settle her, stop the spinning in her soul from the flight, the shock, and the horrible ache that came from the realization that for the first time in her life, she was truly alone. Even the moon had abandoned her, its thin light concealed by the clouds overhead. She rubbed the bridge of her nose, willing the loop of events to stop spinning through her mind, yet the pictures remained sharp as blades, begging her to fight, to avenge, to do something. But she didn't know how or where to start. She only knew why.

It'll be better in the morning, she thought.

To top it all off, the jackbirds were gone. The trio of gargoyles had guarded her family for hundreds of years, animated by an ancient magic and charged to protect the family. In the confusion of her aunt's disappearance, Emily hadn't missed them at first. They were often still and moved around at random. As long as she'd lived there, they'd never left the grounds before. Emily watched the sky, hoping they'd swoop up the driveway and into the house. Shaking her head, she pulled the edges of Aunt Maeve's bathrobe closer; it was a shade too tight across the shoulders. She frowned and searched her mind for a shred of meaning, or some reason why all of these things were happening to her. All she found was a memory.

***

Emily was only seventeen years old when her problems with love began, and at that time, her greatest hope was that she'd never meet the man of her dreams. After all, he'd been nothing but trouble. For three weeks, he'd visited her every night while she slept. He'd also commanded her attention during the day when she was too bleary-eyed to concentrate on her classes. She'd tried to stop the visions on her own with no luck. She had tried chants, prayers, and even a sort of cosmic apology with no luck. The worst thing about it was that Emily knew she deserved the punishment. She had learned her first important lesson: that spells had consequences and that magic did not forgive.

Emily wasn't quite sure if she was dreaming or awake. She closed her eyes. Her skin still burned from the memory of his touch. The memory of his voice echoed through her mind as he again tortured her with his gentleness, his touch, and the hard velvet planes of his body. He stretched his hand to her, and when she took it, he pulled her into his arms.

"This is right, this is real, you are . . . everything," he said. He looked at her with his warm, chocolate eyes. She stroked his back, and he whispered her name as he ran his hands through her long, dark hair and covered her mouth with a slow kiss. Just as she circled her arms around his neck, the vision began to fade.

2

"Damn it!" she whispered as she opened her eyes and found herself lying alone underneath her patchwork quilt. She rubbed her eyes and tried not to cry. She clicked on the table lamp and squinted into the light.

"He's not here," she said. "It's just the spell."

Just to be sure, she leaned over the mattress and peered under the bed, but there was nothing but a lost shoe and a couple of dust bunnies. *It was only a love spell,* she thought. *And it backfired, and they already humiliated me for it. Why do they keep punishing me?*

I told you this could happen, a voice said.

"I know," Emily said.

You were warned, the voice said.

"I know!" Emily said. "Stop lecturing me and help me out! Is he still in here?"

Silence.

Emily huffed and pulled herself out of bed to investigate. Everything seemed normal. The band posters, ticket stubs, and a program from the ballet company hung on the wall, same as always. Her book bag lay against the shelves balanced high with piles of books. Her bed was a twisted mess of covers. As she padded toward the window, the smell of dried flowers and herbs wafted through the floorboards. She yanked open the closet door and pushed past her clothes, but there was nothing there either, just an ancient brick wall and a sparkling black prom dress that she'd stuffed in the back corner two days ago.

A familiar tune began to play, and Emily pulled herself from the closet and listened. The music changed and there was talking, then the tune started again. The room echoed with the notes from the theme song to her aunt's favorite movie. The door creaked, muffling the words of the song, *da da dee dee dah dah . . .*

She heard me.

"Emily, are you okay in there?" her aunt called.

3

"I'm fine," Emily said.

Aunt Maeve is still awake. If I keep banging around in here, she'll be knocking on my door. Then what would I say? That I've botched my training and broken a major rule? That a spell made me crazy, and now I'm tossing my closet in search of a naked man in the middle of the night?

Frustrated, she reset her alarm clock and buried herself under the quilt, with her long braid trailing down the side of the bed. She stroked the sheet in the place where he had lain and vowed that the next time she tried magic, she would play by the rules.

Too soon, an obnoxious beep filled the room, and Emily groped blindly to silence the alarm. She hauled herself out of bed, looking for her uniform. *Catholic school,* she thought, *the irony.* She pulled on her white blouse, plaid kilt, and navy blazer, stifling a yawn. The place between her shoulders ached, and her throat felt dry and scratchy, like she'd spent a lot of time screaming. Maybe she had been screaming. She grabbed a comb and ran it through the top part of her hair to the braid, then tied the braid and pinned it with a silver clip, a Celtic knot. "It'll do," she told the cat curled up on her bed. "It's not like I have anyone to be pretty for."

Emily trudged down the back steps into the kitchen and plopped into a creaky chair that always threatened to break, but never did. She watched her aunt's long braid move against the pale pink print of her back and dreaded the conversation that was coming. Aunt Maeve poured her a steaming hot coffee: milk, no sugar, then sidled up to her with her own cup, adjusting her robe as she leaned to Emily. Emily clutched the ancient yellow mug and stared into it.

"What in the stars was going on in your room last night?" she asked, handing Emily the cup. "Are you sneaking someone in through your window?"

"No."

"Nightmares?"

"Sort of," Emily looked out the window and across the yard where the dark gray waves of the river sat below an equally gray sky, concealing the far bank in a thick mist. Emily shuddered. She wanted to crawl back into bed and sleep.

"Want to tell me about it?" Aunt Maeve said.

"You already know something, don't you?" Emily said, reading the expression on her aunt's face.

"Well, you've been talking in your sleep for the better part of a week," Aunt Maeve said. "Not to mention moaning, growling, and one time, you even sang."

Emily felt the color rise in her cheeks.

Aunt Maeve smiled and continued, "Tell me the details. Don't worry, you won't embarrass me." She set her cup down, plunked her elbows on the table, and rested her chin on her hands.

"The whole thing is just so weird," Emily said.

Aunt Maeve winked at her, then patted her arm. "You don't have to tell me about it then. You're entitled to your secrets." Maeve rose from her chair and walked to the kitchen window. "Looks like it's going to be a dreary day."

Emily frowned and held her breath in an attempt to force the tears back, but that only made her snort with an airless half-sob causing Aunt Maeve to turn and wait until she was calm. She handed Emily a box of tissues.

Emily blew into the tissue. "Sorry," she said.

"What is it, Em?"

"I screwed up, big time. I need your help."

Maeve crossed her arms and tilted her head to the side.

Emily sniffed. "I'm having visions. I can't sleep at night, and I can't think when I'm awake. You need to help me make it stop. I feel like I'm losing my mind."

Aunt Maeve crossed her arms against her chest and sat back in the chair. "How did it start?"

"I cast a love spell."

Aunt Maeve looked confused. "I was wondering when you'd give that a try. Everyone does it. Was there something strange about the spell?"

Emily sighed. "It wasn't just a garden-variety spell to bring love into my life. It was a spell for someone in particular that I wanted to notice me. I knew he didn't like me; he was dating someone else, but I didn't care. At least, I didn't care about it then. So I worked the spell to make him break up with his girlfriend and date me instead."

"Oh . . . yes, that would change things," Aunt Maeve said, scratching her chin. "And who was this spell for?"

"It was for this guy Jared in my math class. He sits in front of me. I've liked him for years, and I really wanted him to notice me. I wanted him to take me to the Prom. I used his picture, and even a lock of his hair for the spell. I bent his will. And it worked. Then the magic caught up with me, and now I'm being punished."

Aunt Maeve's frown deepened, but Emily continued, "I know that it's against the rules to use our magic to manipulate people, but I did it anyway."

"What happened after that?" Aunt Maeve asked.

"The spell worked fine for a few days," Emily looked down at the table, "and a few nights, actually . . ."

She took a deep breath. Since she was confessing, she might as well tell her aunt everything. "I wasn't on a hiking trip with the girls from my class a few weeks ago. I was with Jared. We spent the weekend camping at the lake, and well, you know."

"I hope that you were careful," Aunt Maeve said. Before she could get started with a lecture, Emily interrupted.

"We covered that base, at least. The rest of it didn't go as well. The spell didn't even last a week. Jared stopped talking to me out of the blue two weeks ago. I've left him messages and texts, but he won't answer. He won't even look at me when I see him in the hall, but I guess he told all of his friends that we'd slept together, because now everyone at school knows, and they're all saying that I'm a . . ."

She couldn't bring herself to say the word. Emily brushed her eyes with the back of her hand and sniffed. "And on top of that, I keep having *these dreams.* Not about Jared, about some other guy, someone I don't even know. I can't make it stop. I tried everything that I could think of, but nothing's worked."

"Is he cute?" Maeve said.

Emily frowned at her "I'm serious! Even the House is lecturing me!"

Aunt Maeve suppressed a grin and opened her arms. "I know, sweetie. I'm sorry. Come here," she said, and Emily curled into her arms and sobbed on her shoulder. Her aunt held her tight and stroked her hair.

"Aren't you going to yell at me?" Emily asked into her shoulder.

Aunt Maeve laughed and patted her back. "It seems like you've paid for your crime already. No wonder you've seemed down for the past few weeks. I bet the kids at school have been awful."

Emily nodded into her robe.

"Besides, you're not the first girl I know who thought a love spell would solve her problems. Look at this." Aunt Maeve patted her shoulder and walked into the pantry. She came back holding a small bottle. "Know what this is? It's a potion for the minister's wife. She thinks her husband is cheating on her, and she wants it to stop. She wants a true love potion to bring him back to her."

"What if he's not her true love?" Emily asked, wiping her eyes and sniffing. "Won't the spell have awful consequences? Like with me?"

"I told her that when love spells go wrong, they go very wrong," Maeve said as she swirled the potion, "but she's

7

convinced that he's her true love, and she's determined to have him back. Either way, she'll be better off."

"Why doesn't she pray instead of using a spell?"

"Ha!" said Aunt Maeve. "She's probably been praying for months. When their prayers aren't answered fast enough, they come here. That's how it's always been."

"Is there something in the closet that can make my dreams stop? I've learned my lesson about love spells."

Aunt Maeve bit her lip. "I'm not so sure that these dreams are a consequence of your spell, Emily. It might just be coincidence. I can give you something to help you sleep, but are you sure that this is what you want? You may be suppressing part of your natural magical talents, you know."

Emily snorted. "I don't care about that," she said. "My talents aren't worth a damn anyway; look at what happened with this. If I had any real magical gifts, they would have shown up by now."

"You don't know that," Aunt Maeve said. "Brewing a faulty love spell doesn't mean that you're powerless, not at all." Her aunt's face arranged itself into the stubborn expression that made her look as if she were carved from ice, and Emily knew better than to pursue the argument.

"I just want to be able to sleep," Emily said. "I need to concentrate; I've already failed two tests this week. I'll lose my scholarship if I don't fix that."

Aunt Maeve's face softened at this. "Well, I can mix a potion that will suppress your dreams, but as for the boyfriend part, I don't know. You're always by yourself, it's not good. How about another spell, a good one this time? I have the ingredients in back. It would only take a day or two to get a good brew made for you."

"No thanks," Emily said, "I've got enough going on in my life without adding another spellbound boyfriend to the list. And as for love, I'll just wait for things to happen the normal way. Never."

"Cheer up," Aunt Maeve said. "Maybe you've been getting a look into the future, did you think of that?"

"Do you really think that there's any chance of the dream coming true?" Emily asked.

"That's the tricky part. The truth of the dreams really isn't the point. The point is that you shouldn't limit your experiences at such a young age. And yes, your dreams might very well come true. It might not often be in the way that you expect, and you never know when. But that doesn't mean that you should discount your gifts."

Here we go, Emily thought, *another lecture on gifts. It figures.* Emily only possessed a few small talents, nothing that she would really call magic. Maybe her aunt was right, and the visions meant she had acquired some other power, something more impressive, like clairvoyance or divination. Emily stared hard at the tan liquid in the cup, willing it to reveal its secrets, then looked up at her aunt.

"You can only do that with tea," Maeve said. "But honestly, Emily, why didn't you tell me all this sooner?"

Emily groaned. "You're better off not knowing the inner workings of my mind. I can barely handle the knowledge myself. Besides, the whole thing is just plain embarrassing."

"Oh Emily, you're such a prude. I hope you'll grow out of that. It's an annoying trait in a woman. Besides, you're not the first one to have dreams like that, I remember when I was a girl, I had this crush on my economics teacher, and every night I'd dream that we—"

"The bus is coming," Emily said, cutting her off mid-sentence. "Just get me out of this mess, and I promise I'll never use magic again."

Aunt Maeve made an exasperated sound. "I'll leave your potion on the counter; just drink it when you get home tonight. You're at a crossroad here; don't let this mistake determine your destiny."

"Yeah, yeah, the power's only as good as the craft," Emily repeated in a singsong version of Maeve's voice, "the power might be limited without the craft, but the craft is also limited without the power. And you don't know anything about being powerless." Emily drained her cup of coffee and thunked it on the table for emphasis.

"Are you sure you don't want a ride?" Aunt Maeve asked.

"That's all right. Besides, it looks like the lady is here for her potion."

The door slammed shut as Emily raced past an old silver Buick to the school bus.

***

Emily shook herself, bringing her thoughts back to the present. Any way she looked at it, she felt responsible for her aunt's disappearance. Aunt Maeve had always been there when Emily needed her, but Emily had never returned the favor.

When she'd shown up on her aunt's doorstep, heartbroken, with a suitcase and a cat carrier under her arm, her aunt had welcomed her back with open arms, found her a job at the State Museum and helped her get back on her feet. Aunt Maeve had been wonderful. She'd listened, she'd sympathized, and she'd never once said "I told you so."

She'd never thanked her aunt for that, not once. Instead, she'd thrown herself into her new job, working long hours and ignoring her aunt's pleas to talk, too stubborn to admit she'd been wrong. Then, when Mr. Not-So-Right had called from Chicago, she'd decided it was time to go back, collect the rest of her things and move on.

Maeve had leaned in the doorway, her arms folded as she'd watched Emily pack her suitcase. "I don't know what you saw in him in the first place, Em. For God's sake, you need to remember who you are!"

"I was tired of being alone," she'd said.

When Emily had knocked on the door of their old apartment, she'd done her best to put on a brave face. He was standing there with her: that blond, perky woman he'd left her for. She told Emily that it was all for the best as Emily nodded like an idiot and tried not to break anything. When Emily had lived there, the apartment had been full of lush, green plants, but they were all gone now, probably dead. At least they'd been decent enough not to throw out her father's record collection. When she arrived back at her hotel, the police were waiting with the news. Her aunt had disappeared. They'd found her car, and according to the police "it didn't look good."

Maybe if she had stayed, her aunt wouldn't have run off in the middle of the night with the Paladin and she'd still be here. Emily swallowed hard and looked out into the night, catching her reflection in the window. She'd grown thinner, her features were honed and sharpened, and the glare of the fluorescent light above the sink hollowed the shadows under her eyes. Abandoning her mug on the counter, Emily walked through the hallways in search of her cat. She left the kitchen light on out of habit, as if she was still waiting for her aunt to return.

CHAPTER 2

Nicholas Flynn sat in his SUV, keeping time with the pulsing beat of the radio as he belted a solo into the gold cap of his new fountain pen, pretending that he wasn't nervous. The lady in the lane beside him stared. Nicholas winked at her and blew a kiss before he sped into the night, chuckling at the scandalized expression on her face, before his thoughts turned dark again. He needed another distraction.

He put the pen in his shirt pocket. With this one small tool, he had the ability to slice, whip, wand, net, and incinerate his prey all at the click of a button. It had come in very handy that night. He reached for his phone. He dialed and sighed impatiently at the sound of the multiple rings and the message on the other end.

"Hey Kane, Nick here. Where the hell are you? The jackbirds are apprehended, well, two of them anyway. One got away, but I don't think it'll make it far; I clipped its wing. I'm heading over to the lab to drop them off. Call me."

Since he had time, Nicholas stopped at a drive-through on the way to the lab. He slurped a chocolate shake as he drove, very proud of himself. No one had ever bagged two live jackbirds before, he was sure of it. They'd been circling the river around the VonPeer residence all afternoon. Dalgreth might promote him; hell, they might even give him a medal for this. A nice token for all the people with nasty whispers about how he'd really gotten his position with the Paladin. Not that he cared about what those people thought. Even so, his victory was tainted by the nagging pang of guilt that kept him flicking his eyes to the rearview mirror.

The two creatures were wrapped together, their black tails entwined, eyes pleading. They were Third Level demons, conjured beings according to the textbook, but intelligent. And they were still dangerous. A wild impulse to let them go kept popping into his mind. They hadn't really harmed anything or anyone; they were just trying to escape his shots. They were remarkable specimens as well: small, animated dragons that looked like stone statues when they were still. It must have taken powerful magic to produce these creatures.

Nicholas sobered at the thought of their destination. *I'd have been better off killing them than bringing them here*, he thought. He cut the engine as two men in long, black coats hailed him with excited looks on their faces. The shorter one was bouncing on the balls of his feet and rubbing his hands together. Nicholas sighed as he hit the button to open the back doors of the vehicle. He jumped out to greet the men, who were already peering at the cage. One of the beasts hissed and huffed, and the tech threw back his hand just in time, escaping the small jet of fire. The creature snapped hard at the cage as a third man joined them.

"Dr. Wagner," Nicholas said, placing his hands together, prayer like, in a brief salute.

Dr. Wagner smiled and returned the salute. "Excellent job, Agent Flynn, I haven't seen specimens like this in years. It's about time you lived up to that name of yours."

Nicholas cringed as his dreams of accolades melted into dread. *Of course that's what everyone's going to say about*

13

me, he thought, *the perennial screw-up.*

"Come on guys," Wagner said to the techs, "get that cage inside and get it processed. I just got a call from another field agent. We'll have another delivery within the hour."

The techs placed the cage on a cart and wheeled it to the door. The smaller of the beasts caught Nicholas' eye, but he turned away. *They're too valuable. No one's spotted creatures like these in years, and the presence of even minor demons like these could signify trouble,* Nicholas thought. Unless they found a lead soon, people would die.

A tech pounded the side of the crate, and he swore as a stream of flame singed the sleeve of his coat. The men hustled the cage through the entrance to the lab, and Nicholas wrinkled his nose at the waft of clinical smells permeating the night air.

"Oh, and Agent Flynn, feel free to stop by anytime. We always love to see your people at the lab." The techs laughed. Nicholas frowned at the double-speak: the lab at Paladin was both the base for live demon study and the morgue for the agents who died by their hand. He saluted again then turned his back on them.

Ghouls, Nicholas thought as he shuddered and climbed into the truck. He could still hear the jackbirds cawing from the cage as the door slammed with a metallic thud behind them.

Before Nicholas had time to think, another call ripped through the radio. It was a Class Four investigation, a demon attack, their third this month. He thumped the speaker as the details at the scene faded in and out on the radio, but he managed to hear the location.

He dialed the phone again. "Hey, it's Nick again, I heard the call, and I'm heading to the river. I'll probably see you there."

He sighed and dialed another number, Gabriel Stanton, his new boss. He hated it when he had to dial up the ladder, but it was protocol. He was relieved when the call went straight to voicemail. "Dr. Stanton, this is Agent Flynn. The jackbirds have been apprehended, and I'm on my way to the call at the river. Thank you sir, goodnight."

Putting the phone down, Nicholas gunned the engine and headed to the scene: the lower banks of the Hudson River, near the north end of the nature preserve. The radio continued to crackle, but it wasn't telling him anything useful, so he turned it off.

He parked under a bridge that even in the daytime was a rumored meeting ground for dealers, junkies, and others who traded in things bought and sold, but they were all gone tonight, chased off, no doubt, by the small swarm of gray robes that dotted the riverbank. Nicholas got out of the truck, hailed the first familiar face he saw, and joined in the search.

The agent who greeted him was a short man in a long, gray cape that blended into the surrounding scenery. Two gashes marked his left cheekbone, indicating his role as a senior agent of Paladin. The man placed his palms together and pointed his hands at Nicholas in a quick salute that Nicholas returned without thinking.

Nicholas crept behind the other agent with some difficulty, alert for signs of danger. "Watch where you step," the man said. "Follow me. And stay armed, that thing might come back."

Nicholas couldn't remember the man's name; it was either Jones or Johnson. He'd met him yesterday with a half-dozen other imported agents. The recent string of supernatural activity had Paladin transplanting help from all over the country, and it was hard to keep track. He'd even heard whispers that they were pulling old agents out of retirement for this case.

Everyone knew Nicholas, though. Not wanting to draw attention to himself, he pulled his hood over his head, though it offered him only a small bit of anonymity from the other agents. He was one of the tallest among them, broad through the shoulder with an athlete's build, but the cloak hid his chin-length, blond hair.

Their boots squelched in the tall grass; twenty yards into the scene, they were soaked to the waist. The air was chill, and carried the threat of snow on the breeze. His only warmth came from within, from the steady burn of the focus that filled him every time he began a new investigation. He passed under a tree, and a loud squawk made him jump. An interrupted crow flew out of the tree to a higher branch, watching the scene with obvious interest. The man beside him smirked.

"I hate it when they do that," the agent said. "They're always hungry; the smell must have attracted it."

The bird cawed again and flapped into the distance.

Taking a deep breath, Nicholas steadied himself as he watched the surroundings, relying on his primary senses before he attempted to use his powers.

The beast had chosen its site well; this forgotten plain between the river and the highway provided little escape for potential prey. Like the other agents spread throughout the field, Nicholas swept the ground and the sky for clues with his othersight, fighting the wind and the occasional bursts of rain that failed to be a storm.

He realized he didn't even know who, or what, they were searching for; given his day, it was better not to ask. It didn't matter what they were looking for, if there was a clue in this field, he'd know it when he saw it. His othersight would take care of that. But as he moved toward the team, his regular senses flew into high gear; a burned, acrid stench filled his nostrils, causing him to choke.

"What is that smell?" Nicholas asked. "It's disgusting." The wind carried his voice away, unheard. He jogged a few paces closer to the other agent. The wind changed and the scent vanished.

"Never mind. There's Kane, I'll have him bring me up to speed," Nicholas said to the man, who nodded and moved off in another direction.

Agent Kane scoured the area with a handheld device lit with yellow and green sensors. He looked up and nodded as the wind blew his hair. The green-cloaked researchers intermingled with his teammates, scribbling on notebooks and pounding on other small devices that measured the magical energies at the gate. About a quarter of a mile in the distance was John's place, the small carriage house that was both his post and his home. The light was on in the kitchen window, as usual.

As Nicholas walked toward Kane, the smell hit him again, and his head rang as his power gathered in his hands in an instinctive defense. He walked toward the smell, cursing the direction of the wind. He lowered his hood as a courtesy; everyone working in the field had sensed him as he approached.

"Where have you been, I've been trying to get a hold of you all night! Is there any news?" Nicholas said.

Kane looked up from his handheld and bit his lower lip. "No, nothing yet. We've been taking measurements all night. It seems there's some type of interference that's messing with our devices, so we had to turn all the phones off."

Nicholas frowned at Kane's response, confused. Before he could think about it, a small, round figure barreled in between them. The agent pulled down her hood, and Nicholas groaned. Arneth Moon was a squat redhead with a big mouth; Nicholas knew her well. He'd been dismayed when she'd been reassigned to his post a few months ago. Luckily, their paths didn't cross often, as she usually avoided fieldwork.

She looked at him and frowned. He locked eyes with Moon for a moment, but she bit her lip and turned away.

"Where've you been?" she asked, handing him the file

"Fighting jackbirds," Nicholas said, with a hint of pride. "I got two of them; they were flying over the river near the VonPeer property. They must have been guarding something or someone pretty powerful."

Nicholas flipped the file open and skimmed the words on the page, seeing the important details of the case: two victims, proposed demon activity, and an absence of a viable explanation for either.

"Where're the bodies?" he asked.

"Nicholas, what are you doing here? Dr. Stanton said that you were *not* to be a part of this investigation."

"Why not?" Nicholas asked.

Moon stared at him for a long moment. "Maybe he thought you couldn't handle it."

Nicholas scoffed. "A call went out on the radio. I was close, so I responded. I've been trying to get a hold of someone all night, but John's gone, there's something wrong with my radio, and I couldn't reach anyone by phone, so I left Stanton a message. What are you doing here, Moon? Shouldn't you be holed up in a library with a book somewhere?"

"Dr. Stanton sent me. He put me in charge of the readings at the gate. You should go back to the office; he wants to talk to you."

"He can wait," Nicholas said.

"Fine," Moon said, stomping away, "Don't say I didn't warn you."

He turned to Kane. "What's with her?"

"Hang on a sec," Kane said. The small box in Kane's hand glowed, and he tapped furiously at the keypad, swearing under his breath. Kane pursed his lips. Nicholas looked at him harder and Kane's feelings began to emerge in his mind. *He's angry and there's something else, sadness? No, not just sadness, grief.* Nicholas thought, *but what . . .*

"Stop it," Kane said.

"Sorry, man, I was just trying to —"

"Stay the fuck out of my head!" Kane said. "It's crowded enough in there already."

Moon stomped back to them and grabbed Kane's device. "What have you got this time?" she said. Her foot bobbed up and down impatiently.

Kane shook his head. "It's the same. There's not even a faint trace of a breach anywhere on the grid. I can't tell you where the thing came from, Arneth, but it wasn't the gate." He ran his hand through his jet-black hair leaving the front standing on end. Nicholas could sense his agitation. He'd known Charlie Kane since the Academy, and he was a perfectionist.

Still, everyone made mistakes, and Kane didn't look like himself right now. He was normally fastidious about his appearance, and he always looked like a professional, except that he normally wore a royal blue stripe in the front of his hair. Today, the color had faded into a silver gray. Also, Nicholas noticed, Kane's robe was rumpled, like he'd slept in it, and he seemed frustrated. So did Moon, who was chewing on her pen cap.

"It's not like a couple of jackbirds did *that*," she said, gesturing behind her.

Nicholas stepped past Moon's shoulder. It took a couple of moments to see where she'd pointed. He walked down a small embankment and around the undergrowth, where a few agents stood pointing and shaking their heads.

At first, Nicholas thought that he was looking at a stump or an old burned out tree, but as his othersight adjusted his vision, Nicholas felt his hands start to shake. A sour smell burned his nostrils as his mind repelled the scene in front of him.

Impossible, he thought, *it must be a trick.*

They stood together beside an outcropping of stones

19

near the gate. The scorch marks on the ground formed an intricate pattern that surrounded the corpses. The man stood upright with his weapon in hand and ready to strike, the woman stretched her bare hands toward the sky in a conjuring position. Both were ashen statues of themselves, grotesque sand castles in the middle of the blackened field, already eroding from the wind and the rain. Their faces, what was left of them, were terrified, yet resolute; they saw the thing that had killed them. Nicholas stared into the eyes of the figure nearest him. Even then, he kept shifting his eyes from the ground to the eyes of the corpse, willing it not to be true. John Dalgreth, his best friend, mentor, and the closest person he'd had to a father in years, was dead. Nicholas shook his head in disbelief, though he couldn't erase the scene in front of him. The gods had seen fit to take away yet another person he loved.

A hand was on his shoulder. Nicholas willed himself to breathe and barely heard Moon's words. "No one told him what happened?" she said. There was only silence, except for Moon swearing under her breath. He turned to glance at her, and she put her hand over her mouth. "Oh, Nicky . . ." she said.

"I thought he knew," Kane said. "He always knows everything."

Nicholas could feel their eyes burning holes into his back, waiting for him to react. Beyond that, there was nothing. Kane stepped beside him and tapped his handheld. Nicholas grabbed the device and threw it as hard as he could into the distance. When Nicholas spoke his voice sounded far away and distant.

"Well, I do know this: you're not finding evidence of a demon, Kane, because a demon didn't do this," Nicholas said. He brushed the ashes from his sleeves. "Look at the wards and the sigils burned into the ground. They're still smoking, even though the corpses are cold. This is magic, probably the work of a witch."

There were a few gasps behind him.

"Paladin does not hunt people," Kane said, stiffening a little.

"Unless it suits their agenda," Nicholas said, rubbing a scar on the back of his hand. He turned on his heel and strode back to the truck. His teammates followed.

The need to strike anyone and anything would have overcome him but for his years of training. He stopped and forced himself to control the blue light gathering in his arms and fingertips. It wasn't worth it, though. He took a deep breath, and a hand rested on his shoulder. Nicholas shrugged, but he didn't feel like brushing it away.

"Come on," Moon said. "Let's head back to the office. There's nothing else we can do here right now."

"Give me your keys," Kane said. "I'll bring your truck back."

Nicholas nodded, handed Kane the keys, and then allowed Moon to lead him to her black SUV. Nicholas slumped into the front seat and rested his head against the window. The engine started and the truck carried them through the city. The wipers swished, blurring the signs and streetlights of downtown. Nicholas closed his eyes.

He barely noticed as the SUV swung into an empty space in front of the brick building. The group walked toward the small, shabby, white-lit sign that glowed by the front door: PALADIN ENTERPRISES: PROTECTION AND SERVICE GUARANTEED. Moon punched the entry code to the lock beside the door and pulled it open. The small corridor was unremarkable, gray walls, scarred linoleum, and a bench that had seen better days. She pushed the button to the elevator, and they filed in.

When the doors opened, they walked into a magnificent white room made entirely of marble and filled with giant columns that soared forty feet above them. They walked down the cavernous corridor to the Grand Staircase that led to the conference room. As they descended the stairs, the carved faces of a thousand animals, both real and imagined, watched them. When he was a child, Nicholas had spent hours sitting on these steps, memorizing the faces of all the animals. He could feel them looking at him now, and he held the rail for support, even though he couldn't bear to meet their eyes.

The stairs led to a central corridor that was crowded thick with researchers, investigators, and other members of the Paladin team. Their faces were set, but their hushed conversations echoed throughout the hallway. Nicholas could tell from their tones that the news of Dalgreth's death had preceded his group. The people who passed them said nothing, they stared in sympathy and one woman, a senior researcher, hid her face when she saw Nicholas, though a muffled sob escaped her lips.

At the center of the hallway, a white marble angel stood wielding a spear. The statue was surrounded by a fountain where more agents sat, pointing and arguing with one another. Some held books, others scrolls. Men and women nodded and bowed in deference as Nicholas walked by them, though he didn't hear what they said.

The room was long and narrow, with blue, plush carpet and carved hardwood on the walls. A fire roared in a marble fireplace at one end of the room. Nicholas removed his damp cloak and hung it on a nearby hook, then sank into a chair beside the fire. He watched as the flames consumed the wood with a bright orange light. Moon sat beside him. Kane paced the room with a nervous energy that would normally irritate Nicholas, but right then, he didn't care.

A door opened at the other end of the room, and a tall man with caramel skin and graying hair walked in. He paused when he saw Nicholas, then shook his head, walked to the window, and with his back to them, forced it wide open. The agents looked at one another in question until he sat on the window ledge and lit a cigarette.

For a while, he just sat there in a cloud of smoke, puffing in agitation like a disgruntled dragon. He met their eyes in turn; daring one of them to speak to him, to say anything to give him an excuse to tear them apart, but they all knew better. The room was silent.

Stanton and John had been team members, years ago. And yet, despite Stanton's obvious distress, here he was, as stoic and cold about the death of his old friend as he was about all business. Nicholas watched him out of the corner of his eye with grudging admiration. Gods, he was tough.

Stubbing out the cigarette, Stanton finally addressed the team. "We've had a blow tonight. Our best information told us that that the creature was heading for the Northern Gate in the mountains. That was where we stationed our highest concentration of agents. It appears that it attacked at the River Gate instead, and that Dalgreth died attempting to prevent a breach. We are unsure about the involvement of Maeve VonPeer, but it seems likely that she was an innocent bystander at the time of her death."

Kane raised his eyebrows. "I met Maeve VonPeer once when I first started as an Agent, and trust me, sir, innocent bystanding is not her style. Are you sure that she didn't call that thing herself?"

Stanton shrugged. "Dalgreth didn't think so, but at this point, anything is possible. Obviously, his loss requires an immediate reassignment of his duties."

"Are you disbanding us?" Kane said, "You can't do that, we want to catch the thing that did this!"

Stanton stared Kane into silence. "I will be taking charge as the leader of this team, but there will be a few changes around here. Number one is that I expect you to let me finish my sentences."

Kane sat back in his chair, sulking.

"Next, I'm promoting Agent Moon," Stanton said. "This case requires an experienced researcher. She will assume the research duties of the team. I will also be assigning new agents to the case. "

He stopped and looked at Nicholas.

"What about me?" Nicholas said.

Stanton didn't meet his gaze. "After some discussion with the Elders, it was decided that Agent Flynn would remain on the team as an investigator. He will also be taking the station at the Gate; we need someone there who has the ability to fend off another breach. Fortunately for us, what Flynn lacks in manners, he makes up for with magic. He'll reinforce the wards at the Gate." With a flick of his wrist, Stanton tossed a file to Nicholas. Nicholas frowned as he flipped it open.

Moon cleared her throat, and the men turned to her. "Actually, sir, we didn't find any evidence of a breach. If a demon was there, it didn't attempt to open the gate. Could it be something else?"

Stanton shook his head. "It would be a large coincidence that tonight is the dark moon, two people were dusted in the manner that is the hallmark of a Fourth Level demon, and that our best agent was apparently powerless to do anything about it." He patted another cigarette from the pack, but didn't light it. "What is it you think we're looking for?"

"It looked like magic," Nicholas said. "There was spell-work all over the site. It also explains the presence of the jackbirds. Those types of demons are usually human creations."

Stanton frowned. "Dalgreth said there was nothing to suggest it, but he was keeping an eye on Maeve Von Peer just in case."

Nicholas coughed. "I think Dalgreth knew Maeve personally, sir." Nicholas said. "He mentioned her the last time we spoke. He didn't sound quite . . . professional about his relationship with her."

Kane whistled again. "Think he brought too much of his work home with him?"

"I don't know," Nicholas said, sighing and running his hand through his hair. "John would never compromise an investigation, though. Still, we've got a lot of information on the VonPeers, and Maeve VonPeer dabbles in love spells . . . he's been alone for a long time . . . I just think we should take another look."

"Do you have any evidence to support your theory, Agent Flynn? Other than your hunch, that is?" Stanton's face grew colder with each word.

"No, it was just a thought," Nicholas said. "Since there was no breach, there might be other explanations for what happened tonight."

Stanton pursed his lips and tapped the cigarette against his hand. "Well, I don't like it. I can't gamble my agents on sloppy theories. That's how people die, as I'm sure you remember."

Nicholas clenched his jaw so tightly that his teeth hurt. He looked over at Moon, who was biting her bottom lip and nodding.

Stanton continued, "I also see that you went to the investigation despite my instructions. Didn't Agent Moon notify you of my orders? You know we don't like family members involved in cases."

Nicholas nodded, feeling the flame of embarrassment under his skin. "Technically speaking, he wasn't my family, sir. Just a family friend."

Stanton's expression was stony as he lit his cigarette. Nicholas watched the floor, certain that he was about to be removed, possibly physically, from the room.

Stanton opened his mouth to speak, but Moon interrupted, "It was my fault, Dr. Stanton. Dispatch got confused with my order, sent a general call on the radio and Nicholas responded. It really wasn't his fault this time."

Nicholas nodded.

Stanton looked from Nicholas to Moon, suspecting a lie, but his expression softened. He stubbed out the second cigarette. "Well, I guess it saves the explanation; as the situation turned out, I had to bring you on anyway due to your familiarity with the local wards. Flynn, see to it that the gate is watched and locked. Above all, you are the first line of defense in case anything tries to enter or leave through the portal. And as for your witch theory, I don't buy it. Dalgreth researched that angle very thoroughly. We're sending agents disguised as police to the museum to inform Emily VonPeer of her aunt's death; their family tradition dictates that Ms. VonPeer will now be the sole guardian of the estate."

"Who's questioning her?" Nicholas said.

"We have chosen not to engage her in the investigation at this point, although you will keep an eye on both Ms. VonPeer and her house. We will upgrade the securities around the perimeter of the Gate, and assign roving guards. I'll be sending senior agents out to back you up and help you select your team."

Nicholas cleared his throat. "Dr. Stanton, with all due respect, isn't it a little premature to just dismiss Emily VonPeer as a person of interest in this case? She seems like our only lead so far, and you're telling us that we can't even talk to her? That thing just dusted her aunt; she might know something that we don't. At the very least, we should be doing more than just watching her."

The room grew cold with both silence and Stanton's barely concealed anger. Someone kicked Nicholas in the ankle. Nicholas glared at Moon, who raised her eyebrows at him—S*hut up!* She mouthed, but Nicholas ignored her. Stanton lowered his chin and studied Nicholas over the top of his glasses. He walked to the table and stood over him, slightly menacing. "The last time I checked, I didn't need your approval for my orders. I have my reasons, and I'll thank you for not questioning them."

"This is bullshit," Nicholas said under his breath.

"What was that?" Stanton said.

"Yes, sir," Nicholas said and sank further into his seat. Moon and Kane were watching him, but he didn't look up. He wouldn't give them the satisfaction. Stanton took a step back, cleared his throat, and again spoke softly, though they heard him clearly. "Agent Flynn, I will let your disrespect slide this one time because of what you've been through tonight. But make no mistake about this: you'll do what you're told, or you'll be turning tarot cards at the county fair; I don't care whose kid you are."

Nicholas felt his hands ball into fists under the table, but there was nothing he could do. Anyone else who dared challenge Gabriel Stanton like that wouldn't find work cleaning the toilets at Paladin.

"It won't happen again, sir," Nicholas said.

Stanton took a few steps back as he regained his composure.

Kane turned to Nicholas. "Well, I'm glad we have that settled. Besides, I already checked on Emily VonPeer, when this whole thing started. Dalgreth was right. The VonPeer girl's got nothing; she doesn't even have the aura of a magical."

Moon cleared her throat. "Theories aside, we're still looking for a Level Four being. Nothing else could explain the pattern of death by incineration. We need to start by following the magic."

Stanton nodded. "Well said, Agent Moon. Kane, go to the police stations and get all the information you can find on disturbances and sightings in the area, all the routine stuff. Go back as far as you can, pick up where Dalgreth left off."

He paused for a moment, looked at Nicholas, and

continued. "Find out everything that you can on Maeve VonPeer, just in case Flynn is right. Flynn, head back to the Gatehouse, secure the area, and look for anything that might help inside John's house. Moon, stay behind, I want to brief you on some of the research aspects of the case."

Stanton nodded, dismissing them. As Nicholas got up to leave, Stanton blocked his way.

"I'm not a big believer in second chances," he said. "But if you handle this case well, I will consider rescinding my statement from your trial, and work to get your record expunged."

Jackass. Nicholas thought, but said nothing. Stanton and his mother were the reasons that he had a record in the first place. Stanton's head snapped up. He'd heard the thought, and Nicholas ducked his head. He hated that his thoughts were never his own in the company of Paladin. Everyone was a damn mind reader. Stanton shot Nicholas a suspicious look as he walked out the door, but then, Stanton had never liked Nicholas much; it was an old prejudice.

CHAPTER 3

Since her aunt's death, Emily's dreams had returned with a vengeance. She'd been avoiding sleep when she finally collapsed in her bed with a book, exhausted.

Then the dream came.

At first, she was in the familiar and exciting vision of her youth. There he was, her hero, the one with the wheat-blond hair and chocolate eyes, the one that in her waking life, she'd compared to every man she'd ever met and found them all lacking. *He lowered his head to hers, brushing her lips with a kiss that deepened as she threaded her hands through his hair. She backed away from him, studying the perfect planes of his face.*

"I've missed you," she said, and he grinned. He pulled her closer and moved to kiss her again. Emily curled her head on his chest, reveling in the familiar comfort of his arms.

Then the vision of him began to spin in her mind, rearranging itself into a new and terrifying image.

This time, she was crouched beside him in the undergrowth. He was disheveled and bleeding through a bandage wrapped around his arm. Emily was afraid.

PREMONITION

"Nicholas," she said, and he turned to her.

"Stay here!" he said. His face was pale, and his breath came in short gasps. Though he swooned when he stood, Nicholas managed to right himself and draw his weapon. The Gate swirled in a portal of light, and in front of it, another man, the killer, stood with his arms raised. The gate glowed bright as the man began to chant in a language she didn't understand. Nicholas took two more steps toward the gate and raised his arm, aiming at a spot between the man's shoulder blades.

"Just one good shot!" he said. "That's all I need."

"You can't do this!" she said. "You'll die!"

"Some things are worth dying for."

Nicholas took a deep breath and charged, flinging a stream of blue lightning at the portal. The man growled and turned to face Nicholas. He held a red ball of light between his hands. For a moment, the two men were face to face. Then the other man threw the orb at Nicholas, and Nicholas shot at the orb instead of the man. Emily screamed to warn him, but her voice was gone. Before Nicholas realized what was happening, the man grabbed him by the neck and held him in the air. Nicholas strained and struggled, but he could not escape. The man pulled a blade from his belt, and smiled at Nicholas. Emily ran to his side, but she was too late. The man stabbed him in the chest, then set him down on his feet and walked away without a backward glance. Nicholas staggered forward and clutched his chest before he crumpled into a pile beside her, bleeding from a gaping wound just above his heart.

"No!" Emily cried, placing her hands over his heart, trying to close the wound. It didn't work. She pulled him into her arms, cradling the upper half of his body.

Nicholas coughed and shuddered as he spoke, "I almost had him."

The man saw her and began to laugh, a deep unearthly

30

howl, as if he had just heard a good joke. He rubbed the knife on the leg of his pants.

"No!" she screamed, but there was no one to help, only another round of laughter in the darkness.

The man walked toward Emily and Nicholas; the glint of his silver knife reflected the fire behind him. Emily was frozen in place, too scared to breathe, too scared to move. She felt the man grab the hair at the nape of her neck to hold her still. The cold metal of the blade drew close to the side of her neck.

Emily gasped, holding her throat. The fire was gone and she was alone, tangled in a web of bed sheets. She tried to steady herself, but her hands were shaking.

"It's only a dream," Emily told herself over and over, clutching her knees as she rocked back and forth. She could feel a drumbeat sounding in her head, and she fought the urge to vomit. Only then did she remember that she'd downed the last of Aunt Maeve's dream suppression potion three days ago. She'd forgotten to make more. Her face was wet with tears. There were tissues on the nightstand, and she grabbed a handful, smeared them across her face, and wondered if there was any aspirin in the House. Aunt Maeve wasn't a big believer in normal remedies, and Emily was in no mood to investigate the herbals for a cure. She threw back the quilt, shoved her feet into slippers, and headed to the bathroom to investigate.

On the way, a door creaked open and Emily paused. The House had kept this room locked since Maeve's death, and no key on the chain in the kitchen would open it. Emily pushed the door open, wondering why the House had finally decided to let her in. When she saw the neatly made bed and the thin film of dust on the nightstand, the grief flooded her. She sat down on the bed, feeling like she was going to cry. The tears she felt remained stubbornly behind her eyes; it seemed that she had already wasted all of her tears on the stranger in her dreams. So she put on her best brave face, the one she used at the office. She walked around the room and told herself that she needed to be strong. It almost worked.

She stopped to touch the familiar things on her aunt's dresser, the silver comb and brush set, the hand mirror, half a dozen painted ceramic boxes filled to the brim with sparkling jewelry, some costume, and some real. The book that Aunt Maeve had been reading lay on the nightstand, its pages splayed and face down in the way that always made Emily cluck and scold. Emily picked up the book and made a frustrated little sound in her throat when she found a leather bookmark lying underneath it. She put the marker in the page, snapped it shut, and laid it back on the nightstand. The top pages of the novel flapped upward like a fan, and Emily pressed the cover of the book, knowing that she couldn't fix it. The spine was broken.

"I've cried enough tonight," she told herself, and held her breath as she closed the door to her aunt's bedroom, willing herself to be strong. Strong for what though? There was no one left to be strong for.

"I just need a few hours of sleep," she said. "Maybe there's something stronger than aspirin around here, maybe a tea or a tincture would do the trick."

Emily thought of the dried plants on the top shelf of the tearoom, used only for desperate circumstances and lost causes, plants that had the power to kill. *It would be so easy,* she thought, *a few leaves in a cup of tea to end the last of the mighty VonPeer dynasty.* But even as she considered this option, her mind rejected it. In the small sliver of moonlight, Emily chose to live, even though the loss of her aunt had left her without friend or purpose.

That's not true, and of course you're not going anywhere, stop thinking those thoughts, a voice said to her.

Emily smiled and patted the wall, surprised. The House hadn't spoken to her in years, not since she'd left for college.

She traced the faded gold patterns of the wallpaper with her fingertips, acknowledging her oldest friend.

"It's been a long time, hasn't it?" Emily said.

You stopped listening, the House said.

Emily moved toward the main staircase. To the right, the hallway opened into an ornate two-story foyer. Emily put her hand on the banister. She felt a small tug from the House, and smiled apologetically.

She never said goodbye, the House said.

"I know, I feel the same way," Emily said. "I won't leave you again, I promise. Though gods know what kind of a mistress I'll be. Look at this place, it's filthy. I'm sorry I haven't been up to cleaning lately," she said, wiping her hand on her nightgown.

The House murmured back to her, it understood. With a soft swishing noise, a light moved across the wood of the banister, leaving behind a glass-like sheen and a faint odor of lemon. Emily raised an eyebrow.

"I always thought Aunt Maeve did that," she accused, and she felt a wooden chuckle emanate from the House.

I stood in spite of Maeve, not because of her, the House said.

"Another secret of yours?" Emily said. "You're full of them, aren't you? Tell me how you do it, we'll be famous." She felt the House laugh again, and then she felt a warm breeze wrap around her body with a slight squeeze. It was the House's version of a hug. Its intention was comfort, but Emily still felt the tears stinging the place behind her eyes.

You still have a family, the House said. A picture began to form in Emily's mind: it was her aunt, smiling and scolding her in the same pink bathrobe that Emily now wore. Her aunt opened her mouth to speak, but before she said anything, Emily shook herself, and took her hand off the banister.

"Not now," she told the House, "not yet. I just can't

handle this tonight. I'm not ready." She felt the House give her a slight mental nudge; it really wanted to talk to her.

"Soon," she promised, patting the wall as she walked down the stairs, "just not tonight. The dreams still have me reeling. I need more time to think about things."

The House prodded her, but Emily closed her mind.

She sighed. Although she was an orphan, she'd never experienced loss of this magnitude. Her parents had died in a plane crash when she was three, and she barely remembered them. Aunt Maeve had been there ever since, and she had served as parent, teacher, and Emily's best friend and tutor. She had forced Emily to read all of the family books, to learn their spells, and to practice their magic. When it turned out that Emily was the least gifted witch in the history of the VonPeer family, Aunt Maeve was unconcerned. "Some powers take time to develop," she'd said, and continued to instruct Emily daily on the secrets of life, love, and the ancient house that was her friend before it was her legacy.

Though it looked like Emily would never have any real talents, she'd still have the House and all the powers that went with it. She was finding out that being the mistress of this place would be as much burden as blessing. The House had a mind of its own. Already she could hear it protesting her decision to remain silent as she descended the stairs.

Emily snapped a light on in the closet-like room behind the hallway that led to the kitchen. She was greeted with the familiar whiff of mingled herbs and flowers. On either side of her, shelves rose above her head, stuffed with glass jars, earthen jugs, and occasional oddities like hand mirrors and feather dusters. After searching and sniffing several canisters, Emily found a jar that contained her favorite blend of tea that Aunt Maeve had dried and bundled last summer.

She looked at the clock. Maybe she'd drive over to see Jessie and Steph. They would have just closed the coffee shop, and they never seemed to sleep. She decided against it. Emily didn't feel like hearing their concerned voices and their thousand kind ways of asking her if she was all right without ever asking her if she was all right. There was no use pretending; no one could fill the gaping hole left by her aunt's death.

Emily turned on the ancient stove and lit the burner with a match. After a moment, the kettle began to hiss with life. Emily reached to the cupboard for the cups, and instinctively pulled out two. She studied the faded patterns of china roses, and sighed as she put one back. She studied the single cup. Another word, her aunt's, came to mind, the word she'd been avoiding in her mind: *Scion*. Emily sighed as she pushed the thought and all its meaning to the back of her head. "I don't want to think about it now," she said, pouring the tea.

She looked out the window. In the distance, she saw a light on in the neighbor's cottage. A new emotion bubbled to the surface of her mind, burning its letters into her consciousness.

"Paladin," she said, spitting the name out like a curse. Until recently, Aunt Maeve had spoken of them or to them only when necessary. All of their dealings with the people at the gate had been laced with the slightest undertone of threat; any appearance of their hooded forms had ended with her aunt reinforcing the wards on that side of the House. She'd warned Emily to stay away from them, to have no exchange, to give them no excuse to interfere with their lives. It was sage advice that Maeve herself had ignored. In the past few years, Maeve had become very close with her neighbor, John Dalgreth, a decision that Emily regarded as highly suspect.

And now this, Emily thought. *Paladin*, she thought with a laugh. It meant guardian. Ironic, considering that it was their fault that her aunt was dead. Emily's jaw set and her resolve hardened. She would get even with them, somehow. She stood at the sink nursing her tea. A swish of black

35

shadowed the window and was gone.

Emily frowned slightly and rubbed her eyes; was something moving out there? She waited and it happened again, a subtle shift of the shadows in the garden. She grasped the edge of the sink and peered out the window, trying to get a better view. *Probably an animal*, she thought, *a raccoon in the garbage, or worse, a skunk.* Emily wrinkled her nose at the thought of cleaning up spilled garbage. The House shifted, uncomfortable. *Maybe I should go take a look,* she thought.

All of the doors in the House slammed shut at the same time. *Stay inside!* The House said.

Emily shivered, the apprehension of the House moved through her hands like an electric shock. She pulled away from the sink and jumped as the teakettle screamed. The blinds on the windows snapped together, blocking her view of the outside. Emily looked around, half expecting to see someone standing with her, but she was alone. Emily took the teakettle off the burner to silence the noise.

"Forget it," she said out loud. "I'll stay here."

Not that she had a choice.

Emily tiptoed to a small closet near the pantry and opened the door. She groped blindly on the top shelf until she found the case she was looking for. She set the case on the table and opened it. Bedded in the gray eggshell foam was a revolver that had belonged to her father.

Emily grabbed the gun, moved to the bathroom in the hallway, and opened the medicine cabinet, where a dusty box of bullets sat on the top shelf. She returned to the kitchen with it and sat down at the table. Though it had been years since she'd done it, Emily opened the cylinder and loaded the gun. It was another one of her aunt's lessons, a woman alone needed to be able to protect herself. She set the gun on the table, but left her hand on it, just in case. There was nothing else she could do, so she sat very still and watched the kitchen door for the rest of the night.

CHAPTER 4

Nicholas stood in front of the fireplace at the Gatehouse, watched by pictures of the dead. Stanton must have known that this assignment would be as much punishment as privilege for him. He picked up a framed snapshot on the mantle, ten years old, and studied his family. John had taken the photo during a weekend excursion to the mountains with the other members of his father's team. He thought of John back then, lanky and dark-haired with a permanent grin etched onto his face. Even Stanton had smiled often in those days; at the time, he was a quiet and kind man who never raised his voice. Back then, both John and Stanton had been permanent fixtures in the Flynn household, a normal part of the family's otherwise abnormal existence.

In this shot, Nicholas' father was still healthy. His arm was draped around his mother's shoulders. Nicholas barely remembered his father like this; he was so different than the sick, bald shell of the man in the hospital that had replaced him in Nicholas' mind. He'd died five years ago from cancer, an extraordinary man felled by an ordinary disease.

Beside his parents was his brother Ben in his newly earned Paladin robes. Ben always looked so proud in pictures: he was always the biggest, the best, and the one that Nicholas could never live up to, not then, and certainly not now. Last and least was Nicholas, the summer before his senior year of high school, standing apart from the rest of them with his arms crossed and an annoyed look on his face. Of all the people in the portrait, Nicholas was the only one left.

Well, there was also his mother, but she didn't count. He hadn't spoken to her since the day of his trial two years ago.

It didn't matter that it wasn't his fault, he knew that now. Ben was dead, and he could have stopped it, of that much Nicholas was sure. He thought about that night when his brother had approached him for a favor. They'd been sitting on the couch in the living room watching a football game with a bowl of chips between them. Ben was engaged then, and he was about to be promoted to team leader, but he needed more combat time to give him an edge over the competition.

"Come on, Nicky," he said. "They'll never find out, I promise. They're out looking for wedding decorations. I need you on this one."

"It's against the rules," Nicholas said. "We'd be out on our asses if they ever found out about it. Not to mention Mom, I'd rather face a demon than have her find out."

As usual, Ben talked him into it. Ben was an expert at steamrolling people. If he hadn't been a Paladin, he would have made a fine linebacker at a big college.

Nicholas sighed as he rose from the chair and walked to the kitchen. He grabbed a red ceramic bowl from the shelf that his mother had used for salads and filled it with water.

"Come on," Nicholas said. "Get the door for me."

They moved down the stairs from the back deck and into the woods beyond the house. In a small clearing was a patio with a round wrought iron table. That was where Nicholas set the bowl. He began to concentrate on the water.

"I'm not even sure this will work," Nicholas said. "I've only done a few minor spells so far. It could be dangerous."

"I'll do the dangerous stuff," Ben said. "You just need to find it."

Nicholas sighed and continued to focus on the water.

"Do you see anything?" Ben asked, looking over his shoulder.

Nicholas pushed him away. "Let me concentrate," he said. He leaned closer to the water and softened his vision, letting his othersight take hold. After a moment, he could make out a smoky cloud of light. The creature swung to face them, displaying two red, glowing orbs that pierced the darkness. The creature turned in the glass, facing him in the water as if it could see him. It stretched its long neck closer and closer to Nicholas so that the only thing between them was the thin glass of water in the bowl.

"Something's wrong," Nicholas said, "it's getting closer, it shouldn't be doing this. Scrying is like watching a television, it shouldn't be able to see us, but it looks like —"

"Oh shit, Nicky, stop, Mom and Arneth are back."

Nicholas was dimly aware of the lights flashing behind him as the creature blasted through the water and appeared in front of them. Before he knew what was happening, Nicholas was pinned to a tree, unable to move or breathe. Ben was shouting and blasting the thing behind him. He could hear his mother and Moon yelling in the distance before everything went black. Nicholas awoke in a bed two weeks later in the secure unit of the Paladin hospital. Ben was dead, and Nicholas was under arrest.

His mother and Stanton had wanted him out, his powers bound, his memory erased, and his contract to the Paladin dissolved. Moon had been silent through the whole ordeal, her eyes puffy while she spun Ben's engagement ring around on her finger.

Nicholas was never convicted of a crime. Instead, John Dalgreth had interceded on his behalf. Nicholas was too powerful to be banned from the organization, he'd argued. Under the circumstances, Dalgreth recommended a note of censure to remain in Nicholas' file for five years, and then he volunteered to take Nicholas as a member of his own team, banding him with the other misfits of the organization. Despite Lillian and Stanton's protests, the rest of the disciplinary counsel had agreed to keep Nicholas. Upon hearing this news, Nicholas' mother had turned in her resignation in protest and transferred to a remote post in Brazil. Nicholas had done his best to stay out of everyone's way.

The people who didn't know were convinced that it was his mother's influence that had him fully reinstated to the organization, and that her resignation was a concession to her own bad decision to keep Nicholas. It was a rumor that still haunted him despite his stellar work in the Agency.

Nicholas sighed and turned the picture on its face.

He'd spent weeks pacing the small living room in John's house. The research team at Paladin had offered to pack up John's belongings, but Nicholas wouldn't let them, not yet. So John's pipe still rested in the ashtray, and the onyx chessboard on the coffee table still held their last match. Nicholas stopped mid-pace and looked down at the board for a minute. He moved a pawn, and then frowned. There was a piece missing, the white knight; he'd have to look for it later.

He stretched his legs. Although Nicholas hadn't broken Stanton's rule to stay away from the VonPeer property, he was about to bend the hell out of it.

For the last few nights, Nicholas had found himself eyeing the property with increased interest. Odd lights were flashing around the place, and though he'd reported this, no one seemed to find it noteworthy. It was after all, the home of a witch, and a little stray magic was to be expected around wards like the ones surrounding the house. Though his orders remained to stay away, his instincts told him that something was amiss next door.

He decided that the best way to investigate was to go for a run. It was a scant quarter of a mile jog to the VonPeer estate. He decided to run by the place and take a look around for potential leads. Maybe he would find something useful about the case, and if not, what Stanton didn't know wouldn't hurt him. He folded a few essential sheets of the file and his weapon, disguised as a pen, into his jacket pocket and started to jog down the road.

The road was little more than a rocky path surrounded by underbrush and dotted with occasional copses of trees that gave way to the cleared fields, which had once been the sprawling VonPeer farmlands. The stone Gatehouse where he lived had once been servants' quarters for the farmhands and indentured servants who worked those fields and stables. The house itself was still secluded, surrounded by a small island of ancient hedges and forest that concealed it from prying eyes.

Nicholas ran close to edge of the road, waiting for a glimpse of the infamous estate. From the description in the file, he expected the VonPeer estate to be the typical Albany finery—a gabled clapboard mansion with swooping porches and well-kept grounds. What he found was an aberration: a low, sprawling, whitewashed structure, half concealed by overgrown gardens and ivy on a small clearing surrounded by woods. Despite its size, the place had the look of an overgrown cottage, with odd rooms and wings and porches jutting at angles across the lawn. Far from Americana, it was the sort of place where people disappeared and didn't come back: serene, natural, and a little weird. It was a home worthy of a witch. He paused to catch his breath and focused his othersight on the front porch. A blue car was parked in the driveway and the porch light was on, but Nicholas had the feeling that there was something else out there, watching him. He ran faster, eager to put some distance between himself and the house.

The whole property was enveloped in magic. Dozens of wards and spells shone around the place like thin spiderwebs of light, warning intruders of both the magical and mundane variety to keep out. Surrounding the magic was a long, untrimmed hedge that snaked the perimeter of the property and ended at a faded black and white sign that read LAUREL GROVE. It might as well have read KEEP OUT. The magic was so strong that those who couldn't see it would be able to feel it.

The cold air filled his lungs, and he let his mind lapse, mesmerized by the graveled rhythm of his steps. He continued this way for several miles, then turned around and started home as the night deepened. When he passed Laurel Grove on his way back, he felt a sense of tension in his stomach. It could have been the wards making him nervous, even from the street; the protective magic gave him a shivery feeling like a bug was crawling up his back. As he passed the driveway, a stream of light flashed around the far side of the shrubs on the edge of the property. Nicholas stopped and turned around, wondering what he'd just seen. The blaze returned, this time it passed within a few feet of the road. Nicholas froze, half in fascination, half in terror.

"I knew it," he said to himself. "She's conjured a demon."

Nicholas followed the light with his eyes and cursed himself for leaving his phone at home. He began to sprint for the Gatehouse, eager to report his findings. At the place where the road turned and led into his driveway, he stopped dead. There was someone standing in the middle of the path, blocking the way. Although he looked like a man, Nicholas could see that this being was something else entirely. The blue light he had seen now perched in the air beside the man. Though it would be invisible to others, Nicholas perceived this being as a cloud of blue light, nearly the same size as the man. Nicholas grabbed the pen from his pocket and pushed a button. It began to glow with a dim light, and Nicholas clutched it, ready to fire should the need arise.

"What do you want?" Nicholas yelled to them.

The man was tall and his skin was very pale. His long hair was dark. The expression on his face was neither kind nor menacing, just still. Nicholas aimed his weapon, but the man inclined his head, and Nicholas could feel his own hand begin to shake. He clasped both of his hands around the weapon to steady them and thought of running, but there was nowhere to go.

The man twitched his wrist, and Nicholas dropped to his knees. Nicholas froze as the man began to speak quietly in an unknown language, and the cloud of light moved forward until it hovered a few feet in front of Nicholas.

Nicholas shivered. Fear flooded his senses and overtook his thoughts. He felt like a rabbit in the thrall of a lion. The man stood where he was as the blue light descended on Nicholas.

Then there was pain, worlds of pain. Nicholas could feel his body as it began burning from the inside out. Somewhere in the distance, he heard himself screaming. The man walked up to him, set his hands on Nicholas' shoulders, and pulled him backward out of the light.

"That's enough," the man said, and the blue light moved away from them both. "I want to see him fight."

Nicholas stood before him, shaking with pain, but even in the depths of his misery, he felt his hand clench around his weapon. He swung his fist upward, and a blast of electric magic flew from the pen and struck the man's jaw. The man took a step back, appalled. He touched his lip in confusion and inspected his hand for blood. Then he began to laugh.

"This one's got a temper," he said to the other creature, "I like that. Do you think we should keep him?" He nodded to Nicholas and gestured him closer, seeking a fight. Before he knew what he was doing, Nicholas clenched his fists again and threw himself at the man, snarling, eager to land a hit. He again found himself on the ground, pinned under the man's boot and unable to move.

"He's brave, but he's not very bright," the man said. The cloud of light hovered, motionless. The man shrugged his shoulders and seemed to lose interest in Nicholas. Taking his foot off his throat, the man turned his back on Nicholas and walked up to the blue light.

"Never mind, I still like the other one better. Get rid of him, and then go back to the original plan," the man said as he disappeared behind a tree.

The demon flew at Nicholas, who scrambled upward, then ducked as it flew by him, leaving a crater in the ground where it had landed. Nicholas grabbed his pen and shot a streak of blue magic that looked like an arrow as it hit the beast. The force of the blow knocked it into the gutter, buying Nicholas some time. He planted his feet and put both of his hands on the pen, igniting a beam that looked like a long club made of blue light. When the creature emerged, Nicholas swung his arms like he was hefting a baseball bat, aiming for its core. It worked. He landed a heavy blow that sent the thing backward, reeling into the ditch. Regaining his footing, Nicholas made a flinging motion with the pen. The blue light shifted from a club into a cord that shot a net of magic through the sky, surrounding the monster. He pulled the trap tight as the blue cloud surrounding the demon melted away. Nicholas had to remind himself to hold his ground as it stood, appearing before him in its true form.

Nicholas swallowed as he felt his mouth go dry. The thing was monstrous, probably twelve feet tall. He wasn't sure if his magic would be enough to hold it. The creature sniffed at the air and bared its long teeth, staring at Nicholas through the giant, blank orbs that were its eyes. It looked something like a man with some of the body parts stretched and set at odd angles. As it moved, it twisted over on itself in a very unhuman way. Its long neck undulated like a serpent in the net, a solid ball of limbs and winged muscle. The rest of it, the claws, the teeth, and the spikes on the tail, seemed to be comprised of razor-sharp blades that, given half a chance, would slice him to ribbons. The creature struggled and hissed, but it could not break free. Nicholas pulled downward, attempting to ground the net so that he could call for backup. He pulled the net backward across the road, keeping himself as far from the monster as possible.

"Gotcha," he said as it snarled and struggled.

As Nicholas pulled the net, the thing snarled at him again, and he heard a grinding sound of rocks against the pavement. He dove backward just in time to avoid being hit by an oncoming delivery van. He swore as he fell into the ditch and landed in a fen of stinking mud, dropping his pen for only an instant. It was enough to sever the magic though, and the demon disappeared as if it had never been there. Nicholas jumped to his feet and raced up the bank. The van twenty yards in front of him.

A thin man jumped from the van, his eyes wide as saucers. Nicholas felt his gut plunge as the man removed his glasses. He dropped to his knees as the man pulled out a green handkerchief and wiped his forehead.

"Sweet Lord Almighty!" the man said to Nicholas, whistling through his teeth. "It's lucky we happened to be driving here, that thing would have turned you to dust in another second or two. What were you thinking, working alone like that? That creature is worlds stronger than you are."

Nicholas looked up, stunned and a little annoyed.

"I was doing fine, actually. I would have had it if you

hadn't driven your damn van through the energy field!" Nicholas protested. The man reached out and helped Nicholas to his feet.

"No need for kneeling, we don't stand on ceremony that much anymore," the man said, wiping his glasses with the bandana. He put them back on and looked Nicholas up and down.

"And neither do you, I see," he said, looking at Nicholas' torn running shorts. "Don't your people usually wear robes?" he asked.

"I was out for a run and that thing attacked me," Nicholas said. "What are you doing here anyway, mister, sir, I mean . . ." Nicholas paused, waiting for an introduction.

The man extended his hand. "Call me Steph," he said, shaking Nicholas' hand.

"Nicholas Flynn," he said.

"I know. I'm here on official business, but it looks like you beat me to the punch. Dammit, I've been chasing it for weeks, now I have to start all over again. It travels with a companion, did you see it?" Nicholas nodded. "They won't be back here tonight. They'll be harder to find now that they know we're hunting them. These things act tough, but they're really opportunists at heart. You have a lot of magic, you know; you'd have made an excellent snack." He shook his head and went back to the van. As he opened the door, he yelled back at Nicholas.

"Do you need a ride?" he asked.

"No, it's fine," Nicholas said. "My house is right here. I'm just going to go inside and get cleaned up a bit. Thanks anyway, though."

Nicholas limped down his driveway and into the house.

As soon as he was inside, Nicholas grabbed his phone and hit the speed dial for Paladin. He peeked through the window, noticing that the van was still parked on the road about fifty yards away.

PREMONITION

"Dr. Stanton?" Nicholas said. "This is Agent Flynn. You won't believe this, but I think I just met an angel."

CHAPTER 5

Emily lifted her head from the kitchen table and groaned. She must have fallen asleep. She'd been stuck in the House all night, most of it spent in a wooden chair glaring at the back door. The House had refused to let her out, telling her over and over that it wasn't safe for her to leave. As she rubbed her eyes, she noticed that the shutters had cracked open and the House seemed content. Even so, Emily was nervous. She rose from the table and walked to the window. The morning mist from the river was only beginning to lift, and it concealed her view of the grounds.

Everything is safe now, the House whispered, and Emily relaxed slightly. After a moment, she walked upstairs, showered, and got dressed for work, but she kept the revolver nearby. She walked with it as she continued her normal morning routine, but decided to replace it after she nearly shot her own reflection when she passed by a mirror in the hallway. She went down to the kitchen, made herself a cup of coffee, and lingered over it. Now that she had her freedom, she was afraid to leave. She looked out the window as the rising sun colored the sky pink and revealed the silvery expanse of river in the distance. Emily slipped into her shoes and coat, and walked outside with her coffee, stepping carefully on the mossy brick path.

It was a glorious morning, cold, but with a fragrant breeze that carried with it the scent of new green leaves and the light aroma of the tulips scattered haphazardly around the property. In defiance of her aunt's neatly planted flowerbeds, a single yellow tulip had sprouted in the middle of the back yard. Emily smiled in spite of herself; she'd always loved the rogue flowers that had the nerve to escape the garden. As she stood over the tulip, inspecting it, a tingling sensation ran down her back. At first glance, she saw nothing. But then she noticed some shattered flowerpots at the edge of the herb garden. The red geraniums and rosemary that Aunt Maeve had potted on either side of the garden's entrance lay among broken shards of the clay pot.

"Damn," she said under her breath. That would need to be fixed before she went to work. The herbs were part of the magical protections that her aunt had put in place around the House. Inspecting the plants, Emily realized that it was unlikely that they'd fallen over on their own. Some of the flowers were scattered around, but the pottery that held them was shattered into a million tiny pieces, so that they looked like they were circled by brightly colored piles of sand. She lifted the rosemary. A few of the fronds had turned to a gray, ashy color, as if they'd been burned. There was an old adage that said rosemary in the garden protected a home from evil. It was a phenomenon that she'd heard about but had never seen. Her hands shook a little as she entered the shed and brought out some new pots, a broom, a dustpan, and a small bucket to contain the mess. There was a movement to the side of her, and out of the corner of her eye she saw him, a stranger at the edge of the garden, standing on the border of the ward lines.

Emily kept her eyes down, trying to form a plan. He was closer to her than she was to the House, and she cursed herself for putting the gun away so quickly. He stood about fifty yards from her, a tall man, youngish as far as she could tell. He had a muscular build, and was wearing a dark green sweatshirt with a hood that concealed his features. A telltale blue light glowed around his figure.

He's one of them, she thought. *Paladin. This morning is not beginning well; first the plants, now another one of those jerks.* Emily kept her face sober and her head down as she swept the pieces of the broken pot into a bag and carried it back inside the shed. She grabbed an old pitchfork, steadied her shaking hands, and instead of returning out the door, she climbed out the large garage window that was concealed by a hydrangea bush. The trick worked. He didn't notice her until she was standing in front of him, brandishing a rusted pitchfork.

"Who are you, and why are you here?" Emily demanded, menacing him with the steel points. Her hair escaped from her braid and blew around her face.

"How did you do that?" the man said.

Emily's eyes narrowed. Raising the pitchfork, she took a step toward him. He suppressed a grin, and she scowled as she noticed that he was fighting the urge to laugh at her. It was true; the situation was ridiculous. He was head and shoulders taller than she was. It would be nothing for him to pull the pitchfork from her hands. Yet he put up his hands in front of him in a gesture of harmlessness and lowered his hood. He brushed back his wheat colored hair and extended his hand.

Emily nearly dropped the pitchfork in her surprise. It was him, the man from her dreams.

"You can put that thing down now," he said. "I'm your neighbor. I work for John Dalgreth, well, I did anyway. I'm one of the investigators looking into his death." It worked; she relaxed her grip a little bit, and stood up straighter, though the air around her still seemed charged.

51

"Agent Nicholas Flynn," he said. He extended his hand, then dropped it to his side when the gesture wasn't returned.

"Well, you certainly don't have John's manners," Emily said, with a feeble attempt at recovery. "Haven't your people ever heard of a telephone? Or do you just like to stalk defenseless women on their way to work? Were you the one who broke my flowerpots?"

"Our people?" Nicholas asked, incredulous.

"Paladin, you're all so damn arrogant," Emily said, her voice low and shaking. "You, John, the men in Chicago—the last agents I saw were dressed as detectives—as if I couldn't tell the difference. They told me that Aunt Maeve was the victim of a brush fire. They told me she died of a heart attack from the smoke and got caught in the fire. Do you people really think I'm that stupid? Unless you have a better story, go away. I don't have anything you want. You've already ruined my family."

Nicholas just stood there watching her with a stricken look on his face. Then his expression hardened. He stood a little taller and puffed out his chest. "Well then, I guess we can skip the formalities. We've tied your aunt's death to possible demon activity and you're part of the inquiry," Nicholas said.

Emily's eyes snapped to his. She stared at him, surprised.

"You think a demon killed my aunt?" she said, then shook her head in disbelief. "Well Agent Flynn, enjoy your investigation but stay off my property. I have to go to work now." She pulled her small heels out of the mud one by one, and turned away.

"Look," Nicholas said, "I want to help; I saw something circling your house last night. I don't know what it was, but it wasn't human, and it seemed to be looking for you. Maybe it was something that your aunt called?"

Emily turned around and, before she knew what she was

doing, lunged at him with the pitchfork. In less than an instant, she had him pinned against the tree with the pitchfork at his throat. Nicholas leaned into the tree bark, keeping his distance from the rusted tine that she held inches from his eye.

"Whoa!" he said, holding his hands in the air.

"Thank you for your concern, Agent Flynn," Emily said, "but my aunt was an herbalist, not a demon summoner; there's a rather large difference between the two, in case you didn't know." The windows of the House began to glow behind her with an eerie light. "And as you can see, I can take care of myself. If you're looking for a murderer, maybe you should start with Paladin, it's probably part of your initiation. How many people have you killed, Agent Flynn?"

She saw the anger flash in his eyes as he reached out and grabbed the pitchfork from her hands. She took a step backward and stumbled on a rock, landing on her backside with a thump. Nicholas crouched above her. He moved close to her, then, as an afterthought, threw the pitchfork to the ground. He offered his hands, and she took them as he pulled her to her feet.

His face was earnest and a little bit angry. "I'm not a murderer," Nicholas said. "I'm a messenger. We don't know who or what killed your aunt and John, and until we find out, you need all the help you can get. There are creatures around this place; I saw them myself. If whatever killed them is looking for you, you'll need more than a pitchfork and a beat up old house to fight it."

"Is this you coming to volunteer your services? Because your delivery could use a little work. I have nothing to say to the Paladin," she said. "Just go."

Nicholas was silent. His expression intensified, and Emily looked down and realized that she was still holding his hands. Embarrassed, she let go of him.

"Have a lovely morning, Agent Flynn," Emily said.

"Give my regards to the thugs."

Emily flinched as Nicholas turned on his heel and stalked away from her. He exited into a copse of trees, and Emily suddenly found herself wishing that he would stay. But she squelched the thought.

"What a jerk," she muttered, pulling a strand of grass from her braid. As she brushed the grass and dew from her outfit, she realized that her hands still felt warm from his touch. That annoyed her. She squared her shoulders, willing her feet to work. There was no way that she was going to let him know that he'd scared her. Grabbing the pitchfork, Emily marched to the shed and put it back on its hook. As she emerged from the shed, she was aware that Nicholas was still there, watching her from the woods, scrutinizing every step.

"Don't trip," Emily whispered to herself. "Fine help you were," she said to the House. The House said nothing. She grabbed her shoulder bag from the stairs and walked to her car. As she opened the door, she glared at him. Nicholas stood at a safe distance on his side of the property line, leaning against a tree with his arms folded, watching her. She frowned at him. It didn't help that he was better looking in person than in her dreams.

Their eyes met, and Nicholas watched her for another moment before he shook his head and walked back to the Gatehouse.

She dropped into the seat of her car and started it, but she remained parked at the edge of the drive, sagging in the seat, her mind spinning in a thousand directions.

Dreams never turn out like we expect, her aunt had said. That was an understatement. She cursed Nicholas, banging her hands against the steering wheel in an attempt to stop the tingling sensation. As she'd suspected all along, his arrival brought nothing but trouble.

So let's take stock, she thought shakily, *I've got a*

murder, a monster, and the man from my dreams on the doorstep. I'm under investigation by the Paladin, and I'm ten minutes late for work. She sat and thought about what she could do, until a pair of unlikely faces floated into her mind. She pulled her phone from her purse and dialed.

"Are you guys around this afternoon?" she asked. "I need to talk."

"Of course, sweetie, anything for you," her friend Jessie said on the other end of the phone. "Is everything okay? You sound a little rattled."

"Everything's fine," Emily said. "I just need to talk."

"You know where to find us," Jessie said.

Emily smirked as she heard a dish crash in the background of the call.

"Oh shoot, I've gotta go, we've got another mess on our hands in the kitchen. Talk to you soon!" Jessie said.

Emily set down her phone and smiled.

Still, her heart sank a little as she drove down the small road and caught another glimpse of Nicholas, who was unlocking the door to the Gatehouse. "Better that he's gone," she said to herself, "I have work to do. If there is a monster out there, then I'll have to figure out a way to take care of that too." She wished, for the thousandth time, that she had the power to back up that promise.

CHAPTER 6

Nicholas spent the better part of the morning pacing the perimeter of the property and telling himself that he was looking for clues. He kept his back stubbornly turned away from the small forest that separated the Paladin property from the VonPeer's, and although he was doing his best not to let his mind drift, he found it difficult to concentrate on the case.

The scenery wasn't helping matters. The place was idyllic. The river bent in a way that concealed the proximity of the city and the industry of the Hudson River on either side, granting him a long view of forest and a few clearings dotted with houses like his own. The property for the nature preserve began about a half mile in the distance. But for the burned circle on the ground, no one would ever guess this place was a crime scene.

He needed something to distract himself from the mess he'd just made. Over the phone, Stanton had told him to look around, to search for remnants of the demons in and around the property. Stanton had made no remark about the angel sighting. He suspected that Stanton didn't believe him. No one in Paladin had spotted an angel near a case in a hundred years. He rubbed his hands together in agitation. They had been tingling in an odd way since he'd helped her from the ground. The Paladin had definitely been wrong about one aspect of this case. Emily VonPeer was anything but powerless.

Yet none of these things bothered him as much as the comments that Emily had made about him.

"She said that I didn't have John's manners," he said, remembering Emily's fiery expression. "She thinks I'm a murderer." He paced through the field, talking to himself as he kicked the burned ground, knowing that both of her accusations were true.

John Dalgreth wouldn't have been caught at the back of the VonPeer property like some kind of stalker. Emily was right about the second thing too: he was a murderer, for the most part. His brother's face floated to his mind. Nicholas rubbed the scar on his jaw from the place where Ben had punched him that time he'd called his mother a sellout for taking over his father's position at Paladin. Nicholas shook his head, wondering why he'd never learned to control his big mouth.

He rubbed his hands together again. Maybe she'd put a spell on him. He kept calling her face to mind, suspecting her of some kind of magic.

Concentrate, he told himself sternly. *Stop imagining things. You're only making that connection because you want to see her again. This is just your body telling your brain that it's been too long since you've gotten laid.*

Nicholas drove his hands into his pockets, stepped backward, and tripped over a rock concealed in the high grass. He clutched his leg and swore. In a fit of annoyance, he kicked the rock and turned it over. There, among the dirt and the bugs that scampered away, lay the missing onyx chess piece from John's house, the white knight. He picked the piece out of the dirt and wiped it on his sleeve. Nicholas cradled the tiny toy in his palm, frowning.

"How did this get out here?" he muttered to himself. John was not the kind of man who lost things, especially not something as precious as the pieces of a chess set handed down through his family. Nicholas held the piece up to the light and examined it closely. The chess piece was imbued with an almost imperceptible blue light. As he turned it in his hand again, the light around it shimmered green. He sat for a moment among the tall grasses examining the piece.

He heard the SUV before he saw it, slowly twisting its way up the thin strip of gravel that barely counted as a road. Nicholas turned around and headed back toward the Gatehouse. He shoved the chess piece in his pocket as the car pulled into the driveway. Nicholas walked up to the vehicle slowly, wondering if news of this morning's exchange with Emily VonPeer had already reached headquarters. Kane and another, older, man emerged from the car.

"Nicholas, this is —"

"Markham," Nicholas said, surprised. "I thought you'd retired."

"I did. They pulled me out and dusted me off for this case though. Not many of us remember this type of situation." He pulled a cigarette out of his pocket and lit it with a battered blue lighter. "The river's in front of you, forest to the side, there's a cleared field over there. Too bad the place is crawling with monsters." He took a single, long drag off the cigarette before he stubbed it under his shoe.

"What are you two doing here?" Nicholas asked. "I talked to Stanton this morning; he didn't tell me you were coming."

Markham shrugged. "I guess he changed his mind. We're just following up on your call from last night, taking some readings around the area, but we haven't found anything so far," Markham said.

"I could have told you that," Nicholas said.

Markham shrugged and ran his hands over his bald head. "Well, I've still gotta do what I'm told. Have you noticed any changes in the gate today?"

"Seen any more angels?" Kane quipped with a wink, but Markham hit his arm.

"Shut up," he said to Kane. Markham continued. "This is a tough assignment, I wouldn't want it. It's too quiet here, kind of creepy. Is everything going all right with you, you know, since . . . Stanton thought that the assignment might be getting to you?" Markham's face was sympathetic.

Nicholas frowned, confused. Then a thought dawned on him.

They think I'm cracking up out here. It happened to other agents sometimes, when the burden of a case began to stress them. Nicholas stared at them stoically and crossed his arms. "I'm fine," he said. "The gate's fine, and the wards are firm, as usual," Nicholas said. "Why didn't you guys just call?"

Kane shifted almost imperceptibly, an odd look on his face. His instrument beeped in a staccato rhythm.

"Because I wanted to show you something," Markham said as he walked to the back of the SUV and opened the trunk. Nicholas looked inside. A small gray animal lay stretched on a blanket, dead.

"The third jackbird," Nicholas said, stunned.

"Moon got it this morning," Kane said. "We told her we'd drop it at the lab."

"Really?" Nicholas asked. "I've never known her to be much of a shot." As a matter of fact, it was the only class at the academy where he'd scored higher than Moon. "Did anyone tell her we're not supposed to kill them, just hit a wing, trap them, and bring them back to the lab?"

"Well, when she heard you bagged two of them, it probably motivated her," Markham said. "She doesn't like to be outdone. You know how she is. Given their limited range, there's only one place this thing could have come from." Markham pointed to the gate. "We've got to take another look around, just in case."

"What does your gadget say?" Nicholas asked Kane.

"Nothing," Kane said. "It's been acting up though, I still can't get a good reading at this site. Mind if I try it at the gate again?" he asked Nicholas.

Nicholas shrugged and followed them down the path. They walked across a grassy clearing with the river on their left and down the hill along a copse of bushes surrounded by an old, rusted chain-link fence with a metal, yellow No Trespassing sign bolted to the gate. They took a right along the riverbank and walked toward a small wooded area.

"It looks the same as it always does," Nicholas insisted, "I tested it this morning, but please, don't let me get in the way of Stanton's orders." He stopped at two small, rather unimpressive columns of stone that stood about six feet high. The columns had been there so long that they were nearly part of the forest, covered in trails of ivy and moss.

"Geez, it's even worse in the daytime," Kane said.

"It looks that way for a reason," Nicholas said. "We don't want people to see it and suspect what it is."

"Stand back for a minute, Kane," Markham said, placing his hand on the gate. Markham brought out his pen that with a whisper shaped itself into a long staff. Kane joined him, still holding his device in one hand.

Markham whispered an incantation to check that the wards were secure. After a moment, he dropped his hand from the gate and turned back to face Nicholas.

"Satisfied?" Nicholas asked, crossing his arms.

"Just do it," Nicholas heard Markham whisper. Kane dropped his sensor and, weapon in hand, spun to face Nicholas. Nicholas hit the ground as a stunning spell flew over his head. He reached to his back pocket for his own weapon. In a moment, he pinned Kane against the fence with a spell. With another shot, Nicholas disarmed Markham.

He kept his distance from the two of them, ready to strike should either of them make another move. The two men froze.

"What the hell was that about?" Nicholas said.

"It's nothing personal, we're just following orders," Markham gasped, clutching his chest. "Did you really need to send a shot that strong? I'm an old man, for Christ's sake."

"Whose orders? Did Stanton tell you to do this?" Nicholas spat. The two men looked at each other, guilty expressions coloring their faces. Markham swore under his breath.

Kane sighed. "I told her it wouldn't work."

"Your mother wanted us to help with your reassignment," Markham said. "She wants Stanton to move you off this project, thinks it's too dangerous, but he refused. So she called in a favor with us. She wanted us to escort you back to her base in Brazil; she said she'd make it right with Stanton and not mention our names. Now, your mom and I go back thirty years, she helped me pass my finals at the Academy. She told us that you wouldn't leave a case and there was no way you'd go see her without our help. I figured a quick stunning spell would do the job, no harm to you, and you'd wake up on a plane to South America. She's a legend, the best there ever was, so of course we were happy to oblige."

Nicholas swore under his breath. "My mother hired the two of you to kidnap me and take me to Brazil? That didn't strike you as odd?"

Markham sighed. "Sure it did, but your mother has always had her own methods. Kind of like you."

Kane was still pinned to the gate. "Look," he said, "no one needs to know about this. We'll just tell her that Stanton caught wind of things and the plan didn't work."

"And where does that leave me?" Nicholas said. "Looking over my shoulder all the time to make sure that my teammates aren't going to hunt me down as a favor to my mother?"

The alarm on Kane's sensor emitted a high-pitched screech from the ground. Nicholas released the two men and they picked up their weapons, the argument forgotten for the moment. Nicholas took a few steps toward the field, not sure what he was looking for. Kane grabbed the device, tapping buttons and frowning.

"I can't turn it off," he said. "It's never done this before." He unloaded the batteries, but the machine continued to screech. Kane tapped the screen, "I don't know where the energy is coming from. It shouldn't be running." The screen glowed yellow, then red. Markham put his hand on the chain-link to pull himself up, and the blue light of the gate suddenly surged around his hand.

"Do you feel that?" he asked Kane.

Kane put his hand against the gate and nodded with a curious expression on his face. Kane frowned as he turned to his calculations, still jabbing a single button with one hand in an attempt to quell the alarm. "The energy's not coming directly from the gate though, it's almost like . . ." Their expressions turned from concentration to panic.

Markham screamed. A blue streak of lightning shot between the men, and Nicholas jumped backward.

"What is it?" Kane asked as the stream of light swooped between them. Markham watched the path.

"Holy shit, it's a demon!" he said. "A big one! Kane, quick, call headquarters, tell them to send backup. They're not usually active during the day."

Kane had the phone in his hand and was dialing for backup when the beast descended.

"Back away from the gate!" Nicholas yelled. He fired a defensive spell to shield them, but the spell hit the blue streak of light and dissolved. After that, it was too late.

In a flash of pain, Nicholas was on the ground. He writhed and tried to break free. Fire was eating his skin from the inside, and he squirmed helplessly as the screams of the two men punctuated his own terror. The pain clouded his concentration and the vision of the beast flickered between his primary and othersight.

Through slit eyelids, Nicholas again saw the huge blue cloud, but his othersight showed him the outline of the monster. It was built like a man, moving like an animal, emanating energy fields that looked like lightning bolts from its hands. It heaved a breath and blew a cloud of blue energy that surrounded Markham and Kane. The creature raised its arms and lifted the cloud and the men from the ground. Their weapons fell to the ground. As Nicholas watched, it blew again, this time lighting them both on fire with a blue flame. Their cries stopped abruptly, and Nicholas watched in horror as the beast moved its long, bony fingers like a puppeteer, ripping the white light of their souls from their bodies and disintegrating them into piles of ash as it took their magic into itself. When the beast backed away from the remains of Kane and Markham, it seemed to grow larger and more powerful. It turned to Nicholas.

As Nicholas fumbled for his pen, his hand closed on the chess piece that he'd found. He pulled both from his pocket and clutched them in his hands while he aimed his weapon, praying he'd be quick enough to land a shot.

Nicholas reared as the beast approached him and fired a feeble incantation. He saw the beast raise its hand and a fiery blue light sailed at him.

This is it, Nicholas thought, bracing himself for the onslaught. *I'm about to die.* He closed his eyes. He could hear the beast's approaching footsteps.

Help me, he thought as the fire rushed toward him.

A warm rush of air blew toward him. Nicholas opened

an eye, shocked that he wasn't hit. A blue flash streaked over his head as the beast hurdled over him and sped toward the Gatehouse. Nicholas looked up and saw that a green light encased him like a bubble. He rolled over and pulled himself from the ground, puzzled by the magic that surrounded him.

At the gate lay two piles of smoldering dust, all that was left of Markham and Kane. The thing had sucked away their lifeblood and energy, the typical death by demon. Dusted, Stanton called it. No hope of recovery, your ashes got sent home to your family in a jar, if they could be identified.

The creature rounded into the driveway, running lopsided on all fours, its arms shorter than its legs. A deafening crash sounded, and Nicholas ducked as the SUV in the driveway exploded. The beast made its way into the carriage house and blew it up from the inside. It emerged from the wreckage, still searching for something.

It doesn't see me, Nicholas realized. *But it knows I'm here.*

Aching with pain, he searched for an escape route. The beast began to move forward, heading in his direction as it cast flames a hundred yards to either side of it. Nicholas ran with all his might as the creature gained speed behind him, and with a gasp of desperation, plunged himself off the riverbank. He hit the water and felt a sharp crack as his ribs made contact with a rock and knocked the air out of him. The dark water closed over his head, and he felt himself caught in the undertow. The current dragged him beneath the waves, far away from the Gatehouse, the monster, and the light of the spring afternoon overhead.

CHAPTER 7

When Emily opened the door to the concourse, she was greeted by a thousand flashing lights that stopped as quickly as they started.

"It's not him," someone said. The reporters turned away from her, muttering, and began to pace.

Emily attempted to push her way through the crowd, but the jostle of reporters, cameramen, and high dangling microphones surrounding the raised platform was too thick; there was no way that she was getting past them. Emily frowned as someone pushed past her, nudging her with a camera. The underground walkway was big as a shopping mall, but it was already as crowded as a concert. Whatever was going on, it must be big. She looked to the right – there were probably a few hundred people between herself and the door to the basement office of the museum where she worked, and more were pouring through the door she'd just entered. She figured she might as well stay to see the show. Spotting two familiar faces, she walked over to join them, glad she wasn't the only one caught in the throng.

"It's a travesty!" Dr. Staats said, slinging an unzipped leather briefcase stuffed with documents and books over his shoulder. "The flashbulbs could damage the integrity irreparably, but will he listen?" He shook his head in frustration, occasionally stopping and raising himself on his toes, attempting to see through the gathering crowd.

"At least you've got it under the glass, it should be fine. These dog and pony shows never last long. Besides, most of the cameras will be directed at him, he always makes sure of that," Senator Blevin said.

The microphone screeched as the Museum Director introduced him, "the man of the hour, a true patron of the arts, Senator Jack Diamond." Diamond appeared from a side door like a game show host, shaking hands and winking as a cameraman subtly angled the camera. Rumor had it that the senator didn't like to be shot from the left because of a telltale facelift scar along his hairline that makeup couldn't conceal. Satisfied, Diamond began his speech:

"Thank you, Mr. Silverstein, for the generous introduction. As you all know, we are a city rich in culture and steeped with the heritage of mighty people. Although they are no longer with us, their history and legacy remain true. I come here today to present you with a piece of this legacy, a map discovered as we paved the way for the Riverwalk, a new chapter in the history of this great city."

"He forgot to mention that they dug it out of the foundation of an ancient church they were demolishing," Staats said under the cover of the echoing applause. Emily covered the silent "O" of her mouth, and Blevin shook his head.

Diamond gestured and a staff member lifted a velvet cover from a large easel on the stage, displaying an elaborate, and clearly ancient, map. Emily immediately understood Staats' indignant attitude. This map was obviously a treasure. Paper tended not to survive the pressures of time; it burned, melted, or was claimed by mold or water. Emily's eye had become trained in recent months

66

on the identification of historic documents. The specimen behind Diamond, if authentic, was exquisite.

A man behind the senator shifted, and Diamond's words faded as Emily studied him. He was clearly trying to place himself in the background, but his appearance, at least to Emily, made that impossible. This man was too expensive for small-time politics. He was pale; his hair was jet black and long in the front, though it was slicked with comb lines as if he'd recently left the shower. He was dressed in an immaculate navy blue suit, white shirt, and red tie. His eyes darted around the crowd, and then stopped when they fell on Emily. They held the stare for a moment. He winked at her and grinned as Diamond finished his speech and the hands of reporters shot into the air. Emily blushed, absently sliding her locket on its chain. Her view of him was concealed as reporters pressed toward the stage abandoning all pretenses of manners.

"How old is the map?" one of them yelled.

"We've dated it at 1652," Diamond said with a quick glance into his hand. He was reading a note card.

"What language is it written in?" another reporter asked.

"Mostly Latin, but some of the notes are in Dutch," Diamond said.

"What are you going to do with it?"

"This map will be translated and authenticated by our team of museum experts, and will then be displayed at a location to be determined in the future," Diamond said.

"That means he wants it in his office," Blevin said, and Staats again pursed his lips and shook his head.

"Senator Diamond, how do you respond to the allegations that the map was uncovered when Diamond Construction began digging in historic property protected by a court order?"

"No more questions," another one of Diamond's

handlers snapped.

Senator Diamond shrugged his shoulders in a "What can I do?" expression, and smiled as the crowd stirred, pressing for more answers. The man in the suit held the door for the senator as several others flanked him, leading him out of the conference. A reporter tried to follow the senator, but the door slammed in his face; he pulled at it, but couldn't get through, someone had thrown the bolt on the other side. For a moment it looked like the man would be crushed against the door in the throng of wires and cameras, but someone yelled, "Let's get him at the limo!"

Blevin grabbed Emily's and Staats' arms and backed them against the side of the marble walls as the reporters ran to the large staircase behind them. He held the two of them protectively with one arm as the stampede passed.

"They'll kill you over a story," Blevin said. "One of the interns was shoved down the Million Dollar Staircase last month when he tried to interview the governor. He was damn lucky that they only broke his leg."

Several of the aides stood by as Staats rushed to the stage to inspect the map.

"We can't forget the easel," he said as the intern struggled under the weight of the huge map. His back arched with the effort, and a small grunt escaped his lips as his hands shook in the attempt. Dr. Staats and Senator Blevin leapt to his aid, and the three men managed to gently guide it back into the office, instructing the intern to open the door as the crowd began to disperse. Emily felt a tap on her shoulder and tried not to gasp as she came face to face with the man in the blue suit.

"Did you have any questions?" he asked her.

"No, I'm not a reporter . . ." Emily said, fumbling for words. She was not good around handsome men. He waited for her to say something else, and there was an awkward silence between the two of them. Emily racked her brains for something to say, but she was so stunned that this man had noticed her that no words would form in her mind.

"Can I get you a cup of coffee?" he asked her.

"No, that's okay, there's coffee in the office," Emily said. The man's eyebrow raised a quarter of an inch before she even realized what he was asking her. Another awkward silence followed.

Yes, Emily thought, *I am that stupid.* She felt the color spreading to her cheeks. His voice was less confident this time.

"I'm sorry; you must be very busy with the map. Another time, perhaps?" he asked smoothly, offering her a way out.

Emily burst into a big grin. "Sure," she smiled, "anytime, I like coffee, I'm Emily."

He offered her his hand and she took it. He grasped her hand in both of his, holding the handshake for a moment longer than he should have, while staring into her eyes. It was a cheesy, old political trick, and it would have been ridiculous from anyone else, but Emily smiled as he spoke.

"All right then, Emily-who-likes-coffee, I will take you up on your promise sometime soon," he said. The man turned from her and strode down the hallway, while she spun around and nearly tripped. She pulled open the glass door, shaking her head.

That was smooth, Emily thought. She hadn't even gotten the man's name. She turned back and watched him through the glass doors. There was something strange about him. She tilted her head, thinking that she saw a vague shimmer around him, but she was sure that this man was no Paladin. Before Emily could focus on him, he'd turned the corner and was gone.

Maybe it was just a reflection from the door.

Blevin, Staats, and the intern were still maneuvering the map through the common area toward the document room.

Emily walked up to them.

"Who was the man in the blue suit?" Emily asked the men in front of her. "Has Diamond got a new press guy?"

"Didn't see him," Staats muttered gruffly, "I was watching the map."

The intern shrugged. "I just got here yesterday," he said, "I don't know everyone's name yet."

Blevin said nothing, but he wore a thoughtful expression as they continued into the office.

"What are you doing here?" Emily asked.

"Secret mission," Blevin said, smiling.

"Really?" Emily said.

Blevin grinned. "Nah, I'm on the Museum Board. We're putting together a display on antiquities from my District. I speak a little Latin from my days in the Ivy League, and they brought Staats in for the Dutch translations. We've been helping James select documents for the display. Mostly they just put up with me because I like old maps and sign their paychecks."

Emily grinned.

Blevin dropped to a whisper. "They promised Staats full access to the map until he completes the translations, but then Diamond decided he needed a prop for his press conference. Staats is half out of his mind thinking they'll damage it. So I'm also here for moral support."

Emily shook her head. Between his brown coat and red face, Staats reminded her of an angry rooster walking in front of them.

"Morning, Mary," Staats said as they angled the map around her desk. Mary, their new receptionist, smiled at them from a stack of files, clearly frazzled as the telephone rang on three lines at once. All of the lines on her phone blinked frantically, ringing faster than she could answer.

"Please hold!" she said about five times before she paused to talk to one of them. "Someone upstairs re-routed all the switchboard calls to my extension, and now there's no one at the desk to fix it or take the calls," she said.

"Yeah, they do that," Staats said, unconcerned. "Those folks at the upstairs desk like to take a breakfast break, a coffee break, two lunches, an afternocn snack, and then it's time to go home. I'm surprised you've lasted this long with it."

The phone rang again. Staats wandered away from her, and Mary shot a murderous look at his back.

"I'll see if I can help," Emily said.

They left Mary in the distance as she repeated the words: "State Museum, how may I direct your call?" over and over into the telephone.

Emily went to her own phone. She tapped the buttons, sent the main calls to voicemail, and managed to get through to the desk upstairs, where the operators had magically reappeared.

"Thanks," Mary said from her desk, sinking her head into her hands.

Emily grinned, then set out in search of coffee. By the time she got back to her cubicle, she was ready for the stack of files that greeted her, where she could lose herself in the details of her work. She stretched her fingers over the keyboard as she flipped to the place she'd left the night before.

Emily willed herself not to think about Nicholas, but it didn't work. She shuddered as she thought about the good part of her dreams, his eyes, his breath on her neck, the perfect way that their bodies fit together. For a split second that morning, when she looked into his eyes, she felt an abrupt end to the emptiness she'd felt since her aunt's death. She told herself that she'd made the right decision when she chased him away. Some dreams, she reasoned, were better left unrealized. Besides, maybe now she had a second option. Just as her mind began to drift toward the man in the blue suit, a hand tapped her shoulder. Emily jumped.

"How's the catalogue coming along?" Her boss, James, was suddenly beside her. She smiled as he wiped the coffee from his large, snow-white beard. His crumpled blue shirt was buttoned the wrong way and a shade too tight across the stomach, and his brown tie hung limp and too short against his chest. The staff joked that he looked like Santa's badly dressed brother, but the concern on his face was unmistakable. Emily smiled back, aware that he had caught her daydreaming.

"I'm waiting for my brain to start working," Emily confessed. "Rough night."

James was holding the coffee pot in his hand, and refreshed her cup.

"Take a break," he told her as he set his coffee cup down on her desk on top of the document she'd been reading. Emily frowned at him, but he didn't notice. James just spread his arms wide and stretched, revealing a hole in his shirt with a patch of white undershirt beneath.

"Come with me," he said, "we found something that you might find interesting."

Emily suppressed a sigh. James' idea of something interesting was usually a pile of old letters or government scripts, the kind that filtered their way out of estate sales and into the state document room. She took another hurried sip of her coffee, then placed her cup beside his on her desk before following him. There was no coffee allowed in the document room. She nodded at the security guards, and they held the door for her as she walked in. The room was sterile, dry, and a little too bright.

Dr. Staats was buzzing around the map like an angry beetle, pontificating about historic objects and photosensitivity.

Blevin stood beside him, suppressing a grin. He turned to Emily. "So, how are things at the old homestead these days?"

Staats stopped mid-sentence to listen to the conversation. Senator Blevin had been a good friend of her aunt.

"It's quiet," Emily said.

"I'd imagine," Blevin said knowingly, giving her a pat on the shoulder, "if there's anything you need . . ."

"You've helped so much already. I can't thank you enough." Emily said.

"How's everything else?" Blevin asked.

"I'm doing all right," Emily lied in a clipped tone and Blevin dropped the subject, but not the concerned expression.

"So what did you want to show me?" Emily asked, turning to James as Mary came in the door, holding a stack of documents to be re-filed.

"It's actually about this map," James told her. "The museum's restoring the old church off Water Street, part of the new Riverwalk Project. Diamond's people found an old Bible in a wooden box under the floorboards, and sent it over here for cleanup and preservation. This map was tucked in the back of it."

"What's the Riverwalk Project?" Mary asked conversationally, shuffling the papers. The other two men looked up from the map at Mary, while James chuckled.

"Mary just moved here from Iowa," James explained, they nodded and turned back to the map. James told her, "The Riverwalk is Senator Diamond's latest attempt to revitalize the tired downtown of the State Capitol while lining his own pockets. Coincidentally, his brother's company, Diamond Construction, won the bid for the project. Don't ask me how he swung that one; it's a huge conflict of interest. There's going to be a bike path, gardens, and a pavilion for concerts and weddings, that sort of thing."

"Don't forget the big fat statue of Diamond on the

walkway," Staats snorted, and the men laughed.

"Aunt Maeve told me about that," Emily said.

"Yeah, your aunt was livid about the way they plundered the riverfront," Blevin said. "She put a real wrench in the plans when she started campaigning to save the church. Initially, it was marked for destruction, but your aunt and her historian buddies stepped in and got a cease and desist order before it could be torn down. Don't ask me how she did it, but your aunt made some calls, and managed to have the church declared a national landmark before they could tear it down. I've never seen anything get done that fast in the government. After that, Diamond founded some sort of fund, and now he's got another few million dollars to devote to the preservation of the church and the dedication of his Riverwalk Project that saved it from demolition."

"Talk about a shell game," Emily said. "So now Diamond's the new champion of historic preservation?"

Blevin shook his head. "It would seem so. That's what a good press team can do for you. The last few weeks, Diamond is acting like the restoration of the church was his personal idea, and is milking it for every bit of publicity he can get. The map is just one of the things they've uncovered in this project."

"We sent the Bible off to the Smithsonian last week for preservation. They'll probably end up keeping that, it's in excellent condition, and there are only a few missing pages in the back," James said.

"That's because they were afraid that if Diamond got a hold of it, it would burst into flames," Blevin said. The three of them grinned.

"This map is a lesser artifact," Dr. Staats continued, "but very valuable nonetheless, and it will make a fine addition to the museum."

James pulled his reading glasses from his head and placed them on his nose. "As far as I can tell, it's one of the route maps from the Dutch West India Trading Company, and it's remarkably well-preserved, a treasure. But the interesting part for you is here," James said to Emily, pointing to a certain spot on the map. He handed her a magnifying glass. Scribbled on the map was a barely legible word, *Van Peer*, beside a dot on the river.

"That's your land," he told her. "It's also the old spelling of your name, it must have changed somewhere over the years."

Emily smiled as she glanced at the map. She knew there were several similar maps framed in a forgotten bedroom at home, but she didn't dare mention this in front of Dr. Staats. She was already fending off his eager pleas for a tour of the House, a favor that Aunt Maeve had always denied him.

Emily inspected the small clearing on the map around her name through the magnifying glass, but stopped as a small ink mark beside the homestead caught her attention. What she had taken to be an age spot on the map was in fact a small circle followed by some scribbles in Latin. The letters were faded, but Emily managed to decipher a single word, *Porta*, it meant gate or entrance.

"It's that old," she said thoughtfully.

"Excuse me, dear?" Dr. Staats asked her.

"Nothing," Emily said, recovering herself. She moved the magnifier around the map some more, and her eyes fell on another spot, farther inland. At first glance, it was only a smudged circled with smeared writing beside it, but as she looked, the shape of the spot resembled a face with horns coming from its head. She pointed to the spot.

"What's this?" she asked.

"It's the church," Staats said. "It was the first thing the settlers built. Too bad we can't make out the writing anymore, I'd be interested to know what it said."

"There's one more thing," Blevin said, drawing Emily's attention to the bottom corner.

Staats frowned. In the bottom, right hand corner of the map were more scribbles in Dutch, and she again saw her last name, a date, and some words that she didn't understand.

"What does this mean?" Emily asked.

"We haven't authenticated that yet," Staats argued.

"But we will," Blevin said. "The language confirms that this map and probably the Bible belonged to Peter Van Peer, which would mean that both of these items technically belong to—"

"We haven't authenticated it yet," Staats argued.

"—they probably belong to you, Emily," Blevin finished.

"It is our hope that if these pieces are determined to have belonged to Peter Van Peer, you'll consider donating them to the State Museum. These pieces really belong in a place of honor for everyone to enjoy," Staats finished.

"Thank you for showing me this, Dr. Staats," she said. "If it turns out that way, I will certainly consider it." The sincerity in her voice was unmistakable, and Staats smiled back at her eagerly.

Senator Blevin grabbed a fountain pen and a pad from the inside of his jacket pocket, and started to scribble some notes.

"This really needs to be saved. Here's what we'll do to keep it out of Diamond's hands for the time being," Senator Blevin instructed. "Take the map, do whatever it is you do in terms of preservation, and mark the bill to my attention," he said. "The State Treasures and Antiquities Task Force has a small discretionary fund for document preservation and restoration. And mark it in the library under this call number. In the meantime, see if you can find another map to lend to Diamond's office; maybe that will pacify him," Blevin said, handing a slip of paper to Staats.

"Will do," Staats told him.

"Why the secrecy?" Emily asked him.

"It's a personal pet peeve of mine, kiddo," Senator Blevin explained. "Every time one of these maps shows up, they frame it and hang it in an office or boardroom of someone important. The documents hang around for a few years until the office is painted or redecorated, and then the document is replaced with cheap prints and photography from the districts. We've lost hundreds of valuable documents this way over the years, from common thievery. Diamond himself has been doing this for years, and I don't think it's right that campaign contributions are recompensed with state treasures. The bastards will take anything that's not nailed down around here. We're going to try to keep that from happening."

Emily's jaw dropped, but she shouldn't have been surprised. She'd heard about the corruption in the Capitol, but it was more real when she heard it from someone she trusted.

"Welcome to New York," James said, raising his eyebrows. Staats started muttering again.

"There is another thing that I wanted to mention. Your family has lived on your property for hundreds of years. I'll bet there are a lot of things in that house that now belong in a museum. Can I expect a dinner invitation soon?" Staats asked Emily.

Emily laughed. "Never," she told him. "I'm the proprietor of the estate, but that does not mean I'll be giving away its contents. I can keep secrets too."

The men laughed, and Senator Blevin shook his head sadly.

"I told you she'd be stubborn, Staats; she's just like her aunt," he said.

CHAPTER 8

"So let me get this straight," Jessie said, "this gorgeous man that you've been dreaming about for years appeared in your yard this morning, offered to help you find out about the one thing you want to know about in the whole world, and you . . . ran him off your land with a pitchfork?"

"It sounds so much crazier when you say it," Emily said with a smile. She settled deeper into the black velvet chair and took another sip of her coffee. "I was scared, something outside broke the pots in the garden, and suddenly there he was in the yard. It was him, the guy from my dreams." Emily sipped her coffee.

"You should definitely brush up on your flirting skills. Apparently, you're having a little trouble with the idea of subtlety," Jessie said. Her eyes crinkled behind her purple cat-eyed glasses.

Other than her house, Grind was Emily's favorite place in town, for the atmosphere as well as the company. The coffee shop's exposed brick walls were covered with squares of abstract art, and a couple of baristas were cleaning the pristine black bar. A few customers sat in stools at the counter, sipping their coffee and reading newspapers and novels. Steph was piping his latest band over the speaker system, and the two tattooed baristas were deep in a conversation bordering on an argument. A woman at the counter batted her eyes, cradling her to-go cup as she made small talk with Steph, who was both patiently listening and trying to get away.

"See you tomorrow," he said, as the woman finally got the hint and nudged her way out the door, still babbling pleasantries. Jessie rolled her eyes.

"Nothing like a handsome boyfriend," she said with a grin. She took another sip of her drink, spotted the two girls arguing behind the bar and shot them a stern look. Jessie watched the scene for a moment as the pair fell silent, and one of them handed a sloppy cup of coffee to a short woman at the bar. Jessie rolled her eyes again and turned back to Emily.

"That's Lauren and Alex, our newest headaches. Steph thought it would be great to hire a couple," she said. "They both came in with job applications, and we only needed one, but he hired them both anyway. They've broken more coffee mugs in the last two months than all the other staff combined, but they never call in sick, and they're mostly decent to the customers, so what can we do?"

Steph made his way around the bar with a coffee mug in his hand. He looked like the kind of guy who'd own a coffee shop, Emily thought. His arms were covered in colorful tattoos, and he was wearing a black T-shirt with a green question scrawled across his chest, "GOT DEMONS?" His dark-tinted, square glasses framed his jaw and prematurely salt-and-pepper hair. Steph's quirky good looks drew the admiration from men and women alike. He always looked so cool.

"Flirting with the customers again?" Jessie said.

"How else can I get them to pay five bucks for a latte?" he said. He winked as Jessie smiled. Steph sank into the loveseat beside Jessie, and wrapped his arm around her with an affectionate squeeze. He took a long and unceremonious slurp of coffee, smiling broadly at the girls' disgust. His knee bobbed independent of the rest of his body, until Jessie put her hand on it to hold it still.

"What's up?" he said.

"Just talking about our staffing problems," Jessie sighed.

"Ah, yes, the drama twins," Steph said comfortably. "What can I say? They're better than Armando at least. Remember how he used to think it was funny to speak French to the customers and pretend he didn't understand the orders? I'll take drama over pretension any day." He took another, quieter, sip of his coffee.

Emily grinned.

"Speaking of drama," Jessie said, "Emily was telling me that she chased another one of those spooky magical dudes off her property with a pitchfork."

"Really?" said Steph, leaning forward and slopping some coffee on his jeans. "Another one of the guards you were telling us about? Why didn't you call us?"

"Paladin," Emily corrected. "It just happened this morning. And yes, they've been turning up everywhere since, you know . . ."

The three of them were quiet. Steph leaned in with a whisper, "Did you go all medieval on him and poison him with your witch's brew? Because that would be seriously cool, and it sounds like the guy deserved it."

Emily laughed. "I've told you a million times, I don't do that. If I could, I'd have slipped Jessie some poison for your coffee a long time ago, something to render you silent for a few days."

Jessie smirked. "Are you sure that you can't do anything like that? Seriously, what's the fun of being"—she lowered her voice—"well . . . you know, gifted . . . when you're not allowed to do any of the fun stuff?"

Emily shrugged. "It doesn't work that way, not in real life. No dungeons, no hocus pocus, no—"

"Chasing magical cops off your property with a pitchfork?" Steph interrupted. "Nah, that's all in a day's work for most of us." Steph's face broke into a big grin that changed to a look of annoyance as the small crash of a coffee cup hit the stone floor. "Shit," he muttered, standing up again. "We're going to be serving coffee in cereal bowls if those two have their way. Time to go be the authority figure."

Jessie turned back to Emily. "Back to business, what are you going to wear tonight?"

Emily groaned. "I didn't say that I was going."

"Don't be silly, of course you're going with us, it'll be great," Jessie said, her ponytails bobbing.

"What if Steph wants a romantic evening with you alone?" Emily objected.

"Oh, please!" Jessie smirked. "Steph suggested it. No more arguing," she said, snapping her blue fingernails at Emily. "They have an outfit in the window at The Web that'll look great on you. Besides, I need you to drive. I have to get some new tights and Steph needs the van for some deliveries."

Emily grinned with a halfhearted smile.

"Oh all right, go get your purse," Emily said, and Jessie bounced behind the bar for her purse and a goodbye kiss from Steph.

CHAPTER 9

Later that night, Emily was sitting on the edge of the back seat of Steph's van. She leaned forward into the front to talk to Jessie and Steph. "I can't believe I said yes to this," Emily told them, pulling at her fishnet stockings. It had been a long time since she'd been out on the town. She drummed her hand against the window of the van. Steph turned around and winked a black-rimmed eye at her.

"Eyeliner, Steph?" Emily said. "Isn't that a bit much?"

"Says the girl in the black leather bondage gear," Steph said. "Where's your whip?"

Emily tugged at the corner of her dress. Maybe it was a little too much.

"Leave her alone," Jessie said. "She looks wonderful."

Emily smiled nervously.

"Magnifico!" Steph said, either in agreement to Jessie's comment, or to the car that slid from a parking spot half a block from the club. Steph pulled the van into the spot, turned off the engine and stepped onto the sidewalk. He slid the back door open and offered Emily his hand, a necessary kindness due to her new spike-heeled boots, another idea of Jessie's. Emily was nearly six feet tall in them, and she wobbled slightly as she smoothed her dress. Her hair, unbraided for once, rippled down her back in smooth ebony waves. She pulled down the edges of the skirt. A crowd of boys in college sweatshirts and baseball caps walked past them. Spotting Emily, one of them snapped around, walking backward with his friends. He let out a low whistle and made a rude gesture with his hips.

"Keep walking," Steph said under his breath, and the boy turned around and high-fived his friend.

"There you go," Steph said, turning back to Emily. "That's all the validation a pack of drunken frat boys can offer. Let's go, shall we?" He offered an arm to Jessie, and the three of them walked down the street to an old storefront with blacked-out windows.

The music vibrated outside as they waited in line. A burly man in a black T-shirt checked their IDs while leering at Emily with a suggestive smile. Emily looked at the ground as they descended the concrete stairs.

The club was hot and crowded, and Emily, Jessie, and Steph moved through the crowd single file in search of an empty table. By some miracle, they found seats in a dark corner on the other side of the dance floor. Steph proceeded to the bar after taking their orders for drinks. Seated on a stool, Emily watched the people around her. It was a darker crowd than she was used to, all of them sporting steel and leather, gyrating together to an industrial beat by a band that she'd never heard.

"What do you think?" Jessie said into her ear.

Emily wanted to say that it reminded her of a high school costume party, but she could see that Jessie was excited about this place. "It's a little scary, but I like it," Emily said, and Jessie nodded. They sat in silence, nodding to the hypnotic beat of the music for several minutes before Steph returned with their drinks.

"Amaretto sour with three cherries," he said, handing a

drink to Jessie. "And a merlot," he said, handing a dusty glass to Emily. She sniffed the wine tentatively. It was suspect of course, but to her surprise, the first sip was smooth. She smiled at Steph and raised her glass in appreciation. He nodded at her in return, took a large sip of his own drink, ginger ale with a twist (Steph never drank), and offered his hand to Jessie. Jessie, in turn, offered her hand to Emily, but Emily shook her head in refusal and took another sip of her wine.

"I'll hold the table. Go dance with Steph," she said into Jessie's ear.

Jessie grabbed Steph's hand and followed him into the crowd on the dance floor. Emily grinned as she watched them. She laughed as she saw Steph, with his back to her, elbow a man in the side of the head by accident. She only caught the occasional glimpse of Jessie's bobbing head among the crowd. Emily was so absorbed with watching them she didn't notice the stranger who'd sat down beside her until he leaned in for a conversation.

The man was easily in his late forties, his hair was slicked back, and the red rims of his eyes indicated he'd been drinking for a while. He yelled something unintelligible in her ear, but the only thing Emily noticed was the scent of cheap cologne, sweat, and the rotgut in his hand. Her eyes flitted to Steph, but his back was still to her.

"I asked you if you wanted to dance," the man said in her ear with a hint of belligerence.

"No, thank you, I'm fine," Emily said back. The man put his hand on her leg, and Emily firmly removed it, getting up from her place at the table and pushing herself into the crowd before the man could follow. She darted through the crowd, searching for an escape. Emily saw the sign for the ladies' room and, making a motion of brushing her hair to the women in front of her, managed to skirt the line and shove herself through the door.

There were a few dirty, red stalls and a group of women crowded around a long mirror trying to fix their makeup. The mirror reflected the buzzing fluorescent lights that made them even paler than their ivory makeup allowed. Pushing toward the mirror as politely as possible, Emily looked in it and raked her hands through her hair. She wet a paper towel in the sink and sponged her hairline. A woman turned to her and petted her hair with admiration. Emily turned with surprise, but found only a slip of a girl behind her.

"It's real, isn't it? I thought it was a wig, it looked so perfect." The woman continued petting Emily's hair. Emily stepped out of the woman's reach with a polite and uncomfortable smile as a few of the other black-lipped women turned around and nodded in admiration while Emily nodded and thanked them.

"Want some candy?" another woman asked her, holding a white tube between her thumb and forefinger. "I'll give you two lines for forty. It's good stuff."

"Um, maybe later," Emily said as she backed out of the bathroom door, hoping that the big, sweaty guy had found someone else to bother.

Their table was empty, and Emily stood on her tiptoes looking for Steph and Jessie in the crowd. As she began to push her way back to them, a hand grabbed her arm and Emily spun, ready to face her drunken suitor with a shove or even a knee to the crotch. But it wasn't him. Emily's jaw dropped as she found herself again looking into a pair of bright, blue eyes. It was Diamond's guy, the one from the press conference. As he took a step closer to her and smiled, Emily could feel her knees begin to shake.

"I don't think they have coffee here, but may I buy you a drink instead?" he said.

Emily nodded. The crowd at the bar seemed to part in front of them, and he handed her the exact thing she wanted, not red wine, but cold, sparkling water in a blue bottle. Emily smiled at him, and he led her toward a leather-lined booth that a group vacated as they approached.

He wore a black shirt open at the collar. It exposed his skin to the place just above his heart. He sat too close to her, but Emily liked it. She could feel the warmth of his body against hers. His black hair was messier now, and he seemed more relaxed. When he smiled, there was a small dimple in his right cheek that she had the strangest urge to trace with her fingertips. She sat on her hands, blushing at the thought. She fluttered her eyes to his, and he was staring at her with obvious appreciation. The music was so loud that he put his arm around her, pulled her close to him and spoke in her ear.

"So, you're a librarian by day and a gothic goddess at night?" he whispered into her ear.

Emily grinned and whispered back, "Everyone's got a dark side."

His eyes sparkled. "Very true," he said.

"Speaking of monsters, how long have you worked for Jack Diamond?" Emily said.

He grinned. "Diamond contracted me for the legislative session, so I'm only here until June, but he'll keep me if he needs me. I've seen you around the Capitol, and I've been trying to work up the nerve to introduce myself for a while," he said, and Emily's eyebrows shot up in disbelief, but his expression was sincere. "I saw you once or twice, but then you disappeared. I thought you were gone, until I saw you at the press conference. I was hoping I'd run into you again soon."

"You were?" she said, hearing the stammer in her voice and hating herself for it.

"Of course, don't you know that you're the talk of the Capitol these days? The mysterious woman who hides in the basement of the museum?"

"Really?" Emily asked. She glanced into his face, startled. Then she relaxed as he laughed. He was joking.

"Don't mind me, I'm an easy mark," she said, and the man laughed even harder. He took a sip of his drink.

"That's not what I meant!" Emily said, flustered.

"You certainly have a way with words," he said.

Emily laughed. "Yeah, I say dumb things when I'm nervous; it's a particular gift of mine."

He shifted so that he was closer to her, and Emily shivered. His face was only inches from hers. For a moment, Emily thought he was about to kiss her. She pulled back from him, and he grinned.

"Who are you, exactly?" she demanded, and his smile widened. He pulled her close to him and began to whisper in her ear: "My name is—"

Just then, Steph slid into the booth on the other side of her. Jessie stood behind him with an odd expression on her face. If she were a cat, her fur would have been bristled on end.

"So we leave you alone for a few minutes and look what kind of company you're keeping. Aren't you Jack Diamond's new guy?" Steph said heartily.

The man looked at Steph blankly. "Have we met?" he asked.

"I deliver the bagels to Diamond's office," Steph said proudly. "I'm good with faces, and names. But I didn't catch yours. My name is Steph." Steph wiped the sweat from his brow and offered his hand to the man, who didn't take it. Nodding coldly at Jessie and Steph, he returned his attention to Emily. Then his phone rang. He pulled it from his jacket and stared at the screen.

"It's Diamond. There must be a problem. I have to go. Another time," he told Emily. He took her hand and pressed it to his lips for a moment, then released it.

"Buh-bye," Steph said, waving his hand with a mock-sad face as the man left.

Emily turned to Steph, annoyed by his comment. "What

the hell was that about?"

"What?" Steph looked confused.

"You just got rid of the best prospect I've had in months!" Emily said, and Steph shrugged, wiping his eye with the back of his hand, smearing his eyeliner.

"Like I control his phone? Honestly, Emily, do you think I'm a magician? Diamond owns that guy. Besides, I've told you to stay away from those legislative types. Most of the time, they're pure evil," Steph said, still concentrating on the door.

Emily's expression turned fierce.

"Emily, come dance with me," Jessie said. She offered Emily her hand with an impish smile on her face. Emily scowled at Steph, but allowed Jessie to lead her onto the floor. Steph stretched out in the booth, watching the door.

After an hour of dancing, both Emily and Jessie were sweaty, tired, and a little tipsy from a couple more stops at the bar. Drinks in hand, they plunked into the booth beside Steph. Steph batted his eyes at Emily.

"Am I forgiven yet?" Steph asked her.

"I'll think about it," Emily grumbled.

"You know, Steph," Jessie said, "I could really go for some Chinese food. That place on the corner should still be open; do you want to check it out?"

Emily was about to protest, she'd finally started having fun here, but something in Jessie's expression made her relax. Then Emily realized she was famished, and Chinese food sounded very good.

Steph grinned. "That sounds great, I'm starving."

Emily stared at him, thinking again that something in his voice sounded a little phony. He stood up and took Emily's arm, and he led them out of the crowded club in a single file line, pausing to look at the sky as they reached the street.

"Steph, what is it?" Emily asked him.

"Hm?" he said, his reverie broken. "Nothing, I just couldn't help but notice the moon."

Emily looked up. "There is no moon tonight, only clouds." She stared into the sky. "It's still a pretty night though."

Emily turned back to them and caught Jessie and Steph having a silent conversation. She could see that something significant had passed between the two of them that she didn't understand.

"I'm freezing!" Jessie said. "Leave the van there; the restaurant's right down the street, and we won't find a better spot." Jessie crossed her arms over her chest, and put her head down against the cold, trudging in front of the two of them toward a neon-lit dragon at the end of the block.

Emily rushed to catch up with Jessie. This neighborhood, full of offices and businesses by day, had a reputation for being a crime-ridden ghost town at night. The trees planted along the sidewalk concealed what little light the streetlamps provided, and there were constant rumors of muggers in the park that was less than a block away. Emily put her head down, dug her hands deep into her pockets and began scouting in the shadows for signs of trouble. Of course, it was only a moment before her heel wobbled on the uneven pavement.

Steph caught her before she went down. "Easy there!" he said, placing her back on her feet. He stuffed his hands in his pockets, but offered her his elbow, which she gladly took. Together, they made their way down the street. Emily was listening to the sound of her heels clicking against the pavement when a loud caw rang from a nearby tree. She looked up and saw a crow preening itself in a nearby branch.

"That's strange," Emily said. "I didn't know that birds flew at night."

Jessie, still a few steps ahead, turned on her heel and looked back at Emily and Steph.

The crow cawed again, and Steph and Jessie exchanged another meaningful glance.

"See what I mean?" Steph said to Jessie. "Stay close." Noticing that Emily was shivering, Steph took off his jacket and wrapped it around both of the girls, giving them each a big bear hug in the process.

"Is something wrong?" Emily said, noting the worried expression on his face.

"No, everything's fine," he said.

"All good," Jessie said.

"Let's go," he said, gently herding the girls without a backward glance. "I'm hungry."

The crow cawed one more time, and then flapped into the night.

CHAPTER 10

The first drops of rain fell as Steph dropped Emily off in the driveway. She wondered why they'd seemed so paranoid; all through dinner they'd been half listening to everything she said, keeping one eye on the window. When she'd pressed them for an explanation, they'd gone out of their way to reassure her that everything was all right.

Emily sighed. At least she was home. She doubted she'd have any trouble sleeping tonight. Emily groaned in satisfaction as she shucked her boots and stockings and replaced them with her slippers. She was halfway upstairs before she noticed that the House was disturbed.

Everything looked normal. She peeked into the front room to make sure that she was alone. The living room was in its usual state of comfortable disorder, just as she'd left it that morning. Her cat, Malkie, was curled up, asleep in the rocker in front of the fire, oblivious to the House's tension. Emily ran upstairs to check the rest of the rooms. She took a deep breath and tried to look for trouble using her instincts, and she felt a sharp push in return. Where the night before the House had shut her in, this time it was pushing her out the front door toward the gardens.

PREMONITION

The shoving feeling ended at the walkway. Emily shot the House a dirty look, annoyed by its impulses. She was getting soaked to the skin in the cold rain. She spun on her heel, and ran back to the House, only to find that the door was locked behind her; this time it pushed her back, so strong that she lost her balance and landed in a puddle. Emily swore, and kicked the door.

"Easy," Emily said. "This dress is new and expensive— I don't need it covered in mud."

You need to go out there, the House told her. The rain poured in sheets as the House directed her attention to a small path outside the garden. Emily staggered onto the small path that led toward the riverbank. Taking a few steps, she turned back to the House. The sky cracked, and the rain began to pour in sheets, soaking her.

"You'd better have a hot bath and some clean pajamas ready for me when I get back." The House nudged her again, and Emily made a face.

She started down the path slowly at first, and then she could feel what the House felt. Someone was out there, in trouble. Emily tripped over the stones as the path sloped downhill onto the small beach and docking area. At first, she saw nothing; her eyes swept the darkening sky and the river below it. A small rowboat bobbed beside the dock, and the waves lapped gently onto the beach. She paced the perimeter, looking for anything out of the ordinary.

A small noise caught her attention, and Emily walked to the opposite side of the dock. There, crumpled against a piece of old driftwood, soaking wet and covered in river slime, lay Nicholas Flynn, unconscious and by the look of him, badly injured.

Emily's heart lurched, and she swore under her breath. She moved to Nicholas, crouched beside him, and ran her hand along his neck looking for a pulse and listening for his breath. A pulse, dull but steady, greeted her fingertips. She ran her hand along his face, pushing the wet hair from his eyes. A small scrape on the side of his face was the only damage to his otherwise perfect features, but he was very still and cold from the river. His chest heaved. Coughing water, he spluttered and then gave a sharp intake of breath. His head lolled toward her, and he opened his eyes.

"Emily," he sighed, with the ghost of a grin on his face, "I was just dreaming about you." His eyes closed, his head dropped, and he was again unconscious.

She held him for a moment, waiting for him to return to her. No luck. His hair was plastered against his head in thin lines. His eyebrows were golden brown. Long, dark lashes framed his closed eyes. His mouth was full and soft. She wondered what it would be like to kiss him, and a grain of self-reproach bubbled to the top of her mind. That would be the wine talking.

A shard of lightning hit the river, and sent blazing waves of electric light shimmering through the water. A second streak of light shot over her head before she had time to move.

She shook Nicholas' shoulder. "Can you move?" she said.

Nicholas groaned, but after a moment, he rolled to his side and pulled himself onto his hands and knees.

"Come on," Emily said, scurrying under his arm. He was much larger than she was, and the muscles in her legs and back screamed as she heaved upward and began to stagger with him toward the back door. Nicholas, injured and still not completely conscious, did little to help her efforts, and their progress was painfully slow.

Another blue streak of light shot over their heads, and Emily screamed as a tree limb and half of a sparking power line crashed in front of them, blocking the path. She swore as she stepped off the path, lurched, and landed them both in a muddy flowerbed. Emily pulled herself to her knees, cursing the sky. The sky returned her complaint with a mighty crash of thunder, and rain poured over them in frigid sheets.

She had gotten about halfway to her feet when she saw a blue comet lighting the sky, hurtling toward them at top speed. Emily's eyes grew large; there was nowhere to run. She threw her arms around Nicholas, attempting to shield both of their heads.

She ducked as a blinding flash made impact somewhere above her head, so powerful that the ground heaved under their feet, and they were again pitched to the ground. Emily looked up and saw the spidery webs of the wards surrounding the House shimmering in a capsule of sparking, rainbow lights. The magic of the House had somehow blocked the comet.

Get inside! The House said.

Nicholas seemed to rally for a moment, and Emily pulled him up with all her strength.

"Move!" she yelled. Amazingly, he began to put one foot in front of the other, surely if not steadily, and Emily, still supporting him, managed to drag him inside, through the back door, and into the sick room before they both fell into a wet, wretched heap on the bed.

Emily wiped her hand across her head, sweating and shivering at the same time. She didn't know how she'd done it, but as she heard the back door crash shut, she knew they were both safe.

Nicholas' arm was still around her, but the second he'd hit the bed, he again lost consciousness. His arm and shoulder hung over her like a dead weight that pressed her into the mattress. She shoved him off her and rolled him on his back. She lifted his leg from the floor so that he was completely on the bed. He groaned in response and began to shiver. She put her hand on his head and frowned. His skin felt too cold. There was no telling how long he'd been in the water, but he was soaked through. Emily shucked his boots and peeled off his soaking clothes as he began to shiver. She pulled the wet quilt from underneath him, and he shifted on the flannel sheets. She had to get him warmer somehow.

From a nearby shelf, she grabbed several more blankets, unfolded them, and threw them on top of him. Then she walked into the kitchen and started a fire in the woodstove. Her hands were shaking, and she had to strike three matches before she could get the wood to light. Soon, she had the fire blazing, and she went back to check on Nicholas. He had turned on his side and was snoring softly. His shivering had diminished to an occasional slight tremor. She placed another pillow under his head and studied him for a few more moments.

She felt his cheek again. He felt a bit warmer. That made one of them. Emily's teeth began to chatter, and she looked down at her mud-spattered dress. She'd lost a slipper and the one that she was wearing felt like a slimy sponge on her foot. She took the slipper off, grabbed the pile of Nicholas' wet clothes, and dumped them into the washing machine before she trudged up the stairs to her own room.

Before she got there, the bathroom door swung open, and Emily was greeted with a steaming hot bath, filled with lavender. Her robe and a fluffy white towel lay on the chair beside the tub. Emily almost cried with relief as she pulled off her clothes, stepped into the tub, and sank into the hot water.

"You did good," she said to the House.

So did you, the House said back, and Emily sank deeper into the tub and closed her eyes.

She'd think about Nicholas later. "What was that thing outside?" Emily said.

I don't know, but it's gone for now, the House said.

After a few minutes, she emerged from the tub, her skin pink with the heat. She dried herself and pulled on the robe.

Then she walked to her dresser and put on her warmest pajamas and a pair of wool socks.

She crept back down the stairs to check on Nicholas. He had stopped shaking. His hair was still damp, but his face had lost its pallor, and his cheeks and nose had turned rosy. She touched his forehead with the back of her hand, then checked his hands. Much better. She decided that he would last the night, but she stocked the woodstove to make sure that his room would stay extra warm before she went to bed.

CHAPTER 11

Nicholas woke up comfortable in a strange bed. The rain pounded on the roof overhead, and he was overcome with a cozy, safe feeling. He drowsed for a moment longer before he shook his head and tried to remember where he was. Nothing looked familiar here. The narrow, wood paneled room was dark except for a small punched tin nightlight in the corner. He had the impression of a calm protection surrounding him. But then his mind focused on the last things he remembered: the riverbank and Emily. As he shifted, he noticed that he wasn't wearing anything beneath the covers. He sat up in bed, wincing in pain. He lifted the sheets and looked down to see a neatly taped square of bandages covering his side, and another on his ankle, which he noticed was swollen and throbbing in competition with his ribs. He tried to sit up, but the merry-go-round in his head forced him back to the pillow. He groaned. Just then, the door opened.

Emily peered in at him, backlit by the light from the hallway. Nicholas was mesmerized. A silver locket lay in the flat place between her breasts. He couldn't help but notice that there was nothing underneath the pajamas, and the material highlighted the slim curves of her body. Her hair was unbraided, and hung down her back in a heavy, dark cloud. In his distraction, he stared at her, and she flushed when she met his eyes.

"I didn't think that you'd be awake," she said. "You've been asleep."

She was carrying a handful of dry pressed clothes, a towel, and a small jar filled with a brownish liquid that had flowers floating in it. She set the clothes on the chair and sat on the edge of the bed, opening the jar. Dousing the towel with the liquid, she pressed it to the wound on his face.

"That stinks!" he protested, even as the pain in his face began to ease. "What is it?"

"The stink is good for you. You probably swallowed some river water, and this will help both your scrapes and your lungs. Press the towel against your face," she said. "And lie down, let the medicine work."

He obeyed, sinking into the soft pillows propping up his head. Nicholas looked at her with the eye that wasn't covered with the cloth.

"Try to inhale as deeply as you can," Emily said.

Nicholas tried, but his ribs hurt with every breath. "How do you know about healing? I thought you were powerless," he said.

"So you have been watching me," Emily said.

He said nothing, but the expression on his face told her what she needed to know.

She shook her head at him, but continued. "This isn't magic. It's herbal medicine. Anyone can learn it, but most people have forgotten it," she said, swirling the bottle in front of him. "It's just like cooking; it's all about finding a good recipe."

"Why are you bothering with me?" Nicholas said, "I can call Paladin; they'll come and get me."

"No you can't," Emily said. "The House won't let you.

As soon as I got you in here, she closed the place down. We're stuck here. She thinks that there's something dangerous out there. Magically speaking, we're in a sort of bubble right now, so nothing's going in or out, not even an ambulance. I tried to call for help earlier, but the telephone isn't working either. The storm must have done it."

"The house is holding us hostage?" he asked her.

Emily shrugged, placing the stack of clothes in front of him. "So it seems," she said. "Your clothes are in the wash," she added. "They were a mess, so I had to run them through a second time. You can put these on until they're ready, when you feel up to it." She laid the clothes beside him, a gray checked shirt and brown pants. The scent of the clothes was oddly familiar.

"Whose are these?" he said.

"I don't know. I found them hanging in a closet downstairs. Knowing Aunt Maeve, they could be anyone's. They looked like they'd fit."

The flannel shirt caught his attention. Nicholas heaved himself up with an effort, the blankets falling around his waist. He willed his head to stop spinning as he reached for the clothes. Both the scent of the shirt and the small pouch of tobacco that fell out of the front pocket seemed familiar. These clothes didn't belong to just anybody. They belonged to John Dalgreth.

You old devil, he thought, examining the clothes. There had been something between John and Maeve VonPeer.

Nicholas looked up as Emily grabbed an afghan. Then she sat down in the chair beside the bed. She stared at the floor, absently fiddling with the locket at her neck, doing her best not to look at his half-naked form.

She's pretty, Nicholas thought. It amused him that she was this shy. Still, she had managed to get all of his clothes off, and while he was asleep, her hands had been all over his body. He shivered at the thought. He turned his eyes to the window, searching for another subject, and a question came to mind.

"How did you get me in here anyway? Can you transport people too? Or was it another one of your non-magical family tricks?"

Emily looked concerned. "You don't remember?"

Nicolas shook his head. "I remember falling in the river," he said. "I sort of remember walking in the yard. Then I woke up here." His right hand was balled into a fist, and he realized that he was still clutching the chess piece. There was a red mark on his palm in the shape of a tiny horse.

"Hang on a second," Emily said. She walked out the door, then, after a moment, came back holding a small flashlight.

"Look at me," she said. She shined the flashlight in one eye, then the other. Then she frowned. "I don't really know what I'm looking for, but your eyes seem normal to me. You lost a few hours yesterday. I think it's common for that to happen with both a head injury and shock. I should have tried to keep you awake longer. I guess I'm not much of a doctor."

"I'll recover," he said, rubbing the side of his head. "And you did a great job, really. I could've died out there without your help last night."

"Your other injuries don't seem serious," she continued, "a few cracked ribs, a sprained ankle. But being submerged in the water this time of year is no joke; you probably have a touch of hypothermia. How did you fall in the river?"

"It seemed like a better option than the demon," he said.

"Was it the same thing that you think killed my aunt and John?" she asked, sitting up in the chair.

Nicholas hesitated for a moment, not knowing what he should tell her, and her expression grew stony.

"It's okay," she said. "I don't want to compromise your investigation or anything. But I think I saw it last night when I was helping you into the House."

He sighed, and decided to trust her with part of the truth; after all, she'd just saved his life.

"It came out of nowhere, during the day no less. No warning, just a big streak of light, and then it was on us. I've never heard of a demon attacking in the middle of the day. It caught us off guard."

"Was it trying to get through the portal?" Emily asked.

Nicholas stared at her. Clearly, the Paladin had underestimated her. He'd have to mention this when he got back to headquarters. He sighed, then continued.

"That would be my guess. Demons have to travel through a gate to get to this sphere; it's the only way for them to pass between their world and ours. It got two of my teammates."

"How did you get away?" Emily asked him.

He showed her the chess piece. "That's the other part that doesn't make sense. I don't know why it let me live. I should have died with the others; that certainly seemed like its intention. It started to run toward me, but it leapt over me at the last second like it didn't see me. I grabbed my weapon and shot, but the spell didn't do any damage. I found this token," Nicholas said, "when that thing came at me, this sort of shielded me; it lit the field on fire, and I jumped into the river. I didn't even have a chance to fire a second spell." He fell silent, ashamed. His words made him sound like a coward.

Emily sat in the chair by the bed, leaned over, and turned on the bedside lamp. She took the knight from his hand and held it under the light.

"Do you know what it is?" he asked.

Emily turned the object in the light, studying the green and blue glow. "It's called a fetch," she said. "It's an object empowered to do someone's magical bidding; in your case, it seems that it was empowered as a token of protection."

"I thought fetches were like voodoo dolls," Nicholas

said, trying to recall his murky education on the subject. He'd never paid much attention in his magical history class at the Academy.

Emily nodded. "That's the standard, but they can be anything. I've never seen anyone use a chess piece before. Does it mean anything to you?"

"It was John's," Nicholas said. "That's a piece from his chess set. We always played when I was a kid."

Emily concentrated hard on it, and twisted it in another direction, making it shine blue.

"John empowered it," Nicholas said. "I'd recognize his magic anywhere."

Emily nodded and turned the object counterclockwise. "Look at it this way though," she said. "See the green aura? It's got my aunt's marks all over it as well." Emily's face was thoughtful as she studied the dual shimmer of the little object. "The weird thing is . . ."

They stared at each other, each begging the other to voice the same hopeless, crazy thought.

Nicholas' eyes grew wide. "The magic dies with the witch or wizard," he said.

And Emily nodded, hardly daring to believe his words.

"Which means," she finished, pausing to conceal the hope in her voice, "Nicholas, is there any way that they could still be alive?"

Nicholas saw the hopeful look in her eyes. He wanted it to be true as much as she did, but his logic fought against it. Whatever had happened to John and Maeve, they were probably dead. And yet, when the beast had attacked Kane and Markham, it had sucked in the light around their beings, disintegrating them as it went, leaving no husk or evidence behind. The two scenes were different enough to give him pause.

"It's unlikely," he said, "but not impossible." He paused choosing his words carefully. "When I was at the crime scene, I didn't think that a demon had killed them. Their bodies looked like statues when I saw them, then they crumbled. It was the first time I've ever witnessed that kind of crime scene, but something seemed inconsistent about the way they died." He left out the last part of his theory, that a witch had killed them. He wasn't sure about it, and there was no need to make her angry.

Nicholas tucked these thoughts into the back of his mind as he noticed Emily watching him. In his distraction, the quilt had slipped even lower, exposing his hipbone. Their eyes met, and he pulled the blanket higher around his waist.

"I'll tell you what, you get dressed and I'll make some coffee," she said. "Then we can figure out what to do next." Her gaze flickered over him for another fraction of a second before she turned her back on him.

We, Nicholas thought. The Paladin would not like this turn of events. He'd gotten himself into yet another mess. Not the least among his problems was his instant attraction to Emily VonPeer.

Nicholas threw back the covers and stood, stretching. It seemed that her medicine had helped. He felt, if not like a new man, definitely not as bad as he should have felt. He put his feet on the rag rug and stretched more deeply, feeling far better than he should after only one day of rest. His ribs and ankle still bothered him, but the pain was bearable. He looked out the window. A barely visible net shone across the outer perimeters of the land. It was a perfect sanctuary, he thought. Or a cage.

His watch, keys, and wallet lay on the nightstand. Nicholas stared at the objects for a moment. Where was his pen? His nerves tingled as the reality of his situation became clear. A sick thrill went through him as he placed his hand on the door, wondering if Emily was holding him hostage. Hastily, he pulled on the pair of jeans and the shirt she'd left.

He opened the door and found himself in the kitchen. It

was a large, low room with two walls made of rough-hewn lumber. A massive oak table covered with a red-checked cloth stood in the center of the room. To his left was an ancient black beast of a woodstove, and beyond that another door and a hallway. There were two doors on either side of a large green stove, a new model designed to look like an antique. From the far door, Emily emerged, holding his weapon in her hand and frowning.

"What are you doing with that?" Nicholas demanded.

"I must've missed it when I tossed your clothes in the wash; I heard it thunking around in the dryer. Lucky it didn't have any ink in it, it would have ruined—"

Nicholas snatched the pen from her hand and frowned, shaking it experimentally.

"Hey," she snapped, "lighten up. It was an accident. I've never been very good with the laundry."

Nicholas watched as she pushed past him and climbed on a footstool to open a cupboard door. Emily stepped from the footstool and plunked two brown coffee cups onto the counter.

"There's some sugar in here somewhere," she muttered, cups clanking. Closing the door, she emerged with a cracked blue sugar bowl. She turned to him, still frozen in the middle of the kitchen aiming a pen, and raised her eyebrows as she poured two cups of coffee.

He spun around still armed, thinking he heard a noise behind him; it sounded like laughter.

"Do you take milk?" she asked him, bringing the cups to the table and heading to the fridge, appearing with a small carton. Sitting at the kitchen table, she pushed a chair toward him with her foot. Nicholas eyed her steadily, waiting for her attack.

Emily arched her eyebrow at him, half a smile on her face. "So you've decided to spare me? Your magic won't work in the House, you know," she said.

104

His jaw set as he reached for the milk carton.

"What is that thing, anyway?" Emily asked. "You seem pretty protective of it, so I'm guessing that it's not just a pen."

Nicholas grinned. "This is my Paladin multi-tool," he said. "It slices, dices, cuts energy fields, and transforms into about a dozen different weapons. Best of all, it seems to be immune to washing machines," he said as the pen began to glow with a blue light.

Emily made a face as he spun the pen around his finger and blew on the end of it like a gun.

"So now what?" Nicholas asked.

Emily picked up the chess piece.

A cupboard creaked open, and the old blue ironing board crashed out of it, making both Nicholas and Emily jump. They studied the ironing board for a moment, and Emily stood. "Oh my gosh," she said, feeling both excited and sick at the same time. "It's so obvious, how could I not have known? We need to ask the House."

CHAPTER 12

Emily felt like kicking herself. Amidst her grief, it had never occurred to her to ask the House about the details surrounding Maeve's death.

"You know what happened to Aunt Maeve and John the night they died, don't you?" she asked the House. The House rumbled, scolding her for waiting this long to talk.

She never said goodbye. They always come back to say goodbye, all of them. Maeve would be no different in that respect.

"You mean when they die?" Emily said.

They always say goodbye.

"Can you show me the last time you saw her?"

Emily closed her eyes and pressed one hand, then the other, against the wall, and let The House's emotions run through her.

She let her mind relax, and the images became clearer. At first, she drew flashes of the House's history. The texture of the floor under her bare feet shifted from the wood floor to bare earth, and her hand no longer touched wallpaper, but timbers sealed together by mud. She saw a woman crouched over a large hearth that no longer existed, and children running in the door. The picture faded, and then a young man in a three-cornered hat hugged his parents and marched out the door, on his way to war. Next, she saw that same young man grown, clutching the hand of his wife as she held a new baby.

"Can you move forward a bit?" Emily said to the House.

Years of these images flashed by, until she saw herself as a little girl run through the front door and sit at the kitchen table, Aunt Maeve at the ironing board with a smile on her face. And then it flashed forward, to a scene that was unfamiliar to Emily.

It was nighttime, and her aunt was standing at the sink, looking out the window. Emily could tell by the pitch black of the sky in the window that it was very late at night, and she watched as her aunt paced the kitchen in circles, stopping at the window each time she rounded the table. Her face had a determined look on it, but her eyes were worried. Emily watched her as she breathed a sigh of relief and rushed to the door. She opened it, and John came inside holding a small backpack and a banking envelope in his hand.

"Are you sure that we can trust him?" Maeve asked him.

"Maeve, he's one of my oldest friends; I've known him for twenty years. He has experience with these things, and the vibrations from the rest of the place should throw them off. Where else can we take it?"

"Why not leave it in the House?" she said.

"It's trying to breach the House; it's almost succeeded. Even with our work, I don't know how much longer the wards can hold. We need more people. I'm hoping if we leave and take it with us, we can draw it away from the House. He'll put it in a place where it's safe," John said.

But Aunt Maeve waved him away. "If something happens, it needs to get back to Emily somehow. There must be some other way, another place . . ."

Aunt Maeve left for a moment, and then returned

holding her traveling cloak, a small purse, and a silver knife called an athame. The real tool of a witch was the athame, a knife used not as a weapon, but as a tool for directing and manipulating arcane energies in a precise fashion, the heart of true magic. Aunt Maeve carried a small one to conduct daily rituals, but she only brought the silver, jeweled knife out for special rituals and holidays. It was an heirloom brought to the new world by Peter Van Peer, though even then, the knife had reputedly been older than dated time.

Emily had only seen the athame three times in her life, but she knew that the House kept it safe within its walls. It had not occurred to her to look for its whereabouts until she saw it in Maeve's hand. How could she have been so foolish as to not look for it as soon as she got back home? How come the House hadn't told her of its disappearance until this moment? And what was she supposed to do about it now?

The visions began to fade, and Emily found herself staring at the kitchen wall. "Where is the athame?" Emily asked. The House showed her a picture, a circle with horns on its head. It was a mark just like the one she'd seen on the map in her office. She pulled her hand from the wall and sat back down at the table.

"Did it tell you where they are?"

Emily shook her head. "No, but she gave me a place to start looking. I have to get back to the map in my office."

"But a map won't tell you where they are if they're still alive."

"I know," Emily said. "The House doesn't know where they are, but she seems to think Aunt Maeve might still be alive."

"What's her basis for that?" Nicholas asked.

"She says that when a VonPeer dies, they always come back to her to say goodbye before they go. She showed me what happened the last time she saw them. Then she showed me some kind of a symbol, something that I saw on a map at

108

work. But the House said something else—John and Maeve were going to move the athame and leave something with one of the Paladin."

"Which one of the Paladin? I know almost all of them," Nicholas said. "Does the House talk to people outside of the family? Do you think she'll talk to me?"

"She generally doesn't like strangers. For some reason, she let me bring you inside though. Maybe it was because you were hurt and needed my help."

"May I try it?" Nicholas asked.

Emily gestured toward the wall. "Go ahead."

Nicholas frowned in concentration, and he placed his hand on the wall. He stood very still for several minutes listening, and then dropped his hand. "I don't feel anything," he said. "Maybe it's a family talent."

"It must be, I've never had much magic of my own," she said. "I have some small tricks, a few skills, but no real power. I couldn't even tell that the House needed to tell me this, until now."

"So why is she holding us here now, if she just told you where to look?" Nicholas asked.

"That I don't know." Emily squared her shoulders and walked back to the kitchen wall and placed her hand on it. She stretched her hand to the wall. "Why are you holding us here?"

Again, the House showed her the picture of the horned face. *It's unsafe,* the House said. *They're looking for you, and the magic that protects you is growing thin.*

Emily frowned. "I don't know what that means. Can you tell me anything else that might help us find out what happened?"

The House showed Emily her own locket.

"What about it?" she asked, spinning the locket on her neck.

You need to know about yourself, about your power.

"Power," Emily scoffed. "Since when do I have power?"

You've always had power. It's faith that you lack.

Emily detached herself, listening to the House, and an unknown vibration ran through her mind. It took Emily a moment to recognize the emotion. It was fear. The green aura of the House changed and began to flash an angry red. Emily tried to remove her hand from the wall, but it held fast.

"Let go!" she said, trying to pull her hand away, but it stuck there, gluing her to the wall with an aura of blue light. She struggled to free herself as Nicholas rose from the table.

This had never happened before, the connection always moved with her hand. Before she knew what was happening, a hand reached out from inside the wall, grabbed the top of her arm and pulled her into a room of the House that she'd never seen before; a long hallway built in between the walls of the kitchen and the dining room.

Emily hit the floor with a hard thump and moaned in pain. She found herself in a dark, skewed, wooden corridor. A blue light sped across her field of vision, and then disappeared. Emily scrambled backward, horrorstruck. She opened her mouth to scream, but no sound would come out, there was just a vague whistling sound that came from the back of her throat. The light stopped and hovered on the other side of the room. The beast hulked in the back of the corridor; then it began to move toward Emily.

The creature walked upright like a man, but that was where the similarity ended. Its limbs hung at odd angles from its body. Its front paws were split into four long digits that ended with talons it clicked together. Behind it, its tail swished the air, reminding Emily of a hungry cat. Above its shoulders was a long, snakelike neck that ended with a head comprised mostly of large black eyes lit like lanterns. The rest of it was a swirling mess of blades that seemed designed for tearing things to shreds. With a small leap, the creature stood beside her, and moved its head with a serpent like motion, studying her. Emily scrambled back toward the end of the hall, but this room seemed to lack both doors and windows. Spotting a small hole to the outside, Emily ran for it, but the beast flew over her head and crouched in front of her, blocking her exit. It towered over her, stretching its lithe muscles with obvious and effortless strength, shimmering with an unearthly glow.

Emily froze, unable to think. The beast held her in its gaze, and she could feel its emotions: anger, hunger, and a childlike eagerness. Emily could do nothing as it edged slowly toward her, sniffing the air. It reached out its hand to touch her, licking its lips. Emily was paralyzed, aware that she was its prey. The beast leered at her, relishing her fear like a meal. It spoke a deep, guttural language, but its meaning was plain to her.

"Lovely girl," it crooned in a low whispery snarl. The thing grabbed her hand, and pulled her close. She trembled and turned her head away from it as the cloying smell of burned flesh seeped into her nostrils. It held her arm with the lightest possible grip, making her aware that the smallest exertion would be enough to sever it from her shoulder. It sniffed the air again and hissed.

Its tongue lashed her wrist, and slowly wound a burning trail up her arm. Emily screamed with pain.

"Delicious," the beast said, gently moving back her hair and exposing her neck. Its eyes caressed her, and it murmured as it moved toward her. "There is pleasure in the pain."

Emily closed her eyes, trembling. She felt a sting on her neck, and cried out as the thing touched her again.

There was a banging noise behind her and then a blast; the beast screamed and dropped Emily on the floor. A blue light flashed over her head as it pounced away from her, clutching its eye. Emily rolled quickly as the beast landed in the place she'd just left. Another flash of blue light shoved it backward to the breach on the other side of the corridor.

Emily looked up, and Nicholas was standing behind her, his face contorted into a sneer. His magic haloed around him with an effect that was both beautiful and a bit frightening. In his hand, his pen looked like it was comprised entirely of white light. With a flick of his wrist, the magic lashed whip-like from the weapon and throttled the beast. It hissed and fell backward from the jolt of the blow. In a split second, the creature righted itself and then pounced at Nicholas, looking for a weakness in his defense. Nicholas stepped around her, and Emily slid away from the battle, putting her back against the wall, shivering in pain as she clutched her arm. Nicholas stood between her and the beast, his face set.

The creature swung its neck toward her, and she closed her eyes as its jaws snapped close to her face.

Before it could grab her, the light from Nicholas' weapon blazed in the fiery darkness, and the beast again fell backward. Nicholas moved toward it, his face grim, terrifying, and lit with magic. The beast hissed and circled Nicholas, crouching and waiting for an advantage. Nicholas moved with an agile grace that suggested his training, a calm light in his eyes; he knew what he was doing.

As the beast lunged, Nicholas blasted it with his weapon. He pulled the beast toward him, ready to strike a second blow. The creature hissed, and thrusting its arms outward, twisted itself out of the binds. Nicholas cast again, and the whip lashed the beast's back, landing a blow, but missing its intention to bind. The beast turned and charged Nicholas, but at the last instant, he dove to the ground out of its way. Nicholas rolled and rose to his knees as a burst of orange flame shot over his head, missing him by inches. Nicholas fired back, and the tip of the lash caught the beast squarely in its face. It howled in pain, and darted back through the tear it had created. As it left, the House shuddered and turned to its usual color of green. Emily propped herself up with one arm.

"I guess we're even now," Emily said with the shadow of a grin, "a rescue for a rescue." Her stomach wrenched, and she lay down with her face against the wood floor, trying not to be sick.

CHAPTER 13

It was still dark outside when Senator Keith Blevin found himself walking through the ornate halls on the third floor of the Capitol building. He flinched at the sound of his footsteps echoing on the marble floor. Even at this time on a weekend, he might stumble upon a security guard, scheming staff members, or a late night tryst, and he didn't want to be seen. But as he passed office after office, no heads bobbed from the doorways, there were no subtle door clicks; the only thing that he could hear was a sort of windy breath that constantly permeated the building. He'd come here to make a deal with a demon.

The buttressed ceiling soared thirty feet into the air, and the long hallway was polished to a sheen that reflected the giant, crystal chandeliers overhead. Soft classical music piped from hidden speakers in the ceiling, and Blevin wondered why they always left the speakers on. It was creepy. He passed a dark hallway that led to other dark hallways. A chill ran down his neck as a thirty-year-old warning resonated in his head. Blevin remembered the motley collection of whispers from the guys, the delivery boys and pages who smoked in the alley, and their dire warnings to never walk alone on the third floor past midnight.

"Bullshit," Blevin had told them, taking a drag of his cigarette. He'd been a young man himself then, laughing and making woo-woo noises as he carted press releases through the building.

If only they could see him now.

Checking for followers one last time, Blevin knocked softly on the door at the end of the hallway. Not waiting for an answer, he pushed into the office. He closed the door and locked it behind him, checking the lock several times. Satisfied, he walked through the reception area, and then took a left into the offices.

He entered the conference room. Although he was ten minutes early, the other two men were waiting for him. Jack Diamond stood by the window in his shirtsleeves with a lollipop in his mouth. He nodded in acknowledgement.

The third man wore an impeccable blue suit and the comb tracks in his hair made it look like he'd just showered. He was slumped comfortably in the black leather chair with his elbows on the arms. His hands were folded, and he pressed his index fingers into his bottom lip, his face expectant. He was young, around thirty, but the look on his face made Blevin feel unsettled. This was the man that Diamond called his protégé in public, though the title was far from the truth. Here, behind closed doors, it was painfully obvious that Diamond, like Blevin, had no idea what he was doing, and that the young man in the blue suit was the one in charge. Blevin shot a sidelong glance at Diamond, wondering how on earth they'd gotten into this mess, and how in the hell Diamond planned to get them out of it. Yet his face remained neutral as he greeted the man.

"Malphat," Blevin said, nodding his head to the man.

"Sit down, gentlemen," Malphat said, gesturing to the chairs beside him.

Diamond lifted his chin. "I'm fine here, thanks."

"Is there something that you'd like to say to me, Jack?" Malphat asked.

Diamond turned to look at the two of them. He looked like he was ready to explode, but the words died on his tongue as Malphat leaned forward.

"Nah," Diamond spat, "I just want this whole thing over with."

Blevin fumbled with a large, black portfolio bag. "I had to wait until everyone left before I could get this thing out of there. Staats must've set the alarm a dozen times before he left tonight." Blevin opened his portfolio bag and pulled out a large black cardboard folder. He deposited it in front of Malphat.

Diamond pulled the lollipop out of his mouth and joined the other two at the table, his face disdainful and a little bit frightened.

Blevin untied and opened the portfolio bag, revealing the map. Then Diamond unrolled a new map beside the first that included the projected path of the Riverwalk. The line was crosshatched in the place where the construction had ended, less than a quarter of a mile from the VonPeer property line.

Malphat traced the ancient map with his hands. He pointed to a place marked with a circle below a half circle, a face with two horns.

"Here," he said, pointing to a place on the ancient map, "this site is where we will conduct the ritual," he said. "It's less obvious than the other sites, and it lies along an ancient ward line, a break in the grid that Paladin won't remember or expect. We'll work here."

"Do you have everything you need?" Blevin asked.

"I will soon," Malphat said. "Don't worry about me. Your job is to gather the other materials and information necessary to make the ritual happen."

Blevin looked annoyed, but said nothing. Malphat turned to Diamond.

"What say you, Jack?" Malphat asked, pronouncing Diamond's name in a mocking tone. Diamond glared at Malphat, suspicious, and Malphat produced a maniacal smile that was at once charming and terrifying.

Diamond shrugged his shoulders. "Now that our, ah, situation has gone away, the protestors have lost their steam. The equipment's running, no one's messing with the site anymore, and the paperwork problems have melted away thanks to the donations. It's like I said, we took away the head of their tribe, and the rest of them are running scared. It all looks good so far—the construction is going as planned, the builders are doing their jobs, and the statue arrived late last week."

Malphat smiled. "Excellent," he said.

Blevin snickered, but quickly disguised it as a cough. Diamond glared at Blevin.

"And what's happening with your people?" Diamond said.

Blevin shifted in his chair, scratching the back of his head. He paused before he spoke.

"It looks like everything is going as planned on my end as well. The Paladin are moving some people around to account for the deaths, and this time it looks like they're heading the investigation in a new direction, but these people are the elite, we won't be able to keep them away for long."

"What about the girl?" Diamond asked Malphat. "The niece? Did you see her at the press conference? What are you planning to do with her?"

Blevin leaned forward, interested.

Malphat smiled again. "Emily VonPeer," he said. "There was a slight interruption in my exchange with the girl, but the situation has turned in our favor."

"You're not going to kill her, are you?" Blevin asked.

"Emily isn't part of the plan; she has nothing to do with this. Besides, she's powerless. I thought you said that you wouldn't harm any innocents in this deal."

Malphat raised his eyebrows. "Innocents? I love how you throw that word around, Blevin. No one is innocent. Don't worry though, I have no intention of killing her; doubtless she will live a long and productive life."

The two men relaxed as he said this.

"We still need to find the VonPeer athame. We've paid a visit or two to the House, the athame is no longer present within its walls," Malphat said.

Blevin shook his head. "They won't tell me where they took it," he said.

"Well, then, we need to persuade them a little harder, don't we?" Malphat said.

"They'll die before they tell us," Blevin objected.

"Make sure that they don't. We need the two of them as well. Use whatever means necessary to get them to talk, short of death. Find out where the athame is and bring it to me."

Blevin felt sick as Malphat continued. "Now, gentlemen, you must give me some credit. I've been doing my share to keep our problems at bay."

Blevin cleared his throat. "That's another thing," he said. "The dead agents are piling up; that will only increase Paladin's resolve to locate the demon. And it might expose us in the process."

Malphat spun a full circle in his chair. He stopped the chair with two hands on the board table, and pushed himself up so that he was standing over the two men.

"What happened to the agents was beyond my control. Besides, your compensation will account for the casualties."

Diamond and Blevin exchanged uncomfortable glances.

"We're not used to dealing in other people's lives," Blevin said.

"Don't make me laugh," Malphat said. "You two may not be adept at taking lives, but you've both ruined your share of them. The demon needs to eat. I can't stop that. If you have an alternative food source, I'd be happy to hear it." He looked pointedly at the two men until even Diamond was shaking in his wing-tipped shoes.

Having made his point, Malphat nodded at their silence. "Well, then, if you have no other questions, I'll take my leave of you both," he said. Malphat straightened his suit and walked out the door.

Diamond looked at Blevin, pulled the lollipop out of his mouth and crossed himself as Malphat left the room.

"I don't like this," Blevin said. "What the hell have we gotten ourselves into?" he asked.

"He's temporary," Diamond assured him, attempting to regain his composure. "We'll be done with him in a week or two."

CHAPTER 14

Nicholas stood in the hallway between the walls, gasping from the fight. The beast screamed in the distance as Nicholas threw ward after ward into the gap where it had entered the House. Satisfied that they were safe, he rushed to Emily. She was on the floor, and although she lay very still, her eyes were open and she was breathing. Gently, he lifted her up and walked her back through the hole he'd blasted in the wall to the kitchen. Once they were both safely in the House, the gap began to seal itself. The House sewed itself together with a bright green light until it was nothing more than a small crack in the wall.

"I didn't know that room was there," Emily said.

Nicholas lay her down gently on the kitchen floor and checked her injuries. He heard a screech outside.

"Emily?" he said. She mumbled an incoherent response. "Are you all right?"

Emily groaned. "My arm hurts," she said.

"Stay here," Nicholas told her. "The House's defenses have been breached; I'm going outside to try and fix them."

The pain ripped through his side and his ankle with every step; he hadn't been ready for a battle. Nicholas didn't care though. He stopped at the bottom of the back stairs and stretched his othersight outward toward the land surrounding the House. It took him several moments to find the creature's point of entry; it was a small tear in the web of wards by the garden to his left. Nicholas began to chant, and pointed his weapon in the direction of the breach. Then he shot a spell directly at the opening, covering the torn threads of the ward with the strands of his own bright blue magic. He shot spells over and over, reinforcing his work. The result was a web of magic woven tightly into the defenses of the House. It wasn't perfect, but it would serve to keep the creature out until he could construct something more permanent.

He limped back inside the House, eager to check on Emily. Of course, she'd disregarded his advice to stay put. She was standing at the kitchen sink, staring in horror at the thin, black line that snaked from her upper arm all the way down to her wrist.

Emily was in the middle of a clumsy process of cleaning and bandaging her burned arm. She had the medicine that she'd used for Nicholas in her hand, and an old metal first aid kit lay open on the table behind her, spewing its contents all over the kitchen table.

"Here, let me do that," he said. He grabbed a clean, white towel from the counter and doused it with the liquid from the medicine bottle. He folded the towel lengthwise along her arm and pressed it gently over the burn. Emily shuddered at his touch, but was otherwise silent. Her face was pale with pain, and though Nicholas wrapped the cloth with an ace bandage as gently as he could, he could tell that even the smallest movement of her arm hurt her.

"Come into the other room, we have to clean the wound on your neck as well and I think you should be laying down for that."

Emily didn't argue, and she moved to lead the way, but stumbled after a few short steps. Nicholas caught her with one arm, then, ignoring his own pain, swept her into his arms and carried her to the sick room.

"I can walk!" she protested.

He ignored her. He laid her on the bed, careful not to touch her injured arm.

Nicholas moved her hair back to inspect the second wound. "This one's not as bad," he said, doing his best to ignore the lilac fragrance of her hair.

She gasped as the cloth touched her neck, scorching her with its medicine. Nicholas hummed a low chant, murmuring half whispers that charged the potion. "How's that?" he asked her. "Does it feel better?"

Emily nodded. "It was awful," she said. "I don't know what happened; it just pulled me through the wall like I was a rag doll. Was that the thing that attacked you?"

"Yeah. This time I got a few shots in, but I didn't kill it. It's too strong. The best that I could do was push it back through the gap, but the House helped. How are you feeling?"

"I feel like someone threw me on a barbeque," Emily said. "I'll bet that's what I look like, too."

"These injuries will fade," Nicholas said, "I've seen these types of marks before. But this medicine seems really good; your aunt must be one hell of a potion maker."

"What about the House?" she asked.

"She's tough, and the wards were well constructed," he said. "I reinforced the protections and helped reseal the breach where the beast came through. I found the point of its initial attack, there was a small weakness—"

"In the garden by the flowerpots," she said, horrorstruck. "It got through at the place where I fixed the pots the other morning, didn't it?"

"It's okay, I fixed the wards," Nicholas said. "I think that it's still out there, but we're safe inside now that I've patched the House. I'm not going to risk another fight

122

tonight, we're both worn out."

Emily nodded, sank into the bed, and closed her eyes. He watched her for a few moments before he moved to go. Her eyes fluttered open as he moved to leave the bed.

"No, stay here, just for a few minutes," she said. "I feel safer when you're around."

He smiled. She patted the corner of the bed, and Nicholas sat down beside her. For a while, the two of them said nothing, they just sat side by side and stared out the window into the night. Emily began to shiver, and Nicholas stretched his arm across her shoulders and drew her closer to him. She leaned her head on his shoulder, and he ran his fingers through the silky, damp strands of her hair, wondering what to do next.

"Do you think we'll make it through this alive?" she asked.

"I hope so," he said. He leaned his head against hers and continued to look out the window.

He had almost fallen asleep when a shriek above them pierced the night, and they jumped back from each other, startled. A blast knocked them from the bed, everything went dark, and they were on the floor. The lamp and the clock flew at them from the wall, and Nicholas shielded Emily with his arm and shoulder. Emily struggled to stand, but Nicholas pulled her down as another blast shook the House. Nicholas dragged her up and pulled her into the corner of the room, covering her with his body as the blast brought down the small dresser beside them and shattered the mirror in the corner.

Nicholas stood in front of Emily, crouched behind the dresser, his wand pointed at the door, waiting.

"It's trying to push its way through the defenses again," he whispered. He could feel the House gathering its power against the creature.

Emily put her hand on the floor, trying to discern what

was happening. Emily yelped and clutched her injured arm. "The demon is close again, I can feel it."

Stretching his othersight as far as he dared, Nicholas perceived the House's power as a green bubble surrounding them. Emily planted the hand of her injured arm against the wall.

"Help us!" she said to the House.

An explosion of books and knickknacks rained down on them. They looked up as the room began to fill with an unearthly green light. The energy around the room began to swirl around a single center of power over their heads. The energy grew around them as the House raised a cone of power and flung it at the beast. The beast screamed again, a different note in its voice, one of anger and pain. Then everything was still.

Nicholas stood first, and offered his hand to help Emily. He frowned in concentration.

"What happened?" Emily said. The energy of the room changed from defensive to vigilant.

"I think the House chased it away," he said.

"Wow," she said. "I didn't know it could do that. Good job," she said to the House, patting the wall.

"We'd better look for more damage," Nicholas said.

Emily nodded as she stood up and dusted herself off. "You take the downstairs, I'll head up."

Nicholas stepped into a side room, and Emily walked up the stairs on his right.

Nicholas walked past a fragrant room filled with herbs and down a narrow hallway where a large, polished staircase made of gleaming, dark wood descended to his right. He found himself in the main foyer of the House, where nothing seemed disturbed.

He took a left into a large, ornate living room, and stared. It was the kind of room that a person could spend days in and still not see everything. A large chandelier hung in the center of the room. The walls of the room were painted with a rich forest scene that held trees, birds, and a winding river that seemed to be an interpretation of the one outside. On a table beside him, a butterfly flapped happily under a large bell jar. Nicholas tapped the glass, wondering how the creature managed to survive, but he didn't lift the glass.

This room was bursting with other types of collections and treasures: there were Oriental rugs on the floor, Victorian-era collections of pressed flowers, shining bugs in glass cases, and even an old walk-in fireplace taking up the entire back wall of the room. Two overstuffed armchairs sat in front of it, one filled with a pillow and a quilt. A gray cat sat on top of the pillow, asleep. *This is where Emily's been sleeping*, he thought, with a wave of pity.

A French door beside the fireplace opened onto another room. When he looked through the windows, he saw a sunroom filled to the top with all manner of plants, and in the center of the room was a long, wrought-iron table surrounded by chairs.

He walked back through the living room and into the hallway.

"Are you all right down there?" Emily said.

Nicholas looked up and saw that she was hanging over a balcony above him. "Yeah, this is quite a place!" he said.

Emily nodded. "It's a mess up here though," she said. "The furniture's all over the place, there are books off the shelves, and it looks like a mirror broke in the guest room. It'll take me weeks to put it back together. How's it down there?"

"The living room's fine," Nicholas said. He peered into the room across the hall. "So is the room with the plants."

"The conservatory," Emily said. "Good. Some of the plants in that room don't even exist anymore, as far as I know. How's the drawing room? That's the one across the hall."

Nicholas strode to the other room. It was blocked by a large piece of furniture. "This one might need a little work. It looks like a bookcase fell in front of the door."

"Let me check the other bedrooms, and I'll join you in a minute," she said.

Nicholas nodded, and she disappeared over the balcony. With a giant shove, he moved the bookcase away from the door and, careful not to step on any books, walked into another, smaller living area that was mostly occupied by a large billiards table.

Despite the overturned bookcases, pictures dropped from the walls, and general mess, all seemed well. He peered out the window and could see that the wards surrounding this side of the House all looked to be intact.

Behind the billiards room was a dining room, painted dark red and occupied mostly by a long, mahogany table. At one end of the room was another porch, and the other end of the room opened into a butler's pantry that led him back into the kitchen.

This place is a fortress, he thought.

CHAPTER 15

Upstairs, Emily was hesitant as she approached the room at the end of the hall. She stood in front of the large door and whispered the words that unlocked the magical protections to the room. This was one of the places she hadn't entered since her aunt's death. The strong, familiar scent of incense, sweet woodruff, and lavender greeted her. A sliver of moonlight shone through the back wall, which was made entirely of smoked glass windows that looked out onto the riverbank. Plants grew around the window, a little wilted, but it looked like the House had tended them in her absence. The rest of the room was elegant, decorated in teal and gold with brightly polished wood furniture. A large circle was painted in the middle of the room, surrounded by candles. In the center was a podium with the book, in its normal place. The rest of the room was neat and orderly.

As Emily prowled the ritual room, she noticed the hasty preparations for a spell on the altar. The candles in their holders were red and black, a red and black altar cloth lay folded on the table. The potion cabinet was unlocked, and several ornate bottles that held the House's most volatile poisons lay carelessly on the table, some of them spilled. A group of small, corked bottles lay beside them. A crystal decanter was filled with a reddish brown liquid, crusted at the top. Emily opened the top and sniffed, the rusty sweet odor confirmed its contents, blood. Replacing the bottle carefully, she walked to the book, her eyes widened with dread as she read and reread the words on the page: *INSTRUCTIONS ON THE INVOCATION AND CONTROL OF THE DAIMON.*

"Emily?" Nicholas called. She heard his footsteps on the stairs. Snapping the book shut, she placed it on the podium. She hurried out the door and locked it behind her. *Now what?* She thought. *Do I tell Nicholas about this? What if he thinks Aunt Maeve conjured the demon? What if she did? What if John tried to stop her? Why on earth would she need a demon?* She turned the key and locked the door behind her, and her hand shook slightly.

"So, this is the magic room?" Nicholas asked and Emily jumped, startled, and turned to face him.

"What are you talking about?" she snapped, and then she realized that Nicholas was standing at the entrance to her bedroom. Emily flushed.

"Oh, that," she said, relieved. "Yeah, that's my room; it's not much, is it?" She paced toward him, eager to draw his attention away from the door she'd just closed. She groaned when she saw the mess. Her small double bed was dressed in white sheets and patchwork quilts. A braided rug lay on the floor beside an ancient nightstand, and an antique dresser with a mirror stood against the opposite wall. The third wall in the back of the room held a window that displayed the starless night. Beside the window lay the remains of her bookshelves that had crumpled onto her writing desk.

"What a mess," Emily said. She glanced at the clock; it was very late, and she was so tired. She picked up a handful of books, then dropped them as the mark on her arm burned.

Nicholas was suddenly at her side, looking exhausted himself.

"Come on," he said. "That thing is gone for the moment. I think the House must have landed a good shot. If it comes back, we'll know. We're done for the night." Nicholas took her hand and pulled her to her bed, throwing back the covers.

Emily's mind raced as he took her by the shoulders and directed her to the bed.

"Get some rest," Nicholas said.

Emily didn't feel like arguing. She stretched onto the bed, groaning from comfort and exhaustion.

"I'll keep watch."

But Emily saw the pale cast to Nicholas' features and the circles under his eyes. He sank into the overstuffed, yellow flowered armchair in the corner by the window, and Emily sat up in bed and tucked her knees under her chin.

"If you're up, I'm up," she said.

"Suit yourself," Nicholas said.

She put her arms around her knees and leaned against the wall. She and Nicholas stared at each other silently across the room for several long minutes. Then her eyes began to grow heavy and she jerked her head up suddenly.

"I'm not asleep!" she said.

Nicholas had already closed his eyes.

It's safe now, the House said. *Go to sleep.*

And she did. Emily shifted in bed as her dreams overtook her. *She found herself walking on a dark path, following the sound of beating drums to a large bonfire blazing against the backdrop of the river. A cold breeze blew her hair around her shoulders. Voices chanted a foreign tune in harmony. As she drew closer to the flames, the smell of smoke filled her, making her eyes water. Even in the dim light, she could see the white moon punching a hole in the sky above her. She moved closer to the crowd for a better look.*

PREMONITION

Their bodies were dark and spiraled with the red and brown marks of earth and blood. The sides of their heads were shaved, leaving the men with sleek, matching Mohawks decorated with beads and feathers. Some wore animal skins, others skulls, others still wore nothing except the fire's light. Several of the men held spears, others brandished arrows and staffs. Many of them held their open hands to the evening sky. Together they danced in a circle around the fire, raising their arms and repeating a rhythmic chant that grew faster as a green smoke began to emanate from the earth beneath them. The smoke rose as their dance became more frenzied, and it spiraled around them, concealing their features in a ring of green light.

At the height of the dance, a single man wearing the pelt of a coyote on his head stood on a rock; clearly, he was a priest or shaman. Someone from the circle handed him a bowl, and the priest lifted it above his head and sang as he threw the liquid onto the fire. Dropping the bowl, he raised his arms and yelled, and a portion of the green light flew into his outstretched hands. The priest was engulfed in the green light, and with a swift wave of his arms, the power that surrounded him turned into bands that he held like ropes. With another wave of his arms, the bands formed an interlocking net of power that reminded Emily of the wards surrounding the House. He threw the net over the fire and the men in the circle began to cheer.

A hiss screeched from the fire's center, and Emily gasped. What she had taken to be a bonfire was a beast, like the one who'd attacked her. The priest pulled hard at the threads of the bonds, capturing the creature in a net of power. The men in the circle raised their arms and threw the second, larger green ring of power over the net, surrounding the trapped beast in a green sphere of magic. Together the men moved and pushed the creature backward into a pit dug into the earth.

As the creature fell into the hole, the men raced to cover it with dirt, some using tools, and others their hands, never ceasing their rhythmic chant. A huge mound of earth rose as they worked. The priest returned holding another bowl. He held the bowl to the sky and stuck his hand in it, painting a single rune on a nearby rock. He backed away, and there it was, etched in blood: a head with horns protruding, the mark of a devil. Emily looked up and noticed that she was not the only one watching this ritual. Another man was standing at the edge of the fire. He did not belong here, yet he made no attempt to conceal himself from Emily or from the people dancing. He was tall, and his dark hair was tightly bound at the back of his neck. His skin was ivory, and his cheekbones were high, offsetting his dark eyes. His dress was old fashioned, though not like the men of the tribe surrounding them. He wore a plain white shirt open at the collar, tucked into a pair of brown breeches that might have been leather. He turned to her and stared. His eyebrow arched, and one side of his mouth curled into a smile. Whatever she'd done, he approved of her.

Though his mouth never moved, his voice rang in her ears, as clearly as if he'd spoken.

I'll be waiting for you, *he said. He winked at her, turned on his heel, and vanished into the woods.*

Emily tried to follow him, but he was too far away from her already. "Wait. Please. Come back!" she said. She felt his loss like a stab to her heart, and though she ran to the place where he was standing, the scene began to grow dark.

The next thing she knew, Nicholas was holding her by the shoulders. "Emily," he said, "Emily, wake up!"

For a few moments, she couldn't open her eyes, though she could feel the tears streaming from her face. She had to find him. Her body contorted as she babbled in a language that neither of them knew.

Nicholas held her shoulders and straddled her, pinning

her beneath him on the bed. That was when she opened her eyes. She stopped screaming and frowned at him, puzzled and a little afraid.

"Nicholas, what are you doing?" she asked.

He relaxed his grip on her arms, and rolled off her as she rubbed her eyes and looked around the room.

"I was about to ask you the same question," he said. "I was afraid you were going to hurt yourself. You were thrashing around in bed and screaming like someone was trying to kill you."

"Nightmares," she said. "I've always had them."

Nicholas whistled. "Damn, look at you, you're shaking! Those must be some dreams."

You don't know the half of it, she thought.

He still had his hands on her arms, and they looked at each other. A few of the buttons were opened, and he was so close that Emily could feel the warmth emanating from his body. Then he was closer. She looked up at him through lowered lashes, and Nicholas stared at her silently.

"You're all right now," he said.

Emily grinned and looked down, still embarrassed. "I know."

Nicholas moved his hand from her shoulder and brushed her hair from her face, then cupped her face in his palm. She raised her eyes to his and they looked at each other for a long moment, and then Nicholas leaned toward her. She lifted her chin, thinking that he was about to kiss her, but instead, he pulled her into the circle of his arms, and Emily rested her head on his shoulder. They stayed that way for a long time. Emily didn't want him to let her go.

"Nicholas?" she said into his neck.

"Mm-hmm?" he said, pulling away from her. He pushed a stray lock of her hair behind her shoulder and gave her a look that was so smoldering she was tempted to laugh. Instead, she managed a stern expression as she put her hands

132

on his chest and pushed.

"I think that we both need to get some rest," she said.

Nicholas looked at her, incredulous for a moment, and like he was about to protest. He raked his hands through his hair and Emily wondered if any other girl had ever shut him down. She doubted it. He scooted off the bed and sank back into the flowered chair. She thought she heard him swear as he threw the quilt over himself.

"Goodnight," she said reluctantly.

"'Night," he said heaving the word as a large sigh.

Emily smiled as she drifted into a dreamless sleep.

CHAPTER 16

The shutters covering her bedroom window creaked open, and Emily squinted and sat up, alone in her bed. The only thing that she could hear were a few birds chirping in the distance. Everything about her surroundings felt different, safer, though she could still feel additional defenses raised around the House. Emily looked around the room, and then listened for Nicholas, but there was nothing. She threw on her robe and padded through the hallway in her bare feet, stopping at the bathroom.

She combed her hair back with her fingers and splashed her face with cold water. She checked the mark on her neck in the mirror. It had faded into a thin, silvery-purple scar overnight. She looked at herself, then leaned closer to the mirror and looked at herself again. On the inside of her iris was a small, bright purple mark. She rubbed her eye, frowning, but when she opened it, the mark was still there. She washed her face and looked in the mirror again. The mark was still there. It was still there when she looked at her reflection in the mirror in the hallway by the stairs, and it was there when she went downstairs to the kitchen and pulled out a compact from her purse to inspect her eyes again.

"Nicholas?" she called.

Nothing. She walked back into her bedroom and pulled on some jeans, a black jacket, and as an afterthought, a little bit of pink lipstick.

In the kitchen, Emily heard a rattle in the pantry and peeked her head through the doorway. The cat was happily devouring a plate of cat food. On the other side of the kitchen, the coffee pot was on and full, and a cup was overturned in the drainer beside the sink. Her heart leapt, and she suppressed a smile as she looked out the window. He was still here.

Nicholas stood in the clearing in the side yard past the gardens, in the middle of a field full of the wards, which to Emily's eyes, gleamed like small strands of rainbow light. His brows furrowed as he manipulated the lines of the wards, using his magic to strengthen them. She poured a cup of coffee and watched as the net Nicholas created around the House began to strengthen. She put her hand on the countertop, and she felt the House's contentment.

"You like him, don't you?" Emily said. "Against everything, including your normal hatred of strangers, and even considering that he's a Paladin, you actually like him."

Our hero, the House said. *You like him too.*

"It doesn't matter if I like him or not, it's not going to happen," Emily said. "We're putting him in danger. Nicholas is the man in all of my dreams."

That's romantic, the House said.

"No, it's not. My dreams have changed since I was a kid. The last time I dreamed about him, I saw him killed. I don't know what it means. I don't even know if it's real, but I don't want to put him in danger."

So what are you going to do? The House asked.

"I wish I knew," Emily said. "It feels different in here, better. We're safe now, aren't we?"

PREMONITION

For now, the House said.

Emily rubbed the scar on her arm absently. It didn't hurt, but there was a vague tingling sensation from her wrist to her shoulder, almost as if that portion of her arm had fallen asleep. Knowing that Nicholas was safe in the garden, she retrieved the book from the ritual room. This book had been in her family for centuries, and she cringed a little as the leather bindings crackled when she opened it. She would have to remember to rub a little oil into the covers of those old books; it was one of the chores she'd been neglecting.

On the second page was a single name scrawled in the middle of the page:

Lady Jane White Van Peer.

The first page read like a diary.

It is upon the event of the death of Peter Van Peer, a good Christian and my beloved husband that led the town to level these accusations against our family. Tom Goodkind, a farmer and a gentleman of good esteem, yesterday brought evidence to the town stating that I, Lady Jane White Van Peer, was seen aiding a devil on the way home from the markets on 15 February. Bereft of family and my dearest husband Peter, I will be placed on trial. There will be no other record of my innocence save the one that I write today.

Then there is the matter of the stranger in the sick room in our home. As a Christian woman, I did knowingly take this man into the House and administer medicine in an attempt to save his life, but I fear that I have also failed in this endeavor, and it is likely that I will face the additional charges of adultery and murder.

The accusations leveled by Goodkind and the Church will likely be enough evidence to merit a conviction of death. Please let this passage serve as testament of my innocence for our son, Samuel Peter Van Peer, and to those who will come to care for him. Though I am blameless in the eyes of God and man, I fear that my fate has already been decided.

Emily turned the page, waiting to see what had happened to Jane, but the next page was an elaborate drawing. The inner margin was decorated with a murder of crows. In the center of the page was a beast, a man with the head of a crow. Behind him were a gate and an army of monsters and demons. *Legions*, it said.

She turned the page and found another sketch taped into the pages of the book.

This picture was different, just a simple pen and ink drawing of a young man scratched into the page in simple brown ink. He was extremely good looking, with long braided hair and high cheekbones. He wore a white shirt with the collar open at the neck.

The caption under this picture said: *MALPHAT, D. 1688.* It was the young man from last night's dream. And also, she realized with a start as she studied the picture, he bore an extreme resemblance to the guy from the bar, Diamond's assistant.

As Emily was thinking about this, the House shifted again and relaxed its defenses.

The Paladin does good work, the House said.

Before Emily had time to think about this, she heard a screech outside. Slamming the book shut, she hid it in the herb room, laying an old stack of dishtowels on top of it for good measure. She'd move it later. As she ran to the kitchen window, she looked out just in time to see a black van tear into the driveway and slam to a halt an inch from her bumper. Emily hurried to the back door as Steph and Jessie spilled out of the van and raced each other up the porch stairs. Jessie burst into the kitchen as Emily reached the back door. She wrapped her arms around Emily, bursting into tears. Steph threw his arms around them both.

"You're all right!" he said, holding Emily at arm's length and inspecting her. He hugged her again, and Emily winced in pain.

"But you're not all right, you're hurt," he said.

"It's just a scratch. I'll be fine. What's the matter?" she said. "You're white as a ghost."

"We weren't expecting to find you alive in here," Steph said. "Between the monster, the Paladin, and the war going on outside, we were sure that something terrible had happened to you."

Before Emily could interrupt, Jessie jumped into the conversation.

"We've been here all night. We saw the creature breach the wards of the House. A few minutes later, we saw the House fling the beast outside—how on earth did you manage to fight it by yourself?" Jessie asked.

"Wait, how do you know about all that . . . and what were you doing here last night?" Emily said.

Before she could get an answer, Nicholas ran through the door and looked at the three of them, his face alarmed. His hair was a mess, and his shirt was unbuttoned. He held his weapon, prepared to fire.

Steph grinned wickedly at Emily. "So is this the guy you forked the other day?"

Jessie covered her face with her hands.

Emily hit him on the chest and felt the heat rising to her cheeks. "Don't be rude, Steph. This is Nicholas Flynn; he lives next door."

Steph shook his hand. "Hello, again, Paladin. I'm glad to see you alive as well. Your people are still next door sorting through the chaos at the gate from the other day. It was a good thing they were there last night; they saw the beast and helped us drive it away from the House. I heard one of them say that they recovered remains from the battle;

138

I assumed that they were yours."

Emily looked between the three of them. "Would somebody please tell me what's going on here?"

"We met the other day," Steph said. "It appears that our jobs are overlapping at the moment." He turned back to Nicholas. "Now I'm the one who owes you for saving my charge."

"Your charge?" Emily said. "Steph, you run a coffee shop."

Steph took her by the shoulders and looked meaningfully into her eyes. "Emily, you may not know this about me, but there is more to me than just coffee. I've been called to a higher task than mere refreshment. I don't know if you'd call me a hero, or even a legend, but it's time you knew that I'm different than I used to be. I'm special."

"That's an understatement," Emily said, rolling her eyes.

Steph grinned over the top of her head at Jessie. "That was good, wasn't it? I've been working on my monologue."

"Beautiful," Jessie said. "But let's get to the point." Jessie took Emily's hands. "We've been keeping an eye on you since your aunt died. First, we'd have done it anyway because we're your friends, but also, we're doing it because now it's our job."

"Your job?" Emily said. "Explain."

"While you lived in Chicago, Steph and I had a sort of, change in status." Jessie said.

Steph pulled a yellowing newspaper clipping from his wallet. The headline read: TWO INJURED IN RENSSEALAER BRIDGE COLLISION. There was a picture of an old, blue van being dragged out of the river. Emily remembered it; it was the same van that Steph had driven all through high school. It was followed by a description of the miraculous recovery of the van's two passengers. Below it were smaller copies of Steph and

Jessie's senior pictures. The article was dated three years ago.

"I told him he was driving too fast," Jessie said.

"Yeah, you're right, I was driving too fast. This is my punishment, going through eternity hearing you say 'I told you so,'" Steph said, and Jessie grinned.

Emily was confused.

"But you're still you! Both of you!" Emily protested. "I've known you both since we were twelve!"

"Yes and no," Steph said. "We were definitely dead. In another place even, at least for a little while. But then they gave us instructions and sent us back. We woke up in the hospital, alive but different. The doctors were amazed; they had no explanation for the fact that we both managed to pull through an accident that traumatic. We're still the same people that you always knew, but in those moments when we were technically dead, we received a promotion."

"Good word," Jessie said.

Emily stopped staring at the article and looked at the two of them. "Let me get this straight, you're telling me that you're some kind of guardian angels? You're helping me through this situation is the two of you trying to earn your halos and wings?"

"Like they'd make him an angel," Jessie said. "Give them a little credit; there is some sort of sense in the universe."

Steph frowned at Jessie, then continued. "Yes, Emily, it's a little more complicated than angels and devils, but to your mind, that is the best way to describe what we're doing here. We're working our way up the celestial ladder, starting with you. Think of me as half an angel—that would be closer. It's our job to help set things right that have somehow gone wrong in the universe, starting with you."

Emily sat down at the kitchen table, her head spinning. Nicholas placed himself between Emily and Steph, using his body to shield her.

"Back up for a minute. If you're so set on protecting her, where the hell were the two of you last night when she was attacked?" he asked.

"We were outside the House's shield, fighting it from the other side, as were several of your agents, though they didn't see us," Jessie said. "The House wouldn't let us in. There are certain things that we can't do and lines that we can't cross. We have been gifted with magical abilities, but we also still have free will, and that makes us fallible. We underestimated the House's wards. Steph almost caught the demon, but it retreated. It keeps coming back here, though."

Emily interrupted, "What about the fact that I'm a witch? Don't the powers-that-be sort of frown on the existence of people like me?"

"You're not very good at being a witch," Steph said. "Maybe they factored that into the equation."

Jessie smacked him on the shoulder and turned back to Emily. "The powers-that-be made you what you are, Emily, and there are no mistakes. That's a human idea of divinity. The whole picture is bigger than people understand."

"Much bigger," Steph agreed. "Just as you are much bigger than you think you are. When we had that run-in with that demon the other night in the club, we got worried. You clearly didn't know who or what you were dealing with. We drove around for a while, debating whether we should tell you the truth about yourself. We were on our way to tell you all this last night when we were waylaid by the demon. But for heaven's sake, Emily, I can't believe that you never figured this out yourself," Steph said, grabbing her locket. "Take it off," he said.

Emily looked at him quizzically and pulled the locket from around her neck.

"Set it on the table." She did as he instructed. "Good. Now, visualize your power," Steph said.

Emily closed her eyes and concentrated, not wanting to tell Steph that he was nuts.

Nicholas gasped as Jessie grinned.

"What?" Emily said, flipping open her eyes.

"Look at you!" Nicholas said.

Emily stared at her hands for a moment, and then blinked her eyes hard to make sure she really saw what she did. Her aura glowed with a bright green light that eclipsed the people in the room.

Emily stared for a moment, and then her eyes grew large with shock. "Is that energy coming from me?" she asked.

"Yeah, that light around you, that's your power," Steph said. "Your magic's been available to you for years; you just got so used to the idea that you were powerless, you stopped trying to access it."

Emily studied her hands in disbelief.

"No way," she said under her breath, but she knew it was true. She looked at the three of them for a moment, then her eyes fell on the coffee cup on the counter. She reached her hand for it, and it flew to her, spilling the coffee on the floor.

"Yeah, you'll need to practice. Untrained magic can be very dangerous," Steph said. "Until you have some degree of control over your talents, you'll need to keep the locket on. You're like a beacon to the other worlds; it's why your aunt gave you the necklace in the first place. It protected you until you found your magic on your own. You've been amazingly slow at finding your powers though. Given the circumstances, you needed a little push in the right direction."

"What can I do?" Emily asked, stretching her fingers outward. A plate on the counter flew across the room into her hand. She barely caught it before it hit Nicholas on the side of the head.

Steph shrugged. "I don't have the instruction manual,

you're the witch. They just told me that it was time you knew about your magic," he said.

"They?" Emily asked.

"We work on orders," Jessie said. "That's all we can tell you about it."

"So now what?" Emily asked. "Wait, do you know if my aunt and John are alive? Do you know how to find them?"

Steph shook his head. "Again, I'm not much help there either. I only have certain pieces of the puzzle, not the whole picture. I do know that you need to find out what happened to them yourselves," Steph said. "But we can help fight the demons while you do it."

"There's more than one of them?" Emily asked, and all three of them looked at her.

Jessie said, "There are two that we know of. We're fighting the lesser one right now. We have to get it out of the way before we can get to its master."

"Fabulous," Emily said.

"I didn't like how the House shut us out of the action. You're lucky that you escaped without a . . ." Steph's eyes fell on the black mark on Emily's wrist. He nudged Jessie. Another one of those meaningful looks passed between Steph and Jessie, but neither of them spoke.

Emily hated it when they did that. "Have you two developed some sort of telepathy as well? I'm lucky I escaped without what?"

"Uh, without too much damage," Steph said.

"Yeah," Emily said, rubbing the mark on her arm. "I only have a couple of small injuries, but Nicholas fixed them. I feel fine. Speaking of luck, the House showed me a symbol that I saw on the map at work. If I can get another look at the map, it should tell us where to start looking for Aunt Maeve and John. Do you think the Paladin will help us out?" Emily asked.

"No," Steph broke in. "We're negotiating with the Paladin as well. Nicholas, you're in this now too, for good or for bad, which means that you're going to have to think up a good cover story to keep them off our tail. You won't be able to speak of your involvement with us should anyone ask. Our case is even more confidential than yours."

Nicholas nodded.

"So what do we do now?" Emily asked.

Steph's phone chimed in his pocket, and he looked at the message. "Emily, you need to find the map. Jessie and I have just received new information on another location for the demon, and we need to make sure that we're prepared. We'll head out now, and re-group later tonight. Come on, Jessie," he said.

Jessie gave Emily a hug and they walked out the door.

Emily sunk into the chair beside Nicholas, her mind whirling and her nerves working overtime. Nicholas put his arm around her, and she put her head on his shoulder.

"Is this what it's like to be an agent?" Emily asked. "Because I feel like I've been turned on my head. I don't know which bit of information is stranger right now, the demons, the angels, the magic, my aunt—"

"Me?" Nicholas asked.

Emily gave him a tired smile. "Yeah," she said. "You're part of it. What are you going to say to the Paladin?"

Nicholas sighed. "I don't know, but I'll stay as close to the truth as possible. I might be stuck there all afternoon. I'll call you as soon as I can."

He paused for a moment, looking thoughtful. "Be careful, though," Nicholas said. "There's a big reason that Steph and Jessie are here, we have no record of seeing any sort of celestial involvement in a case in centuries; their presence alone speaks volumes about the creatures we're fighting."

Emily and Nicholas walked out to the car together. He

took her hand and squeezed it, and Emily's heart began to race.

"Are you sure you're okay to drive?" he asked.

"I'll be fine," Emily said.

He opened the door for her, and she sat down behind the wheel. She tried not to wince as she reached for the seatbelt.

Steph pulled toward the driveway and rolled down the window. "I don't mean to cut the goodbyes short, but your Paladin entourage is on the way, Nicholas, so it's go time. Do you need a ride to your place?"

"No, take the path," Emily said. "It's faster, and the Paladin won't see you leave the House."

Steph nodded and pulled out of the driveway in the van, and Emily closed the door. She started the engine and rolled down the window. She waved her hand out the window, and the brush in front of Nicholas cleared, showing him the way. Nicholas turned and smiled. Emily grinned; she had to try her magic just once before she left. She put the locket back on, rolled up the window, and pulled out of the driveway.

CHAPTER 17

Emily followed Steph's van for about half a mile, then turned right up the hill as she continued to the light and headed uptown to the Capitol buildings. She pulled into the underground garage, ran up the stairs, and hurried through the empty concourse. It was a quiet morning and hours before the few vendors open on the weekend would show up to unlock their stores.

Every footfall echoed in the white marble corridor, and Emily nodded to the security guard who only had eyes for the newspaper propped up on his lap. She swiped her passkey against the sensor and walked inside.

The office was dark, and she left it that way as she padded over the industrial gray carpet to her cubicle. She turned on the desk lamp and fired up her computer on the off chance that someone else came in; James or Dr. Staats frequently put in Saturday hours, more out of boredom than necessity, a habit that Emily had acquired since she'd been hired. At least she wouldn't look suspicious. Emily opened the program and checked to see if anyone else was logged into the museum's system. No one yet, but she glanced at the bottom corner of her computer screen, it wasn't even eight o'clock.

The hair stood up on the back of her neck and a shiver ran down her spine. Nothing moved, and there was no sound except the electric hums of her desk lamp and computer. She tried to act casual, but she knew that someone was watching her.

"Hello?" she asked. No one responded.

"James?" Emily asked. She had her hand on her locket, eager to try her new powers, but decided against it. It was always best to look innocent, especially when you weren't. Emily searched the room for an additional cover for her presence in the document room. A small collection of plastic-cased maps lay strewn across a table beside James' office door. For a librarian, he had a terrible habit of not returning the documents when he was finished with them, a shortcoming that warranted mutiny with most of the staff. Under the pretense of re-shelving the documents, she sorted the stack in her arms and headed back to the document room, a gesture that provided a likely alibi.

Quietly, Emily pushed open the metal door and held her breath. Her view was partially obscured by the bookcase. Three men stood around the map, their backs to her, engaged in a heated discussion.

Senator Blevin ran his hand through his hair, agitated. "You can't take it out of here like this, Jack, people will notice. Besides, Staats hasn't finished the translation work; this is no time to be hasty."

Senator Jack Diamond stood beside him, his hand on the frame of the map. "You can't expect the museum to safeguard a document like this. It's a huge security risk. My office is in the main building of the Capitol, there is twenty-four hour security outside at all times, as well as a hidden locked storage space in the floorboards of my own office."

Diamond continued to argue. His pale-yellow golf shirt highlighted his tanned arms. He was, as always, camera ready, perfectly coiffed and turned out, and if Emily didn't know better, wearing a little makeup in case a stray camera happened to find him even at this early hour. Staats stood beside them, leaning on his heels with his hands shoved into his pockets, looking very much like he wanted to be somewhere else. None of the men had seen her yet. Diamond moved to grab the map, but Dr. Staats grabbed his arm.

"There's still the matter of payment to be discussed," Staats said. "Finding the meanings of these runes will require outside help, and the people who do this don't work cheap."

Emily decided that she needed to be bold if she was going to get a look at the map again. Edging her way toward the room with her arms piled full of maps and her shoulder on the door; Emily prayed that her acting skills were up to this challenge. She felt a light tap on her shoulder and spun around in shock.

"Ohmygosh," she said. The man grinned at her, the man of her dreams, the other one. Malphat. His face was playful as he shook his finger at her in admonition.

"Didn't anyone tell you that it's not nice to spy on people?" he chided.

"I wasn't spying, I work here, I'm always here on Saturday mornings, I . . ." The words died on her lips as his eyebrows rose in amusement. Emily shivered at his proximity, both fascinated and afraid. She set the maps down on a nearby table.

"Is something wrong?" Malphat asked, again stepping too close to her.

Emily stepped back, nervous.

"You didn't seem this shy the other night," he said with a wicked grin on his face.

Emily smiled nervously, and her hand flew to her locket. "I just wasn't expecting to see you this morning," she said. It was a lame excuse, but he seemed to buy it.

"Same here," he said, "I think that you should come in

and say hello to everybody."

Before Emily knew what was happening, Malphat's hand was on her back, and he ushered her into the room. The three men stared at them for a moment, registering shock and on Diamond's face, flat-out annoyance.

"I found Emily walking around outside," Malphat said.

Emily could sense an undercurrent to his words, and the three men stared at her. Emily walked to the far side of the waist-high, gray document cabinet, near where Diamond was standing, and picked up a large dusty volume from the table. She still couldn't see the map.

"I came in to get some extra work done on the catalogue," Emily said, searching for words, painfully aware that all eyes were on her. Staats relaxed, and Blevin broke into a smile.

"Jack, you know Emily's aunt. This is Miss Emily VonPeer, the heiress to the VonPeer estate on the river."

Diamond's face shifted from annoyance to a sad smile. He extended his hand to Emily, and as she clasped it, his other hand closed over the top of hers as he stared meaningfully into her eyes.

"I've heard a lot about you. It's a pleasure to meet you, even under these circumstances. I was deeply troubled to hear of your aunt's death," Diamond said, his face arranging itself into a sympathetic expression. "It was such an unexpected tragedy. You probably know that your aunt and I didn't always agree, but I knew Maeve VonPeer for a long time. She was a good woman and an asset to our community, and she will be sorely missed."

Emily shot a sidelong glance at Malphat, who had a frown on his face. Malphat stepped closer, and Diamond caught his eye. Emily looked down; Diamond was still clasping her hand in his, still blocking her view. His expression was full of sympathy, probably false.

"It's such a shame that you're all by yourself in that big

house—" Diamond began, but Blevin stepped between them. Diamond's interest in her was obvious, and it gave Emily an idea.

"Emily's a tough gal," Blevin said, "just like her aunt. Staats tells us that they rave about your abilities down here. You're very dedicated to be here this early on a Saturday morning."

Emily shrugged. "My work is all I've got right now. I'm just trying to get caught up on everything, the catalogues are pretty backlogged. But it is kind of lonely. I spend a lot of time by myself here on Saturday and Sunday mornings."

"Indeed," Staats agreed, and the men nodded. Emily caught Diamond's eye and held his gaze for an extra fraction of a second. Diamond winked at her and seemed to make a mental note of this information.

What an old lech, Emily thought.

"That's why we're here this morning too," Blevin said, "lots to do, there's a press conference later this afternoon."

Emily smiled as the situation pulled together in her mind. Diamond was here to bully Staats for the map, and Blevin, true to his word, was trying to stop him. Malphat was here to back up Diamond. This situation would probably still end with Diamond taking the map, so it was now or never for Emily.

An idea came to her. Desperate times called for desperate measures, she thought. Emily threw back her shoulders and did what she saw all of the other twenty-somethings in that place do on a daily basis, flirt.

She looked Diamond square in the eye and beamed at him.

"I heard that you've also become an expert on these old maps and historic preservation," Emily said to Diamond, batting her eyes. "A lot of people are saying you're a hero," she said.

"Who told you that?" Diamond said with a charming

smile.

"Just some of the girls," she said, picking an imaginary piece of lint from his shoulder. "You're pretty famous around here, you know." She looked up at him through her lashes. "You've earned yourself quite a reputation." The way she said this conveyed a dual meaning, and Diamond smiled again, looking very much like a cat being stroked between the ears.

"I do my best to keep everyone happy," he said, catching on to her signals.

"I've heard that too," Emily purred, inching closer to him. "It never really hit me until I started working here how long my family's been here. It's amazing to see how some of these maps are hundreds of years old, and yet have our family's estate listed right there in that same spot along the river. And also here in the corner. You know, there's evidence that this map belongs to my family."

"I've heard that rumor myself," Diamond said. "It's quite a treasure. What would you plan on doing with it, should the authentication verify your ownership?"

"I'm a generous woman, Senator," Emily said, pausing for effect and catching Diamond's eye again. "If the map does turn out to belong to the VonPeer estate, surely we could come to an arrangement that would leave us all . . . satisfied?"

Diamond was silent, but she saw his jaw tense.

Bullseye, she thought.

Diamond laid his hands squarely on the table. He didn't move, but he was watching her intently from the corner of his eye.

So was Malphat.

Emily sidled up to Diamond so that her shoulder was barely brushing his.

"What else can you show me?" She asked, lifting an eyebrow. Diamond coughed.

To her astonishment, it worked. In an instant, Diamond had launched into a discussion about the map.

"Dr. Staats, may I have a word?" Blevin asked, and he and Staats left the room.

Blevin tried to catch her eye on the way out the door. She could see his eyebrows knit together in a single line, but she ignored him. She knew what she was doing, or thought she did. Emily kept her gaze fixated on Diamond and the map.

"This," Diamond said, pointing to a section of the map while flexing his tanned arm, "is where they're constructing the new Riverwalk." He pointed to the very place that she needed to see.

She affected extreme interest as she noticed the demon rune a few inches from his finger.

"This is the location of the church they're restoring."

Emily nodded and fixed her stare between his eyes.

"Of course, this sample is very rough compared to the map that I have in my office. My version is newer, but contains a much more detailed view of the city. You're welcome to stop by anytime and check it out." Diamond leered at her.

Emily remembered to smile with encouragement.

"I'll have to do that sometime, Senator," she said, touching his arm.

Diamond smirked.

Blevin cleared his throat as he appeared in the doorway, a cup of coffee in his hand. Emily was on the receiving end of his best overprotective fatherly look. He shook his head at her, and his meaning was clear: *What the hell are you doing?* Blevin shifted his gaze to Diamond.

"Staats has a few other documents that may interest you, Jack. He's in his office," Blevin said. "I hate to do this to you, Emily," Blevin said, "but we have a few things to tie up here, some details that are best discussed in private."

"Are you telling me to take the day off?" Emily asked.

"Very much so," Blevin said. "It's a beautiful day, go out and enjoy it. The library will be here when you get back."

Emily shrugged. "All right then," she said, going to her desk to turn off the computer and get her coat. Malphat followed her out of the room.

"So why are you really here?" he asked Emily.

She frowned and turned to him.

"Why are you playing games with Diamond? Were you trying to make me jealous?"

"What?" Emily asked. "Why would I want to do that?"

Malphat was silent as he stared into her eyes. Emily, feeling brave from her success with Diamond, took a step toward Malphat so there was almost no space between the two of them. Her eyes narrowed.

"I know who you are, Mr. Malphat," she said.

Malphat stepped close to her and put his hands on her shoulders. His eyes gleamed red with a fierce light, and Emily felt the sour taste of terror well up in her throat.

"Do you?" he said, his voice laced with an edge of threat. "Good." As he stared into her eyes, his expression changed from threatening to thoughtful. "I wonder, Ms. VonPeer, if you have any idea who you are?" He ran the back of his hand along the side of her face, and pulled her closer and whispered in her ear. "Because when you figure it out, I'll be here." His breath warmed her neck, and Emily shivered as he let her go. "Goodbye for now," he said, then left her to join the other men.

Emily beat a hasty retreat back down the concourse, a little frightened by Malphat, but also excited with her first real clue. She needed to get to the construction site by the church. She pulled out of the garage and down the road, her hands trembling.

But as she pulled closer to the church, she saw that the site was a mass of moving bulldozers and workers with blueprints. She'd have to wait until that night to go exploring.

"Hold on," she whispered, thinking of her aunt. "I'm coming."

CHAPTER 18

Nicholas was limping down the road attempting to use his waterlogged radio when the black SUV flew by him. It screeched to a halt, kicked hard into reverse and drew back to meet him. The tinted window lowered, revealing a man with slicked back dark hair, sunglasses, and an arrogant expression. *Perfect,* Nicholas thought. He closed his eyes for a second as he tried to arrange his face in a neutral expression; he couldn't stand this guy. He nodded coldly. "Agent Arch."

Arch nodded in return, but said nothing.

Moon leaned over him in the seat. "Nicholas!" she said. "You're alive!"

The window of the backseat rolled down, a voice said, "Get in."

And he did. Nicholas climbed into the back of the SUV and slammed the door. He was met with a stony silence; the only noise he heard was the soft whirr of the air conditioner. Sharing the backseat with him was a woman in her late fifties, tall and lean, dressed in a crisply tailored ivory suit. She looked more expensive than Nicholas remembered her. Her hair was dyed an impeccable shade of wine. Several tasteful pieces of gold and diamond jewelry sparkled on her neck, wrists, and fingers. No introduction was necessary; this woman was the epitome of Paladin leadership, and the most powerful magician and demon hunter the Paladin had seen in a hundred years.

"Hey, Mom," Nicholas said. "How've you been?"

Lillian pulled off her designer sunglasses, revealing catlike amber eyes and three small, pale knicks high on her left cheekbone that indicated her rank. She raised her penciled eyebrows at him.

"How've I been?" she repeated. "I get a call in the middle of the night from Paladin, catch the red eye from Brazil to New York, and drive for three and a half hours only to arrive at headquarters and have them tell me that they have four agents missing, presumed dead, my former partner and youngest son among them, and then you turn up on the side of a dirt road looking like a hobo with a 'Hey Mom' for all my trouble—tell me, Nicholas, how do you think I've been?" She huffed out a sigh, put her sunglasses back over her eyes, and looked out the window, ignoring him.

Nicholas glared at Moon, who turned around in her seat, barely concealing her laughter.

"Kane and Markham, then?" Nicholas asked.

Arch shook his head. "Dusted," he replied. "We identified their remains at the scene. Until a few minutes ago, we assumed that you were killed in the Gatehouse." There was an accusation in his tone and the silence returned.

"The thing chased me," Nicholas began. "I couldn't fight it. It grabbed Kane and Markham. When it attacked, I jumped into the river—"

"Save it for headquarters," Lillian said, rubbing her head. "That way, you'll only have to tell it once. At least you're not dead."

"Aw, thanks, Mom, that means a lot coming from you," Nicholas said. He looked out the other window, sneering.

Some things never change. But the silence gave him time to think: he needed to get his story straight before the questions began.

Arch pulled into the Paladin parking lot, drove to the back of the compound and parked in the underground lot.

Lillian, Moon, and Arch all shook out their long, neatly ironed Paladin robes, and threw them over their suits as they walked to the elevator. They were all groomed to the hilt; but for their robes and the odd piece of ostentatious jewelry, they would have been appropriate for a high-level corporate meeting. Nicholas followed behind the group as his mother eyed his outfit with distaste. John's ragged shirt, jeans, and work boots were a sharp contrast to the crisply pressed cloaks and boots worn by Moon and Arch. He was sore, needed a shave, and was desperately tired after last night, and he knew that it showed. The dull ache in his ribs and ankle made it difficult even to stand straight. Nevertheless, he glared at his mother, daring her to say something, but she remained silent. They crowded in to the small elevator, and Moon pushed the down button.

The steel doors of the elevator parted, revealing an ornate, gray marble hallway. The corridors were filled with agents, and their multicolored robes swirled around the room. The researchers in green, the historians in purple, the healers in brown, there were even a couple of the lab techs cloistered together in their somber black robes, watching their entrance.

They were met with an occasional welcome and nod; a few even bowed in deference to Lillian. Moon wore her best haughty expression, glaring at the rank and file people who came too close to them, and waddled beside his mother with an important little strut. Someone must have announced them, as the doors flew open before they were touched, each with an eager smiling face behind it. Lillian smiled back, gracious and cold as Nicholas' disgust grew. He slunk behind them, and no one looked at or acknowledged him. His presence was a mere footnote compared to his mother's.

They pushed their way through the final set of doors, and were greeted by another sea of smiles. Stanton sat behind them in his office with the door open. He looked at them over the top of his glasses as he fiddled with the files. He stood as they approached his desk, exited his office, and ushered them into the adjoining boardroom.

"Lillian," Stanton nodded, his face grim. His eyes fell on Nicholas, and a look of relief briefly crossed his face. Noticing that Nicholas was shivering, Stanton grabbed a spare cloak off a hook and handed it to him. He gratefully threw it over his shoulders. Stanton nodded at him. He paused in the doorway as Paladin took turns greeting Lillian in the boardroom.

"You okay?" he asked Nicholas under his breath. "Do you need a medic or anything?" Nicholas grinned gratefully.

"I'll be all right, but I could use a stiff drink right about now, Chief," Nicholas said.

Stanton swore under his breath and shook his head. "That makes two of us," he said as they walked into the boardroom where Lillian was already seated at the head of the table. She exchanged her sunglasses for a pair of tortoiseshell reading glasses, and flipped through the file as Stanton and Nicholas found seats at the middle of the table.

"So, what have you got for me, folks?" she asked.

A man Nicholas recognized as an agent named Cross (an agent not assigned to the case) spoke first.

"It looks like we have a Level Four demon on our hands here, Commander Flynn. So far, we have four"—his eyes flicked to Nicholas—"make that three Paladin agents confirmed dead: Senior Agent John Dalgreth, Field Agent John Markham, and Junior Officer Charles Kane."

"Method of death?" Lillian asked, for the benefit of the room. She kept her head down and toyed with her silver pen as the agent continued.

"Dusted. Agent Dalgreth was initially discovered in corporeal form, but his remains were damaged irreparably at the scene after field agents confirmed his identity."

Stanton interrupted. "Officer Cross, Commander Flynn, if I may?" he asked. "Nicholas is our only living witness to date, perhaps it would be better to hear from him than to rehash what we already know?" Stanton shot a harsh look at Agent Cross, who had neither the grace nor the sense to look humble.

Lillian nodded, turning her eyes to Nicholas for the first time since their argument. "So what happened?" she asked him in her agent voice.

Nicholas took a deep breath and looked around the room. The weight of their stares pressed on him like beams, and Nicholas shifted in his chair before he began.

"Agents Kane and Markham came to the Gatehouse to show me that they had located and terminated the last of three jackbirds discovered on the night of Agent Dalgreth's death," Nicholas said. "As we were searching for potential breaches in the gate, we were attacked. The creature, which looked to be a demon of high-level origin, caught Agents Kane and Markham, disarmed them, and eliminated them. It then moved to the Gatehouse—"

"It didn't identify you?" his mother cut in.

Nicholas shrugged. "Not at that point, I was standing apart from them, farther away from the gate. It moved toward the house, and eliminated both the house and the car containing the jackbird. I attempted to shoot it, but missed. The demon charged in retaliation, burning the field as it came. I jumped into the river to escape, but I was knocked unconscious on impact. I woke hours later and found that the river had washed me downstream."

"We looked for you," Moon said. "We couldn't identify your presence."

Nicholas was ready for that question.

"I was washed onto the grounds of the VonPeer estate," he explained, and the agents all murmured to one another. Nicholas continued, "The trip down the river left me with some injuries, and I rested in the boathouse on the bank for over a day. I could see the beast circling the sky at night. It looked like someone was fighting it."

A couple of agents nodded.

"As I discovered, and I'm sure that you all know, the VonPeer estate is heavily guarded by magical sigils and wards. They must have concealed my presence. I camped in the boathouse, waiting for an opportunity to escape. Emily VonPeer spent the weekend alone in her house, and I didn't want to alert her to my presence since you told me not to contact her. I noted that the house was occupied, and not knowing the nature of the wards or protections on the land, I thought it would be best to wait until Emily VonPeer left to leave the land. I had just left when the agents found me."

The agents nodded to one another and Nicholas sighed. It was a neat lie, all truth except for the omission of several critical details; a trick that he had learned when dealing with his mother as a teenager. Something in his mother's face troubled him though. She began scribbling in her notebook, and addressed her next question to the notepad in front of her.

"Did the demon touch you or make contact with you in any way?" his mother asked.

All of the agents watched Nicholas, not daring to move. Nicholas was taken aback by her concern.

"No, why?" Nicholas asked.

His mother's face lost some of its tension as she explained, "You'll need to report to the medical unit to confirm that. These higher-level demons both feed and reproduce through the manipulations of magical energy. Had it touched you physically, it is likely that the demon would have contaminated you, eventually turning you into a creature like itself. There is no known cure for the condition at this time."

Nicholas pressed his lips together, focusing hard so that he could shield his thoughts as Emily's face floated into his mind. A quicker shot, a split second or a better reaction on his part might have saved her from that injury. He pushed the thought away, but it kept floating to the surface of his mind. Contamination. The academy was full of old rumors about agents who'd been injured by this sort of beast but not killed, and the doctors who dealt with those injuries. But the rumors were old, practically legend. To his knowledge, not one of agent in recent memory had been sent to the labs while they were still alive.

"Essential to this case is the VonPeer family. The agents who were on the scene"—she nodded to Moon and Arch, who sat taller in their chairs—"informed me of their opinion that Maeve VonPeer summoned a demon at the time of her death, and theorize that Dalgreth died trying to stop her, resulting in both of their deaths. The demon, however, is still at large."

Stanton frowned, unconvinced.

"And where did said demon come from?" Stanton asked. "It's an amazing coincidence that the creature is manifesting in the direct vicinity of the gate, yet the two facts are unconnected."

His mother nodded. "Our agents theorize, and I believe it is a good theory, that the answers lie in the VonPeer estate. Agent Moon tells me that she has been assigned to tail Emily VonPeer, and believes that she may also be a suspect in this case. The VonPeer estate is clearly our next lead."

Nicholas looked at Stanton who was blatantly trying to control himself. "Commander Flynn," he said, "that is a seriously flawed argument. The file indicates that Maeve VonPeer grows organic herbs to make into teas and soaps.

161

How do you come to the conclusion that Emily VonPeer has somehow colluded or contributed to the deaths of our agents? Or that Maeve VonPeer conjured a demon?" Stanton asked.

"We haven't, yet," Lillian said. "But it's the obvious lead to pursue."

Stanton looked at Nicholas; clearly he remembered that Nicholas himself had made the exact same argument.

Nicholas looked doubtful. "I thought that at first too, Mom—er—Commander," Nicholas corrected as Lillian raised her eyebrows. "But now I'm not so sure. I think that while you were fighting it, the creature tried to breach the House's wards. It didn't get inside, the House wouldn't let it. It looked like the wards were designed to keep demons out, not to let them in." Nicholas caught Stanton's eye, then looked away.

"Commander," Stanton said. "This theory has been discussed and rejected. Six agents, including Agent Moon, have confirmed Emily VonPeer's lack of magical ability. And, as Agent Flynn tells us, the VonPeer land is highly protected. We need better confirmation than a hunch that Emily VonPeer is a potential suspect. I don't approve of the turn this investigation is taking. This Agency has long been opposed to the idea of witch hunts."

"As you know," Commander Flynn said with a smile at Arch and Moon, who smiled back at her, "good agents frequently lead with their instincts, it's how I have personally managed to be here talking to you today."

"I forbid you to proceed on this," Stanton said with an icy tone, but Lillian just smiled.

"As it turns out, Gabriel," she said, "I don't need your authority to pursue this lead." She handed him a business-style envelope. "As of today, I am officially the new lead investigator on this case."

Stanton looked mutinous as he read the letter. Lillian

162

smiled, a look of smug satisfaction on her face. Stanton got up and exited the room, saying nothing.

"Mom, wait, you've got this theory wrong, I have proof," Nicholas said, reaching for his pocket, but coming up empty. The chess piece was gone; he'd left it at Laurel Grove.

"Nevermind," Nicholas said, his cheeks burning. He sank into his chair, defeated.

"Agent Arch, please escort Agent Flynn upstairs to be evaluated by the medics, he's clearly feverish and may not be in complete possession of his faculties right now."

"Were you ever?" Arch said under his breath to Nicholas.

"Oh, and Agent Flynn," Lillian continued as they moved to leave the room, "in light of your injuries and the recent deaths of the two agents, I feel it would be best if we assigned you to a different leg of the assignment."

"I'm fine!" Nicholas protested, but Lillian interrupted.

"You're being reassigned to Magical Antiquities. You can pick up your orders at the desk. Agent Moon, I'm promoting you, you're my new assistant on this case."

Moon's smile widened and she shot Nicholas a look of triumph.

CHAPTER 19

Emily sat at the kitchen table, frowning at the chess piece in front of her. It may have been her imagination, but it seemed that the auras surrounding the chess piece were growing dimmer. Where was everyone? She looked out the window for the tenth time in five minutes, then glanced at her watch, rubbing her arm absently as the clock in the living room struck ten. Everything was ready to go: flashlight, a marble school notebook full of spells, healing draughts, water, a hammer, and a crowbar. All of these she swept into her old, black backpack.

The phone rang, and she lunged for it.

"Emily?" Steph said on the other side of the phone. "We're running late, we had a small accident at Grind. Nothing too serious, just enough of an issue to be annoying and make us late."

"It's all right," Emily said. "Nicholas is supposed to be on his way too."

"Wait till he gets there, then we'll meet you both at the church in an hour," Steph said. "If he doesn't show up, stay where you are."

"Okay," Emily huffed impatiently. "But he'll be here, it

will be fine," Emily said, hanging up the phone. She put her hand on the House. "Any demons out there tonight?" she asked.

The House said no.

"Then I'm just going to have to risk it," Emily said. "I can't wait for Nicholas, not with Aunt Maeve out there somewhere."

Although Nicholas had called her a few hours earlier as promised, their conversation had been clipped and awkward, little more than a time and date. He'd spoken like someone was listening to their call.

Emily sighed. *Maybe he's not coming after all; maybe he changed his mind. Or maybe the Paladin changed it for him.* She surveyed the chess piece. Emily stuffed it into her pocket. She waited for a few more minutes, but decided she didn't need Nicholas with her anyway. She knew where she was going. Besides, now she had her own magic if she needed it. She grinned at the thought. She tugged her locket out of her shirt, checking to see that it was secure. She looked in the mirror again. The lavender speck had formed a tiny, forked line across the gray of her eye. Maybe it had something to do with the magic. In all the confusion with Steph that morning, she'd forgotten to mention it to Nicholas. Grabbing her sweatshirt and backpack, Emily checked to see that all was clear and headed into the night.

At the path to the car, a chill breeze greeted her, and a flutter in the corner of her eye caught her attention. She looked hopefully at the source.

"Nicholas?" she asked into the night. No response. She jumped into her car, bracing herself as she backed it out of the driveway. She held her breath as she moved out of the House's protection. She paused for a moment, expecting a demon. Finding nothing, she raced down the country road toward the yellow lights of the city.

She left her car in an alley a few blocks from the church,

passing back doors littered with bouncers, smokers, and angry waitresses complaining to one another. Emily edged behind the bars. A variety of thumping beats punctuated her steps; they blended into a single undertone as she headed to the construction site.

Although it was not as grand as the buildings that surrounded it, the church exuded a powerful personality. Its windows and doors formed a pious face that frowned at her from across the street. As Emily studied the street, an impression filled her mind. This church housed a darker god, a god of punishment and blood, forgotten under the gilding by the modern Christians. Here was the home of the Puritans, the hunters of all that was evil. Emily was reminded of a favorite saying of Aunt Maeve's: those who know they're doing wrong do far less damage than those convinced that they're doing right. Emily took a deep breath and ran across the street to the church before she lost her nerve.

Luckily, she knew this place; she'd been here dozens of times with her aunt. It looked different at night, and was marred by the construction, but the outline of the graveyard was still the same. Ducking around the bright orange fencing and yellow tape, Emily searched for a clue. She stumbled, and barely caught herself from tumbling into a deep hole guarded by a sleeping bulldozer. Despite this, she left the flashlight in her bag, it was too obvious, and besides, she'd always been able to see well in the dark. She crouched and put her hand on a stone. It vibrated, but she didn't know what that meant.

Emily crouched in the shadows and covered her pale face as a police car swept past her. She picked her way to the back of the site, to an even darker street, the only light was a dim yellow bulb on a building a hundred yards away, not enough to provide her any visibility. The ground here was undisturbed. She felt the soft grass under her feet.

Someone grabbed Emily's arm from behind. She turned

toward it and swung, her hand balled into a fist that was easily caught by another hand. With both her arms turned behind her, the form shoved her against the back wall of the church. Emily struggled, but he was taller, and his grip was like iron.

"Emily, it's me," Nicholas said. She stopped fighting, and he dropped her hand.

"You scared the hell out of me!" Emily said.

Nicholas pulled off his hood.

"And you're late!"

"Sorry about that," Nicholas said. "The medical workup took longer than I thought at Paladin. They just let me go about a half hour ago, but I'm mostly healed now. I stopped by the House to get you, I got there just in time to see you pull out of the driveway, so I followed you here. Why didn't you wait for me?"

"It was late, I thought you weren't coming," she told him.

"You thought I stood you up?" he asked.

"I didn't know," Emily confessed. "Charming as you are, I really don't know anything about you, except that you're a member of an agency that my aunt's told me to avoid my whole life. You can't blame me for second-guessing you." Emily put her hand on her injured arm and bit her bottom lip.

"How's your arm? Are you sure you're okay to do this?" he said.

"I'm fine," Emily said. That part was a lie. Her left arm felt like it was engulfed with a blazing heat from her fingertips to her collarbone. There was also that thing with her eye, but she didn't want to think about those things right now. She had more important things to worry about.

"Then come with me."

They moved to the far side of the church. Something cracked a few feet from them, and Nicholas grabbed the pen from his back pocket.

A few branches snapped in the distance and they froze.

"What's going on?" She held her breath as a faint blue shimmer of power disappeared around the far corner of the church. Nicholas used his weapon to draw a sigil in the air.

"It will help protect us," he said.

"That reminds me," Emily said, reaching into her pocket. "You left this sitting on my kitchen table." She showed him the chess piece. "Hopefully, it will keep the demons away."

"Thanks," he said, stuffing it into his pocket.

They walked to the graveyard and stayed close together beside the wall, eager to keep their cover as long as they could. Nicholas swore under his breath as he slammed his foot on the edge of a grave concealed by the dense undergrowth of the unkempt site. Emily gazed at a tall, stone angel holding a sword; its eyes watched them, forbidding.

"There's no indication of arcane energies here," Nicholas said. "It all looks normal, normal for a gravesite anyway. Are you sure this is the right church? There's about twelve of them in this neighborhood," Nicholas said, frowning as he continued to sweep the gravesite.

Emily crouched beside him, scrubbing back the leaves to read a gravestone. "I'm sure," Emily said.

"What are you doing?" he asked.

"I'm reading the grave stones. If you can't find something magical, look for something ordinary. We're probably looking for the section of ground with the oldest graves." She bent down at a few other graves, searching for reference points.

"It's probably over there," she said, pointing to the far section of the small graveyard, the part that stretched toward the construction site.

As they crossed the cemetery, a chill wind stung their cheeks. Nicholas knelt in the underbrush, studying graves. A small patch of stone lambs greeted him as Emily moved toward the far end of the site.

He knelt down and placed his hand on a statue of lamb. "What are these?" he said.

"Those are children's graves," Emily said, and Nicholas stood and moved closer to her, looking sick.

Though they walked lightly, Emily noticed that Nicholas was preoccupied. He kept looking over his shoulder. The church loomed overhead, and the tombstones rose around their feet like a series of jagged teeth. There was something here, something in the shadows that she was missing, and she didn't know if it meant that they should run, or that they were very close to finding something important. It was probably both.

Emily dropped to the ground fast, causing Nicholas to bump into her. She was holding a flashlight on a tombstone and reading the inscription.

"Here," she said. "This is what the House showed me. This is what she wanted us to find. Start looking, would you?" She turned to the gravestones. She pushed aside a stray vine that had started to make its way over the face of the grave. PETER VAN PEER and a date.

"My aunt fought hard to save this place," she said. "Our ancestors are buried here."

"But the graveyard itself is safe," Nicholas said, confused. "It's the area outside the graveyard where they're digging."

Emily turned and looked at him. For someone with so much magic, he could be surprisingly slow.

"The unhallowed ground outside the cemetery is where they would bury our kind," she said. "More than one of the VonPeers was accused of witchcraft over the years. Some of them are buried inside the churchyard, but there are others interred outside the cemetery's gate."

"How many?" he asked.

PREMONITION

"A few," she said. "Some from witchcraft, but several others were buried there by choice, so that they could rest alongside their family. My great-grandmother is outside the gate. That's how my aunt managed the court order to halt the construction around the church. She had proof that Diamond Construction was about to overturn a gravesite. Over here," she said, pointing in front of them.

They walked toward a large bulldozer sitting alongside the street. Emily stooped. Tangled in the mass of vines surrounding the gravestone was a small stone vase filled with a withered bouquet of flowers. Among the leaves were miniscule grains of phosphorescent light, another mark of her aunt's magic. "Look!" Emily said. She grasped the bouquet. Though it was withered, the scent of the herbs remained, and its fragrant combination made Emily think of the times that she'd been here with her aunt when she was a girl.

Nicholas frowned as she handed him the bundle. Again, he didn't seem to see what Emily saw. He took it and turned it over in his hands.

"What is it?" he said.

"It's flowers from our garden," Emily said. "There's rosemary for remembrance, carnations for love, and sweet pea for goodbyes. My aunt used to bring them here once a month, ever since I was a little girl."

Nicholas looked closer at the bouquet and turned it over in his hands.

"Don't you see the magic?" she asked.

"Maybe just a trace," Nicholas said doubtfully.

"But it's everywhere!" Emily said, making a frustrated noise. "You can't miss it!"

He stared at the bundle again, frowning. "I don't see much here," he said, "but I'll take your word for it. Maybe you're seeing something that I can't." Nicholas looked at her, then away. His eyes fixed on a point in the distance, and

Emily was swept with the impression that he didn't believe her.

"Just a minute," Nicholas told her, staring into the darkness. "I think I've found something!" He reached his hand to her and Emily took it, following him back to the construction site. Jumping the orange construction fence, they circled the church until they found the place where Emily had started her search. He edged himself in front of the blade of the bulldozer, beckoning her to join him.

"Careful," he said, holding her steady.

Their feet were hanging at the edge of the deep hole. Nicholas pointed.

"We just had the wrong angle," he said, pointing downward.

On the edge of the excavation was a wall piled high with stone and wood. The bulldozer had obviously struck one of the fabled sections of the city beneath the city, and collapsed a portion of the stone wall within. Emily's heart lurched when she saw where Nicholas pointed. Amid the crumbled rocks, a single stone stood cracked into five pieces; after all these years, the stone was still marked with the demon rune. It was the burial site from her dreams.

"We have to get down there," Emily said. "They might be inside."

The drop appeared to be about fifteen feet deep, with no likely entrance point. He edged around the hole, looking for a path down to the crypt. He stepped lightly, half walking, half sliding into the pit. Gingerly, he picked his way to the rock, and looked up to Emily, waiting to see her follow.

She dropped beside him, flashlight in hand. With no hesitation, she crawled into the crevice in the side of the crypt and shined the light around the chamber.

"There's nothing here."

"Wait," Nicholas said. "Let's take another look." Nicholas stared at the area with his othersight, and saw a slight twinkle of magic in the far corner of the crypt.

"Look," he said, "a pocket. It's an old Paladin trick. Sort of like a false wall created by magic. It's used to conceal objects." Nicholas reached into the space, and his hand disappeared for a moment, then reappeared holding a bundle.

Emily stared at the cloth for a moment, then took it from Nicholas. She put the cloth against her cheek, breathing the familiar smell of lavender and sweet woodruff.

"It's Aunt Maeve's," she told him, gathering the cloak into a bundle. As she picked it up, something hard hit the floor with a metallic thud. Emily stooped to retrieve it. It was the VonPeer athame, the jeweled dagger she thought she'd lost.

"Why is this here?" she wondered out loud.

"The demon wants it," Nicholas said. "They must've hidden it here."

"How do you know?" she asked, spinning the blade, noting how the hilt fit perfectly in her hand.

"Because this is the last place that it would look," Nicholas said. "It's been caged in here for years, who knows how long? It's not likely that it would return to its prison."

"You think it's a better hiding place than the House?" Emily asked.

"The demon's been weakening the House; it would have gotten inside last night if I hadn't stopped it," Nicholas said. "Maybe it wasn't looking for us; maybe it was looking for this."

"But why?" she asked. "I mean, the athame is pretty, and it's probably valuable, but it's only a tool. I don't see why it would be special to a demon."

Nicholas took the flashlight and shined it on the wall.

"Maybe the answer is right here," he said, "you don't happen to speak any arcane demon languages, do you?"

Emily gasped as her eyes followed the beam of light. What she'd taken to be the texture of the inner rock was small, meticulous handwriting scripted over every inch of the crypt in a repeating pattern.

"We should copy the runes," she said. "You people must have books on this stuff somewhere."

Nicholas stared at her, dumbfounded. "Yeah," he answered, "we do, but look at all of this; it would take years to decipher it." His eyes flashed over the runes repeatedly, noticing the thousands of lines of handwriting sized script that covered every inch of the tomb.

Emily nodded. "My notebook's in my bag, I left it up there, I'll go get it." She placed the athame in her belt, squeezed out of the crypt and was gone as Nicholas found a pencil in his own pocket.

She saw her backpack lying beside the bulldozer. She reached down to pick it up, but as she straightened, a hand was clamped over her mouth, and she was pulled backward by someone she couldn't see. She tried to reach for her locket, but he held her arms down with his other hand. He whispered a few words, and her body was covered in coils of thin blue light. Emily struggled against him, trying to free herself, but the coils moved around her neck and mouth, and she found that she could barely breathe, much less scream.

"Hold still or they'll get tighter," a deep voice said in her ear. Whoever was behind her was dragging her backward, away from Nicholas. "Emily?" Nicholas said, pushing his way out of the crypt. A blaze of light shot past his cheek and struck the rock behind him.

Emily's eyes strained with fear

"There's nothing in there anymore," Arch said. "But you have to give our ancestors credit; it's the perfect place to bury a demon. It will be a good place for her."

Emily struggled to move, but the bonds were too strong.

Nicholas stood still, his eyes wide. Arch smiled. "Look at her," he said. He grabbed her arm and pulled up her sleeve.

Nicholas shook, and Emily looked at her arm. A dark

173

red line of energy had started to snake up her arm toward her shoulder. It looked like a bruise, and as she clenched her hand, it stung.

"Leave her alone, she isn't part of the case," Nicholas said through clenched teeth, pointing his scepter at Arch, who shielded himself with Emily's body.

Arch raised his eyebrows. "I'm not going to fight with you on this, Nicholas. Put down your weapon," Arch said. He tapped the side of his pen and produced a blue point of light that he held to Emily's neck, "Or she dies here and now."

Emily met Nicholas' eyes for a second, then she tapped her foot on the ground, near Arch's boot. The silent communication flashed between the two of them. Nicholas brought his eyes back to Arch, and took a step forward.

Nicholas narrowed his eyes and planted his feet, poised to shoot. "Your call. Who do you think is the faster shot, Arch?"

Arch looked uncertain for a moment and in the second that he shifted his stance, Nicholas rolled and landed a blast at Arch's foot, Arch's return shot hit a gravestone an inch from where Nicholas' head had been, and Nicholas fired another shot, releasing Emily from her bonds. Emily launched her body downward and rolled out of Arch's grasp as she pulled off her necklace. Arch took another shot at Nicholas, but missed. As the locket fell, her power surged, lending her grace as she lunged. She landed on Arch and pinned him to the ground. Her eyes gleamed in wild delight at her triumph. Arch's eyes grew round in terror as Emily bared her teeth. A feral snarl filled the air, and it was a moment before Emily realized that the noise came from her own lips. She was too angry to care.

Kill him! A voice inside her mind said, and it seemed like the most natural thing to do. Emily raised her arm and prepared to strike. Arch screamed. As her blow was about to land, an arm caught her, and she reeled on Nicholas.

Emily growled as she swung to face him.

"Whoa!" Nicholas said, tightening his grip on her as she struggled against him. He was stronger than she was, barely. His muscles flexed, and his face was very still.

"Emily," Nicholas gasped, struggling with her as she bucked against him. "Stop! It's me!"

She squirmed out of his grasp and turned to face him, poised to strike.

Emily grabbed Nicholas by the front of his shirt, and her arm was shaking as her fist clenched. She let him go and crumbled on the ground beside him, curling herself into a ball with the horror of what she'd nearly done.

"Oh my God, what am I doing?" she said over and over, rocking herself in time with her questions.

Nicholas stood as Arch lifted his upper body from the ground, still watching Emily in terror. Nicholas turned to Arch, muttering a few words as he shot a thin pink light from his weapon. The spell hit Arch square in the chest.

Arch's face relaxed into a smile as Nicholas said softly, "You never saw us. Take your weapon and continue your post with nothing to report for the night. Do it now."

Arch pulled himself from the ground, collected his weapon, and turned his back on the pair of them. Nicholas watched him walk to his car and listened as Arch grabbed his radio and told dispatch that he'd seen nothing.

Nicholas lifted his eyebrows. "That was close," he said. "Luckily, I've always been good at manipulation spells."

"What did you do to him?" Emily said.

"I blasted his memory and replaced it with a new one. He saw nothing and is on his way back to headquarters. He's going to ask if anyone wants take-out on the way."

Emily nodded and replaced the locket around her neck. As quickly as her power had come, it was concealed. All that was left was Emily, grass-stained, pale, and shaken. She looked at Nicholas, sick with dread.

"Nicholas," she whispered, "what's happening to me?"

He watched as the taillights of the car disappeared, acting like he hadn't heard her question. "I never thought I'd be able to fire a shot at a teammate, not even Arch," he said.

"You're going to be in trouble for this, aren't you?" Emily guessed.

Nicholas shook his head, incredulous. "I don't know, but I won't let them hurt you," he said. He pulled her into his arms, and Emily put her head on his shoulder.

She wrapped her arms around him tightly and they stood for a moment, still as statues.

"Now what?" Emily said.

He planted a kiss on the top of her head. "It'll be all right," he said, but Emily could tell that he wasn't convinced.

CHAPTER 20

Across the river at Grind, Jessie was in the kitchen, standing on a step stool, slowly stirring a bubbling pot with two hands and whispering an incantation. Lauren and Alex, their two baristas-slash-apprentice-demon-hunters, were at the sink, pouring boiling water over a dish tray filled with piping hot globes made of blue glass.

"We're going to miss them," Steph said as he paced behind them, wringing his hands with a worried look on his face. "Why didn't they tell us that Emily might turn into a demon? Wouldn't you think that's need-to-know information?"

"It does complicate things," Jessie said. "But you have to relax, like you told Emily, we don't know the bigger picture."

"Sometimes people die in the bigger picture, Jessie," Steph said. "Look what happened to us. Clearly, we're not a foolproof solution to their plan. Can't you go any faster?"

"No, I can't, Stop asking! This recipe is fussy and it takes time," Jessie snapped from the stove of the kitchen. "I can't rush this process, Steph, you know that. If the girls hadn't knocked over the first batch, we'd be ready to go by now." Jessie checked the temperature of the brew simmering on the stove and nodded to the two girls beside her. "How are they coming, girls?"

Lauren, the shorter of the pair, yelped, and a small sphere of glass hit the floor and shattered. "Damn," she said, sucking her finger, "they're hot!"

She showed her burned thumb to Alex, who kissed it. "It's okay, we have plenty of bottles," she said to Jessie.

They brought the trays of sterilized spheres to her, and Jessie began to fill each of them with a syringe of iridescent liquid. She corked the top of one and held it up to the light. The potion gleamed like tiny, imprisoned rainbows.

Steph paced back and forth behind them, muttering, "What's the sense of having all this power if we don't know where or when we can use it? There's no logic to this case; it doesn't make any sense. But do they answer? Oh, no— forget about that, they just told us to protect her from the demons and help her find her aunt. That's all. Like that's easy."

Jessie turned to him. "If you want to take your mind off things, you could start helping us," she said. "This batch is ready; start loading them into the briefcases."

Putting on a pair of oven mitts, he scooped a sphere into his hands and gently placed it into the foamy eggshell lining of the briefcase. Pressing the sphere down, he began to create rows of them, ten spheres to a row, four rows to a layer, and four layers to a case.

"How much have we got?" he asked.

"Enough for ten cases," Jessie said. "Until we find its nest, we won't be able to kill it though."

They worked quickly and filled the other cases.

"Take those to the van, Steph. I'll meet you out there," Jessie said. "I have to wash my hands; if the demon catches a whiff of this stuff, it'll be gone again. I think that's why it disappeared the first time."

178

Steph nodded and grabbed the cases.

"Girls, do you think you know what you're doing here?" Jessie asked. "Can you mix up the next batch by yourself?"

"You're trusting those two with a kitchen full of bombs?" Steph whispered to Jessie. "Have you lost your mind?"

"I heard that," Lauren said. "We'll be fine, Jessie, don't worry," she said as another sphere crashed to the floor.

Jessie and Steph turned back to look at them.

"Talk about bad timing," Alex said. She grabbed the broom and started to sweep the glass.

"Don't worry about it, just get them done," Jessie said, pulling off the pink apron and gloves and hanging them on the hook outside the bathroom door. She walked into the bathroom and closed the door.

Steph placed the briefcases on the ground as he fumbled for his keys. As he was securing the briefcases in the trunk bolted to the van's floor, a ray of light flashed beside him, and he turned in time to see the explosion. Steph covered his face as shards of glass burst outward onto the street, showering him in small shards. He ran in the front door as smoke began to pour from the back of the building.

Lauren and Alex pushed out the kitchen door, coughing, covered in smoke, and drenched with the foul smelling liquid. "We didn't do it, honest. It was something else, this thing blasted through. It threw us to the floor and then blam!" Lauren said.

"Get yourselves out of the smoke, I'll go find Jessie," Steph said.

Steph pushed past them to the bathroom as the smoke continued to tumble through the building.

"Jessie?" he called. "Jessie!" He pushed through some overturned shelves in the hallway beside the kitchen. One of them had fallen across the bathroom door, and Steph heaved it out of the way enough to gain a small purchase on the bathroom door. He pulled it open and edged his way through. Water was pouring from the place where the sink had fallen from the wall. The cleaning supplies had fallen from the shelves, and Jessie lay among them with the sink on her chest and her eyes closed.

"Jessie?" Steph said pulling her up from the mess. "Babe? Are you okay?"

Jessie lay very still in his arms for a moment, then cringed and whimpered.

"Ow," she said weakly, and Steph clasped her against himself, half crying with relief. She wrapped her arms around his neck as he picked her up and carried her out the back door.

Lauren and Alex were sitting in the back of the van, wrapped together in an old army blanket, their arms around each other. Steph sat Jessie down beside them.

"Any injuries?" he asked.

Jessie lifted her shirt up to her ribs, revealing a deep impression of the sink on her stomach that began to disappear as they watched. "I'm all right now," she said. "I guess it takes more than a flying sink to get me the second time around."

Steph hugged her. "Well, there's one thing to be thankful for," he said. "Stay here. I'm going to take a look around inside." He walked through the shop to the kitchen, where smoke was pouring from the door.

The gas burner was still flaming amidst the smoke. Quickly, Steph reached over and turned it off. The pot that they'd used to brew the potion was lying in the middle of the floor, charred black. Thankfully, most of the potion was safe. Had he not taken the briefcases to the van, the girls wouldn't have survived the blast. He walked to the storefront and examined the hole in the front window that the beast had left.

"Should we call the police or the fire department?" Lauren asked.

"Sounds like someone already did," Jessie said as they all began to hear the sirens wail in the distance.

Steph looked at his watch and opened his phone. He sighed as the call went directly to Emily's voicemail.

CHAPTER 21

Emily saw Nicholas hesitate when he looked at her. She tried to tell herself that it was nothing, a trick of the light, her imagination. But she kept returning to the same thought: Nicholas was afraid of her. Even now, he said nothing as they sat on the church stairs waiting for Jessie and Steph. *He's so quiet,* she thought, watching his eyes fixed on the spot in front of his feet. *Determined not to look at me.*

He moved forward, and his hair fell in a curtain between them.

"I have to leave," Emily said. "I almost killed you a minute ago." She got up to walk away, but Nicholas grabbed her arm.

Nicholas sighed. "Sit down," he said, "I need to tell you something."

Emily sat beside him, crossing her arms. He put his arm around her shoulder, and looked at her to make sure that the gesture was all right. "When I was at Paladin today, I found out something that I didn't know about your injury. The damage from the type of beast that attacked you is more serious than I thought."

Emily nodded. "I knew something was wrong. My eyes

are changing color," she said. "There are other things too, voices in my head, instincts that aren't mine. It's like I'm not myself today."

"The demon's touch contaminated you. It's the way it reproduces. It chose you for the transformation. There's nothing that I can do to prevent it, but I haven't looked at everything yet, I haven't read . . . there might be an answer somewhere."

"How soon will it happen?" Emily whispered.

"I don't know," Nicholas said, looking at the ground. "We'll fix this, we'll find a way," he said. "The Paladin have worked with these cases for years, but it's been a long time since anyone's seen a case like this. Surely there's something, a cure buried somewhere in one of the dusty books in the vaults."

"It's like my dreams," she said.

"Dreams?" he said.

Emily nodded. "I saw you in my dreams before we met. There was fire and demons. A demon murdered you in my dream."

"Are you psychic?" he asked.

Emily gave him a tired half-grin. "I'm not even sure I'm sane anymore," she said. "The dreams are a tangled mess of visions; I always thought that they were brought on by a backfired spell when I was a teenager. Then you showed up on my doorstep, and now I don't know what to think. But I feel like our involvement might be dangerous for you."

Nicholas scratched his head and shot her a skeptical look. "I don't think it's our job to predict the future. It's our job to create it."

Emily grinned. "You sound like my aunt," she said.

Nicholas squeezed her shoulder. "We're going to find them, I can feel it. Don't worry about your dreams. There's nothing you can do about them. Right now, I'm here to help you out of this mess, and that'll happen if it's the last thing I do."

Emily smiled at him, and he drew her into his arms. He pushed her hair back and tilted her face up. His lips brushed hers and sent a wave of electric shocks pulsing through her body. She put her hands on his chest as he kissed her again. He moved away and put his chin on top of her head.

"Everything's going to be all right," he said.

Her eyes closed and for the few minutes that they were sitting on the steps together in the dark, she believed him. She buried her head on his shoulder, then put her hand to her lips and smiled.

Emily pursed her lips. "First things first," she said in a copy of her aunt's brave voice. "We can still save Aunt Maeve and John, Steph said so."

"Where are Steph and Jessie, anyway?" Nicholas asked.

"Steph called, they were supposed to meet us here. Maybe we should run back to the House and if they're not there, head to Grind."

Emily pulled her phone from her pocket and dialed it.

"They're not answering," she said. She dialed Jessie, but she didn't answer either.

Nicholas nodded. "Let's take my truck, it's closer. I'll drop you off at your car."

Emily nodded, and they fell into step together. He wrapped his arm around her. As they reached his truck, she thought that he was going to open the door for her, but instead, he pushed her against the door and put his arms around her waist. She circled her arms around his neck, and when he kissed her again, the world began to spin and her knees went weak.

He pulled away from her and stroked the side of her face. "I know that pretty much everything is wrong about this, that this is the last thing that either of us should be doing right now," he said. "But I can't help it. You're so . . . everything," he said, pulling her close.

"I know what you mean," she said, burying her head in his neck.

In the distance, a metal door ejected a group of loud partygoers into the street, and Nicholas stepped back from her with a sheepish grin.

"Come on," he said, opening the door. "Let's get you back to your car."

She pulled him back to her one more time, and he kissed her again in a way that made her forget all of the bad things that had ever happened in her life.

"We make a fine pair, don't we?" he said as he pulled away from her.

He walked to his side and got into the driver's seat. He started the car, and they drove in silence for the few blocks back to her car. He parked, took her hand again, and Emily clasped it in his.

"Do me a favor," he said. "Don't let your dreams rule me out of the picture just yet."

"All right," Emily said in a low voice.

The driver's side door swung open, and before Emily knew what was happening, a large man had Nicholas pinned around the shoulders, pointing a fountain pen at his throat. Beside them, a plump young woman in a blue sequined tank top smiled, twirling another pen in her hand like a small gold baton. The woman turned to Nicholas, shaking her head.

"Moon," Nicholas said. "What the hell are you doing here?"

"I knew when you left the medical ward that we needed to follow you," Moon said smugly. "You have a talent for getting yourself into trouble. Of course, your instincts are the best, just like your mother. Unfortunately, your cloaking could use a little work. Not to mention your taste in ah, women."

Emily was shocked—how did Mary from her office know Nicholas? Why did Nicholas call her Moon? She didn't have enough time to piece together the truth.

"Emily, run!" Nicholas said. He struggled to free himself as a flash erupted from Moon's hand, hitting Nicholas in the chest.

Frozen in horror, Emily watched as Nicholas fell to the ground in front of her, clutching his chest.

"No!" Emily screamed, reaching for her locket, but another pair of hands had her arms behind her back before she could do anything. Her sleeve ripped, and Moon's eyes grew large.

"Look at that!" she said, pointing to Emily's arm. "Take her too."

"Help me with him," the first man said as Arch limped toward them with a blank expression on his face. Arch grabbed Nicholas by the feet as a black SUV swung around the corner, stopping beside the two men with a slight tap on Emily's bumper. The trunk door opened, and the two men shuffled toward it and loaded Nicholas in the back.

"Mary?" Emily said. "Is that you?"

"Great," Moon said. "Now my cover is blown. We really have to figure out what to do with you now." The woman who was either Mary or Moon turned to Emily and pointed her pen at her. In a flash, Emily lay on the ground, stunned from the blast, but still conscious. She fought to push herself up, but her muscles wouldn't work properly. Moon crouched beside her as she struggled against the power of the spell.

"It hurts less if you relax. The atrophy spell is very potent; it will knock you out in a minute. You're pretty strong, even for a witch." Moon smiled over her, and patted her arm.

"I'm not a witch," Emily breathed, knowing it was a feeble lie.

"Take her too," Moon said to the men.

Arch scooped Emily into his arms, but hesitated.

186

"Commander Flynn only told us to bring Nicholas," Arch said, rubbing his head and gesturing to Nicholas.

"That's because she didn't know who he was with," Moon said, clicking her wand back into a pen and stowing it in the place where her shirt folded between her breasts. "We need to take her to the lab if that injury's what I think it is. And if I'm wrong, we'll just let her go, no harm done."

Half an hour later, Jessie and Steph were driving around the small city blocks that surrounded the church, looking for signs of Nicholas and Emily. Steph frowned as he dialed Emily's cell number for the thousandth time. The phone rang and then clicked to her voicemail. All he found was Emily's empty car. They parked behind it and got out of the van to investigate.

Jessie found a small bouquet of flowers laying in the gutter. She nudged them with her foot.

"Damn it all!" Steph said.

"Do you think that they went back to the House?" Jessie asked.

"No," Steph said, worried. "But let's check anyway."

CHAPTER 22

Emily woke, feeling dizzy and disoriented. She squinted at the bright fluorescent lights swinging over her head. She moved to shield her eyes, but she was stuck. Her hands were strapped tightly to the side of her body. She pulled at the braces, but nothing happened. She looked down; she was strapped tight to a gurney, immobile. Her clothes had been replaced with a thin hospital gown that barely covered the top of her thighs.

She heard a door swing open, followed by a series of footsteps.

"That them?" a voice mumbled from the corner.

"Kane and Markham, it's them," one of the techs said. "We found the identification implants in their teeth. It's weird how everything burns away except for your teeth, isn't it?"

Emily twisted and a wheel on the gurney creaked.

A man in a black coat with red trim stood over her with a cheerful expression on his face. There was a single notch on his left cheekbone. He was a tall man with uneven teeth, and his hair was a dirty shade of brown. "How's our newest patient?" he asked, smiling down at her.

"Patient?" she asked. "Where am I?" Emily struggled against the restraints, and the strap on her arm loosened. The man in the coat grabbed the end of the strap and pulled it tighter.

"I'm Richard Wagner, the lead researcher on your case," he said, attempting to shake the hand that was strapped to the gurney. "You're at the Paladin laboratories. It's better if you settle down. The sedative is wearing off, but we need you to answer a few questions before we administer more. Don't worry; this will all be over soon."

Wagner turned to the men behind him. "You'll see that the contamination has two entry points," he said, pointing at Emily with his pen. "Here," he said, tracing the pen along Emily's arm. "The smaller but more severe of the injuries is right here on her neck."

Wagner reached over and gently brushed Emily's hair from her face with the back of his hand. The two men he was talking to stood over her, taking notes. One of them, a gorilla-like man with a close-cropped haircut, searched the whole of her body with his eyes, smiling. He stretched his hands, cracking his knuckles with a rude smile at Emily before he addressed the doctor.

"What about Flynn? Do we get him too?"

"No," said Wagner, the disappointment evident in his tone. "According to the healers, he's clean. They have him contained in a cell upstairs, just in case. They'll be monitoring his progress. But there's always hope."

The men nodded, and Emily thought how closely their expressions matched the demon's.

"But still," Wagner said, turning back to Emily, "we're lucky to have you with us tonight." His smile deepened into a leer as he moved close to her bedside. "Such a pretty thing," he said, tucking another lock of hair behind her ear.

Emily shuddered.

"Historically speaking, the demons seem to have a

189

preference for women like this one: mid-twenties, dark hair, small frame, attractive. Did you know that?" Wagner asked as he and the techs pulled on plastic gloves. He turned to a tray of syringes and chose one.

"You'll feel a pinch," he said to Emily as he drove the needle directly into the scar on her arm.

Emily fought the restraints, her chest heaving with the effort to escape. The straps dug into her arms as Dr. Wagner pulled a pale purple fluid from her arm. He changed the collection tube on the needle several times, and Emily grew faint.

"There we go," he said, handing the vials to the assistant, who covered each with a sticker and placed them into another tray.

The assistant surveyed the samples.

"And now one from the other site," Wagner said. "Ms. VonPeer, I encourage you to hold very still for this test so that we only need to perform it once."

Emily shuddered as Wagner put his hand on her chin. She cried as the second needle seared into the place between her neck and collarbone.

"Wonderful!" Wagner said, tapping the vial. "Notice that the concentration is much higher in this fluid sample. This is more than we've managed to get in thirty years. Take these to the lab and get started."

Emily was ashamed of the tears rolling down her face, and she turned her head away from the doctor.

He produced a tissue and began to swab the tears from her eyes.

"Just a few more tests for tonight, don't worry. The transformation progresses quickly, so we need to do as much as we can with you while you're still manageable." He turned to the tech. "Did you find her family information?"

"No family listed," the tech said.

"That makes it easier," Wagner said. He looked at the

clock and nodded to the tech.

"List the official time of death as 1:53 a.m."

"Method?" the tech asked.

"Call it coronary failure," Wagner said.

"I'm not dead!" Emily said.

Dr. Wagner smiled down at her. "Not to us, Miss VonPeer. But to others, well the rest of the world really, you are. Now try to get some rest." He pushed the button on the IV beside her bed, and in thirty seconds, Emily fell into a dark and dreamless sleep.

Chapter 23

Nicholas paced the small cage, cursing and rubbing the side of his head. Close range spells hurt. His teammates had not been gentle when they'd tossed him into the car or the cell. It had been a long time since he'd seen the inside of a Paladin cell, but that time, he'd deserved it. Now, he was ready to fight. Nicholas pounded the side of the wall.

"You fucking traitors!" Nicholas shouted through the glass. "What am I even doing in here?"

Moon walked up to him and stared at him from the other side of the cell.

"My mother already took me off the case," Nicholas said. "Now she's thrown me in prison?"

"Well, there is the small fact that you blasted Arch— you wiped part of his memory, did you know that? That could have messed up the whole investigation. Plus, it's a good thing we showed up when we did—the VonPeer girl is contaminated. Couldn't you see that?"

Nicholas didn't answer. Clearly Moon didn't know the depth of his involvement with Emily, and he wasn't about to give her any more information than she already had. At least his spell had worked on Arch.

"I'm trying to find John," he said.

"John is dead," Moon said.

"No, he's not, I have proof." He reached in his pocket and handed Moon the chess piece. "It's filled with John's magic, even now."

Moon surveyed the piece.

"Put that back in your pocket," she whispered, handing him the piece. "Quick, before Arch gets here. Don't say anything about this in front of him."

There was something in her expression that made him nod in agreement. He stuffed the chess piece into his pocket.

A moment later, Arch appeared in the doorway, carrying a metal clipboard that he handed to Moon. She read the paperwork and signed her name at the bottom.

"This all seems in order," Moon said.

Arch nodded and held the clipboard, shooting an evil glare at Nicholas. There was a bandage on the side of his head.

"Leave it to you to try to bang a demon," Arch said. "What's the matter with you anyway? This town is crawling with drunk sorority girls and slutty interns with low standards."

Nicholas felt sick. "Where's Emily?" he demanded again, though he already knew the answer.

"They took her to the lab," Moon said. "They'll do what they can for her, but you know how it goes."

Nicholas said, "Why do they need her? What are they going to do for her? I thought the contamination was incurable."

"It is," Moon said. "The least that we can do is spare her the transformation. In the meantime, she's useful; we don't have a lot of samples of her type."

"So, let me get this straight, there's nothing they can do for her, so you sent her down to the lab for those ghouls to experiment on her before she . . ."

He couldn't bring himself to say it. The Paladin intended to euthanize her like a sick pet.

"Nicholas, stop being so dramatic. She's already dead, you know that. They'll look for answers and make her comfortable. That's all that they can do at this point."

Arch shook his head at Moon. "I don't know why you're talking to him," he said as he flipped the clipboard under his arm and began to walk down the hall. "He isn't right in the head."

Moon looked at Nicholas with a touch of sympathy.

"I can see what happened; it's why they told you to stay away from her. The VonPeer women have a long habit of enslaving men. The more magical the man, the more susceptible they are to the witch's charms. It's what happened to Dalgreth, don't you see? That's why we need to keep you here. As soon as Emily VonPeer is gone, you'll be yourself again, the same old obnoxious hack resting on his mother's fame. But until then, I'm not going to be responsible for you."

Moon shrugged her shoulders in apology and followed Arch out the door. The door slammed behind Moon and Arch with a sickening thud. Nicholas stalked to the front of the cell and looked out the door, wondering if there was a way out of here. A guard was at the end of the hall, sitting in a chair, half asleep, with his legs propped on the desk. Nicholas placed his hands against the clear wall. The cell crackled like a bug zapper, and Nicholas fell to the ground, swearing. His hands burned with the powerful magic that held him.

The guard yawned and opened a sleepy eye. "Come on, Agent Flynn, you should know that you can't do that. You're lucky that magic didn't knock you out."

Nicholas swore and began to pace again, blowing into his hands to ease the pain of the scorch marks.

Five minutes later, the door clicked open and Moon

reappeared, this time escorting his mother.

"We'd like a few words alone with my son," Lillian said to the guard. "Would you mind waiting outside the ward for a few minutes?" Lillian smiled sweetly as the guard exited his post, then she followed Moon to the cell. Lillian watched to make sure that the door closed behind the guard before she turned to Nicholas.

"What proof do you have that John is alive?" Lillian said.

"On the day Kane and Markham were killed, I found this lying in the field," he said, pulling the chess piece out of his pocket and handing it to Lillian. "It's marked with John's magic."

Lillian spun the chess piece in her hand for a moment, her eyes grew wide. "I'll be damned," she whispered. She continued to survey the ivory knight in her hands.

"It's his, isn't it?" Nicholas said.

Lillian nodded. "He did this once when we were on an investigation together," Lillian said. "It's an old trick that we used in abduction cases, you imbue the piece with magic then use it as a sort of beacon to trace to the source, but its success rate is so slim that we don't even teach it as a technique anymore at the Academy. John would be one of the few people who'd even know to try this trick anymore."

Just then, Lillian's phone rang. "Lillian Flynn," she said. She pressed the phone to her ear as Nicholas and Moon stood and watched.

"We're on our way," she said in a clipped voice, turning off the phone and stuffing it into her pocket.

"There was a break at the document room, they figured out how to activate the map. They'll need your translation services, Moon. Nicholas, we're going to need your talents as well. Moon, be a doll and go find my son a robe," Lillian said, "I need a minute to talk to him alone."

Pursing her lips, Moon ducked her head and left the cell.

She pulled out a cigarette and lit the end of it with a silver lighter. She extended the pack to Nicholas, but he shook his head.

"I quit last year," he said. Nevertheless, his fingers twitched as his mother lifted the cigarette to her lips.

Lillian puffed the cigarette "What's the matter with you, anyway? I'm springing you from jail, and this is how you treat me?" she asked.

"Are you kidding? You swept in here, took over half the organization, and you have Moon babysitting me like I have no sense. Plus, you lifted Stanton's assignment right out of his lap. No wonder he's mad; by your own orders I'm supposed to help him, but thanks to you, Arch and Moon threw me in the brig for no reason."

Lillian's face grew red. She was silent through Nicholas' tirade, but when she finally spoke, her voice was low and lit with anger. "You might not be able to see this, but everything that I've done here has been for your protection. Yes, I threw you in jail, it was a sound decision, and I'd do it again. Your proximity to Emily VonPeer suggested that you may have been enchanted or under the influence of some type of spell. In case you haven't noticed, I have three dead agents, a rogue demon, and a contaminated witch on my hands. The last thing I need is you involving yourself in the mess."

"You're ignoring crucial parts of the case that could save people's lives," Nicholas said.

"So are you," Lillian said. "You've bent every directive you've had in this case so far and compromised yet another investigation," Lillian sniffed. "By shooting Agent Arch, you may have deleted valuable evidence that we're compiling on his treason case."

"What?" he said.

She puffed again. "We think that Maeve VonPeer was in league with some of our dirty agents; her spellwork was found all around the Gate.

"Why would she help the witch hunters?"

Lillian shook her head. "We don't know. They were looking to recover access to the River Gate. We'd already linked Arch to the case when you blasted his memory. We were looking at Kane as a possible conspirator as well, but that's also a moot point now. Stanton had already ruled you out as a suspect when he assigned you to the gate."

Nicholas watched her for a moment, then sunk onto the bench beside him. He rested his head in his hands. "Take me off the case then," he said.

"I can't, we need you. You're too powerful. Besides, you're one of the few people around here that we can trust."

"Then trust me now. I don't think that the VonPeers are involved in this," he said.

"Oh, please, Nicholas. Moon filled me in on your little rendezvous this evening. Don't let your crush on the VonPeer girl cloud your judgment. The evidence we have suggests that Maeve VonPeer used John in an attempt to gain access to the gate; now we have to clean up the mess she left behind. It's not the first time this sort of thing has happened. The VonPeers have their own file drawer filled to the brim with magical offenses of this kind; they deserve what they get."

"No, they don't" Nicholas insisted. "They're not the perpetrators, they're the victims; you need to trust me on this."

"And how do you know that, Nicholas? Really? How? Where's your proof?" Lillian crossed her arms and stepped back, waiting for an answer.

"I just know," Nicholas said stubbornly, and his mother threw up her arms in exasperation.

"Well, if your evidence holds up, then we can have John straighten this mess out himself," Lillian said. "In the meantime, we need to try to locate him without anyone else

197

finding out what we're doing."

"Where do we go next?" he said.

"We need to get to Stanton; he's monitoring our other suspects. This signal is weak, but I'm hoping that between the two of you, you can manage to discern John's location."

Moon reappeared around the corner and handed a robe to Nicholas.

"What about Emily? " Nicholas said. "Is there a way out of the contamination?"

"I have Wagner researching that angle as well. He tells me that it doesn't look good, but he's looking at ways to try to slow the transformation process in any case. She's more useful to everyone alive than dead, so she's safe for the moment. The next thing we need to focus on is finding John Dalgreth."

CHAPTER 24

Emily woke again in the lab, seeing a spectrum of rainbows emanating from the fluorescent lights overhead. She stretched her senses around her, feeling every nerve in her body snapping with magic, but the whole world was heavy and muffled as if she were underwater. The room hummed with unseen machines, and it took her a moment to remember where she was. She flexed her arm, and again felt the bite of the leather restraints, then footsteps.

"She's waking up," a voice said.

The light moved, and she could see. Dr. Wagner move the pole holding a bag of liquid attached to her arm, and she realized that the bag was blood. Her blood. She squirmed and felt the needle slide from her vein. There were scuttles and tweets behind her, and the sound of feet in cages just out of sight. She strained her neck to see, and the man smiled.

"Easy now," he said. "We're almost done with you for tonight."

She flinched as he patted the side of her leg and moved back to his clipboard.

"Let me go," Emily hissed, fighting the restraints.

Dr. Wagner seemed unconcerned.

PREMONITION

As she struggled, her locket slid from her breastbone to the side of her neck. Dr. Wagner bent over her.

"I meant to ask you about this," he asked, fingering the locket. "It's very old. How long have you had this? Where did it come from?"

Emily glared at him and said nothing.

Wagner smiled and brushed her hair back.

"Leave it alone!" she snarled, seeing her opportunity.

Wagner's fingers moved to her neck, and she felt the goosebumps rise in response to his touch. The necklace slid from around her neck. For a moment, he studied the locket, swinging it like a pendulum in front of his face. He was so absorbed with studying the pendant he failed to notice that Emily had already escaped her restraints.

"That was a mistake," Emily said as she jumped from the gurney and grabbed the locket from his hand. She shoved it into her pocket.

Wagner took a step back into the IV pole, and his eyes turned to saucers as he realized his dilemma. Emily stood in front of him, unbound. She wiggled her fingers, testing them against the cloud of power surrounding her hands.

Standing, Emily was nearly as tall as Dr. Wagner. His eyes moved to the melted straps of the gurney. He took a small step toward the back of the room and startled her. She snarled and leapt backward onto the rolling bed, ready to pounce. That was when she saw the red telephone hanging on the wall.

Emily knew Wagner's intention before he knew it himself, and with a lunge she pounced across the room and ripped it from the wall, leaving him no opportunity to call for help. He wasn't getting out that easy. The jackbirds squealed and banged in their cages, hungry for revenge. Emily grabbed him by the collar and lifted him toward them. They stretched their claws through the metal casing, eager to grab hold of the man that had imprisoned them.

Emily was surprised at their reaction. Under normal circumstances, the jackbirds were slow and stubborn creatures, nearly impossible to differentiate from an ordinary gargoyle statue. Only an occasional shift of a wing or claw could give them away as something other than a clever piece of masonry. However, here in this cage, they slithered over each other eagerly, and one of them blew a puff of smoke from its nose. They were very happy to see her.

"Well, I was wondering what happened to you," she said to the jackbirds. "I thought that you disappeared with Aunt Maeve. Do you think that you can help me find her? Wait, where's Grog?" They hissed and Emily had a sinking feeling as a picture flashed from their minds. They'd been shot down and brought here, only Grog had escaped the attack. Grog had been shot later, but not brought here. They knew that Grog was dead. Their malice for the lab was overshadowed by exhaustion and a deep desire to breathe the night air. They begged her to unlock the cage and let them go home.

"Let's have a little fun first," she said, narrowing her eyes, "it looks like we owe him one."

In her mind, she could hear their version of a laugh as she thrust Wagner toward the stacked cages. They got the joke, and snapped their teeth at him in a display of intense ferocity. The doctor yelped, and they hissed in excitement, banging their shoulders against the cage. *Freedom*! They cried, and Emily laughed as the man dangled in front of her, too scared to scream.

"Don't kill me," he whimpered.

Emily tilted her head and studied him, thinking.

The jackbirds hissed in her head. *He was going to kill us! All of us.* The jackbird gestured with a wing.

Emily took a step back. The cages were filled with small animals and other oddities, a menagerie of strange creatures, though none seemed as intelligent as the jackbirds.

The jackbirds hissed again, and Wagner started to cry. She dropped him, and he fell into a pile beneath her, sobbing.

Quickly, the jackbird said in Emily's mind. *They're alive, but they're in trouble, there isn't much time!*

"Where are they?" she asked.

A single image of a water tower emerged in her mind.

"Diamond's behind this?" she asked.

The jackbirds hissed, confirming her question.

Emily opened one of the cage doors and tossed Wagner inside. "Can't have you calling in the troops, I'll bet you're the only one down here this time of night," she said, locking the door. "They won't find you until morning. You can just sit here and think about what you've done."

She opened the doors to the cages above him, and the two jackbirds flew out, ready at her command. They swirled the lab, their wings knocking bottles and tubes onto the floor as Wagner cringed.

Emily spotted her clothes on a table in a large, vacuum-sealed bag. She ripped it, shed her hospital robes, and threw her clothes on as she spoke, "Nobody can hear you. That's usually how you like it, isn't it?" She read Wagner's thoughts and shuddered as the wails of hundreds of victims floated through her mind. If anyone deserved to die, it was this man; but the faint voice of her conscience pounded in her head.

Harm none, it said. It was the cardinal rule of her kind, but she resisted it.

Wagner backed into the corner of the cage, her cage, her name already marked on the nameplate in erasable ink.

There would have been no mercy for me, she argued with the voice. *Or for them,* she thought, as she looked at the jackbirds.

"Years of research," he muttered.

"Years of torture," Emily countered, kicking the cage in disgust.

Just kill him now, another voice in her head said. *What a delight to see him squeal, to make him pay for all he's done and will continue to do when someone lets him out of his cage: one quick snap would bring an end to the suffering of so many.*

Emily shook her head and rubbed her temples, horrified at herself, amazed that she would think something like that.

"Where's the athame?" she demanded, kicking the front of the cage.

"The what? Oh, you mean the knife. The agents took it; I don't know where it went. It's probably in a vault somewhere."

The jackbirds muttered with impatience. *The agents are coming,* they said.

There was no time to find the athame, she'd have to rescue them without it, and there was only one way out: through the front door. The thought of Nicholas flashed in her mind, far away through a mile of bending hallways, doorways, and Paladin agents. No time for him either, she decided.

Emily raced to the door. She'd never been this agile or surefooted; for a moment, she lost herself in the joy of her own grace, an ability that her mundane body usually denied her. The jackbirds flew beside her as she climbed a staircase, raced through a deserted white hallway, and climbed another set of stairs.

The top of the stairs were lit only by the red glowing letters near the ceiling, EXIT, above a white metal door. Emily looked around in all directions, but there was no one there. She pushed the metal bar of the door gently, and held her breath, fully expecting an army of Paladin guard to begin shooting at her.

There was nothing, only the delicious smell of the night air and the image of a single streetlight in a puddle at her feet, reflecting a yellow light overhead. Staying in the shadows, Emily slipped out the door and ran down the empty streets toward the river.

She stretched her mind again, and followed the jackbirds into the night.

This way, they hissed.

Every alley opened itself to her, and she ran with a speed that quickly placed her far away from the Paladin offices.

Silently, she sped across the street and behind a car. The jackbirds dove straight into the water, but Emily hesitated, thinking of how the cold river had nearly killed Nicholas. A siren wailed in the distance, and before she had time to think, Emily ran to the bank, dropped into the water and surfaced under the dock. She dunked her head back under the water, marveling at how the icy water didn't affect her.

Let's go now! The jackbirds hissed. *Stay under for as long as you can.*

Emily ducked, and the water closed over her head. She opened her eyes underwater, and the only thing that she could see were the two shadowy forms of the jackbirds swimming on either side of her.

Keep your head down, they said in her mind, and Emily began to swim through the murky, dark water, letting the jackbirds lead the way. She could hear the spray of thousands of drops of water begin to hit the river as somewhere above her it began to rain.

Emily surfaced, gasping for air. She treaded water and looked around. Her speed was incredible; she'd managed to swim almost three miles in the time that she was underwater. She guessed from the lights on the riverbank that she was about a hundred yards from the shore. The deserted stretch of the riverbank was lined with broken buildings and waste punctuated by dim lights, rusted remnants of the city's manufacturing history. A single bright light spotlighted a pale blue tower etched with a single word: DIAMOND.

Emily swam toward it, hoping that she wasn't too late.

She stopped to see if anyone had managed to follow her, but she was alone. Emily shook for a moment, wringing her hair, and ducked behind a metal shipping container. Footsteps echoed toward her, and she forced her muscles to be still. She grabbed the side of the container and boosted herself to its top, careful not to make any noise, then laid flat with her cheek against the metal.

"She's in here?" Emily asked as the jackbirds swooped.

Maeve was here, they said. *Can't you tell? Her scent is everywhere.*

Emily lifted her nose in the air and concentrated. It was true; her aunt's scent lingered at the door.

The footsteps came closer, accompanied by a stretch of light on the ground. A moment later, a second light joined the first, then both were extinguished.

"See anything tonight?" a man's voice said. A match struck and cigarette smoke furled toward her feet.

"Nah, nothing, same as usual. The big guy's on edge tonight. Something's been bugging him all week."

"Eh, well, it's good work, getting paid to watch machines and empty crates."

"Who says they're empty? They carry all sorts of stuff in these cars," the man said, hitting the side of the container. "I hear they even smuggle animals and people in these boxes."

"Why do you say that?" the second man asked, suspicious. "You seen any animals or people running around here?"

"Nothing really . . . but earlier tonight, I thought I saw something moving in the shadows, like a dog or something, only bigger, over there on the quiet side of the yard, and when I went to look for it, it wasn't there anymore. Who knows? Maybe it was just a shadow or something. I didn't find anything, so I didn't put it in the report."

The other guy nodded. "These jobs, they'll do funny things to your brain after a while, make you see things that aren't there."

Emily tiptoed to the far edge of the container and dropped to the ground without a sound. Racing to another stack of containers, and then another, she stretched her senses, alert for signs of life, or death, other than the night guards. Mentally, she searched the containers, but nothing came to her. She inched along the shadows toward the main building. It was a small construction trailer, faded to a dirty shade of white.

Emily heard the muffled conversation of a man behind the window, talking then pausing as if on the telephone. She peeked through the window and saw Diamond standing over the desk, phone in hand. He began to pace the room, holding the phone in his hand. His expression was tense. Emily leaned closer to the window as she struggled to hear what Diamond was saying.

". . . can't do it tonight, I'm telling you Malphat's onto us, there's not much we can do about it for now"—another pause—"Well, you'd better figure it out quickly, we don't have the time or the supply to keep going like this . . . really? Wait, what about Staats? Are you sure? All right, all right, we'll look into it, just lay low for now. I'll call you back when it's ready."

Emily moved closer to the window as a metallic thud sounded across the yard, followed by a loud curse. Emily threw her body flat against the building and ducked as Diamond approached the window and threw it open. From the corner of her eye, she saw a large, dark form disappear behind a container.

"Go!" she whispered to the jackbirds. "Find help. See if you can find Jessie and Steph."

"What's going on out there?" Diamond yelled into the night.

A moan followed in response, and Diamond leaned farther out the window. Emily held her breath, if he glanced down and to the left, he'd see her.

"Nothing boss," the guard said. "Al tripped over a barrel out here. He's bleeding kind of bad; we might need to take him in for some stitches."

Diamond cursed under his breath. "Damn idiots . . ." he muttered. "Just a minute," he said into the phone. "Wait right there you two!" he yelled into the darkness. Diamond slammed the window shut, and Emily heard the metal of the file cabinet slide and click.

She crouched behind the hedge as the door swung open. Diamond emerged holding a file and a First Aid kit. Emily slipped through the door as he stalked away, mindful of the silence. She focused hard and found that she could hear what Diamond was saying fifty yards away from her.

He threw a set of keys to the guard.

"Take him in, call his wife to meet you at the hospital, and then come back here. Make sure he fills out the comp forms."

Diamond stood with the injured guard as Emily turned to the room, eager to find something that would lead her to her aunt or Dalgreth.

It was the kind of room with dark paneling, metal desks, and plastic ashtrays, a far cry from the senator's white marble offices at the Capitol. This room was a semi-ordered mess of papers, receipts, and metal filing cabinets, clearly the result of someone's personal system. Tacked to the bulletin board were newspaper clippings, each of them illustrating Senator Diamond cutting ribbons, attending groundbreakings, or shaking people's hands. Emily scanned the desk and surrounding area, careful to touch nothing. A yellowed clock on the wall buzzed the time: 1:15.

Emily heard the sound of a vehicle pulling up to the men, and their exchanges as they hauled the injured guard into the truck.

After a moment, Emily heard footsteps walking back toward the trailer. She looked for an escape, but there was no other exit. On the other end of the room was a beat-up, tweed couch. With a lunge, Emily moved the couch a few inches from the wall and squeezed herself behind it. She inched her way to the edge of the couch where there was a small space between it and the side of the low, metal filing cabinet beside it, praying that Diamond wouldn't see her. He entered the room just as Emily made herself comfortable in her hiding place. Looking annoyed, Diamond picked up the receiver.

"Still there?" he asked. The voice on the phone responded.

"Yeah, I talked to Malphat. We can't wait for the perfect moment, there's no other way. Dalgreth is strong, but Maeve will be dead in two days, three tops. The beast is getting too strong for them to resist, and when they're gone, it'll revolt. It's got to be tomorrow night. I'm going to check on the two of them now, then go home and get things ready for the press conference tomorrow . . . nah, it's late, I'll just take the truck over. The Mercedes attracts too much attention in that area."

Emily suppressed a sigh of relief. It didn't sound good, but at least her aunt and John were still alive. Now she had to figure out how to save them.

Tucking his hair underneath a cheap baseball cap, Diamond grabbed an old jacket from the hook on the door and snapped off the light switch as he left. The only illumination came from the shifting lines of the screen saver on the aged computer. She jumped as the phone rang twice and the message played on the ancient answering machine.

"Jack, it's me again," a familiar voice said, and Emily's stomach lurched. It was Blevin. "Call me as soon as you get this message, we have a problem here that needs to be taken care of immediately." Beep.

She peeked out the window, and when it was safe, slipped out of the office. She followed him around the corner of the trailer and watched from the shadows as he opened the driver's side door and got into the truck.

Someone grabbed her arm from behind, and she spun to face her attacker. She snarled, and her eyes glowed red. To her great surprise, she was met with an identical snarl and a pair of red eyes that flashed above her. She relaxed in his grasp, which once she stopped struggling, seemed more like an embrace.

"Forgive the interruption . . ." Malphat said, his handsome face creased with amusement, ". . . but this really can't wait any longer."

CHAPTER 25

Nicholas followed his mother through the winding hallways to a grubby elevator used mostly by the service people. She pushed the call button, and the three of them looked at each other silently until the door opened. Lillian ushered them inside and punched the button for the fifth floor.

When the doors opened, Nicholas was surprised to see a flurry of activity in the typically deserted hallway. The plush navy carpets and mahogany paneled walls seemed to enforce an aura of quiet among the crowd; nevertheless, even the genteel trappings of the Paladin libraries couldn't suppress the activity around them. A researcher in green robes walked by them toting an armload of documents. Robed acolytes stood whispering in the corners, and the whole place was awash in excitement. At the end of the hallway, the large gold door was open, and Nicholas could see several people in the room.

"Come in, sit down, and act like you hate me," Lillian whispered in a low voice. "It shouldn't be much of a stretch for you. Moon, stay close, I might need you."

Nicholas dropped a few paces behind his mother and

Moon. As his mother swept into the library with Moon at her side, Nicholas edged in the door and moved toward the back of the room as quickly as possible.

The library was set up for a presentation, and four or five rows of the caramel-colored leather chairs were set in front of a large table. Lillian and Moon shook a few hands and exchanged pleasantries before moving behind the table themselves. Nicholas dropped into a seat in the back row, wondering how soon he could sneak out of this mess to go find Emily. He crossed his arms as Stanton dropped into a chair beside him.

Lillian looked at them out of the corner of her eye as she told a joke that made all of the people around her chuckle with forced amusement.

"Your mother told me you had information that Dalgreth was alive," Stanton said under cover of the laughter.

Nicholas watched the front of the room and nodded. He reached into his robe and handed Stanton the chess piece.

Stanton examined the small stone knight for a moment.

"Damned if you didn't make yourself useful after all," he said, handing the knight back to Nicholas. "Now all we have to do is figure out which one of these bastards took him. Keep your eyes open, this place is a wolves' den. I have to go join the show up there." Stanton rose and smiled uncomfortably as he made his way to the table, stopping along the way and shaking hands with several people before he reached the front of the room.

Nicholas looked around the room, and his eyes fell randomly on the bookshelf beside him. One book was out of order, and Nicholas moved to push it back in line as he read its title.

A History of Contamination and Possession, the cover read. Nicholas pulled the book from the shelf and began to turn the pages. He skimmed through horrifying pictures of people half-transformed into demons. They were gnarled, twisted, and some of them sported extra limbs. Though he began to skim the passages for something that might help save Emily, every page held the same conclusion: there was no hope for the contaminated.

"Wow, you must really like her if you've resorted to reading to save her," Moon said over his shoulder.

Nicholas dragged his eyes from the page and glared at Moon. "Emily VonPeer is an innocent in this situation, and the last time I checked it was our job to protect innocents."

"Oh, please," Moon said, "don't try to pretend with me, the prettier the innocent, the higher the priority with you. You've always been that way." She sat down in the chair that Stanton had just left.

"Why are you sitting with me?" Nicholas asked. "Shouldn't you be up front hobnobbing with all the important people?"

"I'm making sure that you don't run downstairs to your demon girlfriend the first chance you get," Moon said.

Damn it, Nicholas thought, clenching a muscle in his jaw. He prayed that Emily was still safe. His expression must have shown on his face.

"Don't worry," Moon said. "Wagner's under strict orders to let us know if there are any changes in her condition. Your mother even set him with the task of trying to cure her, if he can. It was a very noble decision on her part, if you ask me. The rest of the Paladin want to entomb her so that they can study her condition as she changes."

Nicholas relaxed slightly, though he was confused by his mother's motives. That, at least, was nothing new.

Someone cleared their throat, and people began to fill the seats.

The man in the silver robes nodded at the door, and two of the younger agents walked in holding a giant map between them that they set on a large easel. The little man in the brown suit wrung his hands and whispered instructions to the agents, making sure that nothing happened to the map. He sat down at the head table with another, taller man that Nicholas recognized from the news.

He frowned and leaned to Moon. "What's the senator doing here?"

Stanton and Lillian approached a podium at the end of the table. Lillian clapped her hands together. "We've had an exciting break in the case," she announced to the room as everyone went silent. "After working closely with the historians and curators at the state museum, Senior Agent Keith Blevin has managed to get us a viewing of the fabled VonPeer demon map."

Several paladin in the audience shifted in their chairs, obviously surprised.

"He's an agent and a senator?" Nicholas asked Moon.

"Yeah," Moon breathed. "I just met him a week ago. He's been undercover for years. He's an expert on the VonPeer witch family and their demon map."

"Demon map?"

"This is a truly remarkable document," Blevin said to the crowd. "It was meant to serve as a warning tool for members of the VonPeer family. The map was housed inside the VonPeer family bible that was dug from the foundation of a local church. It's been buried for many years."

Nicholas looked at the map and was unimpressed. The map looked like a dirty, brown drawing, much the same as every other old map he'd seen. Then Blevin stretched his hand across it, and the crowd gasped. Small grids of light appeared around the map.

"Get the lights, will you?" Blevin asked. The lights in the room dimmed. Blevin pulled a pen from his jacket and with a click, the pen glowed with a pale pink light.

"As you can see," Blevin said, waving the pen across the map, "the map indicates the local ward lines." Everyone in the room gasped as the map lit into a web of glowing multicolored lights. "And also," Blevin said, passing his pen over the map again and this time, a hundred small points of light appeared, "the map indicates the location of all of the magical people in the area, though we can't see their identities." He pointed to a group of dots so bright that it looked like a small red blob on the page. "This, for example, is Paladin. And this," he said, pointing to another glowing form by the riverbank, "is the VonPeer estate."

"Can you use it to find the demons?" someone asked.

"Possibly, though even without the use of the map, our agents have already located a potential demon this evening." The audience began to clap until Blevin raised his hand. "This map has so many more implications than just the demons we're fighting now. Using this tool, we'll be able to usher in a new era of peace for this region. This map gives us the corner market on virtually all of the magical activity in the area. The time has come for us to rise up and lead our magical brethren in a way that will be beneficial to us all. With this tool, we can preemptively guarantee the safety of the people that we are destined to serve."

"Preemptive safety?" Nicholas said. "Does that mean what I think it does? They just want to stop trouble before it starts?"

Moon raised her eyebrows and nodded.

"Holy shit," Nicholas breathed as the room erupted into thunderous applause. The people around him began to rise to their feet applauding. Nicholas sat in his chair, dumbfounded until Moon pulled him to his feet as well.

"Play along," Moon said.

Nicholas looked up, and Arch was watching them from the table beside Blevin and his mother.

Nicholas began to clap in spite of himself. He noticed Stanton leave his seat and walk out the door.

Lillian nodded at Blevin, then followed Stanton out the

door.

The lights came on in the room, and the place was abuzz with activity as the agents all moved closer, with smiles on their faces, eager to congratulate Agent Blevin on his amazing discovery.

"So this guy would have the Paladin going back into the business of witch hunting?" Nicholas said.

"Unless we figure out a way to stop it," Moon breathed.

Moon's phone began to vibrate. She pulled it out of her pocket. "It's a message from your mother," she said. "She wants us to meet her in her office."

Nicholas followed Moon silently out the door. His mind was spinning with a thousand things: the corruption, the greed, the fact that everyone was so willing to go along with it. It was as if everything he'd ever known and loved about this place had been yanked away from him. He was so lost in his thoughts that as Moon led him into his mother's office, he did a double take when he saw Lillian and Stanton sitting in chairs near the open window with an ashtray between them. Before he had time to speak, Stanton cleared his throat.

"So what do you think of all this, Agent Flynn?" Stanton asked.

"Of the corruption, the greed, or the complete subversion of the Agency I've dedicated my life to? Are you guys on board with this?" Nicholas said.

His mother smirked at him with an expression that looked distinctly like pride.

"I told you he'd be on the right side of this," Stanton said.

"What do we do now?" Nicholas asked.

"We find Dalgreth," Stanton said, and Lillian nodded. "Wherever he is, he's in danger. We need you for that, Nicholas."

Stanton and his mother looked at him expectantly, and

Nicholas took a step back. "I don't know about that," he said. "The last time I used divination, Ben was killed. I don't want that to happen again."

As he said this, even Moon looked sympathetic. She paused, and then with what looked like a tremendous effort, she spoke, "What happened to Ben wasn't entirely your fault, Nicholas. I pushed him to get that promotion. I don't think that he'd have asked you to do what you did otherwise. I'm at least as responsible for his death as you are. But there's nothing we can do about the past. You need to find a way to use your gift to help us now. We need you." Nicholas fell silent as he stared at Moon. After a moment, he held out his hand to her. After another moment, she took it, then looked into his eyes as she shook his hand.

Nicholas looked to his mother and Stanton. He dropped into a chair and produced the chess piece.

"Let's do this," he said.

"Moon, watch the hallway," Lillian said. "Nicholas, Stanton's going to help you scry this time," she said. "The aura on the chess piece is very weak, but I'm hoping that between the two of you, we might be able to get a signal."

Stanton stubbed his cigarette and pulled his chair beside Nicholas. The two men sat face to face. "Here's what you do," Stanton said. "I want you to focus on your memories of John, and let those guide you to the place where he is now."

Nicholas wrapped his hands around the chess piece, closed his eyes, and let his mind drift. Under normal circumstances, this practice was against both his training and ethics. It was probably why they didn't teach it at the Academy anymore. He concentrated on his memories of John. There was the time they were fishing with his dad; John standing beside Nicholas at Ben's grave; John walking the fields in his old black boots and a crumpled fishing cap shining with lures . . . the images began to swirl together, forming a whirlpool in his mind's eye that dragged him deeper, until the picture began to right itself again.

He brushed John's mind with his own.

John? He questioned, *It's me, it's Nick. Can you hear me?*

The images began to grow dark. "The connection's slipping," Nicholas said.

Stanton laid his hand over Nicholas' and offered a small push of magic. "Keep going," Stanton said.

Nicholas pushed with his mind until he felt a slight acknowledgement, and continued.

John, you've got to open your eyes and look around, show us where you are.

It took several moments before this happened.

"He's very weak," Stanton said.

Through John's eyes, they could see the room. It was very dark, and a single, weak light shone far overhead. The interior of the room was cylindrical, metal, and fastened together with rivets. John moved his head, and Nicholas could see Maeve VonPeer sitting in the room crouched against the wall.

"Maeve VonPeer is in prison with him," Stanton said.

Where are you? Nicholas asked, but the scene went dark.

Nicholas opened his eyes, disoriented, his blood pounding in his head.

"What'd you get?" Lillian asked.

"Not enough," Nicholas said. "They're in a cell of some sort."

Stanton shot Nicholas a sidelong glance. "They're housed in a large cylindrical structure, approximately ten feet in diameter, twenty to thirty feet tall, comprised entirely of riveted sheets of metal. There was a light source overhead, natural light by the look of it. The floor was made of earth, but there was some kind of grain in the corners of the room."

Nicholas looked at Stanton, impressed. "Whoa," he

said.

"He's the best," Lillian said. "It sounds like we're looking for some kind of silo."

Stanton got up. "I'm going to get my laptop, establish a perimeter, and start looking for buildings that match the description in a ten-mile radius of the disappearance site."

"You think they're somewhere near the place where they were attacked? Hidden in plain sight?" Nicholas said.

"That's usually the way," Stanton said. "These creatures are not native to our world; they operate by necessity and convenience. The fact that it keeps turning up at the River Gate suggests that it's hiding nearby."

There was a tap of boots on the marble floor. Moon walked to the door.

"Blevin's coming," she said, peering out.

Lillian nodded to Stanton, who disappeared into a side office. Lillian dropped into the chair beside Nicholas just as Moon smiled and escorted Blevin inside.

"Please, have a seat," she said, gesturing to the two empty chairs, but Blevin shook his head. "Have you met my son, Nicholas?"

Nicholas stood tall, put his hands together and saluted Blevin, who returned the salute.

"No, but it's nice to meet you, Son," Blevin said.

Nicholas cringed at the word *son*, but managed to retain a respectful expression.

Blevin turned to Lillian. "Has there been any change in Emily VonPeer's condition?" he said, looking concerned.

Nicholas wondered why he cared.

"No," Lillian said, her eyes darting quickly to Nicholas. "But I have Wagner on standby."

Blevin nodded, looking thoughtful. "What a shame. Such a good kid."

The phone on Lillian's desk rang. "Excuse me," she said as she went to answer it. "Lillian Flynn," she said.

They could hear the panicked tone on the other end of the phone, but not the words. Lillian's face looked grim, and she dropped the call, then dialed another number.

"This is Lillian Flynn. I want you to put the building on lockdown immediately. No one gets out except for the agents that I'm sending through the front doors, is that understood?"

Lillian replaced the receiver and stood up. "That was the lab," she said. "The techs came back from a break and found the doors open, specimens everywhere, half the lab destroyed, and Wagner locked in one of the cages. Emily VonPeer is missing."

The phone rang again, and Lillian answered it.

"Emily VonPeer was spotted on foot near the riverbank."

"She must be headed back to her house," Nicholas said.

"Well, Blevin, let's put this map of yours to work," Lillian said. "Has everyone cleared out from the conference?"

The group walked the short distance down the hall and back into the library where three agents stood guarding the map.

Blevin moved to the table and produced his pen, waving it over the map. At once, a thousand points of light shot from it.

"How do we know who's who?" Moon asked.

"The ones that are moving might be a good bet," Blevin said. He pointed to a pinprick of light. "I'll bet that's her. Are there agents there?"

"It wouldn't matter," Nicholas said. "They'd never be able to break through the wards of the house alone."

"What about the VonPeer athame?" Blevin said. "It's very powerful; it should unravel the wards on the house and allow us uninhibited access to the entire place. With any luck, we can bring in Emily and the jackbirds for Wagner."

"What does Wagner want with her?" Nicholas asked.

Blevin tapped the map. "The site where we found Emily was a demon tomb. After looking through our records, we found that former orders of Paladin warehoused their demons in places like this before the technology to eliminate them was possible," Blevin said. "We think that Emily might be able to help us study them." He waved his hand over the map, and a series of bright green circles emerged.

"I thought the demon tombs were a myth," Nicholas said.

"So did we," Blevin said. "We'd like to see how the former Paladin system works, so that we can safely study the creatures housed in other tombs in the area. It's unlikely that we can cure her, but Wagner thinks that a combination of sedation and restraints will allow us to use Emily for this purpose as she transforms."

Nicholas thought he was going to be sick. He looked at the faces around him, trying to keep his expression neutral, though inside he seethed with fury. "So this is why you all want Emily unharmed?"

"Well, there is also Laurel Grove to be considered," Blevin said. "It's a veritable treasure trove of magical information. Your involvement in the project has become critical to us, Agent Flynn; we need you to help us capture Emily VonPeer so that we can obtain the magic necessary to gain access to the house."

Nicholas clenched his fists. So much for honor. Hell, this man was nothing but a scavenger looking to break into Emily's house. Blevin was stroking his chin like a cartoon villain, for Christ's sake. Nicholas wanted to wipe that smirk off his face, but he knew that he needed to stay cool or he'd end up right back in the lockup.

"Look," Moon said, changing the subject. "There's a dot moving in the center of the river too. It's huge!"

"Then that's where we'll go," Lillian said. "It may be the other demon. We'll take a few more teams north along both sides of the river, then scour the area to see if we can find that thing. If we hurry, we should be able to surround it. Stanton and Blevin can investigate Laurel Grove. Nicholas, Moon and I will take our teams and follow the leads up the river."

"No, I want to go to the house to find Emily," Nicholas said. "If she's there, I can bring her in by myself. She trusts me."

His mother looked at him and shook her head.

Moon pushed her glasses higher on her nose. "Why should we trust you?"

Nicholas cracked his knuckles. "I have a score to settle with Emily," Nicholas said. The lie tumbled from his lips so well that everyone looked impressed, even Moon.

Lillian paused, then looked at the others. "Alright," she said. "But be careful, all of you. These creatures are highly dangerous."

The men moved to go, but Lillian grabbed Nicholas by the elbow before he left. "This is me trusting you," she said. "Don't screw it up."

Nicholas looked at her for a moment, then nodded his head as he walked out the door.

CHAPTER 26

Emily shivered as Malphat clutched her arm. He was going to kill her; she knew it. Malphat waved to Diamond, and Diamond stopped and rolled down the window.

"What do you need?" he said.

"Just a ride," Malphat said.

Diamond leaned to the passenger side and opened the door. "Get in."

"It's a nice night, and I have some things to discuss with Ms. VonPeer," Malphat said. "We'll ride in the back." He slammed the door shut and Diamond rolled up the window, muttering something about being a chauffeur.

"Don't worry about Diamond, he'll do what I tell him," Malphat said. "Please," he gestured, and Emily leapt onto the bed of the truck. He followed her.

Maybe she could jump; she'd probably survive the fall. She wondered if he had a gun. No, he wouldn't need that. For a moment, she thought about trying to fight him, but abandoned the thought. His power far outstripped hers. He moved closer to her, and Emily knew that she should have been afraid of him, but she wasn't. She could feel the power exuding from him in waves, but the sensation was comforting rather than malicious. Diamond's truck rumbled and began to move. Without a word, Malphat raised his magic around them in a glowing red bubble that obscured all sound. He made himself the center of a universe that contained only the two of them.

Malphat put his hand on her leg and she slapped it away. "Get away from me. You're a monster."

He shrugged his shoulders. "So are you, almost. I need your help. You're the only person on this side who can open a gate, and I need a way home. I've been trapped here by your friends for long enough."

"My friends?"

"Your wizard friends, the Paladin. They're after you as well, you know."

Emily shifted as she considered his words.

"But how?" she asked him, "Nicholas—"

"Is the scion of a very old and powerful family, much like your own. He seduced you into believing that he was your ally."

Emily blushed at the word. Seduced her, is that what he'd done? "That's none of your business," she said. "And it's also no reason for me to trust you."

Malphat inched closer to her. "You need to trust me because you don't have a choice. The Paladin know about your transformation, and they'll come for you as well; they don't care who you are, they care about what you've become," Malphat said. "When they caught me, they were making it a practice to kill anyone else who possessed our kind of magic. It's why they killed Jane Van Peer, your ancestor. They trumped up a charge of witchcraft and murdered her before anyone was the wiser. I'm trying to prevent the same thing from happening to you."

Emily was silent for a moment. "What does Jane have to do with this?"

"Jane," Malphat said, his face sorrowful. "She didn't

deserve what happened to her. But I've had much time to think about these things. Much time."

"What happened?" Emily said. "Who are you?"

"I'm not a human," Malphat said. "But I'm not a monster like they believe me to be. I was chasing a monster when I came here. The Paladin closed the gate behind us. I couldn't get home. And then they began to hunt us, both the beast and myself. I ran for days and managed to escape the agents. I was sick and starving, and the magic from your house called to me. Jane found me near the side of the path, and I scared her, she thought I was a robber. She pulled a wand from her basket and slashed the air with a protective spell, and I was saved. That small bit of magic gave me what I needed: food."

"You feed on magic?" she asked.

"It is the only thing that can sustain me in this world," he said. "Without it, I survive, but only barely. Jane, her mother-in-law, and her son, Samuel, spent days restoring me with their magic. Together, we used our magic to entomb the first beast, and then we tried to open the gate to send me home. It didn't work."

"The Paladin were mighty then. I wasn't strong enough to fight them. They overpowered me and Jane and threw us in prison. They accused us of witchcraft and at that time, they were the law. Even Jane's family was powerless to interfere. Her brother came to visit us in prison. The Paladin attempted to seize the land and the House. The lands were only preserved by titling most of the land and the river gate to the Paladin, a bribe that they hoped would save our lives. The Paladin promised to release us the morning after the papers were signed. Instead, the minute they owned the land, they brought us to the church, where they convicted us both of witchcraft."

He paused. Emily's eyes grew wide with horror. "Then what happened?" she prompted.

"They enlisted the help of the natives, who used powerful and ancient spells to subdue me. I was thrown into a tomb outside the churchyard, covered with earth, and left there. They did the same to Jane. I could hear her crying for a few hours, but my magic had been so diminished that I was powerless to stop it. She died, but I continued on in the dark, unable to live and unable to die."

"How did you get out?" she asked.

"By accident," Malphat said. "A bulldozer went digging in the wrong place and struck my tomb. At first, I did not know that I had been released. I did not remember the daylight, and the outside sounds were strange. A small wind blew into my tomb, and for days I lay there, just feeling the wind on my face. A few more days passed, and I heard thumping sounds. I waited until night and then escaped my grave only to find that the beast was awakened before I was, dug out of the quarry amid the rocks that are now paving the street. I followed it to the good senators. Diamond and Blevin recovered the creature, and were placating it by feeding it small amounts of magic. They did not expect that the beast would grow. At first, they could control it. But, as it grows stronger it needs them less and less, and now it is killing for sport and searching for a mate." He stopped his story and stared at Emily for a long time.

"It chose me?" she asked, not wanting to know the answer.

"You are the only one with the power to help it. As its mate, you would be unable to destroy it. It was a sensible choice."

"How do we get rid of the beast?" she asked him.

"With the athame," he said, "you're the only one who can vanquish the beast and open the gate."

"If you're so concerned about my family, why didn't you save my Aunt Maeve?"

"I tried, but the beast overpowered me. Diamond was

the one who decided to take your aunt and Dalgreth for its sustenance. Blevin set up a spell to make it look like they'd been dusted. He thought their magic would be enough to placate it, but the demon only grew stronger, too strong for anyone to control."

"And now it's taken to dusting the Paladin?"

"They're the people with the most magic," Malphat said. "But it's running out of food, which is why it needed you under its control."

Emily gulped the cool night air, and tried to steady her hands, which were shaking beyond her control.

"I can keep you from falling under its sway. Your transformation is advancing quickly now," he said, stroking her hair. "The evidence of the transformation shows in your eyes, did you know?"

As he said this, Emily felt a wave of pleasure rush through her body. It was an unusually clear night, and she lay back in the truck bed and studied the patterns in the stars as if she were seeing them for the first time. She suddenly wasn't worried about Diamond, her aunt, or anything else. She was possessed with the overwhelming urge to stay where she was, to watch the night sky until the sensation passed. A sleepy feeling overcame her as the sensation gently but methodically erased her fears, enveloping her in a warm cocoon of peace.

"That's right," he said. "Relax, just let it happen," Malphat said.

She sighed as her nausea was replaced with rhythmic waves of warmth. Her toes curled as each turn of his hand through her hair brought a heightened sensation of pleasure. She closed her eyes, a sleepy grin on her face. Her fears, her worries, and her sense of purpose were eclipsed by a gentle but persistent demand ordering one thing: surrender.

High in the night, a bird soared among the stars. Emily watched the bird as it circled the trees above her in an arc, swooping lower and lower in circles. The bird dove beyond her sight, and her mind was filled with a terrible scream. The bonds holding her to the truck released. Then a voice, familiar as her own breath, echoed in her mind. It was the House, Emily marveled.

Emily, the House said, *you have to fight him. They're still alive, but there's not much time! You must . . .*

The voice of the House was silenced, and Emily struggled to regain control of her own body. Her ears rang and her heart began to pulse in an unfamiliar rhythm. Emily felt the skin on her hands crawl, and she looked at them, seeing her own hands one minute, a smooth paw punctuated with razor talons the next. She watched her hands in horror, too terrified to scream.

Fight it, the House whispered, snapping Emily to her senses.

Malphat held her by the shoulders and she was still, entranced. He smiled at her then, and she felt her knees grow weak. She smiled back at him. He traced her lower lip with his finger, and she closed her eyes, not wanting him to stop.

"Forget your old life. I'll bring you with me," he said. "To my world. You'll be safe there, there are many like us where I am from."

Emily purred under his touch, and he smiled. She didn't think about his magic or her abrupt shift in affections, all she could feel were his fingers, now trailing down her neck to her collarbone. When his lips moved to hers, she did nothing to stop him. Everything in her body screamed for Malphat as his tongue passed her teeth. He moved his hands down her back, pulling her close to him, strong and confident. He kissed her again, harder. When he pulled away, his face was more beast than man, his desperation and wild need so different than . . .

Nicholas, Emily thought, and his face blew into her mind, bringing with it a cold breeze of reality that was enough to remind her of what she was doing. She realized how this new side of her personality was overshadowing her mind, her emotions, and her true feelings. Most of all, they were keeping her from her mission. She retreated into the space of her mind that she could still call her own, seeking her own powers. "You're perfect," Malphat murmured, gently kissing her neck as she fought not to give in to his persuasions. "The best creation I've ever seen—"

Diamond's truck ground to a halt. Emily felt the light of her magic bubbling inside her before she saw the green aura gather in her hands. As Malphat moved to kiss her again, she flung her light straight at his shoulder. He didn't flinch; he just stared at her.

"That didn't even injure you, did it?" she said.

"A little sting," he said, rubbing his arm. "It's no use to fight me on this, though. You're holding onto your human identity very tightly. Don't worry, that instinct will pass."

He reached for her, and Emily scrambled backward. She fumbled in her pocket and closed her hand over the locket, engulfing it in green light. She prayed that the spell would work like she thought it would as she secured it around her neck. Her hand closed on the small object, and she feinted and jumped from the side of the truck just as Malphat reached for her again.

"Emily?" he asked into the darkness, his voice soft and pleading.

She didn't move, didn't dare breathe, but marveled at the power of the locket. With this single tool, her aunt had shielded her from everything, including, she realized, creatures like him.

"Where are you?" Malphat asked, and began to fire random shots into the darkness in an attempt to snare her. "Emily, you need to come back, it's dangerous. They followed us here!" Malphat backed away from the place where she stood, muttering about where she'd gone. His departure left an ache in her heart, and part of her wanted to call him back to her, to beg him to take her with him, to do what he would with her.

Emily hauled herself into a nearby tree, and watched Diamond exit the truck. He looked over his shoulder several times as he retreated into the woods.

"Emily?" Malphat called in her mind.

She turned and stared at him. She could still see him standing a hundred yards away. He looked worried as he disappeared into the woods, glancing back over his shoulder. She saw Steph peer from behind a tree, beckoning to her with a small pocket- knife. Emily sped through the branches of the trees to meet him, keeping one eye on Diamond.

She put her hand on his shirt and he jumped. "Can you see me?"

"Yep, but that cloaking spell is crazy," Steph said.

"How did you get here?" she said.

"Keep your voice down, I don't want your companion to know that we're here. We tried to meet you. We went to the cemetery first, then to the House to find you, but you were gone. The creature was circling the House again. We managed to track it here to this place."

Steph pointed and Emily saw a blue light flash in the distance.

"Where's Nicholas?" Jessie said, appearing from behind a tree.

"With the Paladin," Emily said. "It's a long story, but he's probably better off there."

"Let's see what the good senator is up to. I always heard he was a creep, but I wouldn't have guessed him to be in league with a creature like this," Steph said.

Diamond paced through the field with purpose. This lot was different than the first, less industrial, and lined with woods. The place had the look of an abandoned farm. It seemed at first that his destination was an old metal outbuilding.

"Follow us," Steph said, "but stay a few steps behind, just in case." She held her breath; after a moment, he led them to a small trail on the left of the building. Jessie followed. When they were out of sight, Emily ran after them, ducking to the side of the stable. She crouched on the ground, sheltered by the building's shadow, and peered around the corner.

Diamond headed toward another building, a tall garage padded with rusted, blue tin siding. Emily watched him ascend a set of metal stairs that led to a steel door and step inside. She took a few tentative steps toward the building, then thought better of it. The stretch of field was too open, and she had the distinct impression that something was looking for her here.

"Steph," she breathed. "Where are you?" There was no response.

Emily skirted the property, nearing the building at the edge of the woods. Her aunt and John were close; she could feel them. She studied the building and could not believe her luck. There were several barred windows at the ground level on this side of the building. She was about to race to the window when she felt a hand on her shoulder.

Steph tipped an imaginary hat. "At your service."

Jessie was already curled under a tree, checking a briefcase filled with small globes that looked like Christmas ornaments.

"What are those?" Emily asked.

"Trade secrets," Steph said, as if it were the most rational explanation in the world. "We couldn't let you have all the fun fighting the demons. Besides, that thing in there blew a fifty thousand dollar hole in our coffee shop. I figure we owe him one." He wielded his small silver knife with an expert spin.

"And what exactly are you planning to do with that?"

Emily asked, pointing to the knife. "Fight a demon? That knife wouldn't cut toast."

"Lucky for me, I am not planning on making toast," Steph said. "Hasn't anyone told you that size doesn't matter?"

Emily grinned in spite of herself.

Steph sniffed the air. "What exactly are you doing here?" he said.

Jessie sidled up to the two of them, throwing a belt covered in potions over her head and shoulder. The potions glowed.

"Aunt Maeve is in that building, and I'm going to save her," Emily said.

Steph's expression changed immediately. He and Jessie again exchanged glances; Jessie's expression had changed from amusement to anxiety.

"I guess it's really good that we're here then," Steph said. "If you're trying to rescue your aunt, you're going to need our help. And if we're going to get the demon, we're going to need your help. The whole situation works out rather nicely."

"It usually does when we're on the right track," Jessie said.

"But Steph," Emily said, "maybe you shouldn't go up there. I'm not normal anymore, what if something happens to you two because of me? The Paladin doctor said that my attack is turning me into a demon. What if the beast does the same thing to the two of you?" she asked. There were a million things that she wanted to say, warnings that died on her lips when she saw Steph's expression of confidence.

"Shh," Steph said, pressing his finger to her lip with an exaggerated gesture.

Emily frowned.

"I'll explain it all later, slowly, so that you can understand. It's time for you to trust me. The beast is out of control, drunk on its own power."

A slithering sensation twisted down her arm. She shuddered and tried to suppress it by clenching her fist.

Steph handed Emily a backpack, and pulled on his own army issue hiking pack adorned with patches that looked like they belonged on the book bag of a twelve-year-old girl. He brandished his knife, and again, Emily was forced to smile. He was so ridiculous. Jessie approached them, similarly attired, her purple streaked ponytails bobbing with excitement.

"Let's go," Steph said, and the three of them ran quietly toward the building.

CHAPTER 27

Nicholas sat in the passenger seat, feeling a sense of dread as they approached their destination.

"If it's even possible to get past the protections on Laurel Grove, I'll be the one to do it," Nicholas said.

Blevin sat in the backseat, holding the athame with the reverence of a priest.

The three men sped down the hill. Stanton ignored the stoplights on the empty streets. Nicholas laid his head against the cool leather of the seats and closed his eyes. His head throbbed from the weight of the night and the hard reality of the task that lay before them. He was resolved that no matter what happened tonight, he'd do his best to save Emily, though it might require that he surrender his job or even his life. With any luck, it wouldn't come to that. He opened his eyes and watched the sky, looking for any sign of the demons.

A thin rain began to plunk the windows, and the soft swish of the wipers blurred the way to their destination. The city streets turned into country roads, and Nicholas felt a brief moment of doubt—what if it didn't work, what if it didn't let him in?

Blevin sat tall, anxious as a child. Stanton leaned deeper into the seat, calm as a man driving to get a doughnut. Nicholas' eyes shifted between the two men. Letting out a sigh, he prayed for some magic or a miracle that could save Emily. Either one would do.

Stanton swung into the long driveway and killed the lights. "Whoa, I've never seen this place at night," he said. "The wards are easier to see now."

Nicholas nodded. When he softened his vision and summoned his othersight, the House was cocooned in a tangled web of glowing light pattered across its perimeter like a series of glowing rainbow spiderwebs.

"It's amazing," Stanton agreed. "Do you think she's inside?"

"We'd never know from here," Nicholas said, opening the car door. Nicholas was the first one out of the SUV. He approached the House with caution, hands aloft. Stanton whistled to him and handed him an extra pen.

"Just in case," Stanton told him. "We don't know what we're dealing with here."

Nicholas walked toward the House, trying to quell his apprehension. The House had permitted him entrance before, but things were different now, Emily was gone. Nicholas approached the House with his hands up, well aware that since he'd fixed the breaches in its defenses, the House would be able to strike them dead before they could pull a potion from their robes. He cast his othersight, attempting to summon the voice of the House.

The wards glowed at the entrance to the path like a net of multicolored light, and Nicholas was overcome with a powerful desire to turn away. The thought patterns of a dozen generations greeted him, and Nicholas stepped forward with the feeling that he was greeting an enemy army.

"Hello," he said cautiously to the House, "I need your

234

help."

The wards of the House grew stronger and more suspicious. The two men watched Nicholas expectantly, and he tried again.

"Look, I hope that you can understand. Emily is in danger, and I need your help to save her. Is she inside?"

In response, a single ward glowed white, and the House prompted Nicholas to grab it. He moved his hand toward it. The wards of the House grew even brighter as Nicholas closed his eyes and put his hands on the protective net that shielded the House.

In his mind's eye, he met the spirit of the House for the first time. She was a beautiful woman with flowing, dark hair banded with a simple, beaded headdress. She had deep copper skin; her clothes were white and made of deerskin. She was crouched in a fighting stance, a javelin aimed at Nicholas' heart. Her eyes were intent, waiting for the least sign of a threat. Her eyes flicked briefly over his shoulder and then back to him. Nicholas slowly moved his head over his shoulder. Stanton and Blevin were behind him, watching him.

"It's okay, guys," Nicholas said to the two men. "Just give me a minute."

The two men relaxed their stance slightly.

She motioned to Blevin. "Bring me the athame," she instructed. "It's mine! It belongs to our family!"

"Just a minute," Nicholas told her. He broke his grasp on the wards and moved to confer with the two men.

"The House wants the athame," he told them, skipping the prelude.

The two men spoke at once.

"Give it back then," Stanton said.

"Absolutely not," Blevin argued. "We need it to fight the demons, and we'll never get it back once it's in that house."

The two men glared at one another, then turned to Nicholas. Since both men were of equal rank, they were at an impasse.

"Well, there are three votes here. Break the tie, Nicholas," Stanton said.

"I'm sorry, Agent Blevin," Nicholas said, reaching for the athame that was still in his hands.

Blevin complied, his jaw tight, but he held the athame for a moment too long before he released it to Nicholas. Nicholas stared at Blevin, and then his eyes flicked to Stanton, wondering briefly if it was safe for him to turn his back on the two men. He marched to the House, offering the athame in front of him as he went.

Nicholas took a breath and stepped into the light of the wards, stretching his othersight so that he could again see the woman. He knelt down beside her, and offered her the athame. She released the javelin to her side, walked to him, and laid her hands on his forehead.

"You have helped our family several times, and for this reason, I have chosen to offer you my protection." She christened Nicholas, imbuing him with a little of her own light. "Kindred," she whispered. Then she chanted words in an ancient language.

He looked up at her and she smiled.

She took him by the hands, and he rose so that the two of them were face to face. She kissed him on the cheek, and as she did so, whispered in his ear, "Do not tell the other men about this." She looked meaningfully into his eyes.

Nicholas nodded his head a fraction of an inch. He already knew what the House was trying to tell him.

"Help me," he breathed to her, as she kissed his other cheek.

She smiled, and with a wink, handed him back the knife. "Rise," she said, "come inside." The wards surrounding the House fell, and Nicholas turned to the two men.

"She invited us to come inside," he said to the two men. "But put your weapons away, it's disrespectful." The House hadn't told him to say that, but he could feel her approval at his words. He strode toward the front door, and the two men fell in behind him. The front door swung open before Nicholas touched it, and Stanton whistled, impressed in spite of himself.

Blevin was more cautious as he approached the House. "I've been thrown out of this place two times before," he said, looking around carefully as he walked up the steps. He followed Nicholas through the front door.

"Whoa," Blevin said. This room of the House was like a church, carved in polished wood and filled with plants.

"Exquisite," he murmured, reaching his hand to touch the ornate banister, carved from bottom to top with silhouettes and faces of hundreds of people, generations of the VonPeer family.

At the center of the wood on the second story, Nicholas recognized a single face with an expression gentle as the moon. It was the image of the House herself, watching them, and bidding them to step inside. A heavy wooden door opened to the right of them, and they entered another wood paneled room even more fantastic than the first.

At the House's instruction, Nicholas laid the athame on the table in the foyer and backed away from it.

Go to the kitchen.

"In here," he said to the men.

They walked down the hallway past the parlor door, stepping as quietly as they would in a church.

Pausing to survey the room, Blevin gasped. "Priceless," he said, "all of it. Every piece in this room is a treasure." Blevin rubbed his hands together, his eyes darting from one object to the next in rapid succession, absorbing the wealth that surrounded him.

Nicholas noticed the greedy gleam in Blevin's eye, and

Stanton clapped Blevin on the shoulder.

"No wonder Maeve VonPeer never let you in, this would be a goldmine for an antique shop," Stanton said. "She would never have gotten any peace at night."

Nicholas was several paces ahead of them, searching for the oldest rooms, the low rooms where he'd stayed with Emily to wait out the monster's attack.

There was a small thump in the next room, and the three men drew their weapons. Nicholas grinned as Emily's cat, Malkie, appeared around the corner with a plaintive meow.

"I'll be right back," Nicholas said, picking up the cat and marching into the kitchen. He could hear the men moving through the House behind him as they exclaimed over the artwork on the walls.

Nicholas set the cat down and reached into the cupboard for a tin of cat food. He opened the tin and dumped it into the cat's dish. He stepped back as Malkie rushed to the food and bumped his shoulder on an open door of a dark room.

In here, the House said.

He stepped into the pantry and pulled a cord that lit the small room.

The room was an old butler's pantry, lined on three sides with whitewashed counters and drawers. The shelves above him were stacked high with dozens of glass jars, each of them clearly marked and containing a number of leaves. Some of the herbs hung from pegs driven into the shelves, dried in bunches and ready for use.

His phone vibrated and he checked his messages. It was his mother.

Perimeter secured, located the creature, need backup.

Yes. Emily not here, on our way, he wrote.

"What's this?" he said. He shifted the dishtowels to the side and picked up the book that was lying on the counter in the pantry.

"May I?" he asked the House.

238

Please, the House said. *I need your help. Emily is in danger.*

He began to flip through the pages. The book was large, and many of the pages contained recipes, pressed flowers, and other oddities.

Wait, the House said. *This is what she was reading before she left.* The book splayed open and the pages began to flip. When they stopped, Nicholas stepped to the book and read its contents.

"This is the second demon?" he said.

He is our enemy, the House said. *Malphat. He was defeated and imprisoned many years ago, but now he's escaped.*

He doesn't need to use the gate because he has the power to create his own, Nicholas thought, flipping the pages. *But he needs the scion to wield the athame. That's why they attacked Emily.*

He spoke in a low voice so the men wouldn't hear him. "Can you show me where she is?"

A door swung open in the kitchen. Nicholas placed his hand on the countertop and was silent.

Even with his magic, his request to the House was large. He focused hard on the thin thread that he'd attached to her mind, begging the House to help him. Nicholas felt the energy in the House's wards drop around him as his mind twirled with the loss of time and space, until he found her, Emily.

Nicholas shuddered in panic as he saw a picture of Emily in his mind. She was running up a flight of stairs, about to be attacked. The House panned outward, and Nicholas saw a large blue water tower, stenciled with a single word on the side DIAMOND. Beside the tower was a large silo.

Stanton ran into the kitchen and grabbed Nicholas by the arm. "Run!" he said, shoving Nicholas toward the back door.

Nicholas yelled as the filament connecting his mind to the House snapped suddenly, and he fell backward onto the floor. As his mind floated back toward his body, he heard a distant sound, *pop, pop, pop*, and then a thump. Then he was in his own body, enveloped in warmth. His arms and legs felt heavy. His upper body was supported by what felt like a warm tree trunk. He cracked open his eyes. Blevin was nowhere, but Stanton was immediately above him cradling him like a child.

"Hang in there, kid," Stanton said, tightening his arms around Nicholas. "The bastard shot us both."

"Shot?" Nicholas murmured, "I feel all right, why am I all wet?"

"Stay with me!" Stanton said. "Nicholas! Nicholas!"

Nicholas murmured something incoherent about a book, not realizing that the seeping warmth was the feeling of his blood leaving his body. The last thing he noticed before everything went black was the vibrating phone in his pocket.

CHAPTER 28

What a nuisance these creatures are, Malphat thought as he stalked through the woods. First, he lost Emily, and now the hunters had followed them. That was one problem easily solved, he thought. He walked into the middle of the road and crossed his arms. The air began to hum with the approach of a vehicle, and Malphat made no motion as the black SUV ground to a halt in front of him. He continued to stand his ground as four of them emerged from the vehicle, clad in the gray robes of the Paladin.

The tallest of the men walked toward him. He pulled down his hood to reveal himself. His hair was blond and cropped closely to his head.

"Excuse me, sir," the man said, "but you're blocking the road. We need you out of the way."

"As it turns out, I need you out of the way as well," Malphat said.

The men didn't even have time to draw their weapons. With a single motion, Malphat conjured an orb of magic between his outstretched hands. The orb expanded as he threw it, casting a glowing red barrier over all four of the men. They didn't scream, they didn't run; the magic prevented it. The only thing that the men could do was watch in horror as Malphat extended his hands again and walked toward them. One by one, he pulled at the threads of their auras, using his hands to draw the energy of their magic into himself. Malphat smiled as the last man crumbled into a pile of dust on the ground. He walked over to the car, where the keys were in the ignition, and drove it off the road into the woods.

Now to retrieve Emily, he thought, as he drove toward the tower.

CHAPTER 29

Emily, Steph, and Jessie ran up the stairs of the ancient warehouse in search of the demon. The potions on their sashes clinked slightly as they ran. They each carried a briefcase filled with more bottles of the potion. At the top of the stairs, Steph moved to kick the door open, but Jessie stopped him.

"Wait," Jessie said with a low hiss. She turned the knob, and the door swung open.

"It would have been cooler my way," Steph said in a whisper.

They snuck through the door, their weapons ready. The room was dark except for the soft glow of emergency lights scattered above their heads. It was a large warehouse-style outbuilding; littered with pieces of old farm equipment as well as boxes and piles that partially concealed their view of the room.

"Where is he?" Steph breathed.

The door closed behind them in response. Jack Diamond walked to the three of them, a puzzled expression on his face.

"Can I help you?" he asked them, dusting off his hands,

his eyes darting from one face to the other. His look of confusion turned to anger when he saw Emily. His reaction was only momentary; he crossed his arms, and his expression turned stony.

"I think you know why we're here," Steph said, and Diamond again feigned surprise. He was, after all, an accomplished liar.

"Can't say that I do," he said, "but this building is old and dangerous. You three had better get out of here before somebody gets hurt." Although his voice was still smooth, Diamond took a step toward them.

"Where's my aunt?" Emily snarled back, taking a step toward Diamond. She was a head shorter than him, but her expression was deadly.

Diamond's eyes grew wide for a moment before he recovered himself. "I don't know what you're talking about. You're obviously a very confused young woman. You need to leave; I don't take kindly to trespassers." His eyes shifted once to the double doors on the other side of the room.

Emily strode to the doors and stood in front of them. "Open this," Emily said, placing her hand on the doorknob.

"I don't have the key," Diamond said.

A screech erupted in the air and they all jumped backwards as a crash on the roof knocked dust from the rafters and made the overhead lights swing. Steph and Jessie snapped into action, each of them grabbing a globe from their belt and uncorking it. Diamond extended his hand to Emily.

"Come on," Diamond said, even as they heard the footprints snaking across the roof. "There's nothing here to see. You should leave now, while you can."

Steph was looking up, following the sounds coming from the roof. "Over there," he said to Jessie, pointing to a space behind a large concrete beam.

Jessie ran to the place behind the beam and snapped

open her briefcase, revealing round bottles filled liquid encased in soft, gray foam. Steph ran to her, grabbed six of the globes and faced the window. Diamond watched them for a minute, apprehensive.

The creature appeared in a cloud of fluorescent blue light, shot through with bolts of lightning in a display that made Emily freeze with terror. She swallowed hard, but found that she was unable to move, paralyzed by the feeling that they were all about to die. Even so, she couldn't take her eyes from the beast. The way it moved terrified her, and she clutched her arm as she watched it approach.

It flashed so close to her, her hand crackled with energy. She took two steps backward and bumped into Steph, who patted her shoulder.

"Your aunt might be back there," he said.

That was the only thought that allowed her to move. Before she could think, Steph pressed a bottle into her hands. She uncorked it and launched it at the beast. The potion missed and broke against the wall, spraying it with a splash of iridescent liquid.

"Step back," Steph said as the potion began to hiss and smoke.

The explosion was small, she thought, not much different than a firecracker, but everywhere the potion had touched had evaporated, and in the place that once held a wall, Emily could see a small patch of the evening sky.

"Try not to stare right at it," Jessie said. "It'll only make things worse." She pressed a potion into Emily's hand. "Aim for the middle and stay out of the range of its tail," she said.

Steph stepped into a defensive posture, ready to strike. Jessie edged to the briefcase, her eyes never leaving the beast. The thing locked eyes with Emily, its expression hungry. Diamond, at ease now, shrugged his shoulders.

"You should have left this alone," Diamond said with a fake sorrowful look on his face. "They're dead anyway, and

I can't let you go now either." Taking advantage of their concentration on the beast, Diamond slipped out.

Emily heard a deadbolt snap with a sickening finality, and she wondered if any of them would make it out of here alive.

"Brace yourselves!" Steph said as the beast leapt.

Blue flames erupted from the creature's mouth. Steph ducked to one side and threw the uncorked bottle at the beast's side, where it burst into a small explosion of glass and smoke. The creature shrieked as Jessie threw a second potion, this time hitting it on the neck.

Emily threw a third potion, then darted back as the beast reared and sent a small shard of glass flying across her cheek. She clutched her face and stumbled into a stack of boxes. The beast opened its mouth and shot a flume of glowing blue fire in her direction, singeing a lock of her hair as she rolled away from the blast. The creature craned its neck and stared at her. The large red orbs if its eyes glowed like lanterns. It swung its neck, snakelike, preparing to strike, but before the creature could move, Steph jumped in and landed a potion squarely on its right side. The beast craned its head up and filled the room with the sound of its pain. Emily attempted to dodge the beast as it thrashed in her direction, clutching its eye and howling. Steph ran to her and grabbed her arm.

"Time to move!" Steph said, half lifting, half dragging Emily away as a stack of wooden crates came crashing down on the place she'd been standing. He tightened his grip on her, accidentally pressing his thumb against her injured arm, and Emily cried out in pain. Steph looked back at her.

"Are you all right?" he asked, but Emily waved him away.

"Fine," she said, never taking her eyes from the beast.

The room was ablaze with the blue fire and smoke, and they crouched in the corner with Jessie, who pressed more bottles of the potion into their hands. Emily darted behind a large steel beam, trying to take aim.

Steph ran to the other corner of the room. Emily met his eyes, and he gave her the thumbs up sign. She crouched, ready to spring as Jessie threw a potion — the beast reeled backwards. For half a second they watched one another; Emily tilted her head a fraction of an inch.

"Now!" he said, and Emily ran as close as she dared to the creature, throwing four potions at once. Jessie and Steph did the same. The creature's scream sounded so human it sent shivers of terror down her spine.

Jessie jumped onto a stack of boxes and threw four more potions at the beast. The beast heaved with a deafening shriek, and as it flailed in pain, its tail smashed against the bottom of the stack of boxes where Jessie stood. She stumbled and fell onto the ground.

Before they knew what was happening, the creature was on Jessie, throwing aside boxes and debris, searching for her. Moving like lightning herself, Emily jumped to the place where she lay.

"Run!" Emily said, pulling Jessie to her feet and shoving her out of the way as the beast blew another blast of liquid hot fire. Emily barely had time to throw her arms over her head as the fire rained down on her.

She was only vaguely aware of her own screaming as the full blast of the magic struck her. She could hear Steph gasp and Jessie shout "no!" as the blue lightning crackled around and through her. Emily screamed and threw herself to the ground as the flames burst around her. It was then that she realized the fire hadn't hit her; she was safe underneath a shield of bright red light.

She looked up and could see that their potions fell on the creature like rain, but the beast blew its magic again, encasing Emily in another cloud of blue fire. She stood unsteadily, angrier than she'd ever been.

She could hear Jessie sobbing even as Steph yelled to

her.

"Keep fighting!" he said as the potions continued to fly, landing all around in multicolored explosions of light.

Emily threw the boxes out of her way, eager to find the beast. She snarled as she came face to face with the creature. She pushed her hands together and drew them apart, creating a flaming red ball of light between them. This she hurled at the beast, who stumbled back from the force of the blast.

Jessie emerged with another half dozen potions. She gave half to Steph. They threw them quickly, in tandem as Emily paced toward the creature. Steph and Jessie were a half step behind her, landing as many potions as they could on the injured creature. As they closed in on it, the beast leapt upward, swishing its tail in a way that caught Steph's leg and knocked him to the ground. Steph hit his shoulder, and his knife flew into the middle of the floor.

Emily launched another blast of her magic at the creature. The room echoed with its screams. With another word and a blast, Emily lit the beast on fire. It hissed and rolled on the floor in agony, unable to escape Emily's magic. Spotting Steph's knife, Emily grabbed it and approached the beast with murder in her eyes.

In a few slashes, it was all over, the beast was gone. The demon shrunk beneath her into a pile of dust. All that was left was Emily, battered and disheveled, limping to the far set of double doors the beast had been guarding.

"Looks like we got him," Emily said, taking an inventory of her wounds. "What?" she said as Jessie and Steph stared at her, horrified. She felt her magic begin to recede, and that was when the pain started. Considering the fight, her injuries were not as bad as she thought they'd be. Her arm was scraped from the fall, her knee was swollen, and there was a dull throbbing in her head that might have been from the aftershocks of the battle.

"Where did Diamond go?" Jessie asked.

"We'll worry about him later," Steph said. "Let's see what's behind the door."

The double doors opened onto a balcony, and Emily stepped onto it and looked down on a large, square room. The large shadows of dump trucks, bulldozers, and other machines filled the cavernous space. She was silent for a moment, training her senses beyond the electric hum of the large fan at the far corner of the room. They were here; she knew it. Though the danger had passed, she tiptoed down the metal stairs, reluctant to make a sound. Steph and Jessie followed behind, each of their boots making a reassuring thump on the stairs behind her.

She began to search under the vehicles, looking for trapdoors or a cellar of some sort, though she doubted something that simple could contain her aunt and Dalgreth. Unless they were dead. She immediately squelched the thought.

"I don't think there's anyone here," Steph said, scratching his head.

"No, we're close, I just know it, can you feel the wards surrounding the room? They wouldn't be here if there weren't something that needed guarding," Emily said.

"What are we looking for?" Jessie asked her, also crouching under the cars.

Steph was moving boxes in the corner and running his hands along the walls. Emily watched him for a moment, and then remembered the way the beast had attacked her through the House's wards.

"Let me try," she said. She placed her hand on the wall and directed her energy inward. Immediately, she perceived the tangled net of wards protecting the room. The wards were like nothing Emily had ever seen or experienced. Where normal wards resembled a net, these were woven thick as fabric and encompassed the entire room. Their intricate lacing indicated that they had been cast by someone with profound ability, someone, she reasoned, who must be even more powerful than the demon they'd just defeated. But even so, there must be a weak spot, a gap in the defenses. She only needed to find it.

Emily studied the glowing net of lights in front of her, testing it with her mind for signs of weakness in the magic. Her instincts led her to a side of the room, nondescript but for a minute length of green thread woven among the red lines. The small green line was almost invisible in the sea of wards, but it was there. Using Steph's knife, she executed a snip of this thread, and then handed it back to him. The wards began to unravel around her, revealing a portal to a place that was neither here nor elsewhere, a pocket between the worlds that by the most convenient definitions did not exist. In the space behind the threads lay a wooden door. Emily ran to the door, but before she touched it, Steph's words made her stop short.

"Emily, wait!" he said. "You can't just open a door when you don't know what's on the other side. What if it's not your aunt and Dalgreth? What if you just release another demon?" He put his hand on hers, and pulled it from the door. His face was kind but resolute.

Emily turned to Steph, with the ghost of a snarl on her face, something in her expression made Steph back away from her. "So what is your suggestion, Steph? Do you really think that I'm going to walk away, now, after all this? Stand back," she said. "I'm not going to let them die in there, not if I can help them."

Emily saw Jessie bite her lip, her expression rife with apprehension, but Emily didn't care. She was outnumbered here, but she couldn't leave the door unopened. The wards defending the door melted under her grasp, and it swung open. Then Steph, ever the gentleman, pushed Emily aside as he produced a flashlight from his pocket. He shined the light into the darkened room. Emily said nothing, just pointed. The room had no floor.

Or at least, the floor was not where it should have been.

"Give me the flashlight, quick!" Emily said. Grabbing the light from Steph, she shined it into the hole where the floor should have been. The first thing she saw, about twenty yards from her, was a roost, a bed of clothes and other scraps dented in the center like a nest, probably the place where the demon had lain. Below that, and far below the three of them, was a floor and two bodies stretched out on a pair of cots, neither of them moving.

"Aunt Maeve?" she yelled, her voice echoing off the metal walls. "Is that you? John?"

There was no answer.

There was a ladder going from the door to the floor, and though she'd always hated heights, Emily threw herself into the gap and shimmied down the metal rungs one by one until she hit the ground.

Emily raced to John Dalgreth, who was nearest her. She could hear his ragged breath, and more importantly, his heartbeat pounding a steady, albeit faint, rhythm in his chest. Emily patted his arm. Then she moved to the second cot, and took a deep breath as she approached her aunt.

Gently, she patted her aunt's arm. Her arm, like John's, was still thankfully warm, and there was no mistaking the ragged pattern of breath that escaped her lips. With tears on her face, she shouted up to Jessie and Steph.

"They're alive!" she said, as Steph landed beside her.

"Bring the van around," he said, looking up at Jessie.

She nodded, and disappeared.

"Steph," Emily said. "There's no door? How do we get them out of this place?"

"I wouldn't think that would be much of a problem for you, Madame Demon-hunter," Steph said.

"All right, but step back," Emily said. She focused her energy between her hands, forming a glowing orb of magic

251

between them. She concentrated on a place in the wall, and then blasted a hole in the side of it, roughly the size of a door.

Steph peered out the hole into the garage and waved to Jessie, who backed the van up to them.

"Have you got any medicines or potions that heal?" Emily asked them. To her great relief, Jessie nodded.

"I have a few things that should help restore them. Though they'll still need plenty of rest. I shifted the equipment around so they can lie down in the back," Jessie explained, "luckily, we're always prepared for a stakeout." She unrolled two sleeping bags and pillows.

Steph lay Maeve in the back, and then turned to help Emily with John. They managed to prop the two of them in the van as another set of lights flashed on the horizon.

"Go!" Emily told them as the lights came closer. "Take the two of them and get out of here, I'll deal with the others."

Steph and Jessie tried to protest, but Emily held up her hand to silence their protests.

"I'll be fine," she told Steph and Jessie, "it's what I need to do. The Paladin agents are closing in, they'll take care of everything else."

"What do we do with them? They need a doctor," Steph asked, nodding to their passengers.

"Take them to the House," Emily said. "The door will be open. Put them in the bedrooms on the ground floor. Beyond that, the House will know what to do. Listen to her. I'm going after Malphat."

She said this with such conviction that Steph didn't bother to question the odd set of instructions. He looked at Emily with affection and punched her on the shoulder, a bit awkwardly.

"Take care of yourself," he said.

She and Steph locked eyes for a moment, and his brows knit with concern; something in his face told her that he knew what was happening to her. She sighed and nodded at him, half in apology, half in resignation.

Steph took her hand. "We'll take them back to the House, and then come back to help you fight him," Steph told her, but Emily shook her head in resignation.

"Just go!" Emily said. "It's the way it has to be, I can feel it."

Steph nodded once, climbed into the driver's seat, and thunked the van into gear. She watched the taillights as the van sped into the darkness. Heaving a sigh of relief, she turned to her next problem, the pair of approaching headlights.

She darted away from the lights and sped into the forest, half-afraid, but also exhilarated. She could feel that Malphat was near, and that even now, he was waiting for an opportunity to get close to her. It was a clear night, and she knew she would not be able to hide from Malphat for long. Their connection was growing stronger, so strong that the locket would soon be useless against him. He would find her, and the new part of her mind danced with excitement at the thought, but she decided she would surrender on her own terms. There was nothing else for her to do.

Emily stalked deeper into the woods, holding tight to the last parts of her human self. It was like trying to hold a handful of sand underwater, every new wave made the pile smaller, and the more she clawed to hang on to what was left, the faster it melted away. She wondered what Malphat would do to her. *Everything*, said the voice in the back of her mind. His connection to her was growing stronger. The fire had returned to her body, and this time she couldn't stop it. She turned her hands, and saw the green glow of her own magic overcome by the red magic of the monster that she'd become.

The moon was laced with clouds, and as she felt her mind begin to slip away from her, she thought of Nicholas, who had, at least, survived their encounter. Emily turned to the stars. She'd always loved them more than the moon itself; they were distant, colder, and present, even when the moon had disappeared.

In all the mess, she'd done a few things right though. Her aunt and John were safe. Hopefully, so was Nicholas. She wondered if she'd done the right thing by avoiding his advances. Maybe she'd changed the course of her dreams and bought him back his life. Or maybe her dreams had amounted to nothing after all. Either way, he was better off without her. No one could have counted on her destiny changing like this.

"Nicholas, take care of yourself, wherever you are," she whispered in the dark, then laughed at herself for her stupidity. Then she pulled the locket off and put it in her jacket pocket.

Perhaps it was the locket that had slowed her transformation, but now that it was off, her entire body blazed bright red in the darkness, calling Malphat to her. The power overwhelmed her and made the world spin in Technicolor detail. A car door slammed in the distance, and she could see Malphat walking toward her. Emily took three steps out of the woods, and he said a word, forcing her knees to the ground. The grass around her began to burn black, leaving only ash as the flame spread in a small circle where her foot had been as Malphat closed the distance between them.

CHAPTER 30

Nicholas could feel his magic leaving him, even as Stanton tried to quell the blood pouring from his side. They hadn't been expecting a tool as simple as a revolver, but it had done its work well. Stanton struggled to murmur the incantations to heal Nicholas, but his own wound prevented him from drawing the proper amount of magic. Stanton frowned as he tore up his shirt and removed it, using the material to staunch the wound in Nicholas' side.

"So much for being the hero of a generation," Nicholas said sleepily, and Stanton barked a quick breath of laughter.

"It's not over yet," he said. "You'll be all right, you'll see. I don't know how he got out, why didn't the House kill him?"

"The magic is different once you're inside. Plus, he could have cut his own way out with the athame; it would have melted the energy barriers."

The look in Stanton's eyes told Nicholas that he was merely trying to keep him calm. Already, Nicholas could feel his hands and feet growing cold, it wouldn't be long now. He closed his eyes.

Nicholas felt Stanton shift his arm as he heard the screen

door slam.

"And look what happens when I leave you to look after yourself for a few weeks," a tired voice scolded. "I walk in the door to find a pair of Paladin agents bleeding on my kitchen floor. Well, that's one thing that's easily fixed, at least." She peered down at the two of them and surveyed their wounds. "Thankfully, the person who shot you has no idea how to use a gun."

In his mind, Nicholas saw her face and smiled sleepily. Somewhere in the distance he heard voices, but they came to him as sounds underwater, muffled and insignificant. A slap across his face caught his attention, and he muttered sleepily.

"Five more minutes," he said, thinking for a moment that his mother was waking him up for school. He was so comfortable, and so tired.

Nicholas was dragged, not gently, to his feet. His head lolled against a shoulder, and he was supported by another arm, but he was still unable to open his eyes. He heard a ripping sound, and he began to shiver violently.

"Get him to the cot, that's it, just stretch it out in the corner there," the voice instructed. "And then get me a chair and some tea."

"You shouldn't be healing anyone," another voice cautioned.

"Yes, well, given the choice, I wouldn't. But if I don't, we'll lose him entirely. And it's much easier to bring them back when they're still alive than when they're dead."

Then Nicholas smiled as sleep washed over him. *Finally,* he thought, *a moment of rest.*

It was the sting that woke him. That and the smell. Nicholas moaned as his side began to burn. He muttered a string of curse words, his eyes still closed.

"Of course it hurts, the pain means it's working," the voice said, clearer this time. The voice seemed so familiar.

"Emily?" he murmured.

"Close," the voice responded. "I'm Emily's aunt. See if you can open your eyes for me."

Nicholas grumbled and attempted to go back to sleep, when he was attacked by another sting on his side. "Stop doing that!" Nicholas said, and another familiar voice laughed, though the command was serious.

"Open your eyes, Agent Flynn; we need you to get back to work."

Nicholas opened his eyes a crack, and as he came to his senses, opened them fully. The shock of hearing John's voice helped him. John grinned at him, his eyes tired, but crinkled up in their usual friendly expression.

"John?" Nicholas said, amazed, "but how, why, I mean, what happened?" Too soon, he sat up in bed. He groaned and laid back down again, his head spinning.

"Don't try that again," Maeve scolded.

"Bastard always was a lousy shot," Stanton repeated, nursing a bandaged arm. Stanton swore and Nicholas smelled the medicine again. Nicholas wanted to sit up, he didn't like these people sitting and standing over him.

Maeve put her hand on his chest. "Easy now, let the herbs work, it won't take long," she said. She was holding a bowl of stinking purple ointment that she swabbed onto his side. With a whispered incantation, his wound began to close. When she finished, all that remained was a small opening. Nicholas felt his strength begin to return.

"Prop a few pillows under his head," Maeve said to Jessie, who was standing beside her. Although it took a slightly painful struggle, Nicholas was half-upright in the bed by the time they were done.

"Here," Maeve said, holding a cup to his mouth.

Nicholas took a sip of the hot broth, then made a face. "What happened?" he said

"Emily found us, then we found you," John said. "Thank the gods for that. It looks like Maeve's ointment does wonders for a gunshot wound. You've lost a lot of blood though, and you're still weak, but we need your help. The demon has Emily."

"What's left of her," Steph said. "Her transformation was almost complete; we had to leave her. Who knows what we'll find when we get back to her?"

"There's always a way out of these problems," Jessie said. "We can't leave her out there in her condition, and I won't even think of the alternative . . ." her voice trailed into silence, not wanting to voice the words they were all thinking.

"Her condition?" Steph said. "Jessie, it's not like Emily's caught a cold, she was about five minutes away from becoming a demon!" Steph said. "Alternatives are what we need right now!"

Nicholas shuddered. They couldn't kill Emily. Not after all she'd done for them. It wasn't right.

Steph spun his knife between his hands in an unsettling manner. "If the Paladin agents find Emily first, there will be nothing that we can do for her. They'll shoot first and figure it out later."

"Then we have to find her," Maeve said. "I don't care what we have to do, there's got to be a way to save her, there always is, what we have to do is go back."

"You two are not going anywhere," Stanton said, his voice rife with authority. "Neither of you are in any condition to be hunting demons; unless I'm greatly mistaken, that's what got you two into trouble in the first place. Besides that, Emily has given everything to save you two; she's given her life in place of yours. Getting yourself killed after all she went through to save you would be a bad way to repay her."

"Then you don't think that we're demon conjurers, witch doctors, or something else? We're not going to be dragged in on some trumped up charge, as is the hallmark of your people?" Maeve said, and John nodded, his face concerned.

Stanton sighed and shook his head. "Yeah, well, I've never been much for unfounded theories," Stanton said. "The trick is to keep you all alive until we sort it out with the rest of the Agency."

Maeve started to rise from her chair beside Nicholas, but hissed in pain before she was upright. She sat down hard, exhausted.

"See what I mean?" Stanton said. "You'll do more harm than good on this task. Besides, even though I believe you two, no one else will. The story is too convenient. The Paladin still think you conjured that thing, and until they don't, you'll only make yourself a target."

"That's my niece out there!" Maeve snapped. "I'm not her mother, but she's certainly my child, and I can't just stand here and let her be—" She stifled a sob.

John put a hand on Maeve's arm. "We're not going to let anything happen to Emily," he said. "Especially not if we can figure out a way to save her. We're not monsters."

"I'll reserve my judgment on that until I have my niece back, thank you very much," Maeve said. Then her face turned pale, and all of the fight left her. She was still very weak. Maeve rose and steadied herself against the wall for balance. She mumbled something else under her breath, conferring with the House, and frowned when she received her answer. "Well, I guess it's settled then," she said, her voice plaintive, "but I don't like it, I don't like it at all."

Have a little faith, a voice said to her.

Nicholas blinked. "Wait, do you know how to save her?" he asked Maeve, a flame of hope lighting in his eye. "I thought that the damage was irreversible."

Maeve turned to Nicholas, and then to John, rolling her eyes as she hobbled back and opened the door to a long pantry. Nicholas heard bottles clinking on the shelves.

PREMONITION

"That's one of the many things I've never liked about your agents," Maeve said, emerging from the closet with a dust bunny in her hair. She was holding a leather volume and a bottle in her hands. "You take it for granted that you know everything."

CHAPTER 31

Rising from the grass, Emily sniffed the air. A thousand scents greeted her, but one scent called to her in particular. It was fear. Diamond's pickup truck was parked in the clearing beside a white SUV, and Blevin and Diamond trudged in the distance with their shoulders hanging, clearly wondering whether they would live or die. Emily squinted to see them better. Even from there, she could see and smell the sweat beaded at their temples. It made her want to laugh. With her new vision, the landscape took on the sparkling, surreal quality of her dreams. Everything was magnified, and she was possessed with an overwhelming feeling that anything was possible.

She realized that she'd been holding her breath since she first saw Malphat. He was behind the other two, but walking in her direction, moving silently behind the drag of the men's footsteps. They were speaking frantically in hushed tones. Emily looked at the ground. Her eyes bulged at the burned cinders of grass that circled the area where she'd crouched. The red cloud of her magic surrounded her hands, and she stretched her finger to a leaf. It withered under her touch.

Malphat stepped from the woods into the clearing, and

the rest of the world receded in the halo of his light. He was dressed as a man, but this was the first time that Emily could truly see him. The beauty of his human form was a fraction of what she saw behind the disguise. His skin was pale and luminous. The closely cropped hair of his disguise lengthened to a thick dark mane that hung in an intricate braid down his back. He was tall, taller than most men, and his body rippled with powerful muscles, visible even under his clothes. He wore a white tunic that glowed as he moved, and cream-colored breeches interrupted at the knee by high brown boots. A metal belt surrounded his waist, and from that hung a silver dagger that made Emily gasp as her eyes fell on it. His weapon was the VonPeer athame. When she finally pulled her eyes to his, his stare was beautiful, ancient, and fixed on her. He looked the same as he had in the club, high cheekbones, blue eyes, beautiful smile and a square jaw, but his magic lit his features in a way that made him seem angelic. Her body pulled to him like a magnet, even though she knew he could destroy her at the slightest whim.

She could feel the red light glowing in her hands, capable of power she'd never known. Malphat smiled at her as he stood still in the clearing. Emily was the one who closed the gap between them. She couldn't help it; she had to be near him. It was the only thing that mattered.

Though his mouth never moved, his command rang in her mind. *Let me look at you,* he said.

Emily fell to the ground on her knees, obeying him without question or thought. Keeping her eyes on him, she slid her hands down the smooth sides of her body. She let her jacket slip down her shoulder as she watched him, her fingers moving rhythmically across her collarbone. She stroked the lace strap of her tank top. He wanted her. She knew it. The sense of her power intoxicated her, and all at once, she wanted to jump, to fly, to test the boundaries of her new self, but he stared at her, compelling her to remain still.

Malphat stood above her, and his eyebrow quirked as he circled her, appraising. Emily cowered under his gaze, expecting anything, even death. Instead, he took her hand and lifted her from the ground. He tilted her chin to his eyes, and she shivered, caught between fascination and fear. Somewhere far away, a stray thought buzzed in her mind, warning her to run, that she was in danger, but the larger part of her remained still, anxious to see what he would do next. He broke the stare as he lifted her hand to his mouth and kissed it.

"You're exquisite," he said, in the velvet tones of his real language, and she immediately understood. "Better even than I'd dreamed." He moved his mouth up her wrist along the scar. Her body felt a pleasure so strong that her knees gave way, and his arm was around her back supporting her so that she wouldn't fall. He kissed her neck and murmured into her hair.

Emily squeezed her eyes shut. Her mind spun with ideas that kept leaving her before they were fully realized; every time a thought of her own bubbled to the surface, the new part of her replaced it with nothing but thoughts of obedience and a desire to serve. Instead of fighting, she found herself stepping closer into his grasp, eager to close the gap between them.

Malphat sighed, pleased with himself. "You are a magnificent demon, Emily VonPeer. Even so," he said, pulling away from her, his expression unreadable, "you need to be trained. Above all, you'll need to obey me or you will die. You're undisciplined. You used the power that I gave you and turned it against me, you hid from me when I bid you come; these things will not go unpunished."

Emily sensed his intention a second before the shot was fired, and she was in the air, eager to dodge his rage.

His magic caught her, and she crashed to the ground, screaming for it to stop. The pain radiated from her injured arm, pulsing white-hot fire through her body. Her back arched, and her teeth bared. The pain stole her voice, leaving her too weak to scream. She prayed for it to end, for him to kill her, anything was better than this. Another wave of pain shot through her system, rocking every inch of her body with violent spasms she was powerless to control.

Wave after wave of blazing pain attacked her body, and she closed her eyes, seeking any form of retreat. There was no fight, the red blaze of her power belonged to him, and it was that power that tortured her now. Her body and her magic were in that moment her enemies. In the back of her mind, she saw a small green light, the small kernel of herself the transformation had not taken away from her. Unable to move her body, her spirit raced to the small, cool piece of her existence that was still Emily.

In her mind, she was elsewhere. Although she could still feel the pain coursing through her body, she was apart from it; it couldn't harm her. She put her foot on the second step, and then the third, descending deeper into herself. At the bottom of the tenth step lay the door. Emily, the real Emily, wanted to cry with relief. At her core, she was still herself, or she wouldn't have been able to find this place. She knocked on the door three times, and it swung open. She was about to enter, but turned back at the sound of a familiar voice.

"Stop it! What are you doing to her? You're going to kill her!"

The conversation stopped abruptly and Emily heard a soft thump on the ground beside her, but she couldn't move to see what it was. The torture had stopped, leaving Emily with only a slight electric twinge in the scar on her arm. She couldn't move a muscle, and the tears streamed from her face as she tried to brace herself for another round of the pain. She took a ragged breath and opened her eyes, then pushed herself up with her elbows, her eyes on Malphat.

With a sorrowful look, he bent and scooped her into his arms. He ran his hands through her hair, cooing with concern over her injuries as if he hadn't just inflicted them himself. He stepped over Blevin, who was shivering in the grass with a look of distaste on his face.

"You lied to me!" she hissed. "You said that the beast was evil, that I was to be its mate, but that wasn't the plan at all, was it? You'd marked me from the start."

"I didn't lie, I merely held back part of the truth—that I mastered the beast, and that I was the one who commanded your transformation. Everything else is completely true."

Her aunt's words crept into her mind: *Never trust a demon,* she'd said. *Their logic and justice are very different than ours.*

Emily didn't have the power to twist out of Malphat's arms, but she steeled her eyes at him, though he looked over her head to the men behind him.

She turned to see what he saw. Blevin was still cowering on the ground, and Emily felt sorry for him. He looked so old, so scared, so human. Diamond pulled Blevin to his feet and handed him a handkerchief. Blevin pressed the cloth to a bleeding gash on the side of his face.

"This wasn't part of the agreement," Diamond started, but Malphat interrupted.

"The others are approaching. Lead them to the quarry and do as I said. There are preparations to be made, and I don't want the Paladin in the way this time." Malphat held Emily tighter, snuggling her to his chest like a trophy. She snarled at him, and he laughed.

"Are you still angry?" He grinned. This time, pleasant warmth radiated through her arm, and a wave of pleasure as extreme as the pain had been, coursed through her, overwhelming her with a sense of comfort and well-being. He strode to the group of buildings from which she'd released her aunt.

PREMONITION

Emily relaxed in spite of herself, but her expression remained stony. She didn't like being carried around like a doll. At first, she thought that Malphat was bringing her to the roost where he'd imprisoned Aunt Maeve and John, but he walked around the building and deposited her in the front seat of his car. He slid into the seat beside her, and his eyes gleamed red, offsetting his slightly maniacal smile. He cupped her face with his hand, and trailed his fingers along the side of her body, not allowing her to brush them away. He reached forward and kissed her, his hand on the back of her neck.

CHAPTER 32

The kitchen looked like a hospital ward, Nicholas thought. He tried not to breathe too deeply, it hurt, but he held himself in the chair as if nothing was wrong. That's what John and Stanton were doing. Stanton had been shot twice, and John was a shell of himself. He stared at the table and noticed John's hands – they were dirty, and his right hand was missing two fingernails.

Maeve and Jessie circled the kitchen, trying not to bump into each other.

"Maeve, sit down!" Jessie said. "Let me do that!" She took a bottle from Maeve's shaking hands and set it on the table. Maeve shot her a stubborn look, but sank into a chair, relieved. She pointed to the counter. "Hand me my book please."

Jessie grabbed the book and thumped it down on the table in front of Maeve.

Steph paced along the far end of the kitchen, muttering to himself. He walked to the door and put his hand on the doorknob, then pulled it back, cursing. He looked at Jessie. "They won't let us go! They say we have to wait here. It doesn't make any sense! She went straight to the demon. She could die!"

"No, you did the right thing by getting out of there," Maeve said. "She could have killed you in her present state, especially if Malphat returned. Besides, it's useless to second-guess yourself."

Steph froze and stared at Maeve. "Did you say Malphat?"

"Yes," Maeve said. "That is the name of the being Diamond released."

Steph tried the door again, but again pulled his hand back. "It's like the doorknob's burning," he said, rubbing his hand.

"Who's Malphat?" Nicholas said.

Steph rubbed the bridge of his nose. "Malphat is the commander of an ancient legion of otherworld hunters. Or at least he was. He was famous for recruiting magicals and enslaving them. The Paladin entombed him hundreds of years ago, but apparently, they didn't account for Jack Diamond's Riverwalk. Shit."

"Was he trying to get through the Gate?" Nicholas said.

"He was after the athame," Maeve said. "With that, he can make his own gate. We need to get to Emily." She stood up, shuffled to the countertop and steadied herself. After a moment, she reached into a cupboard, pulled out a dusty, brown bottle and set it on the table.

Everyone in the room fell silent.

Jessie pulled out a row of shot glasses and plunked one in front of everyone at the table, leaving one for herself. She yanked the cork out of the bottle and poured each of them a shot of the stinking brown liquid. Nicholas cringed as he swirled his glass; his stomach was already revolting at the pungent stench of alcohol and another smell he couldn't identify. As if that weren't enough, Maeve pulled a packet of herbs from her pocket, sprinkling a little into each of the glasses. She spread her hands to the three men. "Drink up," she said. "It will make you feel better."

Nicholas lifted the glass to his mouth and swallowed the concoction. His first reaction was to gag, the drink tasted even worse than it smelled. It took a moment before his hands started to tingle. The brew didn't erase his pain much, but it did seem to restore his magic. Maeve watched him as Stanton threw back his drink.

"Delicious," he said, coughing into his sleeve.

John's face was grave, but his eyes crinkled in amusement.

Maeve muttered something under her breath, and the door opened as the two jackbirds flew in and perched on the top of the cupboards. One of them looked at Nicholas and hissed.

"The jackbirds!" Nicholas said. "They're yours?"

"They're our guards," Maeve said. "And pets, sort of."

Nicholas frowned. "Yeah, well one of them took a chunk out of my shoulder!"

"You probably deserved it," she said, then turned to the jackbirds. "What do you two know?" The two creatures began to move and gesture in a series of hisses and clicks while Maeve nodded. Her lips pursed, and her eyebrows knit together. She nodded and took another sip of her drink. The three men shot sidelong glances at each other, puzzled. Stanton watched the creatures avidly, shaking his head. He hated to be wrong about things. The jackbirds fell silent, and she looked at the three men sitting at the table in front of her.

"It's not going to be easy to save Emily," she said, searching her book. "We've got a lot of work to do, and we can't do it with just the four of us; John and I are useless at the moment, and the rest of the Paladin team is running toward death. We need reinforcements."

"Consider yourself reinforced," Steph said.

Jessie smiled as the two of them began to glow with an incandescent light that made everyone in the room gasp.

"So you really did see an angel," Stanton turned to Nicholas. "I thought you were just losing your mind out there at the Gatehouse!"

Nicholas frowned. "Apology accepted."

"Here we go," Maeve said, pushing the book toward them, showing them an illustration that made even Steph's face grim with apprehension. "Malphat won't kill Emily, he needs her, but if there are agents anywhere in the area, he'll think nothing of using them as a snack." Maeve raised her hands, inspecting the still dim light of her own power.

Nicholas produced the chess piece from his pocket. "Who needs this the most?"

"You do," Maeve said. "Use it to shield yourself so that the demons can't see you. How are you feeling?"

"Better," Nicholas said, shifting his arm. He was still in pain, but it was disappearing rapidly. He turned to Stanton. "Where were the agents headed?"

"They were forming a perimeter along the river. There's a quarry on the other side," Stanton said. "Lillian and Moon took their teams to help secure the demon, but it takes the combined efforts of several agents to generate ward lines powerful enough to do that."

"They're dead if they find Malphat," Maeve said, sinking into the chair. "He's getting stronger, but he can't go long without magic, and he'll need to feed to open another gate.

Maeve turned to Nicholas. "You're going with John and I to save Emily, small help that we'll be. We can at least take you to the scene and keep you cloaked. We'll take the jackbirds with us; they might prove useful."

The ground began to rumble, and Steph stopped and held his ear as if he heard something. "New plan," Steph said. "Jessie and I are being called to the Gate. Something is trying to compromise the wards. Find Emily and the Paladin, and figure out a way to shut it down from the other end. Dr.

Stanton, I need you to come with me."

The ground shook again, and the window glowed with a flash of purple light that erupted in the sky like a firework.

Steph grabbed his keys and ran for the van. "Jessie, how many of those potions do we have left?"

CHAPTER 33

At the center of the clearing was a large fire. In front of that stood an altar fashioned out of a large flat-topped boulder that faced east. There were flatlands and woods surrounding the area, and Malphat stood in the center of a cleared piece of land, etching sigils into the ground with the red fire of his magic. He sang in an ancient language, and Emily shivered; she was the only one who could understand his lyrics of conquest and death. She crouched on the ground, feeling the cool grass between her fingers charring into ash. He walked over to her, crouched beside her and took her hands in his. He lifted her to her feet, then pulled her jacket off her and threw it to the ground. He kissed her collarbone, and she shivered as his breath hit her neck. Then he stared into her eyes, inches away from her, and she felt her knees begin to buckle as she realized that she wanted him as much as he wanted her, maybe more. But . . . no . . . she needed to get away. She shook her head, confused. Malphat began to whisper as he took the athame from her belt and laid it on the altar.

"Watch them," Malphat said, nodding his head toward the men.

Malphat's words bound her in place like iron fists; she had no opportunity to move or escape. So she did what he told her, she watched. Blevin and Diamond stood before him, both of them looking bedraggled, muddy, and exhausted. Blevin looked to Emily with concern on his face, and she snarled deep in her throat. "Traitor!" she spat, straining against her bonds. It was no use though; she stood firm in the spot where Malphat had commanded her to stay.

Blevin cowered, and Malphat stopped singing and looked up at them. "She doesn't like you much anymore," he said to Blevin. "I can hear what she's saying in her mind, you're lucky she won't move until I say so."

"It doesn't look like she likes you much either," Blevin said.

Malphat paused from his workings, looked up at Emily and whispered under his breath. The warmth of his spell overcame her and she relaxed, making a sound in her throat that approximated a purr. He walked over to her and stroked her hair.

"She may hate me now, but that will change with time," he said. "Especially on the other side, she'll need me there."

Emily stared up at Malphat, the look in her eyes murderous. He looked at her and spoke, placing his words in her mind so that only the two of them could hear as he continued to pull his hands gently through her hair: *I'll enjoy breaking you to my will.*

"Just kill me," she pleaded, "I don't want to be a demon."

Malphat shook his head, incredulous. "Kill you?" he asked out loud. "Why would I kill you? That would be such a waste. No, you'll be with me for a very long time. To think I almost took the other one instead," he said conversationally, returning to the altar. "The Paladin. And there you were, right next door with all that power disguised underneath your talisman. Then I intended to have you both, he was on his way to save you, and it would have been nothing for me to initiate him. It's really a shame that you shot him," he said to Blevin. Malphat spoke of this as a minor annoyance, like he'd lost a button from his shirt.

"You shot him?" Emily said. Tears filled her eyes, and she began to cry. A violent ache bubbled in her chest.

Malphat continued, still lost in thought. "Yes, I'd have liked the pair of them, especially given our recent mishap. They're easier to control when they're young."

"This has all gotten out of hand. Let Emily go, I'll take her place," Blevin said.

Malphat laughed, and glanced at Emily, willing her to join in the joke. "You? Why would I trade this lovely creature for a powerless old man? Besides, I've seen what you do with a little power, so forgive me for passing on your offer. No, your job is to go back to the next round of agents and take care of them." Malphat sniffed the air. "They're getting closer. Take Diamond with you."

Blevin took two steps backward.

Emily snarled and tried to lunge at Blevin, but the spell held her back. She shivered, straining against it as much as she could, but it was no use. He was far stronger. Blevin looked at Emily, horrified as Malphat laughed at the two of them.

"See how spirited she is?" Malphat continued. "No, I couldn't possibly let her go; I'm quite attached to her already. Besides, she'll starve to death without me; she doesn't even know how to feed yet." Malphat winked at Emily, she sneered back at him, and he laughed again.

"I'd rather starve," she said.

"Of course you would," Malphat said indulgently. "You're full now, but that will also change. And you'll have to eat, whether you want to or not. You won't starve like a human; you'll just stop, painfully imprisoned in your body until you're able to feed again. It is an unfortunate reality of your transformation."

Diamond stood in the shadows, watching the exchange without comment. His face was expressionless, but he kept wringing his hands and looking to the side. Malphat sighed, and said over his shoulder in a more human voice.

"You might as well do as I say, Jack, there's nowhere that you can run. We had a deal."

Malphat turned to Emily. "Diamond was the one who found your aunt and Dalgreth in the field attempting to stop us. It was his idea to abduct them and make it look as if they'd been dusted. It was a small piece of magic on Blevin's part, but one that helped him greatly."

Emily turned on Diamond. "You took my aunt?" she said. She could feel the heat of her magic rising around her.

Diamond cleared his throat. "I didn't know that he was going to kill them or use them as food, or whatever it was you let that thing do to them," he squawked. "I just wanted her out of the way to continue with the Riverwalk."

Malphat shrugged. "There wasn't enough of their energy left for another meal anyway, it was about to dispose of them when you released them," he said. "They're half-dead from its feedings. Emily's feeding on her own magic at the moment, but she'll need to eat soon," he said. "You'd better get moving, Blevin. Diamond, you can go wait in your truck. I may need you soon."

The men exchanged glances, nodding to one another as if they were going to speak at any moment, but they were clearly too afraid to disobey.

Emily bit her lip to prevent herself from screaming at the men to come back, to not leave her here alone with Malphat. She took a deep breath, squared her shoulders, and thought of ways to buy herself time from his attention.

She turned to Malphat, who walked around her in a circle, making elaborate signs with a stick, sigils that she had never seen, though she could tell by the feel of them that they were evil. He lit a small fire and with a wave, produced a pot. He took liquid from a metal flask on his belt and dumped it into the pot, chanting.

"What are you doing?" she asked.

He looked up at her, crouching on the ground as he made his final marks. "These sigils are the necessary beginning of the ritual."

He was beside her; he traced the side of her face with the back of his hand, making her shiver. "Don't fret so much. You will have everything you ever wanted, you'll see."

Emily crossed her arms and stepped back. "Fine," she said. "Then let me go, release me, and send me home to my family. That's what I want."

Malphat laughed, and she almost smiled back at him. His voice had a way of making her forget the horrible things he'd done: the murders, the kidnapping, and her own attack and transformation. Despite all these things, she still found herself powerfully attracted to him, though maybe she only thought these things because she was now a monster herself.

"You would be a danger to them and to yourself," he said. "You would kill them with a touch, or your desire to feed would overcome you. Or they would try to kill you. You would spend what was left of your life running, hunted by the Paladin guard, or imprisoned and studied, caged like an animal. Do you see those lights?" He pointed to the ridge above them. "Even now, the Paladin are going to reestablish the tomb there to contain you. Those would be your choices if I released you."

Emily thought about it for a moment. He was right. She was trapped. Even if she managed to escape him, the Paladin would kill her.

"I can see that you are loyal," Malphat said. "Yet I do not understand your pity for the Paladin. They've taken your family, wanted you dead, left you alone and unprotected. I will never leave you," he said, drawing near her, and looking deeply into her eyes. She didn't stand a chance against him. Everything about him compelled her.

He kissed her, and she didn't resist. Under his touch, the thoughts of who he was, and who she was, melted from her mind, leaving nothing but the desire for the moment to continue as it was, for the two of them to remain frozen together like this for all eternity. When he overwhelmed her in this manner, there was no choice, only his will that overpowered hers, his wants penetrating the deepest corners of her mind. Emily was unable, and unwilling to resist his advances. She stepped back and her tank top and jeans were replaced with a floor-length red tunic, slit to her hip. Her wrists and ankles sported heavy, carved-gold bracelets and another jewel, a heavy ruby, hung from a gold rope on her chest.

"See?" he whispered as he nuzzled her neck. "I told you that you would grow to like me," he said as he broke away from her.

Her eyes narrowed, and he laughed at her; the cruel notes again penetrated his voice. Emily turned away from him, burying her face in her hands. She didn't dare strike him, he was too strong, and she didn't want to think of what he could do to her. She shuddered. Even the memory of the pain was unbearable.

There has to be a way out of this. Every spell has a loophole, she thought. She wondered if it were the same with his magic. Suddenly, Emily doubled over, hissing in pain. She stared at Malphat, the accusation in her expression.

"You're hungry," Malphat said.

"I'm alright," Emily said, knowing that it was a lie. Her body began to tremble, and she could feel a deep hollow at the center of her being begging to be filled. Already her limbs felt leaden, and she began to understand the urgency of her situation. Even the strain of the bonds became heavy as the hunger became stronger.

PREMONITION

Malphat smiled and continued to stir the potion at the altar, still intent on conversation. "Until you become stronger, I can sustain you myself," he said. "But you will need to feed before we attempt to cross through the gate."

He lifted the cup to her mouth and the smell was repugnant. Emily curled her lips in disgust and backed away from him, though there was nowhere she could go. The bond held firm. Malphat grabbed her hair by the nape of her neck and forced her head back, pouring the drink into her throat. The first sip of the potion was heaven, and Emily grabbed the chalice from his hands, ravenous. When the chalice was empty, he handed her a cloth. She wiped her face and gasped for breath.

Malphat still held the back of her neck. He cocked his head and looked at her wryly. His face glowed with a cold and alien light. She shivered as he opened his other hand and laid it across her heart.

"The second part of the feeding hurts," he told her.

And it did. She was aware of a distant whimper, a small mewling sound that came from her own lips. Electricity shot through her body, not the kind of pain that had emanated from her arm; she had the impression that her entire being was being jolted with power, like jump-starting a car.

As quickly as it had started, the feeling passed. Her bonds dissolved, and she was left weak and weeping in his arms.

He kissed her forehead, wiping the sweat from her brow. She could see her reflection glowing in each of his eyes, shivering from the remnants of the pain. She laid her face into his shoulder, too weak to care about anything but rest.

"The pain will diminish," he said. "Once you have fed on your own."

Emily tried to find her feet beneath her, but she was too weak to stand, and he caught her as she collapsed. He laid her down in the tall grass that again charred to cinders beneath her, leaving her in a bed of burned ash. She lay on her back and watched a single patch of sky that had broken through the clouds. A distant star twinkled faintly in the small diamond. She shivered even as the electric heat of his touch still pulsed within her and wondered if anyone would find her. Her stomach lurched as the pain began to ebb into a new surge of power. She thought that if someone did come to find her, there might not be anything left of her to save.

CHAPTER 34

Lillian cradled her phone, waiting for a message to appear. Nicholas should have been here by now. Something was wrong, she knew it.

"The perimeter is secure," Moon said, ending her call. "There's something in the clearing about a mile from here." She squinted and looked into the distance. "Gods, it's strong; I can feel its aura from here. He's still not answering?"

Lillian held the phone to her ear. "No," she said. "I've texted him about twenty times, but he's not answering. Let me try Blevin again. We might need to go in without them."

A line of old warehouses sported cracked smiles that were the work of long gone vandals. This place was one of a dozen of the industrial strongholds that had rusted into silence. There was nothing here except for a few empty storefronts and cheap buildings that sold parts for cars and computers. *It's the sort of place where no one would hear you scream,* Lillian thought. She cracked the window and lit a cigarette.

"Mind if I smoke?" she asked as it lit.

Moon shook her head no, but cracked her window in what she hoped was an inconspicuous manner and leaned her head against it. Lillian took two long drags of the cigarette before she smashed it into the ashtray, leaving only a swirling cloud of smoke behind.

"Sorry," Lillian said. "You do mind. I quit years ago, but I started again when they called me back here. You need something to do when you're waiting. and I've had enough coffee to keep me awake for a decade."

Lillian shot a sidelong glance at Moon. Moon hadn't changed much in the past few years; as always, she was still bright, ready, and eager to please. She'd have been a good daughter-in-law. Lillian held her breath for a moment. She debated letting Moon out of the car.

"I'm staying," Moon told her again, and Lillian frowned.

"You're very talented," Lillian said. "An asset to the Paladin. You don't need to prove anything here."

But Moon crossed her arms and assumed a mulish look that made Lillian smile. Moon reminded her of herself at that age. No wonder Nicholas had never liked her.

Lillian glanced at her watch again. Half past three. Moon tapped her fingers against the door of the car. Lillian eyed the landscape, darker than it should have been because of the clouds. A series of birds swooped across the night sky, edging themselves into their rooftop nests. As Lillian watched the birds, her eyes narrowed slightly. Everything about this place was too calm; it lacked the sense of dread she'd come to associate with these situations.

"They should be here by now," Moon said.

"It'll be all right," Lillian told her, but the concern in her voice was unmistakable. They sat in silence for some moments when the radio crackled and Blevin's voice rang through the air.

"There was a small holdup at the House, but . . . wait a minute," Blevin said. There was a short pause, and he continued, "Can't talk now, but I'll be there soon."

281

His voice sounded high and faded. Moon's hand started tapping faster as Lillian told him their location. She bit her lip and glanced at Lillian, not wanting to tell her what she was thinking. Lillian snapped the radio off and turned to her.

"What is it?" Lillian asked.

Moon looked thoughtful. "Blevin said that *he* would be here soon."

"What do you mean?" Lillian said.

"Why did he say 'I'll be there soon' and not 'we'll be there soon'? Something's wrong, I can feel it."

Lillian's stomach dropped, bringing with it the sense of dread she'd expected. "I knew they shouldn't have gone to that place," Lillian said. "Blevin has been friends with Maeve VonPeer for years; the Agency's always kept a close eye on their exchanges."

Moon nodded as Lillian continued.

"We have a few minutes left; let's gather the agents. Quick, before Blevin gets here."

Moon signaled the cars behind them and agents appeared, silently stepping into the road. They walked toward Moon and Lillian, leaving the caravan of vehicles behind them. Their faces were questioning until they saw the grim set on Lillian's face.

"Agents Smith and Cross," she said.

The men saluted her.

"We're going to make an emergency change in our directive. I need you to head to the top of the ridge beside the quarry and wait. Moon and I are going to stay behind. We'll meet you in about half an hour."

The men nodded and returned to their cars, heading for the ridge on the other side of the river.

"What about us?" Moon asked.

"We're going to stay here and confront Blevin. Have your shooting skills improved at all?"

"They're passable," Moon said, then hesitated. "But not

great. I'm not as good as Nicholas."

Lillian nodded. "You may have to run backup. If we get into a dangerous situation, you need to promise me that you will leave me and run."

"But—"

"No buts. Just do what I tell you," she said.

Moon nodded and cleared her throat as Lillian looked out into the darkness.

"Nicholas is going to be all right, he's always all right," Moon said. For a moment, Lillian didn't appear to register Moon's comment, but then she nodded slowly.

Lillian sniffed and lit another cigarette. "I thought that about his father and brother," she said.

"This is different," Moon said.

"I know," Lillian said, her face set. A pair of headlights swung into the parking lot.

"Stuff your pen into your boot, Moon, and tuck your pant leg in around it tight. Take this instead," Lillian said, handing her another fountain pen. "Better that you have a backup, you might need it. He's going to try to disarm us, I think. I doubt that he'll think to search our boots."

"You think that he's in league with the demon?" Moon asked.

"I don't know," Lillian said. "I still think that he and Maeve VonPeer had a plot, and that makes me doubly suspicious of her niece. If something's happened to Nicholas, then they'd better pray that they get me with their first shot." Lillian's eyes glittered like a serpent's.

The headlights were bright, but they could see Blevin's outline in the car.

"Just stay calm and pretend that everything is fine, that we don't suspect him."

Moon took a deep breath and fiddled with her collar.

Blevin slammed the door shut, his face weary. Lillian eyed him expectantly, wearing her best concerned expression.

"Emily VonPeer came while we were at the house," he said. "The transformation was complete. There was nothing I could do for Stanton or Nicholas. It all happened so fast."

He's lying, she thought. She could read it on him as well as if he'd told her.

Lillian stared at the ground, not wanting to meet his eyes. Blevin was unusually perceptive, and he was waiting to see if she'd bought his version of events. All it did was confirm her instinct about him. *Let's see who's better at this,* she thought to herself, and when she pulled her eyes to his, they were overflowing with tears.

Moon put a hand on her shoulder in mock reassurance. *Good girl,* Lillian thought. *Play along.*

Lillian's face turned to stone, and she took a threatening step toward Blevin. "You just let my only living son die on your watch and that's all you have to say for yourself?" she said. She pulled her weapon and pointed it at Blevin. She held it there for a moment, then dropped it and turned away from him, burying her head in her hands. "He was all I had left."

Blevin walked up to her and patted her shoulder, hesitant. Her shoulders began to heave as she held her breath and worked up some tears. Blevin took a step closer and put his hand on her back. Lillian grabbed his hand in hers and squeezed it, smiling at him through her tears. With a quick step backward and a snap of her arm, Lillian had Blevin on his back. She stood over him with her weapon drawn; Moon had already moved to cover her.

Lillian whispered an incantation, and bound Blevin's hands in front of him with a thin blue rope of magic.

"Agent Keith Blevin," she said, hauling him to his feet by his collar, "you are under arrest for conspiracy. As of this moment, you are officially relieved of all your duties as a Paladin agent." With a wave of her hand, the scars of office on Blevin's cheek disappeared. Lillian searched Blevin's pocket and came up with a small revolver.

"You are going to take me to Emily VonPeer."

Blevin sighed. He stood heavily on one side; she'd landed him on his hip, and he limped to the truck where he slid into the backseat. With another incantation, Lillian had him contained behind a transparent wall of magic.

Lillian slammed the door shut and met Moon at the hood of the car.

"Good work," Lillian said. "Now comes the hard part, fighting and containing the demons." She spoke into a small radio pinned on her neck, "This is Commander Flynn. Agent Moon and I are going to apprehend the demons, but we'll need reinforcements. Stand by, just in case."

"Here," she said to Moon, handing her the gun. "Hang on to this; we'll need it as evidence."

In the back of the car, Blevin groaned and shifted his sore leg. "Bitch," he mumbled.

Lillian jumped into the truck, and spun around to face Blevin.

"So, tell me," she said, "Where are we headed?"

"Lillian, you don't understand, I can explain."

"Then explain," Lillian said as Moon inspected the revolver.

"There are three bullets missing," Moon said, "fired recently. The inside of the chamber is still warm."

Lillian's stomach lurched, but she wouldn't allow herself to think about Nicholas, not now. She flexed her hands on the steering wheel and took a breath; it had been a while since she'd thrown anyone over her shoulder like that, much less a man the size of Blevin. This was going to be a rough night.

"It was the demons, they compelled me to do their bidding," Blevin said. "I'm a pawn in this whole thing, an innocent. I had to do what I was told. They said they'd come after me, after my family."

"So you decided to come after mine instead?" Lillian said.

"What else could I have done?" he said.

"You could have asked for help, you could have run away."

"You could have died," Moon said.

Blevin gave her a startled look.

"That would have been my choice," Moon said. "I would die before I betrayed the Paladin like that." Moon gave him a disgusted look before she turned to face the windshield.

Always determined to prove herself, Lillian thought.

"Lillian, I never intended for this to happen, I—"

"Save it," Lillian said. "I can tell a pack of lies when I hear them. Just get me to your boss."

They drove across the river and a few miles down a dirt road, and then stopped at a small clearing.

"We have to walk from here," Blevin said.

Lillian and Moon jumped out of the car, pointing their weapons at him.

"You first," Moon said, shoving him in front of her. "Walk in front of us, and keep your hands where we can see them."

Blevin coughed. "Look, you haven't seen this thing, you don't know what we're up against, it's not just Emily VonPeer, there's more—"

Moon sneered at him. "We don't negotiate with traitors."

Blevin shrugged his shoulders. "I warned you," Blevin said.

He paced onto the trail ahead of them. Lillian and Moon followed at a close distance, Moon with her eyes trained on Blevin, Lillian surveying the scene for signs of danger.

Blevin led them around a crop of rocks, and they had a

full view of the clearing. There were demons, two of them - a male and a female, huddled beside a makeshift stone table. A giant bonfire blazed behind them; its light combined with the red cloud of their auras concealed their features. The taller of the pair dropped a handful of herbs into a bowl in front of it, and then lit it on fire; it lifted the bowl to the sky and chanted something in an unknown language. The second figure stood beside him, deferent to the ritual. A third figure stood beside them. Senator Jack Diamond, looking very much like he wanted to run away.

Lillian gasped and stood still as the creatures turned around and moved toward her. She had never seen any being this powerful before. Blevin broke his walk and ran toward the demons, but it didn't matter. Coming to her senses, Lillian fired a blast of light intended to blind them as she pulled Moon behind a rock. The shot was off its mark though, and landed as a harmless puff of smoke at the male demon's feet.

"No," Moon said, slipping out of Lillian's grip. She stepped out from behind the rock and fired a shot at the smaller of the creatures. The creature shrieked as the blast hit its leg, and when it lifted its head, Moon's eyes widened. "The smaller one is Emily VonPeer."

The male demon spoke a word and lifted its hand to Moon. A red shot pierced the air. Lillian watched in horror as Moon fell backward in slow motion, twisting onto her side as she fell, limbs splayed at awkward angles. Lillian looked at her body, her mouth open in shock. She peeked over the rock and saw the creatures move toward Blevin and Diamond, who cowered in the grass at their feet.

"This is Commander Lillian Flynn calling to request backup." She fired a blast of blue light into the sky, wondering if anyone would find her in time.

CHAPTER 35

Nicholas gasped and clutched his side as John hit a bump in the road. He tried an incantation to relieve some of the pain, but the dull throbbing persisted. He lifted his shirt and moved aside the bandage to inspect the partially open wound. At least it had stopped bleeding, thanks to that potion.

Maeve clucked with sympathy. "Those non-magical wounds are the hardest to heal, unfortunately. Blevin must have known that."

"It was my fault," Nicholas said, "I told him that his magic wouldn't work in the House."

"We all trusted him," Maeve said quietly. "He's been a friend of mine for twenty years. I had no idea he was even an agent, much less the lying piece of filth he turned out to be. This whole thing could have been prevented if I'd just been a little bit quicker on the draw."

"Don't beat yourself up about it," John said. "He's good, a professional liar, and he fooled all of us."

Maeve held her hands on either side of the front seats and leaned forward, her head level with the two men in the front.

"Should we cut the headlights?" Nicholas asked.

"Nah, it doesn't see us coming," John said. "Maeve and I don't have enough magic left between us for it to detect us right now, and you're holding the knight, so it can't see you either. Besides, it's not concerned with us. Not anymore."

Not now that it has Emily, Nicholas thought, finishing John's sentence. He didn't say anything though. Maeve was already upset.

"Now watch for the drive, John," she instructed, "it comes up quickly."

They found the driveway, a small opening between the underbrush that was little more than a footpath. The car bumped down the road, and John pulled to the side and killed the engine. The three of them exited the car.

A blue flash of light shot through the trees like a low-level firework, and they paused.

"What was that?" Maeve said.

John frowned, and Nicholas drew his pen as the light faded from the sky.

"It's a Paladin distress call," Nicholas said, moving to run.

John held him back. "Wait," he breathed. "You can't just go running in there, you'll blow your cover."

Nicholas was shaking with rage, but he listened to John's instructions.

The light flashed again, followed by a muffled scream.

Maeve clutched her chest and started to shake.

John grabbed Maeve's arm. "We need to get her back to the House," he said.

"No, we need to save Emily and whoever else is out there!" Maeve insisted.

"I'm going," Nicholas said to Maeve. "With any luck, I'll be quick enough to provide backup to whoever's out there."

"Nicholas, you need to be prepared for this. The Emily

289

that you know may already be gone," John said.

Maeve slapped John on the arm, hard. "You don't know that!" Maeve said with tears in her eyes.

John pulled her into his arms and held her tight. She pressed her face into his shoulder.

A burst of rainbow light began to swirl in the sky, illuminating their faces and making them cover their eyes.

Nicholas was dumbstruck. "What is it?" he asked.

"It's opening up another gate," John said. "I saw a creature try it once before."

"How?" Nicholas asked.

"It takes a hell of a lot of power, and an ancient ritual that is ill-advised to even attempt. We're farther down along the ward lines by the gate and the House, but it would be possible to open another gate along the same lines—though the power from doing so could implode the first gate and release whatever is on the other side. That's why Steph stayed there."

There was another flash of blue light. "I'm still going," Nicholas said. "Maybe I can fight it on this side, or maybe I can distract it or something, but I'm not going to leave Emily out there. There's got to be a way out."

Maeve handed Nicholas the potion from her sleeve.

"Throw this at her when she gets near enough to you," Maeve said. "If she's under the thrall of this being, this potion will bring her to her senses."

Nicholas turned the small vial over in his hand.

A small crackle rippled through Nicholas' consciousness, and he looked to John. He'd felt it too, that small mental tug meant someone had just been cut from his life. He'd felt it when his brother died. Nicholas stared blankly at the sky, and John walked to him and put his hand on his shoulder.

"What is it?" Maeve asked them.

"I think . . ." Nicholas said, not wanting to utter the

words, "that my mother just died."

John opened the back of the car and poked his head in. He held an old plaid blanket where the pair of jackbirds slept in a pile.

"All right, you two," he said, tossing them into the air where they flew. "It's time to get to work. Go see what's going on out there, and then stay with Nicholas. I'll take care of Maeve. Got it?"

"Take Maeve home," Nicholas said, squaring his shoulders. He walked into the forest, afraid but determined. Behind him, he heard the car doors slam, and the engine fire as the car trailed away from the woods.

The jackbirds swooped in front of him, almost playful in their curiosity. Nicholas clutched the chess piece, wondering if it still worked, or if Emily would be able to see him. His throat was dry. He trudged through the grasses, so intent on the light of the chess piece that he almost stumbled as the ground gave way beneath his feet. He grabbed a sapling and righted himself, seeing with sickening clarity the few small rocks that tumbled down the barren hillside. Thankfully, he was far enough away that no one seemed to notice the small landslide he'd created. He crouched by a tree and lay flat on the ground at the very edge of the precipice. The jackbirds were perched in the trees overhead with a hungry look in their eyes.

Two men stood in front of the fire, their shoulders hunched and their heads bent. The demons stood in front of them, and Nicholas' stomach was in his throat. He could see his mother lashed to a burned tree. She was shot through with a web of red magic, but it looked like she was still alive, for the moment. He saw a body lying face down near a pile of rocks some distance from the fire, and he cringed. It looked like Moon had not been as lucky. She lay in the grass, immobile, with not even a trace of the faint blue light surrounding her.

"You have to be careful how much you feed, you nearly killed them both," the taller one said, laughing.

Nicholas saw the beast with its minion, following it like a pet. At first, he saw them as spheres of light, a pair of figures glowing in the darkness like angels among the white lights. Then the shorter one turned, and Nicholas gasped.

The smaller being was Emily and not Emily. Her features were the same, but everything about her was slightly different. Gone was the shy, unassuming girl that he knew. In her place was a goddess. It was as if everything weak about her had been burned away, leaving only her true self at the core. Everything about her posture, her movements, and even her walk exuded confidence and power. Her usual soft expression was replaced with a feral grin, and her once gray eyes were replaced with glowing lavender orbs that shone in the darkness. Nicholas quietly edged down the hill in the grass so that he could better hear the conversation.

Diamond said, "We've done our share here and then some. Let's settle the deal and let everyone go home."

"Yes, Jack," Malphat said. "It is time for your payment. It is time to fulfill my part of the bargain."

Malphat turned to Emily. "Jack's deepest desire is immortality, for his name to be remembered for all time. So be it," he said, waving his hand. "It is justice."

At first, it seemed like nothing was happening. Diamond moved to take a step, but it was impossible, he was frozen in place. The ground turned white at his feet. He flailed for a moment before he froze as the whiteness trailed up his arms and legs.

"Stop!" Blevin shouted. "What are you doing to him?"

"Let me go!" Diamond said, "I changed my mind, I don't want anything, I just want to get out of this place, just let me go and we're even." The white spread to his face and his expression froze.

"He makes a fine immortal, don't you think?" Malphat

asked.

Blevin was speechless. Diamond's face, frozen in his final moment of terror, gazed back at them.

"It's an excellent likeness, don't you think?" Malphat asked, surveying the white marble statue.

Emily protested. "This is what you call justice?"

Malphat turned and took her hand, drawing her close to him. "Diamond is a very bad man, and his punishment fits his crimes."

"Blevin," the beast continued, "it's your turn."

He turned to Emily and took her under his arm again. "Now, you don't know this, but Senator Blevin's wish involved you. His wish was somewhat less grand than Senator Diamond's here, but no less selfish."

"What are you talking about?" she said.

"You see, Emily," Malphat said, "Blevin is a murderer, and were it not for me, he would have been your captor. Do you know what he wanted, in exchange for delivery of the athame? He wanted me to bend your mind so that he could be the master of the VonPeer estate and all that was in it, including you. And he will have you, body and soul. Kill him!"

Nicholas' eyes narrowed. He saw Emily hesitate, then shake with pain as she attempted to defy the order. Emily dropped to the ground, shrieking with otherworldly anguish.

"I won't be your weapon," she said.

Malphat grabbed Emily by her hair and forced her to stand. He drew her close to him, lifted her arm with his own, and pointed her hand toward Blevin. Blevin tried to run, but Malphat moved her arm and whispered.

"No!" Emily said as a red light shot from her hand, dropping Blevin dead a few paces away from Moon. Emily wailed and dropped to her knees.

Malphat crouched beside her, pulling her into the circle of his arms and rocking her back and forth. She struggled to get out of his grasp, but he held her firm.

"It's who we are," he said into her hair, "we deliver justice to the guilty. This is what we are destined to do. In time you'll come to understand that."

Emily continued to sob as he clutched her.

Nicholas took the opportunity to lunge at Malphat, but he was pulled flat onto the ground. A soft breath released by his ear, and he scrambled to pull himself upright; the jackbirds had him pinned by his cloak. Nicholas pounded the dirt with his fist.

"I'll kill him! Look at what he's done to them!" Nicholas said through clenched teeth.

Not yet, the jackbirds said in his mind.

Out of the corner of his eye, Nicholas saw something twitch. He smothered a yelp of surprise when Moon lifted her head a fraction of an inch and winked in his direction.

CHAPTER 36

Malphat patted Emily's arm, and with another squeeze, released her. Emily cringed. She couldn't look at Blevin's body crumpled in the dirt, already forgotten by Malphat, abandoned like a carcass on the side of the road. She looked at Lillian lashed to the pole, her head hanging against her chest. Her shoulders rose slightly, and Emily sighed with relief. Lillian was still alive, at least. Emily had taken a great deal of magic from her, and she could feel the power pulsing in her veins, waiting to do his bidding.

Emily stared at Lillian, wracked with guilt. "She's hurt," Emily said.

Malphat shrugged, unsympathetic. "Your guilt will fade as you gain power, as you come to see the true nature of their souls as I do. I can see their hearts. Most of them are not worth saving. These women, for example, came to us with the intention of killing us. Given the chance, they would have. The overwhelming majority of people here deserve this fate."

"I don't believe that!" Emily said.

Malphat shrugged. "You will."

Emily looked at her captor. Malphat, for his part, stood

with his shoulders thrown back, handsome and confident against the early morning sky. Emily marveled at him. Malphat did not understand sorrow, or cruelty, or any of the human emotions. Nor did he understand why she fought him. She could feel the tendrils of his mind that both caged and caressed her.

"If we're all so evil, then why did you want me as a companion?" she asked him, and he smiled.

"Because I can see inside you," he said. "And you are truly one of the few worth saving. It runs in your family."

Malphat pulled her to him, and again Emily hated herself as she felt her body surge in response to his affections in a strange mixture of fear and desire. She didn't resist as he kissed her. His face was buried in her neck when a small motion caught her attention. The silver strand of her locket trailed from the pocket of her jacket in the distance. She had just enough time to see Moon's hand close over it before Moon and the locket disappeared from view.

"She's gone!" Emily said, and he pulled away from her.

"She stole my locket!" Emily said, feeling her anger rising. *That locket is mine,* she thought. Moon had no right to steal it. Before she knew what she was doing, Emily conjured an orb of red light between her palms and blasted fire from her hands at the place where Moon had lain. Emily lunged and snarled as the fire burned around her, sniffing the air for a trace of Moon. Malphat raced to her side, holding her back as she was about to spring in the air

"Give it back!" she said, from the circle of his arms, and Malphat held her as he laughed.

"That would be your sense of justice at work. No matter that she's gone," he said. "She cannot fight us now; she's too weak from the feeding. The ritual is nearly complete." His light surrounded her, shielding her like a blanket. "We must work quickly though," he said, looking at the sky. "My protections will not last much longer in this sphere."

Emily shook, furious that Moon had stolen her most valuable token.

Malphat strode to Lillian, grabbing a chalice from the altar along the way. He grabbed her arm, and with his magic opened a line in the pale skin along the inside of her bicep. The blood gushed into the chalice.

"The final two ingredients. The blood of a mystic," he said, holding the chalice forth. "And the last ingredient, the blood of a witch."

"Am I still a witch?" Emily said. "I thought I was a demon."

"You're both: all witch and all demon," he said. "And all mine. You're much more powerful for the blend."

Emily inhaled quickly as her arm opened under his touch and her blood pattered into the cup, mingling with Lillian's. A soft white glow emanated from the cup, and he smiled with a maniacal fervor as he raised her arm to his lips and kissed it. She looked at her arm, and the cut was gone. Then he pulled her into his arms and kissed her.

Malphat turned from her and walked to the altar. A single shot fired from nowhere knocking the chalice end over end and spilling its contents to the ground. Malphat snarled as he wiped a trail of blood from his cheek, and Nicholas emerged from the shadows glowing in the midst of a blue halo of power, his face set with determination. He moved toward them and fired off three shots in rapid succession, hitting Malphat square in the chest with each shot. Emily screamed and ran to Malphat's side as Nicholas continued to shoot. Malphat grabbed her, and placed Emily between the two of them. The shots stopped.

Nicholas stepped sideways and disappeared.

Emily screamed as a shot grazed her arm from another direction. Malphat snarled, his voice low and threatening as he threw a shield over the two of them. He clutched Emily to his side.

There was a small flash of light, and the magical binds surrounding Lillian's chest released. Lillian dropped to the ground and disappeared into the night.

"Get her out of here!" Emily heard Nicholas yell, and then she saw Malphat shoot a wave of blue flames in the direction of the voice.

"Find them!" Malphat said to her. He dropped the shield, and Emily ran, circling the woods that surrounded the clearing, searching for their scent. She looked left and right, but there was no sign of them.

There was a flash of light behind her, and Emily turned back to look at Malphat as Nicholas emerged from the shadows on the right and landed three more shots at the demon. Malphat took two uncertain steps, roared, and sent a blaze of fire at the tree where Nicholas had stood. But once more, they found themselves fighting a phantom.

Come back to me, Malphat's voice rang in her mind. She struggled for a moment, trying to break free of his will, but was greeted with a blast of pain. She walked back to him as a shot ripped over her head.

Malphat grabbed Emily and threw her to the ground. Holding her in place, he sniffed the air, waiting for either Nicholas or Moon to strike again. He threw the barrier over them both again, and rested with his hands on the ground, mumbling an incantation.

The earth beneath Emily began to shake, and she whimpered as stones rose from the ground. Under his orders, the rocks became a set of pillars, ten feet tall, and each of them carved with markings as ornate as if they'd been wrought by the gods. Moving to the altar, he grabbed an offering bowl and flung it into the midst of the pillars, raising the energy with his hands until it bounced freely between the points of the gate.

Emily cowered as Malphat called her to him with the athame in hand, mentally dragging Emily with him to the gate. He put the silver athame to her throat.

"Put down your weapon and come to me, or you can watch her die," Malphat said.

Emily was about to protest, but her mouth was clamped shut. She knew that Malphat was bluffing, that he had no real intention of killing her. Malphat was playing to Nicholas' fears, and it was working. The whole thing was a show.

"No," she whispered through clenched teeth, though she could do nothing to deter what happened next.

Nicholas appeared, dropped his weapon, then slowly held his hands aloft. Malphat raised his hand and hit Nicholas with a jet of light, pinning him against a tree. "No!" Emily said. She ran between Malphat and Nicholas, but she heard Malphat's voice in her mind, and she fell to the ground. She struggled to stand, but Malphat held her there. He shot another stream of light, this time hitting Nicholas in the chest. Nicholas clenched his teeth as the light crackled around and through his body, and he began to tremble.

"Stop!" she said. "You're killing him!" Emily threw herself against the bonds in her mind, trying to run to him, to help, to stop Malphat, but she was powerless. She clutched her ears as Nicholas howled in pain, wondering if this torture was intended for Nicholas or for her.

She could feel the tears wet on her face as she pled with Malphat. "Don't hurt him! There's no need! Please!"

Malphat dropped his hand, and Nicholas slumped against the tree.

"Enough interruptions," Malphat said. He waved his arm over his head, encapsulating the three of them, and the gate, in a dome of bright red light. When he was finished, he stepped to Emily and pointed to Nicholas, who was lying on the ground, immobile.

"And here is an even better lesson. This one intends to kill us too. Look into his heart, you'll see it."

Emily looked at Nicholas and then back to Malphat. She

wanted to deny it, but she knew that it was true. There, among the love and the goodness in his heart, there was also fear and hatred. Malphat was right. Nicholas would kill them both if he had the chance.

"But there are other pieces to him," Emily said.

"The other bits don't matter, the intention is there. The Paladin are murderers of our kind; they can't help it. They're predators, just as we are," Malphat said.

Emily could not deny what Malphat said. Her aunt had told her the same thing all her life.

For a moment, there was only silence punctuated by Nicholas' gasps. Shifting his eyes between the pair of them, Malphat began to laugh, a rich booming sound that filled Emily with dread.

"No," he said, stroking her hair, "I will not kill him. This is your next lesson."

Emily looked at Malphat and her mouth went dry.

"Take this," Malphat ordered, handing her a knife from his belt.

Emily's hands covered her mouth, and she shook with the effort that it took to utter the single word. She steeled herself and felt her jaw nearly burst in pain as she struggled to utter the word. "No."

"No is not an option," he said.

Emily wasn't able to resist him. Another round of pain brought her to her knees. She tried not to scream as her hand moved independent of her will to the blade, and she took it from his hand.

"Bastard!" she gasped at Malphat, who looked patient.

"I don't create the pain, Emily, you do. It comes from resisting your instincts and disobeying my commands."

She picked up the knife, and her hand trembled. She fought to drop it, but the blade held firm in her grip.

Nicholas lifted his head, and their eyes met. She could see the horror on his face as she drew closer to him, brandishing the knife. She walked slowly, the blade in her hand, fighting against every step, though her body moved independent of her will. She looked over her shoulder and saw the triumph coloring Malphat's face. There was nothing she could do to fight him, he was too powerful. She stood in front of Nicholas, seeing her own eyes, wide and terrified, reflected in his.

"Emily," he said. "Are you still in there? Please, don't do this."

With a slash of the knife, Emily opened the sleeve of his shirt, exposing his bare arm. His chest heaved, and Emily could see a vein throbbing the rhythm of his heart on the side of his neck. She closed her eyes. Her hand shook as she fought Malphat's instructions, and the tip of the knife drew a small bead of blood from his arm.

"Nicholas, you don't understand. I can't stop it; he's making me do this. I'm sorry," she whispered again as she plunged the knife into the top of his arm.

Nicholas moaned as she drew a line down his arm with the blade of the knife, and a small stream of blood ran from his arm. Malphat drew close with the chalice to catch the blood in the cup. He spun Emily to face him with one hand, and she froze still under the weight of his stare.

"Again, it's your turn, *my love*," Malphat said, placing emphasis on the last two words as Nicholas struggled.

Emily's hand grasped the knife. She bit her lip as she lifted her hand and pulled the blade down her own arm. Malphat squeezed her blood into the chalice. This time, the light from the chalice lit his face, making it glow with an unearthly light.

"This potion is stronger than before," he said, swirling the chalice and inspecting its contents.

Nicholas sneered and tried to lunge, but his binds held firm, and Malphat raised a mocking eyebrow at him.

"Quite the hero. Too bad. If there had been time for

301

another transformation, I'd have taken you with us as well."

With three paces, Malphat threw the chalice into the tower of energy. The wind began to swirl around them. Picking up the athame from the altar, Malphat walked to Emily. For a moment, she thought he was going to stab her, but he turned the blade downward and offered it to her, pressing it into her hands.

"This is your blade," Malphat said, "and you must wield it. Open the gate."

Emily grasped the athame in her hand and walked to the gate.

"Save us," Emily said, drawing her hand back. She drove the blade into a piece of sky inside the gate, and cut a doorway into another world.

CHAPTER 37

Jessie looked worried and Steph paused to grab her hands.

"It's going to be all right," he said, as much for himself as for her. A strong wind had started to stir, and it blew Jessie's pigtails around her face like a pair of wild kites. He pulled her into his arms for a brief second before he grabbed the cases and began to make his way across the blackened path that once led to the Gatehouse.

"Follow me," he said, marching toward the burned remnants of the Gatehouse. When they turned the corner behind the ruin, Steph could see the dim outlines of hooded figures marching toward the gate. Their gray robes whipped in the wind, and the occasional spark of blue magic erupted from their weapons. The Paladin agents were about fifty yards ahead of them, moving toward a sparkling golden light at the end of the field. A flame burst into the air, and the Paladin paused as the flume of light shot toward them like the breath of a dragon. When the fire subsided, Steph and Jessie could see the gate, a gaping pool of golden light framed against the dark sky. The Paladin wards streamed around it like ripped streamers of electric blue magic.

Stanton fell in behind them. "The Agents guarding the

PREMONITION

Gate are straight ahead," he said.

"Hurry," Steph said, breaking into an awkward run. "Malphat must be opening the gate further up the ward line. The surge of magic just blew the Paladin protections off the gate. This place will be demon central if we can't hold the line here."

The Paladin had stopped, and one of them had turned toward Jessie and Steph. He pointed his weapon at them.

"Halt!" the guard yelled, as his pen gleamed with a sharp blue light.

"Stand down!" Stanton said, and the Agent complied, but more of them came running, each of them stopping quickly when they recognized Stanton.

Steph held up his hands. "Your weapons won't work on me." He stepped toward the group. "Fall in behind me, all of you, if you don't want to die."

Steph and Jessie began to glow; the white halo of light that surrounded them caused the men to look at one another in alarm, and one of them even had the sense to bow. Steph took the lead and they approached the gate in silence.

Steph placed the briefcases on the ground a few yards from the gate and snapped them open. He began to affix more potions to the belt on his shoulder. Jessie did the same, then handed each of the men a belt from the briefcase.

"See this?" Steph said, holding a sphere aloft to show the Paladin. "Throw them at whatever comes through that gate."

"But our weapons—" one of the Paladin began.

"Your weapons have about a third of the power of the spheres. There are more briefcases in the van, strapped to the sides of the walls. A few of you need to go back and get them."

One of the Paladin nodded, and three of the agents ran back to the van.

Just then, a small purple orb of light came sailing

304

through the golden liquid at the gate and hung suspended in the night sky. Steph took careful aim, then chucked the potion. It struck the orb and exploded in the sky. Something small fell smoking to the ground, and Steph walked through the grasses and lifted the thing by its tail. It was a small skeleton of a creature that in life might have resembled a winged lizard.

"See this?" Steph said, holding it for the agents to see. "Those are ward demons; they move in swarms, and they'll chew a hole right through you if they get the chance."

The demon shriveled and crumbled to dust in his hands as three more of the orbs shot through the gate.

Steph threw another potion as the ground rumbled beneath his feet.

"On your right!" Jessie yelled, and Steph launched a potion at a streak of purple light that ripped past his ear. Another small, winged creature fell to the ground, and shriveled into dust.

"Duck!" Jessie said.

Steph threw himself to the ground as Jessie threw another potion, hitting two more of the creatures with a well-timed shot.

The Paladin caught on quickly. As the three agents arrived back with more briefcases, the men threw the belts over their chests and hastily armed themselves with the glowing spheres. Before they reached the gate, a dozen more of the purple orbs swarmed into view.

Half of the Paladin began to blast the creatures out of the sky with the potions, while the others stood in front of the gate, weaving the threads of their magic in an attempt to reestablish the decimated wards.

"I hope we've got enough ammunition," Steph said.

"Look." Jessie grinned, pointing at another set of headlights that swung into the driveway. "Reinforcements!"

Lauren and Alex jumped out of the car.

"We bottled more potions," Lauren said. She opened the back door of her car and produced another armload of the briefcases.

"You ladies have earned your paychecks this week," Steph said. "I think we've got most of them for the moment, and the Paladin are resealing the gate; we just have to nail this one—" He swore as he threw a sphere that fell short of its mark and landed in a small explosion on the ground.

The creature made a beeline for Steph, and before he could move, Lauren grabbed a bottle from her belt and threw it in the air beside his head. Steph barely had time to flinch as the creature fell to the ground beside him. The dust from the explosion left a black streak across his face.

"Thanks," Steph said, righting his glasses.

Alex grabbed a potion, held it aloft as she watched the creature, and then threw the bottle so that the creature flew straight into it. The beast dissolved in a small cloud of gray dust.

Jessie wiped her brow with the back of her hand. "Welcome aboard," she said, throwing another potion.

It took a few minutes, but they managed to eradicate the swarm.

Stanton's phone rang, and he answered. "Give me the report." His face was grim, and his chin set as he listened for a few minutes. "Standby for further instructions."

He sighed and turned off his phone. "It looks like we've got things under control here, but we need to get down the river, Commander Flynn is injured and her team needs backup," Stanton said. "Report to Agent Cross for further instructions."

The driver of the other SUV nodded and turned around in the field with a flash of headlights.

Stanton walked to Steph. "We've set up a perimeter around the area the demons are in about three miles down the river, but the reports aren't good. So far, they've been unable to breach the protections the demons have placed on the emerging gate. The demon created a protection that looks like a dome over the entire area. They got Moon and Lillian out before the dome went up, but Nicholas is still inside. We don't know if he's alive or dead. I'm hoping you have an idea on how we can breach their defenses," Stanton said.

"All right then," Steph said. "Executive decision," he said. "We're going to get to them through this gate. We'll travel up the ward lines and surprise them before Malphat can fully cut the passageway to the other realm." Steph looked at the Paladin, who had just finished forming a tight blue netting of magic over the golden pool of light at the gate. "We've got to open it back up," he said.

"We don't go knocking on doors . . ." Stanton started, and Steph turned to him.

"Yeah, I know all about that," Steph said. "You Paladin love your rules, don't you? The problem with that answer is that unless we do something pronto, the whole damn world is going to end. Who's left inside the perimeter?"

"According to my agents, Blevin and Diamond are dead, the demon killed them. When they took Commander Flynn from the scene, Nicholas was still fighting with the demons."

"You mean the demon and Emily?" Steph asked, but Stanton shook his head.

"No, I mean the demons. There is no more Emily VonPeer, as far as we know."

"I was afraid of that," Steph said, his face grim. He chewed his bottom lip. "Well, two of them are easier to fight than a legion. Once we get inside, we can do our best to wrangle Emily and Malphat and dissolve the magical perimeter from the inside. We've got to do something before they call forth an army; with two of them on this side, they'd be powerful enough to do it."

Steph waved his arm and motioned to the group.

"Everyone, come close!"

Steph swiped at a patch of dirt with his foot and motioned the agents down with his finger. The group of them crouched in a circle while Steph drew a picture in the dirt with the blade of his knife. He looked at the sky, which was turning from black to a pre-dawn, purple-gray color.

"We're nearing dawn. When the sun rises, it will be possible for Malphat to cut a new gate between the worlds and unleash whatever's on the other side. Unless . . ." he said, drawing a line in the dirt, "we head him off before he can cut the gate through to the other side."

Stanton frowned. "Where does the gate end?"

"There are two cuts necessary to open the gate," Steph said. "When opened from this world, it will produce a tunnel of sorts, to the ley lines. The ley lines are magical roads to the other worlds. Malphat will need to cross through the first gate into the void before he can open the second door to his own realm. If we open this gate first and travel up the line, then we can beat him to the second gate and use our magic to collapse the wards behind us. At Stanton's cue, we'll have the Paladin attack from one side to distract them, while we run up through the other end of the gate."

"Is that even possible?" an agent asked.

"Theoretically," Steph said. "It's risky though. We'll be walking between the worlds and, as you can see, we're not the only creatures who've tried it. There might be more of the ward demons inside, so we need to be ready. But the distance is short, and we should have a good shot at making it through without detection."

"That is the craziest idea that I have ever heard," Stanton said, shaking his head.

Steph nodded. "That's why it's going to work. The first thing we need to do is start tearing down the fencing," he instructed, pointing to the gate. "We know the gates, when opened, create a fair amount of wind. We need the area clear of any debris that might come flying through. In the meantime, call in the rest of the Paladin," Steph said. "I want the writers, the researchers, the janitors, anyone who's able will do. This is no time to be picky; we need anyone who's willing to fight."

"Is this cleared to your liking?" one of the junior agents asked, pointing at the gate.

While they'd been talking, the agents had worked. Steph and Jessie gaped. The entire area was swept clear of everything, even grass. Steph walked the space with an imaginary tape pretending to measure the parameters of the gate.

"It'll do, soldier. Now, if you'll all stand back," Steph said, cracking his knuckles in front of him. "It's time for me to get to work."

Stanton stepped up to Steph and pressed a small book into his hands. "These are the necessary incantations to undo our wards—" he began, but Steph just brushed him out of the way.

"No need for that," Steph said, holding his knife in the air. "I've got it covered."

A few of the agents looked at him, perplexed.

"Have a little faith, guys," Steph said.

Pushing his glasses up with a finger, Steph paced to the gate. He whistled a small tune, looked sideways, and, with his knife, snatched one of the blue strings that connected the ward. For a moment, he held the shining string of magic in his hand and then, with a flick of his wrist, pulled the knife through it.

"Voila," he said, turning to them, holding the end of the strings.

The Paladin all wore the same expression of shock and disbelief at what he'd just done.

"Everyone arm yourselves. When I drop these threads, it will reopen the Gate. I want you to run into the tunnel and stay behind me. If you see an orb, blast it. Ready?"

The agents nodded and Steph heaved the string and unleashed the netting of wards that surrounded the gates. He moved toward the glowing pool of light.

Jessie walked up behind him and grabbed his hand as he was about to enter. "Are you sure you know what you're doing?" she blurted.

"I never do," Steph said, squeezing her shoulder and planting a kiss on the top of her head. "That's the best way to win, you know."

CHAPTER 38

Emily pushed herself from the ground, still clutching the athame, and wiped her hair from her eyes. The doorway that she'd cut glowed golden against the sky, and Malphat cackled with a bird-like laughter, his expression manic with glee. The sky behind the towers glowed with a red light and a murder of crows swung through the air, yelling their loud caws in response to their leader. Malphat stood in the gateway, shouting instructions into the valley beneath his feet.

Emily took a deep breath and did her best to settle her mind. She inched her way to Nicholas. He was still bound, and bleeding from the place where she'd gashed his arm. Keeping one eye on Malphat, she reached Nicholas' boot and nudged him.

He dragged his head from his chest and looked into her eyes. She cringed as she looked at his bloodstained shirt. *I did that,* she told herself, *and if he dies it will be my fault.* She stole another glance at Malphat, who wasn't paying attention to her. He continued to hover around the entrance to the gate, shouting to the creatures below.

"What is he saying?" Nicholas asked, "Do you

understand it?"

"It's a battle cry," Emily said. "He wants revenge for his imprisonment. It's justice, he says, for what the humans did to him. He intends to lead his army back through the gate."

Nicholas nodded wearily.

"And that's why the gate is to remain closed at all costs," he said to her.

Emily reached up to him. She tore his shirt and wrapped it around his arm, staunching the blood. With a touch, she healed his arm.

Nicholas whispered something, and his pen flew to his hand. He paused for a moment, waiting for Malphat to turn and kill them both. But Malphat was so absorbed with the scene in front of him, that it seemed he had forgotten the pair of them for the moment. Wincing, Nicholas released the magic binding him and slowly inched his way to a crouching position, exhausted by the effort. He grabbed a nearby branch and somehow managed to drag himself to a half-upright position.

"Stay here!" Nicholas warned. His face was pale, and when he stepped away from the tree, Emily was sure that he would collapse from his injuries. Though he swooned, Nicholas held his ground. He took two more steps toward the gate and raised his weapon, aiming at the spot between Malphat's shoulder blades.

"Just one good shot!" he said, "That's all I need. Just enough to push him in and seal the gate . . ."

Emily's face froze in terror. Here was her nightmare in real life. She tugged on his good arm and began to babble in a low and frightened voice.

"Nicholas, you can't do this, you don't understand. You'll die. It was in my dreams." She knew what he was going to say, and the fear rose from her stomach as he uttered the words.

312

"I have to stop him," he said.

"No. Change it all, just walk away. I'll go with him, the dream will change, you'll still be alive this time," she said. "You can't just go, I love you."

They stared at each other for a moment. She'd surprised herself with those words. She stood silent with her eyes wide, feeling very helpless and exposed.

He touched her cheek. "I love you too."

For a moment, she thought she'd convinced him. Then his expression told her she was wrong. She knew what he would say as he said it.

"Some things are worth dying for," he said.

No, she thought, *I won't let this happen. I'll change the dream.* Emily picked herself up from the ground, determined to follow him. She would not let him die; she would change his fate if it killed her.

Nicholas was already five paces in front of her. She could see the blue aura of magic swirl around him as he gathered his powers, and the lightning shot from his weapon flashed just as it had in her dreams. The shot gleamed as it crackled through the night air, a shade too bright and a fraction of a second too soon.

Emily yelled and dove at him, but it was already too late. Malphat waved his arm, and flung her to the ground with a hard thump a few yards away, and the tears were already streaming from her eyes as she pushed herself from the ground.

"No," she whispered.

With another wave of his hand, Malphat held her in place. He charged at Nicholas with lightning speed. For a moment, the two men were face to face. Then Malphat had Nicholas by the throat and held him in the air. Nicholas struggled, but Malphat was too strong. Malphat stabbed, and Nicholas fell into a crumpled heap beside Emily, bleeding from a gaping wound just above his heart. Emily screamed

313

and felt her binds released.

"Justice," Malphat said simply as he turned his back on them, wiping his blade on his pant leg.

"No!" Emily cried. She ran to Nicholas and placed her hands over his heart, trying to close his wound. It didn't work. She pulled him into her arms, cradling the upper half of his body. Nicholas coughed, and shuddered as he spoke.

"I almost had him." Nicholas shifted slightly and began to shake.

Emily reached out, intending to go after Malphat, but Nicholas put his hand on her arm.

"Take this . . ." Nicholas shivered as his breath grew faint. He opened his hand and from it, she took a small bottle.

Emily bit her lip and cried. "I knew that this would happen. I thought that I could stop it, that the dreams weren't real—I don't know what I thought. I'm so sorry!"

"It's okay," Nicholas said. He squeezed her hand, exhaled, and died.

Emily lifted her head and wailed, still holding Nicholas in her arms.

"Come back," she said, rocking him in her arms.

The tears streamed down her face, and she stretched and lay with her head on his shoulder, not caring if she lived or died.

Her wail turned to a snarl as Malphat approached.

"You're a murderer!" she hissed.

He looked at her disdainfully, like she was a child who'd just covered herself in mud. He nodded as he looked down at Nicholas.

"Yes," he said, "he was brave. He might have made a decent demon."

She lunged at him, but he struck her to the ground and laughed, unconcerned. He stood over her, an amused look on his face, his blade at her throat. She lifted her eyes, mustering all of her hatred for him in a single, violent sneer. She didn't care what he did with her, it didn't matter anymore.

The light purple sky was being replaced by pink and orange streaks at the horizon. Malphat backed away from her and pulled her to her feet.

"Enough theatrics over the humans, come with me, now," Malphat said.

She met his eyes for a second, and he took her by the arm, placing the athame in her hand.

He led her through the golden light of the gate, into a swirling tunnel. A series of images began to form in front of her, and suddenly she found herself standing in paradise.

They were at the edge of a lush, green valley that bloomed brightly with thousands of flowers. In front of her, a pair of creatures not unlike her jackbirds gamboled lightheartedly in the air. In the distance was a silver lake and behind it a pale blue castle that looked as if it were carved out of the side of the mountain itself.

"That," he said to Emily, "is our home."

He yelled a wordless call that sounded like the caw of a crow; in an instant, a thousand creatures appeared from the air and gathered in the valley, dressed for war. Malphat held up his hand and yelled, and the creatures looked up at him and began to cheer.

"The first touch of sunlight will link the worlds. When that happens, you need to make the second cut to send us home," Malphat said.

Emily shook as she held the athame in her hand. Malphat put his hand over hers, and poised the athame at the thin window of magic that separated the worlds.

The first ray of sunlight peeked over the horizon, and guiding Emily's hand, the two of them used the athame to rip a passageway into Malphat's realm.

Malphat smiled. "The Paladin are waiting outside the shield. After we depart, my army will dispatch them."

"Unless, of course, someone stops you and saves the

day," a voice said.

Malphat and Emily turned to find themselves face to face with Steph and Jessie, leading a band of Paladin agents. With a motion of his hand, Steph guided the agents and Jessie out through the ward that Malphat had opened.

"Get them ready," Steph said to Jessie. "I'll handle these two," he said. He peered out the doorway into their own world, where the bodies lay surrounding the altar. "That's what I hate about demons," he said conversationally, "your dealings with mortals are always so bloody and destructive, and it never does any good."

Emily didn't know whether she should laugh or cry.

Malphat snarled and lunged, but Steph held up his hand and stopped him mid-flight. Malphat hung, frozen in mid-air, his face wrinkled in a frustrated snarl.

"Anyway," he said, in the same conversational tone. "I have a message for you, Malphat. You have two choices: you can release Emily and cross into the gate and go back with your demon buddies, or you can face the consequences, the consequences being me."

Steph stepped closer to him, and his face shone with a white light that was both beautiful and terrifying. The pocketknife shifted in his hand, becoming a jeweled white sword. Steph spun it in his hands threateningly, and braced himself, ready for a fight.

Malphat sneered at him. Before she knew what was happening, Emily was lunging at Steph with the order to kill. Steph threw her backward through the gate, where she landed with a painful thump. The potion Nicholas had handed her dropped to the ground. Again, she picked herself up, the athame bared, preparing to strike while Malphat watched. Emily took a step back as she realized that she was surrounded on all sides by an army of robed Paladin, standing with their weapons drawn.

"Hold your fire!" Jessie said.

This time, Steph moved his hand, and Emily again flew to the ground hard. She landed inches from Nicholas. She lay panting as Steph ran to her, brandishing his sword. She leapt up, holding the athame in desperation, knowing that Steph could kill her in a heartbeat.

He stood in front of her with the sword held at an angle, ready to strike. He took two steps toward her.

"Is the not-demon Emily in there somewhere?" he asked her, and Emily nodded slightly.

He didn't move, but his pressure on the sword lifted slightly.

"He's making me do this," she said.

"Then I need you to trust me. I grabbed Maeve's potion, but it will only work for a few minutes." Under the pretense of swinging his sword, he uncorked the bottle and threw the potion on her.

Instantly, she could feel Malphat's grip on her mind release. Emily twitched her hand and looked at Malphat from the corner of her eye. She was free.

Her eyes fell on her own blade, and she knew what to do. She looked into Steph's eyes and nodded again imperceptibly. Steph's eyes were compassionate.

"Keep fighting me!" she said.

"It's been a pleasure working with you, Emily," Steph said, with half a grin. Steph forced her to the ground with his blade.

Emily snarled, and crouched into position, then launched herself into the air. Instead of lunging into the fight, she turned at the last second and landed chest first on her own blade.

She could feel the connection unraveling between them as she felt her own life begin to slip away. She could still feel her heart pumping wildly in her chest, and she waited in panic for the moment that it would stop. She didn't want to die.

"It's over," Steph said. He waved his hand and Malphat dropped to the ground.

"No!" Malphat screamed, grabbing his chest as he rushed to Emily.

Emily rolled to her side as he approached her. The energy of her magic poured from her body like blood, and she began to feel very cold. She didn't know if she was alive or dead; she just lay there in limbo, watching the scene in front of her and waiting to die.

Malphat moved to reach for her, but Steph's blade snapped through the air, and Malphat backed away from him. As his hand fell from his chest, a bright wound appeared in the same place as Emily's. Steph lunged again, and Malphat flailed backward.

As the sun rose higher, the gate began to open wide, creating a pathway between the worlds, and with it came a series of hoof beats and metallic crashes that sounded like an approaching army. Malphat smiled at the sound of his armies behind him.

"You're too late," he said, disappearing through the golden pool back into the tunnel.

A moment later, Malphat flew back through the gate and hit the ground with a loud thump. The spirit of the House emerged from the gate, her eyes fierce. She strode to Malphat and stood over him, pointing her finger at him. Malphat cowered on the ground beneath her, his eyes filled with fear.

"You stole lives from my family once, but you will not do it again!" she roared, her voice laced with thunder. She picked him up by his shirt, lifting him from the ground. Speaking in a language long forgotten, she threw Malphat backward through the gate and down into the valley of demons below.

"Kill them," Emily heard him say. "All of them!"

His army began to march, ascending the hill between

their worlds. Dozens of multicolored orbs flew through the gate.

"Now!" Jessie said, and a thousand arcs of blue light shot across the sky. The Paladin began to swarm over and around them in an attempt to fight the approaching demons and close the gate. The spirit of the House moved to Emily and dropped on the ground beside her. She removed the knife and placed it on her chest. She kissed Emily's forehead and the wound left by the athame was gone.

Emily began to glow with a quiet green light. Looking into her face, Emily burst into a grin and wrapped her arms around the woman.

"Who is she?" Jessie asked.

"That's the House," Steph said, "her spirit, anyway. I saw her fighting the night the demon broke in."

Emily said to the woman, "How did you get here—and why?"

"The athame does not spill blood, only energy. Likewise, it is one of your weapons, and cannot be turned against you, even by your own hand," she explained. "When you did what you did, you called me here to your side. Because the gate was open, I was able to travel the ward and find you."

"I don't understand this magic," Emily said.

"Hush now, rest." The spirit pressed her hand to Emily's head, the skin of her hand felt cool on Emily's forehead.

"See what I said?" Steph said, suddenly standing beside them. "Never assume that you have the whole picture. These things have a way of turning themselves right in the end."

"Did you know that all this would happen?" Emily said.

"No," Steph said. "I just knew that everything would work out the way it was supposed to."

Emily glanced at Nicholas, who was lying cold and still on the ground. "Not everything," she said.

The House moved to him, touching his face. "This evil has had terrible consequences," she said, her hand on Nicholas. "His bravery will not be forgotten." She lifted Nicholas and walked to the gate with him cradled in her arms like a child.

"What about these two?" Steph asked her, gesturing to Blevin and Diamond. The House looked at them and shook her head.

"They made a deal with a devil," she said over her shoulder. "And so they paid the price."

The House walked into the gateway and disappeared with Nicholas. Emily watched them leave as Steph pulled her to her feet.

The sky was awash with bottles and potions. Thin strands of light shot from Paladin weapons. Emily watched as Moon slashed a rogue demon that appeared through the gate. Some of the agents charged, firing their weapons into the gap, while others used their magic to sew the breach between the worlds.

Emily sat up on her elbows, attended by Steph.

"Don't they need you in the fight?" she asked.

"It looks like they're doing fine," Steph said, "most of them have been living for this moment, especially the ones who aren't field agents. They're all hunters at heart." As Steph said this, a pudgy, bald, little Paladin in a green robe ducked beside him, snaring a demon as another green-robed agent blasted it. The two men high-fived and ran into the battle, their faces glowing with pride. The few demons that had escaped the gate were being eliminated or pushed backward into the portal by the bright blue weapons of the Paladin agents.

"Besides," Steph said, pointing to the glowing web of light the Paladin had constructed in front of the gate, "they've already sealed the wards. The rest of this is just cleanup and details."

Emily opened her mouth to protest, but what he said was true. Her head ached, and as she raised her hand to rub it, she caught sight of her own magic. She was relieved at the sight of the soft green light surrounding her, but bereft of the adrenaline rush of pure power that Malphat had given her. Her mind flashed to Nicholas, and she only managed to quell the wave of pain by replacing it with something more immediate.

"Rest for a minute," Steph said, taking her arm, but Emily refused.

Rest would bring no comfort now. She limped into the clearing, gathering all of her power into her hands. The crowd cleared as she approached the gate.

"Stand back!" Stanton yelled to the agents, still shooting at stray demons. Flashes of light erupted all around her, but Emily paid no attention to them, if they hit her, so be it. Instead, she focused all of her power into a single band of light. She felt the power building in her hands, and as it reached its apex, she threw her hands over her head, and hurled her power at the gate. Her magic exploded the pillars that Malphat had raised, and as quickly as it had risen, the gate was gone, reduced to a pile of smoking, crumbled rocks. The Paladin agents closed in behind Emily, and continued to weave the fabric of the worlds back together with dozens of bolts of thin blue light.

Emily's arms lowered to her sides, her features expressionless. It was as if the expulsion of her magic had numbed her pain, leaving her drained not only of her power, but of her feelings too. Then she cried out as a blast hit her in the back, and she plunged into darkness.

CHAPTER 39

There was a clink of bottles, and the first thing Emily was aware of was her face against a soft pillow. Her bedroom was dark and comfortable, the same as always. The next thing she knew, her aunt was beside her, stroking her hair the same way that she did when Emily had nightmares as a little girl.

"It was an accident," someone said.

"Accident, my old white backside!" Maeve said over her shoulder. "They should have Moon's job for this! Talk about protecting your own. Another inch to the left and there would have been nothing left for me to do."

Emily shivered, fading in and out of consciousness, as her aunt continued to mutter. Emily felt herself drifting into comfortable darkness until the day came flooding back to her.

"Shhh," her aunt said. "She's waking up. Emily, Emily dear, can you hear me? Say something if you can."

"What happened?" she asked. Her brain was fuzzy, and her throat was dry; she had the momentary impression that she'd been dreaming all this time, and here she was, safe in her own bed at home, same as always.

Then a big pair of hands turned her and arranged her pillows so that she was sitting upright in bed, and she was looking at the weathered faces of her aunt and John Dalgreth. Then reality came flooding back to her. She reached for her locket in an instinctive gesture, but it was gone. Gone, like Malphat, the battle, the forest.

Like Nicholas.

Her eyes remained dry, though a lump formed in her throat. She swallowed hard, but it wouldn't go away. John pulled a new looking pipe from his pocket and cracked the window, rocking back and forth in Emily's chair in the corner, seeming to be lost in his thoughts. She felt her aunt's arm snake around her, and Emily put her head on her shoulder, noticing how thin she'd become.

"Did we win?" she asked.

"We won," John said. "With minimal losses, thanks to you and Steph. And to Nicholas."

"He killed Nicholas," Emily said. "The whole thing was just like my dream, but there was nothing I could do to help." Her aunt's arm tightened around her.

"It wasn't your fault," Maeve said. "We can't change the order of the universe. It must have been his time."

Downstairs, the door slammed and boots tramped into the kitchen.

"That'll be Steph with the rest of them," John said. He nodded to Maeve. "I'll leave you two here to talk." He rose stiffly, leaning heavily on a cane as he hobbled out of the room.

Maeve squeezed her again.

Maeve looked at Emily with tears in her eyes. "There is no one to blame in this situation. John and I found out what Diamond had done, and we were trying to stop him and send the demons back through the gate. But we underestimated a lot of things: Diamond, Malphat, the strength of the threat— we thought we could handle it on our own. We thought that a simple spell would right everything. And then there was Blevin, we counted on him; we didn't know he was a traitor, not at first anyway. And despite our plans, despite our best efforts to leave you and Nicholas out of it, everything went wrong. Well, not everything. Malphat is gone, at least for now. The House took care of that."

"I'm glad you're still here," Emily managed, patting her hand. "It was rough without you."

Maeve smiled and took Emily's hand and squeezed it. "I'm glad you're still here too," she said. "It was touch and go for a few hours, the Paladin weapons aren't meant to injure, they're meant to kill. But I'm going to let you rest now. There are more people who need medicine. Call if you need me." Maeve patted Emily's hand again and kissed her on the cheek as Emily sank deeper into the pillows.

Her last thought was of nightmares, but for the first time in forever, she fell into a hard and dreamless sleep.

When Emily woke again, it was nighttime, and she was alone. The light from the full moon shone through her window, lighting her lace curtains and pooling on the floor beneath her rocking chair. Emily swung from her bed and placed her feet on the floor. Unsteady, she pulled herself to her feet and tottered to the window. She looked out past the garden and saw the gentle swish of the river lapping onto the shore. She felt a twinge in her shoulder and moved to the mirror to inspect her wound.

Emily pulled back the bandage, expecting to see a large gash. To her surprise, her skin was healed, everything but a small blue scar a few inches from her shoulder blade that resembled a star. Emily pulled off the bandage and threw it in the trash. She looked at herself in the mirror: though her light was faded, she knew the bright green aura of her magic would return to her as she healed.

Next time, she thought, *I'll be better. I'll be stronger.* Next time she would be ready, with both study and power, she'd see to it that no one was hurt because of her weakness. And next time, she'd do it on her own. There were worse things in life than being alone.

She sighed. Though she was still weak, she didn't want to sleep. Emily walked down the hallway, tracing her fingers against the wood paneling.

"You there?" she asked the House.

A weak greeting acknowledged her, and Emily patted the wall.

"Thanks," she said.

Silently, she padded down the hallway and into the kitchen, where she could hear several unfamiliar snores. Maintaining her silence, Emily slipped out the back door, careful not to let the screen door slam behind her. Even though she was distracted, she relished the familiar feeling of the wet grass on her feet, and the fact that it no longer burned at her touch.

Emily sat on the bench by the river and watched the moon. It was a beautiful night, and the heavy perfumed scent of the blooming lilacs in the garden hung thick in the air. She didn't know when she started to cry, but after a while, she was aware of the tears rolling down her face as they hit the fabric of her robe. In her whole life, she'd only wished for a handful of things: a little power, real love, and an end to the dreams. She'd gotten everything she'd wanted. It wasn't the universe's fault that everything had gone so horribly wrong, that a future with Nicholas had been snatched out of her hands. But the thought of his face as he died brought a fresh round of sobs, and she couldn't help but think that there was something else she could have done to save him.

Her tears fell more quickly. She didn't try to stop them; it was no use. She needed to cry.

"Nicholas," she whispered, "I'm so sorry."

Something flashed in the corner of her eye, and her head snapped up. She spun to see what had caught her attention.

PREMONITION

Something was moving in the garden. The light flashed again; Emily stood and took a tentative step toward it. Something was trying to breach the wards of the House.

A few moments passed. Emily could hear nothing but the sound of her own ragged breath. She watched as whatever was out there tested the threadwork of the House. She took a few more steps forward then ran toward the garden as one of the ward lines began to unravel in front of her. She wiped her face with the back of her hand. She thought about yelling to her aunt, but there was no time. The thread, one of the blue ones that Nicholas had woven, was unwinding fast. She walked toward the breach, gathering her magic around her. She managed to collect a small green ball of energy between her palms, and she threw the orb at the breach, but the magic made no difference as the ward snaked to the ground and disappeared. Emily, frowned, looking for something that she could use as a weapon. She looked on the ground, hoping to arm herself, but the best that she could do was a round rock the size of her hand. Cocking her arm, she took a step back and waited for the moment to throw it.

A silver orb flew through the opening, growing larger and larger until it was the size of a person. The light faded away, and Nicholas took a step toward her with a tired smile on his face. Emily gasped, not believing her eyes.

"Are you a ghost?" she asked, stammering.

"I don't think so," he said, examining his hands. "I heard you call my name, so I came back," he said.

"Back? From where? You were dead!" she said.

Nicholas nodded. "I remember that part," he said. "But then I heard you call, and they told me that I had to go home, that I wasn't done yet, and to tell Steph that he did the right thing. And then the House opened the ward and here I am." He took another step toward her.

"They? Who's they?" Emily asked, but Nicholas just shrugged, a strange look on his face.

"You know, I could have answered that question until you asked me about it," he told her. "But now I have no idea."

Emily looked behind him, and saw the spirit of the House standing in the gap behind the ward. She smiled at Emily, and zipped the ward back into place, leaving the two of them alone.

Nicholas closed the gap between them and threw his arms around her. Emily put her head against his neck, and it was warm.

"You feel real," she murmured, hugging him tighter. She opened the buttons of his shirt and placed her hand on his chest. His heart pounded underneath her fingertips, steady and fast. He smiled at her, and she marveled at the fact that he was so very *alive*. She stood on her tiptoes, threw her arms around his neck, and began to cry.

He crushed his mouth against hers with a kiss that made her go weak. He smiled as he pulled away from her, leaving both of them slightly breathless. Nicholas kissed her again, and she felt a rushing, spinning sensation. She felt the light of his magic rise and surround her. Then she felt her magic rise to his, and for a moment, the light of their combined auras fused together in a flash of turquoise that haloed them in a cocoon of light.

Dragging her mouth away from his, she took his hand and led him inside, through the House, and up the stairs to her room.

He closed the door behind them and stepped closer to her, and she shifted her weight to her back foot, making them both tumble onto her bed. She could feel the light of her own magic responding to him.

Emily moaned against his collarbone as his hand moved beneath her shirt and ran up her back. Then he lifted it over her head and pulled her close. She clutched him tightly, feeling the impossible softness of his skin and waiting for the moment that he would recede back into the smoky darkness of her mind. He must have sensed her hesitation.

"What's the matter?" he asked, pulling back from her. "You seem nervous."

"We've done this so many times before . . . in my dreams, and it always ends the same, with you fading away, and me alone in my bed." She paused. "Don't go away this time."

Nicholas smiled and pulled her close. "I'm not going anywhere tonight," he whispered in her ear. He kissed her again, "or ever."

He pulled back from her and removed his shirt, then drew her into his arms. Emily moaned in pleasure as every kiss, every touch, and every breath echoed the dreams that had haunted her for the better part of her life. Everything about Nicholas was familiar and close, but every touch was thrilling and new, and most importantly real.

As good as his word, Nicholas made sure that this dream didn't end at the good part. Emily reveled in every one of his kisses, his whispers, and the wonderful sensation of his skin against hers as he moved against her in the darkness. She watched him and realized that she didn't care anymore if she was dreaming or awake; she only hoped that this feeling would last forever.

Emily lay for a long time in the stillness of his arms, watching the moon through the window. She lay with her head on his heart, listening to the soft thumping rhythm that reinforced his presence. His hand scrawled a lazy pattern up and down her back, and she looked up at him and smiled.

He leaned down and kissed her softly.

"Was it as good as your dreams?" he asked.

"Better," she said, cuddling close to him.

He smiled widely, kissed her again, and then closed his eyes. After a few moments, his breathing eased into a regular pattern as he fell asleep.

Despite his assurances, she was afraid to fall asleep. She leaned her head against his chest and listened to his heartbeat. As the first rays of sun broke over the horizon, she finally closed her eyes.

Emily opened them abruptly as a knock sounded on her door. The sun was high in the sky and streaming through the window as Aunt Maeve backed her way into the room, holding a tray in her hands that she nearly dropped at the scene in front of her.

"I know you're probably not hungry, but I mixed up some tea just in case—"

Emily sat up with the sheet wrapped under her arms. For a moment, Maeve opened and closed her mouth with no sound. Emily looked at Nicholas, who sat up halfway beside her; she turned back to her aunt, who was doing her best to recover herself. Maeve set the tray on the dresser and backed out the door, stammering apologies as she exited. Emily looked at Nicholas, who was wearing an amused smile on his face.

"No, no, no," Maeve said, bursting back in the door. "On second thought, this is not a moment for privacy. I'm not leaving until I find out how in the name of the heavens and the earth a dead man is here, very much alive, lying naked in my niece's bed?" Maeve crossed her arms, her expression thunderstruck.

Emily looked from Nicholas to her aunt with a sneaky grin. "It was magic," she said.

CHAPTER 40

Two weeks later, Emily was back to work. She blew a stray lock of hair from her eyes as she continued to type the catalogue. It was going to be another one of those mornings. The alarm hadn't set, her shower was cold thanks to Aunt Maeve's early morning trifecta of a bubble bath, a load of laundry, and a spin of the dishwasher, and to top it off, she had a thin line of coffee trailing down the front of her shirt. And yet, despite all these things, she was happy. She flipped her ear buds into her ears as James began the morning meeting, pontificating for the third time that week on proper document handling. Since her back was to him and her hair hung loose, she tapped on her computer, occasionally looking over her shoulder with a serious expression and a nod.

James drifted toward Emily and continued to talk as he stood by her side. As she caught the eye of another coworker, she felt a tug near her ear, and James, not missing a beat, continued talking with the wire of her earphones hanging from his hand.

"Now that we're all paying attention," he said mildly, tapping her on the shoulder as he passed her, "we need to talk. First of all, it's nice to see that Emily's returned to us after her long bout with pneumonia; what with Mary's resignation at the same time, it's been a rough couple of weeks around here. Although we've had some help from upstairs, they're not as familiar with our systems as you are, and it's much easier than usual for there to be mistakes, and for things to get lost. It's very important that we keep track of these documents. The map was nearly lost in the shuffle of last week's investigation, and it's our job to make sure that things like this don't happen. Thankfully, the map has been returned to the VonPeer family, and Maeve VonPeer has graciously agreed to allow Dr. Staats to finish the translations here to avoid any further mix-ups. We're under the microscope here, folks, so make sure that you don't screw anything up for the next few weeks—and if you do—come see me immediately with a token of penance in hand. Scotch is good."

Emily grinned.

The man from the news office appeared silently and began unloading a stack of newspapers and a copy of that morning's clips of headlines from around the Capitol. James adjourned the meeting as Dr. Staats walked in looking more crumpled than usual, clutching his briefcase.

"Can I speak to you for a moment?" he asked James in a low voice.

James nodded as the two of them walked into his office and closed the door. The rest of the staff had gone back to their usual work, but Emily was curious.

Her phone rang, and Emily suppressed a smile and the little leap in her stomach when she saw the number.

"Hi," she said into the phone, a little too breathlessly, she thought, but Nicholas didn't seem to notice.

"So I'm calling to check on our dinner plans; have you decided where you want to eat yet? Do you feel like a drive? Saratoga, the Lake, or there's this great little place in

Vermont I heard about . . ."

"Surprise me," Emily said. "I'm up for anything tonight."

Nicholas chuckled. "Beer and wings it is, then." Emily started to say something, but Nicholas cut her off.

"I'm just kidding," he said. "I'll meet you at your place at seven."

"Sounds good, I'll talk to you then—"

"Hey," Nicholas cut in. "Could you do me a favor? Could you just keep your eyes open for anything suspicious around your place? I know it's being handled, but I'm still a little concerned—I'll tell you more about it tonight."

"No problem," Emily said. "I'll talk to you later."

She hung up the phone and went back to her typing. *Honestly,* she thought, pecking away at her keyboard, *there are a dozen conspiracies a day around this place, if I spent all day looking into them, I'd never get anything done.* Sighing, she turned around in her chair and looked around the office, expecting to see nothing. Then she paused as a man dressed as a policeman walked in the door. He shimmered with a bright blue aura. He walked straight to James' office, knocked on the door, and walked in.

Another agent? She looked down at the newspaper clips. The front pages were still filled with the news about Blevin's death, the memorial, and the subtle power struggle within the Senate that had ensued.

Although Emily couldn't hear the words, voices were rising behind the door to James' office, but there was nothing new about that. James and Staats were always arguing about something; their bickering was a running joke among the staff. Emily smiled as she brushed the pink and yellow flowers that they'd left on her desk as a welcome back present. It was nice to be missed.

The front door opened, and there was Steph, pushing a cart with a load of coffee and bagels. The staff brightened, and Janie, one of the other librarians, almost fell over her chair rushing to Steph.

"Are you sure these are for us?" she asked. "I don't think anyone placed an order this morning."

Steph scratched his head. "Document Room, Basement, State Museum, ask for Emily."

A murmur of approval went through the room as people stood and stretched, and a few of them raced to the cupboard in search of the paper plates.

Steph winked and Emily improvised an awkward speech. "Um . . . happy Friday! I think it was my turn to buy breakfast." Emily looked at Steph in question.

Steph walked over to her with a clipboard in his hand. "Just sign here," he said, handing the clipboard to Emily.

Emily looked at the pink paper, which was blank. She glanced at Steph to see if there was some mistake, but Steph raised his eyebrows at her and nodded his head. Emily ducked her head and played along, when a loud crash sounded in James' office. Staats whipped the door open in a fury, and Steph put his hand on Emily's arm and stepped in front of her as Staats stormed by them.

"You're being completely unreasonable!" Staats said over his shoulder.

James followed him, hands in his pockets, a sheepish expression on his face. "I'm sorry, Doctor, but there's only so much that I can do here. There are rules with these sort of things, you know. They have a warrant, and they'll need us to deliver the map."

"Look at him," Steph breathed, and Emily squinted, but she wasn't sure what she saw. Staats was certainly projecting an aura of magic, but like nothing she'd ever seen. It was a sort of brownish-orange blob emanating only from his upper body.

"What is it?" Emily whispered, taking advantage of the fact that the rest of the staff was also absorbed with the commotion and watching the drama between James and Staats. "He wasn't like that the last time I saw him."

"I don't know," Steph said, "but it's not good, whatever it is. I heard some rumors at Paladin and came over to check it out. Looks like they sent someone too. Your aunt called me to tell me that they'd be moving the map back to Paladin after all."

Emily nodded, looking at the police officer who stood beside Blevin. "Isn't it a bit of a coincidence that things are happening here around us, now?" she asked.

"Not really," Steph said. "This sort of thing happens everywhere, you're only noticing magic now because you know what to look for. It's a shame you aren't wearing your locket though, it would come in really handy."

She patted the place where her locket had been.

"I do miss it," she said. "Aunt Maeve said that the Paladin asked her to make more of them for their agents."

Steph grinned, "Now that you're all going to be family, they probably figure that that they're entitled to the imposition."

Emily raised her eyebrows in shock. Steph smiled, then looked out the door. "I'm going to keep an eye on things, but call me if you need anything."

"Will do," Emily said.

Steph winked at her and walked out the door, clipboard in hand.

CHAPTER 41

Nicholas walked out of the meeting with a new file in hand. The case was small work, magical cleanup and repair at the gates, mostly. Nicholas was the new head of this committee, and if the work was boring, he didn't complain. He could use a break from dealing with demons. Besides, he had a date tonight. He nodded as he passed a few familiar faces in the hall, including Moon, who stopped when she saw him.

"Nicholas," she said, touching his arm. "Can I talk to you for a minute?"

"Sure thing," Nicholas said, working hard to cover the tension in his voice. He followed her into an empty side corridor, where she turned to him.

She pulled a velvet bag from her cloak and handed it to Nicholas.

He frowned, puzzled, until he opened the bag. Emily's locket spilled into the palm of his hand.

"Technically, I should have sent this down to the evidence room, but it should go back to where it belongs." She faltered. "It's only right, after everything that happened."

"Thanks," Nicholas said, dangling the locket in front of

him. "Emily will be happy to have it back. It's taken a lot of convincing to keep her from coming after it."

"I figured," Moon said. "So you're still seeing a lot of her then?"

"Of course," Nicholas said, suspicious.

"And she seems okay to you?" she asked. "Everything seems back to normal?"

Nicholas rolled his eyes. "Let me guess, you've been talking to my mother again."

Moon looked at him, unabashed. "Yes, but I've also done a lot of studying on this sort of thing, Nicholas—" she started, and he began to walk away, but she followed him. "Will you please just hear me out, and I'll never bring it up again?"

Nicholas spun on his heel and crossed his arms in front of him. "Fine," he snapped, "what is so important?"

"Everything I've ever seen or studied on the issue indicates that there is no cure for contamination," Moon said.

"I know that already," Nicholas said, "but we've also never encountered a tool like the athame before, either, now have we? And gods know we've never had access to the VonPeer library before, have you forgotten about that?"

"No," Moon said, "but nevertheless, there has been research that suggests that there are tools out there that can delay the contamination, and maybe that's all the athame did for Emily. Look, I'm not telling you what to do, just be careful, okay? And call us if you need us?"

"Okay," Nicholas said, softening a little at the earnest expression on Moon's face. "So you've taken the promotion, I assume?"

Moon nodded eagerly. "There was no question, I mean, I know you don't always see eye to eye with her, Nicholas, but nobody in their right mind would pass up the opportunity to work with her . . . except, uh . . . I mean—"

"Except for me?" Nicholas said. "Yeah, you're right;

there is no way in hell that I'm going to work for my mother. I told her so last night, though you obviously know all about that."

Moon looked at him with a guilty expression on her face, but said nothing.

"Yeah, I thought so," Nicholas said. "I'm very happy here, as I told her last night. There is no way that I'm moving three and a half hours to New York City to have my mom as my boss. Besides, they've offered me John's position; he's retiring, did you hear?"

"You mean you're moving back to the Gatehouse?" Moon asked him. "I thought they'd agreed not to rebuild that property."

"No, his old position," Nicholas said. "They're making me a Senior Field Agent. My team gets in next week; they're assembling them from all over the country. They're not going to rebuild the Gatehouse; they're putting me up in a little brownstone near the Capitol buildings instead."

Moon looked impressed. "I don't think your mother knew about that," she said.

"She didn't," Nicholas said. "Stanton and John just told me a few minutes ago. I think that John's telling her now. He said he'd break the news to her."

"Speak of the devil, here they come now," Moon said.

Dalgreth was walking as slowly as possible, though Lillian limped stubbornly along at a fast pace, banging her cane on the marble floor as she went. The look on her face was grim, until her eyes met Nicholas'.

"Hey, Mom!" he said brightly. "How are you doing?"

"I expect you know exactly how well I'm doing," Lillian said, standing up straight and pointing her cane between Nicholas and John.

"Don't think I don't know what you two are up to, creating new teams and positions so that you can stay close to those—" she stopped short as she saw the expression on both of their faces. "You mark my words, both of you, no good is going to come out of either of these situations, and if you'd take my advice—"

John interrupted her. "You've made it very clear about your thoughts on the situation, Lillian," he argued. "Sooner or later, you're going to have to accept the fact that we're both grown men, and we can make our own decisions."

Nicholas nodded, his face set.

"Fine then, good luck to you both. You'll know where to find me when you need me. And you'll need me soon enough. Anyway, I'll be back for the wedding."

She gave Nicholas a cold peck on the cheek and a quick one-armed hug. "Be careful," she said in a low voice, so that no one could hear her, and Nicholas nodded and hugged her back.

"It'll be okay Mom, really," he said, but his mother's expression hardened, unconvinced.

"We'll see," she said, and turned to Moon.

"The car's all ready?" she asked.

Moon nodded.

"Good," Lillian said. "If you drive fast, we can make it there before rush hour hits, you know how I hate sitting in traffic." she drifted off down the hall.

John fell into step beside Nicholas, shaking his head.

"That's one hell of a woman, your mother," he said, half laughing.

"No kidding," Nicholas agreed. "So, what about you, are you all ready for the big day?"

"Absolutely," John said. "Got any plans for lunch? Maeve said they put up a big, obscene marble statue of Diamond at the entrance to the Riverwalk, I thought I'd go check it out."

Nicholas laughed. "Let's go," he said. "What'd they end up doing for Blevin?"

"Some small plaque in a local park, I think," John said,

scratching his head. "I'm not really sure. Funny how those things work out, isn't it?"

Nicholas nodded, and they headed out of the building together.

CHAPTER 42

Later that night, Emily was standing in her bedroom as her aunt zipped her dress. She looked in the mirror for the hundredth time, inspecting herself from every angle. "You don't think it's too sexy? It's not too short?" she asked.

Maeve snickered as Emily tugged at the hem of her burgundy dress. "Is there any such thing?" Maeve said. "Really, Emily, you look beautiful, stop fussing. Doesn't she look beautiful?" she said to the House.

Always, the House said, and Emily smiled.

Maeve picked up a pair of gold hoops from the dresser and handed them to Emily. "Where are you going?"

"I don't know," Emily said, putting the earrings in her ears as she heard a car swing into the driveway. "He said he's taking me somewhere special tonight, and that it's a surprise."

"He's here," she said, and was about to dart out the door before her aunt grabbed her arm and pulled her back to the bed.

"Wait here for five more minutes, spray on some perfume or something. I'll get the door. There's no need to look like an amateur."

Emily heaved a sigh and stood up from the bed. Spotting her wristwatch on the dresser, she walked over to pick it up, catching her own reflection in the mirror. She brushed the hair back from her face, debating on a barrette, but then decided to leave it long.

Something in the mirror caught her eye, and she leaned into the bureau to inspect her eyes. A single spot of lavender light glowed in the iris of her left eye. Emily clutched the dresser in panic.

"Mind if I come in?" Nicholas asked her, popping his head around the door. "Hey, are you all right?" he asked, noticing the expression on her face. He put his arms out, and Emily rushed to him, burying her head in his neck.

"Yeah, I'm fine," she said, refusing to look at the mirror. "I just stubbed my toe on the dresser, that's all."

Nicholas kissed the top of her head.

"You're almost perfect," he said. "But something's missing." He reached into his pocket and pulled out her locket.

Emily squealed with joy. "Finally! Thank you," she said, grabbing it from him and moving to the mirror to put it on. She looked at it in the mirror. The lavender shimmer she had seen in her eye was gone. She turned away and then turned back to the mirror and looked again under the pretense of admiring her locket. Again, all she saw were her own gray eyes staring back at her.

"You have no idea how much this means to me," she said, turning back to him. "I don't know how to thank you."

Nicholas' grin grew wider. "I think we'll figure out something," he said, snaking his hand down her back and kissing her on the cheek.

For a moment, she thought about suggesting they forget about dinner and stay right here, but her aunt called up the stairs.

"Are you two leaving then?" Maeve asked.

"Geez, I guess they want their privacy," Nicholas teased. "The wedding's six months away, but they're already acting like newlyweds."

Sure enough, John was sitting at the kitchen table when they came down. Both he and Maeve were looking at them anxiously.

"We're going, we're going!" Emily said.

"Don't wait up for us," Nicholas said as the two of them walked out the door.

"Don't worry, we won't," Maeve said with a gleam in her eye.

It was a perfect night, and Nicholas took Emily's hand as he led her down the stairs and through the small path to the driveway. The sun had just started to set, and the first stars began to twinkle through the lavender mist in the sky.

As she moved to open the door, Nicholas spun her into his arms and drew her close. As his mouth crushed hers in a kiss that seemed to stop time itself, Emily was reminded of what her aunt had told her so long ago: that dreams don't always turn out as you'd expect them. As Nicholas held her tightly in the darkness, she thanked the heavens that she didn't know what the future would hold.

ACKNOWLEDGEMENTS

Thank you to Maer Wilson and Jen Ryan at Ellysian Press, who spent countless hours helping me revise and polish the manuscript; to Mark Barlet, my technical guru who has helped me put together my website and related materials; and to all of my family and friends who've believed in me and encouraged me to write over the years.

ABOUT THE AUTHOR

Agnes Jayne began her career as a political writer, producing speeches and other government documents for local politicians. A native of Northern New York, she holds a Master's Degree in English from the State University of New York at Albany and an undergraduate degree in English and Political Science from Binghamton University. When she's not writing, she spends her time teaching courses in composition and literature. She lives high in the Blue Ridge Mountains of West Virginia with her husband, son, and a plethora of adopted pets.

ELLYSIAN PRESS

To find other Ellysian Press books, please visit our website (http://www.ellysianpress.com/).

Some of our titles are:

Moth by Sean T. Poindexter

Relics by Maer Wilson

A Shadow of Time by Louann Carroll

Idyllic Avenue by Chad Ganske

Portals by Maer Wilson

Innocent Blood by Louann Carroll

The Boogeyman by Lillie J. Roberts

Magics by Maer Wilson

The *Ellysian Press Catalog* has a complete list of current and forthcoming books. It can be found on our website.

A Shadow of Time by **Louann Carroll**

When young widow Kellyn O'Brien discovers her toddler has inherited the Shadow Ley fortune and estate, she thinks all of her problems are solved.

Unseen, a mysterious guardian dwells deep beneath the house. As the run-down mansion repairs itself, Kellyn is plagued by nightmares – windows into other dimensions that are as confusing as they are frightening.

Not sure what is real or imagined, Kellyn turns to her new friends for help. When they realize that their dreams are connected, they are determined to find the truth behind the unbelievable coincidence.

But the presence at Shadow Ley has something more diabolical in mind. And the friends must unravel the secrets before the insane entity takes more lives, beginning with theirs.

The Boogeyman by Lillie J. Roberts

The nightmare begins…
Two girls lost on a lonely country road.
One killer thrilled with an unexpected opportunity.
Two families desperate to find their lost children.
One girl…lost
One girl remains…
Until a young boy joins her…

And discovers the Boogeyman is real.

Ghosts of Modern Magics: **A Collection**
by Maer Wilson

Thulu and La Fi's clients were usually the dead. The Ghost novelettes detail a few of their more memorable cases.

"Ghost Memory" - An amnesiac ghost hires Thulu and La Fi to find missing money from his home for his aging husband.

"Unwanted Ghost" - The couple inherits a furnished Victorian, complete with its own noisy ghost.

"Ghost Dancer" - Young Danika asks Thulu and La Fi to save her dog from the killer who murdered her.

"Wedding Ghost" - Just before their own wedding, the detectives are hired to find out what happened to another bride ninety years before.

BONUS MATERIAL - "Lost Ghost" tells the story of eleven-year-old Thulu and Fiona's first case.